Du Rose Family Ties

The Hana Du Rose Mysteries

K T BOWES

Would you like to be part of it?

I'm a believer in 'try before you buy.'
There's nothing worse than forking out your hard earned cash on a doozy and regretting it.
I don't want stinky reviews. I want you to love my work and feel like you got value for money.

If you'd like 4 free eBooks as a series starter, you can do that by signing up on my website, ktbowes.com.
I will take care of your email address and won't be sharing it or spamming you.
You can unsubscribe at any time. I promise not to send Rohan Andreyev after you...maybe.

Acknowledgement

I dedicate this novel to my beautiful sister, Rebecca Arden, who
makes me laugh, shares my sorrows and gives me advice.
I lost you for a while there, but it won't happen again.
I will hold on more tightly this time and the rollercoaster of life
will not shake me loose.

1

Bush Emergency

"Something's wrong!" The redhead lifted the reins in her left hand and the white horse halted under her, drawing a cloud of dust from the baked earth. "Did you hear that?"

"Yeah." Her companion stopped to listen, his Appaloosa shifting with impatience and dragging his hooves on the track.

"Three shots mean there's a hunter in distress." She turned in the saddle, her green eyes intense on his face. "Don't they?"

He groaned and ran his dusty hand through curly, blonde hair. "No, please let's not do this, Mrs Du Rose? Your husband warned me you were the biggest distraction on this mountain."

Her inhalation sounded sharp as she widened her eyes and feigned shock. "That's mean! I don't even need you. I know this mountain as well as you do, David Allen!"

"Yeah, well I don't know it that well so get a move on, we need to get the cattle to the bottom before dark." David peered around Hana at the little band of calves who hung around on the track ahead of them. They spread out nervously, tugging at green shoots in the undergrowth, the native ferns unappetising. Their tufty cream and patchy black bodies made them look more like giant teddy bears than the younger members of a lucrative beef herd. "Do a head count. Have we still got twelve?"

"Er, yeah, I think so. They won't keep still."

David sighed with exaggerated drama, pushing his dusty cowboy hat back on his head. His horse snorted with impatience and pawed the ground again. A crackly sound broke into the calm of the bush as the radio on David's saddle projected Logan Du Rose's voice into the air. David winced. He unhooked the walkie talkie and pushed it towards his companion. "You answer it. He's your husband."

"He's your boss!" Hana smiled smugly and tried to count the cattle, growling her exasperation as two kicked up their heels and fled down the track. The rest surged after them.

"Come in, Hana!" Logan's voice held an edge of impatience, blended with an undertone of fear.

"I hear ya." David's voice was low and deep, feigning calm as he spoke into the handset. "What's up?"

"You're late. There's only thirteen calves. It shouldn't take all day!"

David's mouth dropped open in horror. "Twelve. There were twelve up there. That's what Toby said and that's what we're droving."

"We've been back hours now. Toby's ridden up the road twice. Where the hell are you?"

"Er..." David bit his lip and watched Hana's shapely form as she weaved the large mare around the calves on the track, herding them back into a tight knot. Her red hair flowed out behind her, the hair clip shucked an hour ago in the mud up near the Du Rose house at the top of the mountain. Dust and bush debris covered the back of her shirt and David gulped. "We took the scenic route and Mrs Du Rose fell off."

A string of expletives split the air with such vehemence, David fumbled the radio. Then, "Is she okay?"

"Logan, she's fine. She got straight back on. She's just..." David bit back the word and saw Hana shake her head and smirk.

"Don't say it to *him!*" she called up the track. "He won't be so understanding."

"Whatever! You are unmanageable. You're a complete bloody nightmare!"

"Are you talking to my wife?" Logan's voice crackled through the radio as David released the call button and his eyes bugged. He stared accusingly at his finger and tried not to cringe. Hana let out a peal of laughter. "Just get back here. Stop mucking around!" Logan's voice crackled again and David sighed as he fixed the radio back over its clip.

"Great, thanks for that. Now I'm offside with him!"

"No, you're not. He worries about me and I'm fine. You shouldn't have told him I fell off though." Hana reached forward and caressed the soft, furry neck beneath her fingers. "It was an accident. It wasn't your fault, was it Sacha?"

The horse's ears flicked back and forth as the mare nodded her head, snuffling softly and crunching on the metal bit in her mouth. David shook his head and edged his horse towards Hana and the surging knot of calves. "You're covered in muck and you've got crap in your hair. He'd have noticed and then yelled at me."

"Coward!" Hana reached behind her and yanked a fern from her long red hair. It resisted, breaking into pieces and she combed it out with slender fingers. "There's a way to tell my husband bad news and that wasn't it. You'll learn." She winked at David and sensed his unease, relenting and nudging Sacha into a tight turn. "It's fine, David. It was my own silly fault. He won't blame you."

"Yeah, he will." The man sounded fed up. "All those years as a British airman and I never had a sergeant like him. He's ruthless."

"He has to be," Hana replied, her voice wistful. "It's a harsh world and there aren't many breaks for people like us. Loyalty's hard won on this mountain and not everyone we like is trustworthy."

"I know." David pushed his gelding into a lazy trot and rounded up a stray calf pulling at a supplejack vine. "Get on with ya!" He tapped the furry flank with the thong of his bull-whip and the small animal surged forward, nosing into the bunch.

"The gate's round the next bend," Hana said, jerking her head backwards. "Logan wants them in the first paddock so we're done. I'll corral them here if you ride ahead and open the gate, then I'll drive them forward."

David grunted. "Then I'll spend the next six months hearing all the reasons why we should have brought them down by road."

Hana rolled her eyes and tossed her head. The remains of the fern let go of her auburn curls and fluttered into the bush. "Nev told me *not* to take them by road!" Hana protested. "And I'll tell my husband that! Nev said the washout on the cliff would freak them out and make it unsafe."

"Well, get your story straight then!" David bit, urging his horse into a fast trot. He skirted the knot of jittery calves and made for the next bend as Hana's horse ducked and weaved to keep the beasts where she wanted them. She held her bull-whip at arm's length but didn't crack it, not wanting to start a small stampede.

Logan Du Rose owned the mountain, running a hotel, motel units, holiday park and a successful beef and horse stud business. His half-brother, Neville was the farm manager, but their communication skills were sadly lacking sometimes.

"Well, furry babies," Hana spoke to the calves, seeing twelve pairs of brown eyes turn towards her. "Now you've finished eating my front garden, you get promoted to the big paddocks.

It's been nice having you stay, but I wish you'd learned to poo in one place."

The sparkiest of the bunch jerked his front feet as though to make a run for it and Hana moved her bull-whip as the group surged in a circle, pinned by her whip and Sacha's exacting hooves. "I actually won't miss *you!*" She directed her comment at the sparky steer with the glint in his eye as he circled and looked for an escape route. "Come on guys, I bottle fed you all and played mummy to you and this is how you repay me? Ingratitude is one of the ugliest sins, ya know?"

Knotty tails flicked against the midges swirling around in the humid bush landscape and the world was silent, except for the occasional snort or stamp. Sacha's body tensed, waiting for one of them to break so she could give chase. Hana felt powerful muscles shift under her thighs. "Yeah, give me warning next time, Sacha. It's great you know what you're doing, but half the time I don't. I'm not Logan; not even a poor substitute." Hana turned her head a fraction, feeling the tension in the herd increase with the prolonged wait. Something caught her eye on the ear of the smallest calf. "Is that a pink ribbon?" she asked, incredulous. She bit back a smile at her daughter's ingenuity. Her tiny children loved bottle feeding the calves. Two-and-a-half-year-old Phoenix and Hana's son, ten-month old Mac, treated them like huge, furry pets, which was probably the reason Logan decided to move them.

"It's open." David cantered up the track on his leggy gelding and the small herd jerked in alarm. Hana lifted Sacha's reins in an upward direction and lowered the whip. The white mare backed up into the bush until her fetlocks encountered the winding supplejack vine and then she halted, crunching on her bit and watching the cattle through experienced eyes.

"Get on!" Hana clicked her tongue and tapped the furry bottoms gently with her whip. They bunched together, their eyes rolling and frightened, staying close to her as their substitute parent. "Come on babies!" she protested and David snorted. Hana sighed. "Right guys, Mama's gonna play dirty if you don't move!"

Frustrated by David's obvious disdain, Hana released the thong on her bull-whip and moved it out to the side. She nudged Sacha, so she was side on to the cattle and saw the mare's skilled ears flick as her body tensed. Hana raised her arm, keeping the whip moving behind her, waiting until she heard the tail make a familiar swish as it straightened. Then she whipped forward, keeping her arm solid as she'd practiced many times. There was a terrific crack and the cattle surged, running and bucking along the track in a furry, cream rush. The biggest calf made a detour into the rugged undergrowth but changed his mind as the others left him. They hurtled down the narrow track as a bunch, spreading out as they turned the corner and spied the lush green grass ahead.

Hana turned with a look of smug satisfaction. It was wasted. David's strong torso bent over his gelding's neck as he cantered after the calves, his hooves kicking up dust and bush debris behind him. The Appaloosa's tail lifted high in the air as he enjoyed the run, dispelling his pent up energy. David managed his reins in his left hand, his right arm straight with the coiled whip. "Well done, Hana!" she called after him, seeking his approval. He raised his arm in response and over the bull-whip, she spied the fingers making a rude gesture. "Telling Logan!" she shouted into the bouncing air molecules. The tui overhead cackled as David disappeared round the corner.

"Good girl, Sacha. I can tell you're impressed." Hana ran her hand down the glossy neck of Logan's favourite mare, rewarded by a toss of the magnificent head. "Come on then, best get down and face the music. Logan and Nev need to start communicating!" Hana clicked her tongue and the mare danced into action, keen to follow the dappled gelding to the fresh grass.

Rounding the corner, Hana found David on the ground waiting. He held his horse's reins and tapped the coiled bull-whip against the fabric of his jeans. "Nice of you to join us!" He kept the gate closed against the calves bunching around him and Hana tutted.

"Stop worrying, David! Nev told me to use the bush track, so we did. Logan will be fine and I won't involve you."

The stockman ran the back of his hand across his sweating forehead. "Just get in the bloody gate!"

Sacha took a step towards the gate and snorted at the gathered crowd behind it, threatening them with her blue wall eye, rolling in its sinister white rim. The calves moved backwards with slow hooves, not yet feeling their freedom in the acreage which rolled out behind them in a healthy green arc. David tapped the whip, growing more impatient by the second. Sweaty blonde curls poked from under his hat and his biceps flexed, communicating his irritation.

It came again. The echo of three shots fired together in quick succession. *Hunter in distress.*

Hana's head whipped back towards the mountain and she saw the flutter of native birds as they rose from the trees in a sudden flurry, moving away from the alarm. "That's the ridge above the forty-eighth," she said, turning her eyes back to David's worried face. "Someone's in trouble." With a flick of Hana's reins the white mare whirled on her back feet and took off along the track, galloping uphill at a terrific pace.

"Get back here!" David yelled after Hana, coughing in the dust cloud she kicked up behind her.

"Radio it in!" she shouted over her shoulder as she disappeared back into the dense New Zealand bush.

2

Freefall

"They don't give me any credit!" Hana chuntered to herself. She led the horse through the thick undergrowth towards the ridge, getting her legs caught in the perilous supplejack vine and ripping her arms on bush lawyer. She stopped to tie another pink hair ribbon to a tree branch, looping it securely round and tying it. A line of them stretched back the way she came, fluttering in the light breeze and marking her route. "Thank goodness I forgot to put these in Phoe's hair this morning," she smirked. "Now I can pretend I always come into the bush equipped."

Sacha snorted and Hana stroked the white brow with soft fingers. "Sorry, Sach. I'm just gonna shout again," she warned. "Hello!" she yelled, causing the mare to blink and shake her head.

The going was tough and Hana felt scratched and prodded in every available space on her body. She drew to a halt facing the deep gully and turned to the horse. "I think you're done now, girl. You can't go any further." Hana stroked the soft lips surrounding the metal bit and left a trail of blood from the cuts on her fingers. She inspected the horse's legs which looked largely unscathed. "This was a stupid idea, Logan's gonna be livid."

The mare whinnied and stamped her furry foot in impatience.

"I'll shout once more and then go home and face Logan's wrath," Hana sighed. "He'll kill me. And then he'll kill David. Maybe we can be buried together although after today, David's dead body will probably move itself well away from mine." Hana let go of the reins and cupped her hands around her mouth. "Hello!" she shouted, hearing her voice carry across the ridge and into the canopy. It echoed back, disjointed and strange. *Nothing*.

"Okay, I quit." Hana's voice sounded flat as her mind ran through the lecture her husband would give her. Sacha tensed as the thin voice carried up the steep slope, the words unintelligible. Hana held her breath and looked at the horse's blue eye, waiting to see if the sound came again.

"Somebody help me!"

Hana's eyes widened. "There *is* somebody and we've found them!" She bounced on the soles of her cowboy boots with excitement. She peered into the cavernous drop and spied the smallest flash of fluorescent orange before it disappeared. "Stay still!" she shouted. "I'm trying to locate where you are."

The orange shape moved back into view and stayed there long enough for Hana to pick a landmark. She hissed in frustration. "It's a man and he's near the derelict hut. It would've been easier to get there from our house on the other side of the mountain. What now?"

Sacha's tack clinked and Hana bit her lip. "Are you hurt?" she yelled into the space below her feet.

The voice came back to her on the wind, sounding pathetic. "Broken leg."

"Oh great, now I've done it!" Hana sighed at her own impulsiveness. She brought nothing to rescue the man with and no radio to summon help. David hadn't followed her in her recklessness either.

"Help me!" The voice came again, whipped past Hana's face by the up draught.

"I'm coming!" she called back, screwing up her face at Logan's horse. "I kinda have to now," she said to the mare's impassive blue eye. "He's expecting me to do something and I'm already in trouble."

Hana breathed out through pursed lips and made a series of decisions. Sacha blew out her stomach as Hana undid her girth. The heavy stock saddle slipped off and Hana placed it on the cantle against a nikau palm. Undoing the throat lash, she took the bridle from the mare's regal head and let her spit the bit from her mouth. Hana scratched her poll with nervous fingers and looked into the horse's wise face. "Sacha, I need you to find Logan. Can you do that for me? Go home, Sacha. *Find Logan.*"

The mare shook her head from side to side and showered Hana with bush debris from her mane. Hana coughed and stamped her foot. "You know exactly what I mean, so do it, please?"

Sacha shifted her feet and Hana resorted to her badly spoken Māori, knowing it was nothing to do with the language but the tone of her voice. Somehow using her husband's familiar tongue felt comforting. "*Whai* Logan! *Ā kāti, karawhiua atu, hōiho!* Please, Sacha. *Go!*"

Part Stationbred and part Appaloosa, Sacha turned her massive body in the small space at the top of the ridge, dislodging rock and soil which tumbled over the side. She picked her way back through the undergrowth, stumbling over the troublesome vines as she followed the route back to the track. Hana leaned over the ridge. "Help will be a good hour away," she called. "But I'll stay here." She watched Sacha's lumbering flank and gnawed on her bottom lip. "Silly horse could go anywhere now I've upset her," she sighed.

"Are you still there?" the plaintive voice wailed and Hana bit back her exasperation.

"Yes! I'll climb down so watch out for debris!" She eyed the yawning drop before her. "And watch out for me, I might come down with it!" she whispered.

It proved a dreadful descent, something an extreme rock climber might have considered employing ropes and crampons to tackle. Hana didn't realise that until she became stuck somewhere in the middle, too far to climb back up and too high to drop safely to the bottom. She clung to an outcrop with her left hand, the skin on her fingers tearing and her fingernails ragged. Her right arm and both legs hugged an unwilling gum tree trunk as it jutted out from the ridge, blessedly branch free.

"Are you coming?" The voice sounded nearer, hope fading in the weakness of the cry.

"Yes!" Hana spat. "I'm just having a spot of bother and if you keep shouting that, I'm dropping a rock on your sorry head!"

"What?"

"Nothing! Yes, I'm coming!" Hana rested her forehead against the trunk and considered her options. There weren't many. The buckles of Sacha's bridle dug into her body and the leather girth had slipped and restricted her arms. Taking something to brace the man's leg seemed like a good idea as she had wrapped the expensive tack around her body. Slowly it turned into the thing which would kill her.

Hana fought the urge to scream and weep alternately. She prayed instead. "Oh dear God, please forgive my sins before I die. I haven't got time to list them all but there's lots. Please bless my children, the cute little ones and the big ones; Phoenix, Mac, Isobel and Beauden. Please remember he likes to be called Bodie and bless his sorry, stubborn ass, Lord, because he needs all the help he can get. Bless Logan. He's so gorgeous, he'll find another wife but please can you make it someone who does as she's told more than me..."

"You're praying!" The voice became a wail. "You think I'm gonna die!" It sounded younger than Hana previously thought and she tried to steel herself to make the rest of the journey.

"Shut up, I'm just resting! My arms ache!" Hana shouted back, hearing the wobble in her voice. Her ridiculous plan to slide down the trunk of the gum tree seemed really stupid as she clung to it like a panda bear. Hana let go of the rock face and used her limbs to hold onto the tree. She made the mistake of looking at the ground below, swarming with supplejack vine and nasty, sharp boulders. The tree grew out of the bottom of the ridge at a jaunty angle, bending upwards in its efforts to reach the light. It groaned and moved every time Hana shifted her weight and her arms ached so badly, the muscles trembled, making holding on even harder.

Straightening her legs, Hana gripped with her feet, grateful for the rubber soles of her cowboy boots. She bent her body and clasped the tree trunk between her knees and dared to move one hand lower in a jerky movement. She repeated the sequence, *legs, hand, other hand, legs, hand, other hand*. The ground came gradually nearer and Hana concentrated on the childhood skill of tree climbing, not used much in her forty-eighth year of life.

A metre from the ground, Hana tried to stretch her body, finding the action impossible. Feeling ridiculous, she completed the sequence of movements until there was no more tree trunk and she could persuade her hands to let go. She stepped back and bent double, willing herself not to be sick as pain shot through every muscle in her body.

"Can you help me, now?" The young male in front of Hana waved his arms to get her attention. She ran a hand across her top lip and saw blood on the backs of her fingers.

"Yep," she gasped. "Just having a nose bleed. I banged it on the way down." She used her sleeve to mop at it, alarmed when even more came away.

"You look worse than me," the man said, his voice sounding tired. "Where are the others?"

"I don't know." Hana sank to the ground next to him, trying to take stock of his injuries amidst their remote surroundings. Once there, she saw he was a teenager and couched her words with care. "They'll be here. I sent Sacha back to raise the alarm and a stockman saw me ride off in search of the gun shots." Hana released the buckle on the girth and unwound it from around her shoulders. Then she unclipped the bridle, wincing at the pain in her cut fingers.

"You heard that?" The teenager sounded pleased with himself. "I ran out of cartridges about two hours ago."

"How many times did you fire?" Hana asked, shifting her atrophied muscles so she could observe him and check for injury.

"I tried it last night but nobody came. So I waited and did it again this morning. I had enough to do six more shots and that was it."

Hana gaped. "You've been lying here since yesterday." She put her hand up to her mouth as he nodded.

The boy's face looked deathly pale and his hands shook as he tried to rub his face. Dark circles marked the skin under his eyes and his lips were pale and cracked. Hana looked around, seeing nothing but the useless shot gun at his side. "Do you have water, food or supplies?" she asked.

"It's all back at the hut. I went looking for breakfast yesterday morning. A wild pig trotted past and I tracked it here, but it charged me and I fell backwards over that rock." He pointed with a dirty, shaking finger. "The pig ran off, which was good because if it stayed to finish the job, I'd be messed up worse."

Hana looked around warily. "Wild pigs are a hazard, especially boars or sows with piglets." Logan showed her how to spot their tracks and avoid them. Hana exhaled. "How far is the hut from here? I could fetch stuff." She closed her eyes, trying to remember the view from above.

"No! Don't leave me. You'll get lost and we'll both be stuck here. I can't take much more of this." His face crumpled in misery. "Sorry," he whispered and covered his eyes with filthy hands.

"Hey, it's fine. I'll sort it out." Hana cast around, scrabbling to her feet. She took her bearings as Logan taught her, searching for a landmark. "I'm Hana." She forced a smile and the man withdrew his hands and looked up at her, his eyes bleary and unfocussed.

"Sorry, I'm Caleb. Thanks for coming after me." He shifted and let out a groan of pain.

"Okay, sweetheart." Hana knelt next to him, pushing his cap back on his head so she could take a proper look. "How old are you, Caleb?"

"Nineteen," he said, his tone reeking of suspicion.

Hana nodded. "Okay. The stream's just down there. I'll find something to carry water in and a drink will make you feel better. Then I'll use the bridle and do something with your leg."

She returned a few minutes later, dragging the branch from a nikau palm behind her, the dead fronds fanning out like the train from a wedding dress. "Please tell me you have a knife on you?"

"Yeah." Caleb moaned in agony as he delved into the pocket of his sweatpants and produced a knife.

"Thanks." Hana stared at the blade and her brow narrowed, recognising the familiar object in her palm. "Where did you find this?"

"In the hut." Caleb sighed and Hana depressed the button to extend the blade, concentrating on the immediate problem. She pared the branch away from the bulb where it once attached to the trunk.

"I'll collect water in this," she muttered as she wielded the knife in her sore fingers. "Although I'll probably drop it on the way back. There's enough supplejack near the stream to weave a fence."

Caleb gave a watery smile. "Thanks for doing this. I didn't realise you were on your own. I thought...it doesn't matter." He gulped.

"I'm not on my own," Hana reassured him, holding the rough container up for his approval. "My husband owns this property and knows it like the back of his hand. He'll find me. Anyway, I sent Sacha back so she'll bring him here."

"Ah, no!" Caleb laid his head back against the rock propping him up. "You're a Du Rose." He exhaled and the fight left him. "Just leave me here to die."

"Don't be stupid!" Hana's voice sounded harsh. "I'm forty-eight years old and I just scaled a ridge to help you. My husband will be too busy yelling at me to do anything to you. He already thinks I'm a liability so you'll be perfectly safe!"

"I'm sorry," Caleb said again, his voice dull.

"I'll get the water now. But it's denser near the stream, so if you could keep talking, that would be helpful. I'll follow the sound so I can find my way back."

"What shall I say?" Caleb asked, his voice sounding hoarse as he contemplated the long awaited drink.

"Anything," Hana called over her shoulder. "Tell me about yourself. But please keep talking. If I don't answer, it's because I'm fighting supplejack."

"Okay."

Hana crawled, walked and climbed over and around fallen trees, scratched by pockets of bush lawyer and tripped by vines. Twice she returned to the clear stream to refill the container after face planting and dropping it all. She drank straight from the stream using her cupped hands, realising how exhausted she felt, the cuts on her palm and fingers smarting against the cool water. Blood stained her jeans from calf to heel on one leg and a painful splinter bit at her left arm. Hana ignored her own injuries, heaving in a huge breath and starting again, carrying the fragile bowl with its life giving liquid back to Caleb. His voice continued in a steady monotony, guiding Hana towards him. "I left home when I was fifteen and I've lived all over since then. I met this chick in Auckland and lived with her parents for a while but she dumped me two months ago. They kicked me out so she could move her new dude in, so I lived on the streets. I hitched a lift to Rangiriri and walked west for a few weeks. I found this hut and stayed."

Hana crouched next to him and handed over the container with shaking hands, her energy spent. "How do you know my husband's name?"

Caleb sipped at the liquid through cracked lips. He winced and closed his eyes. "Geez, that's nice. I've been dreaming of that water for hours."

"Sorry it's only half full," Hana apologised. "I fell over twice and dropped the lot."

"I know." Caleb smiled and put the cup to his lips again. He drank deeply, draining the bulb. "I heard you swearing."

"How do you know Logan?" she asked again.

Caleb wiped his mouth with the back of his hand. "I don't. I saw one of his workers six weeks ago. He was moving cattle around on the lower slopes. He told me this was Logan Du Rose's land and if he caught me here, he'd make me disappear."

"Nice," Hana said with a smile.

"Will he?"

"What?" Hana watched the empty bowl sink into Caleb's lap and dreaded the trip back to get more.

"Will he make me disappear?"

Hana tutted. "Look love, everyone's scared of him, but he's a decent man. Unless you've been stealing stuff, you'll be fine."

"Stealing? Like what?" Caleb's eyes widened and he chewed his bottom lip.

"Don't know. You tell me?"

"Like vegetables from the garden at the top of the mountain? Tomatoes and stuff and maybe a cucumber or two?"

"Ah, so you're the naughty possum who's been helping himself?" Hana smiled at Caleb's confusion. "My daughter's convinced we've got a pet possum who eats fruit and veggies."

Caleb nodded. "I saw children, but I also saw a guy there once and figured it was Logan Du Rose. He looked real scary. He'll mash me and make me disappear. I was just hungry and didn't know that was his house but I didn't take anything after that. I hunted down here." His eyes lowered to his leg. "Not very successfully."

"There's plenty of vegetables, Caleb. I don't think he'll begrudge you a cucumber and a few tomatoes. He's never killed anyone over a vegetable, I promise." Hana knitted her brow. "You didn't steal the gun, did you?"

Caleb shifted on the dusty ground and met her gaze. "Yes, but not from here."

Hana sighed. "Okay. Let me take a look at your leg and then I'll fetch more water."

It was painful for Caleb as she sawed the elasticated bottom of his sweatpants apart with the penknife. "I'm sorry," Hana said. "I need to cut your pants so I can get to your shin."

"It's fine." He sounded breathless.

Hana tried not to comment as she exposed the break in Caleb's shin. The bone protruded through the front of his leg, splitting the skin like a banana and sticking through for an inch, a jagged, white monstrosity. Hana swallowed bile and breathed quietly. Caleb tried to see the break and Hana's rebuke sounded sharp. "No, stay still. You'll make it worse." Dried blood encrusted the wound and it looked dirty. The skin shone an unhealthy grey. Hana swallowed.

"Sweetheart, I don't want to mess around with this too much. I don't think washing it will help and I can't force the bone back into place. It looks like a green-stick fracture. I'll make a splint to help stabilise it, then get more water and wait until help arrives."

Caleb nodded. "I don't care anymore. Just don't leave me; I'm sick of being on my own."

"Okay, love." Hana foraged in the nearby undergrowth, finding more fallen nikau branches. She lined her equipment up next to Caleb's prone body, separating as much of the leather from the bridle as she could and putting it in a pile. "*Now* my husband will kill me," she said, smiling at Caleb. He looked white and his breaths rasped in his chest. "This is his favourite horse's best tack."

Caleb's vibrant blue eyes studied her movements without reply. Familiarity tweaked a memory in the back of Hana's mind, but it was like trying to knit fog. She couldn't lay hold of it and dismissed it for the moment. Standing, she stripped off her chequered shirt and examined it. The teenager raised a smirk. "Drinks and a show. Luxury."

Hana snorted, her flimsy singlet covering the remnants of her dignity. "I'm trying to work out how to use this as packing between your legs. I don't think it's substantial enough."

Caleb grinned. "Take it all off. At least I'll die happy."

Hana put her hands on her hips. "Yep, that would certainly guarantee Logan kills you." She glanced at the singlet but the thought of being discovered in her bra by a jealous husband and a rescue team, filled her with dismay. "This will have to do," she said, rolling it into a long sausage and placing it between Caleb's legs with care. "Okay, now get as comfortable as you can because you might be here a while."

The poor boy groaned. "I can't. I can't sit here any longer. Can't you just help me out of here?"

"No, sweetheart. It's too rough going. Just do as you're told. Would you rather lie down or sit up?"

"Lie down," Caleb said. "I can't feel my ass."

Hana helped him lay flat, gulping against the pitiful cries he made as he moved his damaged leg. "Sorry, love," Hana soothed. "I know it hurts."

"That feels better," he rasped. "I couldn't lie down before, in case I died. It felt too much like giving up." His chest moved in rapid gasps of agony.

Hana squeezed his shoulder and moved to his legs. "Right," she said. "Tell me more about where you grew up. This will hurt and I'm more frightened than you. So talk for *me*, please. And don't stop." She placed the heel of Caleb's boot into the cup at the end of the palm. It wasn't a good fit, but supported it. He cried out as she moved his leg and Hana cringed. "I'm so sorry. I hate causing you more pain." She sounded tearful and Caleb waved his arm.

"It's okay, it's fine," he panted. "Just do it."

"Talk then." Hana used the knife to break the fronds and push them up the sides of Caleb's injured leg as packing. "You're not helping."

He closed his eyes, his brow knitted in pain. "I grew up in Taumarunui and I thought we were a happy family. My dad left when I was nine and everything went wrong. I loved my dad; he was awesome. He worked as a farm labourer and in the shearing season, won trophies for being the fastest guy in the King Country. He won competitions and I hoped he'd teach me but he went to work one morning and didn't come home. When I was ten, Mum moved her new boyfriend into our house and I resented him. He was my dad's best friend but very handy with his fists. We had a massive show down at the end of last year and I told them both I'd leave and find my dad. Her new bloke laughed and said I'd be lucky because he was dead. When I tried to leave, he beat me up." Caleb dragged his hand over his eyes and Hana stopped for a breather.

"But he's not dead, right?"

Caleb nodded, groaning in agony as the movement rocked his leg. He took a moment to regain control and his face adopted a sickening greyness. "My mate's dad was a cop and I climbed out my bedroom window and went to their house. They hauled the bastard in for beating me up and asked him some questions about Dad. His answers didn't ring true. They asked a judge to extend the custody and began investigating. My dad's body turned up at the farm they both worked at, buried at the bottom of a gully." Caleb snorted in disgust. "Ironic I should end up in one too."

Hana tutted and stroked Caleb's other thigh. "You won't be staying here sweetheart, so don't think that way."

His half smile looked doubtful and Hana continued her makeshift brace around the broken leg, preparing to strap it to the good one and avoiding the torn flesh and jagged bone. "How did your mother cope with everything?" she asked, glancing up.

Caleb's jaw tightened. "No idea. They convicted her boyfriend of murder. In court, my mother testified how the man I called 'Dad' wasn't my father at all." The teenager's chin wobbled. "She had an affair one summer while he was shearing and got pregnant with me. I loved him so much and he wasn't even my dad."

Hana leaned back on her heels after placing a piece of straight branch along the outside of the broken leg. It looked like rimu and was straight enough for its purpose. "I'm sorry, love. I bet that was miserable."

He nodded, his eyes glittering with unshed tears. "You know, don't you? You know what that feels like?" Hope burgeoned in his voice.

Hana shrugged. "My husband does. I discovered last year that my brother wasn't my brother; he was my cousin. My situation isn't the same but my husband could sympathise with you. His uncle died and then Logan discovered he was really his father." Hana blinked. "There's no putting that right."

Caleb nodded. "Yeah, at least I can find my real dad. I know he's still alive."

Hana smiled, hiding the fear in her eyes as she examined the different parts of her hoary looking creation. "Caleb, I'm ready to brace your leg with this branch and then strap your legs together. Sweetheart, it's gonna hurt. Shout if you need to, but keep still."

Caleb's eyes were wide, the whites showing as Hana utilised pieces of Sacha's dismantled bridle. He shouted as she moved his damaged limb to slip the leather underneath, sometimes whimpers and other times, great bellows of agony.

Once finished, Hana paused for breath, feeling sweat trickle between her shoulder blades. "That's much better," Caleb admitted, reaching for Hana's hand as she sat next to him clutching her knees. "It's taken the pressure off my muscles."

"Good," Hana said, her voice trembling. "It's tied at your ankles and thighs. I've used Sacha's reins to make a figure of eight around your feet to hold it still."

"Wait, what?" Caleb's voice radiated shock. The last rays of sun dropped behind the ridge and with a jolt of shock, Hana recognised the dying throes of daylight.

"I said I've strapped…"

"No! Not that! You said Sacha's reins." Caleb's face looked greyer in the dimming light and frustration burned from his blue eyes.

Hana shook her head in confusion and shrugged. "So?"

"You made me believe Sacha was a girl! You sent her to get help and tell your husband where we were." He laid his head back on the ground and Hana saw a tear roll down the side of his face and disappear into the parched earth. "Sacha's a bloody horse, isn't she?"

With nothing useful to say, Hana nodded and crouched on the ground next to the stricken boy. She rubbed his icy fingers and prayed for divine help. The bush grew quieter as night claimed it and Hana worried for her children. It was past their bedtime and she wasn't there to kiss them good night. "Want more water?" she asked to distract herself from maudlin thoughts.

Caleb nodded. "Yes please. And Hana?"

She stopped moving away and turned to face him. "Yeah?"

"I'm sorry. I'm glad you're here and for everything you've done. You're a nice lady."

"Thanks." She lowered her eyes. "Don't give up hope, Caleb. Logan will come."

Caleb swallowed. "Last time I lost hope, a guy was kind to me. It took a day to walk from the motorway and he gave me a lift the rest of the way to his French restaurant. He let me eat there even though everyone stared and I hadn't washed for weeks. That's the nicest thing anyone did for me until you showed up. I thought I'd die here."

Hana bit her lip and smiled. "That was Logan's cousin, Alex. So you see, they're not bad people. You won't die here, Caleb, I won't let you." Hana smiled. "I'm a Du Rose and we don't tolerate failure."

She crawled through the undergrowth in the deepening twilight to the stream. Caleb didn't talk this time and Hana took numerous wrong turns until she found him, using the last light shining from the west to point her back to where she started. There was little water left in the bottom of the disintegrating bulb and she bit back tears. "Caleb, Caleb!" Hana shook him awake and he groaned. "Drink, sweetheart." She propped his head up against her shoulder and dribbled the water between his lips. His face looked ethereal in the dim light, a pretty bone structure with high cheekbones and a strong chin. Hana brushed his ash blonde hair back from his forehead and again, felt the stirring of a memory. Caleb gulped and choked on the liquid. Hana patted his face with the flat of her palm. "Don't sleep, sweetheart. You need to stay awake."

"They're not coming," he mumbled.

"Yes they are. Have faith." She placed her knee under Caleb's head to cushion him from the hard ground and help his breathing. He settled and let out a sigh.

"You got kids, Hana?"

"Yeah. Four," she replied. "My eldest son is twenty-nine, my daughter is twenty-eight and I have two littlies, two and ten months."

"Ah, I've seen them," he sighed, exhaustion leaking through his voice. "They look happy."

"I hope so." Hana ran her right hand across her collar bone, trying to banish the cool air chilling her body temperature. Thoughts of her children induced sadness and a sense of loss. "Actually," she said, injecting false joviality into her tone, "I've got another son who's twenty. He's not really mine - he's Logan's nephew, but he calls me Ma and there's another boy who's seventeen. He's half-brothers with the twenty-year-old, but his mother died last year. I've kinda adopted him too. So I probably have six children altogether." She sighed.

"You're nice." Caleb's words slurred and Hana's concern grew.

"Caleb, don't sleep. You can't sleep. I'm lonely, so talk to me." Panic laced her voice and Hana shook him, causing a deep groan to emit from his chest. "Caleb!" She shook him again and there was nothing. "What have I missed?" Hana doubted herself. "Did you bang your head? I must have missed something!"

Caleb didn't reply, laying with his head balanced on a stranger's knee and his legs encased in the rough contraption made by a city girl. Hana felt the panic, fluttering at first but increasing in strength and volume as she realised how utterly alone she was. "Logan," she whispered into the darkness. "Logan, help us." Hopelessness magnified itself in her chest as a spirit of death hovered over the broken man and his saviour turned victim. Hana's shoulders heaved at the thought of her children being told she was lost forever and her courage snapped. "LOGAN!" she screamed.

It was the biggest sound the slender woman ever made and it took everything. It emerged with disappointment, anger and fear into a shout which echoed off every ridge and rock face, rebounding around her head for more than a second. Shuddering sobs followed it as the last of Hana's hope died and the man cradled in her lap slipped deeper into unconsciousness.

At first Hana doubted her hearing, believing the shouts were born of desperation and a feral craving for her husband. His voice sounded faint at first, calling her name over and over. She felt it ignite in her soul and the connection between them fired. Life became worth living again. "Logan!" she screamed, putting the last of her effort into his name. "Logan!"

"Hana!" His voice sounded above her head and light shone on the pitiful scene at the foot of the cliff.

"Logan!" she cried, sobs of relief punctuating incoherent words. She shook Caleb's shoulders with cold hands, trying to rouse him and fill him with the same sense of reprieve which gripped her. "Caleb, they're here," she sobbed. "Caleb, please wake up."

Male voices shouted questions as lights and confusion added to the *thwack, thwack* of a helicopter overhead. Hana cradled the silent stranger in her lap and wished for her bed, the feel of her husband's strong arms and one more chance to tell her six children how much she loved them.

3
Another Stray

Hana had time for one embrace with her husband before being loaded into the helicopter. Logan's grey eyes looked dark in the flashlights, his body rigid with tension. "I'm sorry about Sacha's tack," Hana sobbed as a medic took her arm and pushed her into the helicopter, thrusting earphones over her head.

Logan clutched the remnants of an expensive bridle and said nothing, his face ashen as Hana's green eyes searched for comfort. She cried all the way to the roof of the Waikato Hospital, still blubbering as medical staff wheeled her to the emergency rooms below. A nurse inserted a cannula into her arm, administering painkillers while she cleaned Hana's many scrapes and cuts. The gum tree was unkind to her, sending wicked shards of bark into her flesh as she slipped down it, one on the inside of her upper arm and another through her jeans into her calf. "They were nasty," the cheerful male nurse intoned, holding up the biggest length of wood. "Do you wanna see?"

Hana grimaced at the size of the shard which had embedded itself in her arm and leaned sideways, vomiting onto the hospital floor.

"Guess not then," he said, sounding disappointed.

Caleb was triaged and taken straight to surgery. Doped up on morphine and other licensed goodies, Hana lay back against the rustling hospital pillows and tried not to think. The registrar sounded American, softly spoken with a southern drawl which was comforting and soporific. His stethoscope dangled from his neck adorned with childish stickers and his white coat sported a dodgy stain near the collar. He pressed a bruise on her forehead and Hana hissed. "What's the date today?" he asked.

"Don't you know?" Hana felt concerned for him.

"How many children do you have, Mrs Du Rose?" he persisted, leaning on his clipboard as he balanced on the bed next to her.

Hana's mind cast back to her conversation in the bush with Caleb and it sounded ridiculous to begin at four and end up with six. She bit her lip and turned to the blonde man, the morphine making her vision blur as she remembered Wiremu. "Seven," she replied. "I forgot one."

The registrar jumped to his feet as the curtain whizzed past his face and Hana's husband stood in the gap. "Can I help you?" the medic asked, intimidated by the visitor's size. His dark wavy hair was peppered with grey at the sides and a covering of stubble graced the lower half of his face. Logan's imposing physique towered over the registrar, bush debris staining his jeans and shirt.

"Na, I'm good." Logan jerked his head towards Hana and the man widened his eyes.

"Mr Du Rose?" he said.

Logan nodded and stole a glance at Hana. "Yeah."

"Your wife had several large pieces of gum tree removed from her limbs; the wounds on her arm and thigh are butterfly stitched. She's had painkillers but seems muddled. I'm inclined to admit her for the night." He stared at Logan with expectation and seemed wrong-footed by the silence.

Grey eyes bored into him, eyes filled with the *mana* of a Māori elder and rimmed by long black eyelashes. "What?" Logan Du Rose said, a hint of aggression in his voice. "She's always muddled. I'm taking her home."

"Always muddled?" Suspicion flashed in the medic's eyes.

"Yep," Logan replied. "My wife rarely knows her ass from her elbow but she looks fine. She's had worse."

"Had worse?" the registrar parroted, "what do you mean worse?"

"Check her medical records, bro'," Logan said, losing patience. "It's late, I'm tired and we're real grateful for all you've done. Thanks for patching her up, but we're leaving now."

The doctor shook his head. "I don't think so."

"Okay," Logan replied. His tired eyes gleamed with challenge in the dim night lights on the ward.

The registrar swallowed and exited the cubicle, glancing over his shoulder and suspecting he had little say in the matter.

"Logan?" Hana said, her vision reducing her gorgeous husband to a dark, swirling shape. "I can't remember how many children I have. This is terrible!"

"Hey, babe. Shhhhh." In two strides Logan Du Rose clutched his wife, crushing her face into his muscular chest and kissing her hair. He smelled of horses and sweat, his white tee shirt stained and ripped and his hair dusty. "I was so worried about you," he breathed into her hair. "When you're feeling better, I'm gonna kill you, bloody wahine!"

Logan kissed Hana's dry lips, holding the sides of her scabbed cheeks and pressing his forehead into hers. "Don't you ever do that to me again!" he rebuked, his voice a husky growl. "Or I swear, I'll lock you up in the house for good."

"He was hurt real bad," Hana wept, the tears running through the antiseptic and the cuts on her face and chin. "I couldn't stop him going to sleep."

"The doctors are asking about him, Hana. Who the hell is he?"

Hana gulped. "I know this will sound stupid, but he needs us. He needs a family as much as Tama and Ryan did. He'll come good, I promise. When he's fixed, can he live at the hotel for a while, just until he's recovered?"

Logan pulled back and shook his head, studying his wife with the familiar Du Rose grey glare. He ran his thumb under her red rimmed eyes and kissed the end of her nose. "Babe, we've got more strays than a bloody dogs' home."

"Not really," Hana sniffed, wiping her nose on Logan's ruined tee shirt. "You already had Tama before we met and Ryan just turned up. But you gave David a home and...Bobby." She gulped, thinking of the blonde stockman who saved her baby son's life. He proved his loyalty to the Du Roses that day.

"Is that why you told the doctor you had seven kids?" Logan lifted Hana's sore chin with his index finger. A tiny smirk lifted the left side of his lips into a lopsided smile. "I wondered if you banged your head, or had stuff you needed to confess." His fingers worked their way around to her back, feeling the softness of her skin through the gaps in the hospital gown. His pupils dilated. He kissed the side of Hana's neck. "Who is this guy, Hana? What do you know about him? He's been living at the hut in Reuben's Gully. Toby says he told him to move on weeks ago. We don't owe him anything."

"Please let him stay, Logan?" Hana implored with her wide green eyes and felt her husband relent. He traced the line of her bare spine with his index finger, chasing away the demons of dread which assailed him earlier. Grounding himself in her strong English resolve, his heart celebrated her survival with a partial capitulation.

"We'll talk about it later!" he conceded. "But right now you need to get it together so I can break you out of here."

The doctor returned with his clipboard and found Hana far more communicative. "His name's Caleb," Hana said. "Caleb

Du Rose." She saw Logan shake his head in a slight movement and bit her lip. "He lives at my husband's hotel in the mountains with us. He went out pig hunting and I heard the gunshots. He was at the bottom of a ridge and I climbed down."

"Did you make the splint and strap his leg?" the doctor asked, raising his eyebrows in approval. Hana nodded, her face and neck blushing in embarrassment. She waited for the medical critique and dismissal of her work. "That was a pretty awesome job, ma'am," he acceded and Hana blushed more.

"Oh," she said, her eyes widening. "Please can we have the leather straps back?"

The doctor eyed her in confusion. "Er, I don't know. I think we got them off without cutting them. What are they from?"

Hana gulped. "I dismantled the horse's bridle," she said. "There's also a girth, an expensive girth." She couldn't look at her husband's face. "We'd like it all back, if possible."

The doctor left the cubicle and Logan leaned forward in the visitor's chair, sighing and pressing his fingers to his temples. Hana felt contrite. "I'm sorry," she said. "Sorry for not waiting and for ruining Sacha's bridle. I'm sorry for everything."

"Hey, it's fine." Logan shifted to the bed, wedging his hip into the small space next to Hana and slipping his arm around her shoulders. She winced as it constricted the wound under her arm. "Nothing matters, apart from getting you back safely."

"Did you find Sacha's saddle?" Hana exhaled, thinking of the combined cost of the handmade tack and the personalised saddle with its ornate stitching.

"Yep. Toby took it back for me. The chopper left and I ran up to the house and jumped in the ute. I think I broke a land speed record or two on the expressway here."

"Why didn't they take us to Auckland?" Hana asked, her fate already inexorably linked to Caleb's.

"Some road accident on the North Shore. They were busy so routed you here."

"Sorry," Hana said again. "You must feel shattered."

"Stop apologising, babe. Leslie and my dad are looking after Phoe and Mac. Leslie was worried sick. Dad helped us search and found those ribbon things you hung on the trees. Very clever." Logan kissed her temple. "Sacha arrived in the stable yard in a right mess, sweating and rearing. She terrified that lad, Rawhiti." Logan sniggered. "He nearly crapped himself. David raised the alarm on the radio so I was already on my way up to him on the quad bike and must have missed Sacha by minutes. David didn't see where you went so we started in the wrong direction. If Rawhiti hadn't radioed for help, we might not have found you until much later. David heard the call and remembered you rode off on Sacha and I went to the stables to get her."

"How did she make you understand?" Hana asked, her voice sounding sleepy. "Was it like Lassie? Did she do hoof movements and neighs which sounded like words?"

"No! She heard the quad coming, jumped the gate into the paddock and charged like a wounded bull. Then she ran off up the mountain. I trusted her and followed. Dad rode up on Methuselah and chased her into the bush on horseback. Some of us had to walk!" Logan chastised his wife with another kiss to the temple.

"There doesn't seem to be a hospital number for a Caleb Du Rose." The doctor whisked the curtain back and stood in the gap, tapping his clipboard with the pen.

Logan gave a little sniff of annoyance and Hana knew he directed it at her. He could have foretold the sequence of events like a fortune teller with a crystal ball. She floundered and he spoke for her. "Yeah, it's not his birth name. He's been with us a while though. It's all legit and he'll sort it when he wakes up." Logan gave one of his winning smiles and the doctor relaxed.

"Awesome. Well, you can go home now, Mrs Du Rose. Your discharge notice is at the front desk."

Hana gaped. "Someone took my clothes; what will I wear?" She looked down at her cut and bruised body and panicked at the vision of herself streaking naked across the multi storey car park in the middle of the night. Logan placed a reassuring hand over hers.

"Find her clothes," he said to the doctor, his authority overpowering in the small space. The man stalked away and Logan heaved a sigh. "Jerk!" he stated. "How did he imagine you'd walk out of here?"

Hana touched her face, an indicator of anxiety. The myriad cuts on her palm smarted and she put it down again. A nurse appeared with a brown paper bag containing Hana's filthy jeans, singlet, bra and socks, resting on her equally dirty cowboy boots. She shoved it on the chair and left without speaking. "Oh, nice," Hana commented, peering into the bag. "Stinky."

Logan helped his wife dress, managing to turn every clasp and button into foreplay without trying to. Hana yearned to lose herself in the big bed at home with him and forget about her disastrous afternoon. She winced as he pushed her arm into the sleeve and caught the white packing over her wound. "Sorry, babe," he said, looking chagrined.

"It's okay." Hana squeezed her eyes shut in pain. "I'm not sure if it's my ass or my elbow. Everything hurts."

Logan smirked. "Neither. But if you don't get a move on, they'll keep you here."

"That's your excuse for dissing your wife?" Hana said, sounding scandalised.

Logan shrugged. "Want me to get that doctor back and tell him I lied? I'd hate to take you out of their care if you're concussed."

Hana screwed her face up, resembling a stubborn Phoenix and drawing a snort from her husband. She allowed him to slide her knickers over her legs without disturbing the wound, tantalised by his dark fingers against her creamy skin. "You're doing that on purpose," she hissed as he smoothed the cotton over her bare buttocks.

"You can go out naked if you want," he whispered back. Hana gulped as her brain returned to the horrible scenario and she behaved while he encased her breasts in her bra and slipped the dirty shirt over her head.

At the desk, Hana picked up her discharge papers, fingering the accident report in her sore hands. The doctor dismissed her with a smile. "How's Caleb?" Hana asked. "Is he out of surgery?"

"Not yet. It was a bad break."

"When can he go home?" she pressed, emboldened by Logan's formidable presence.

"Not sure," the doctor said. "It'll be up to the surgeon. First few days he'll be on pain relief and then we'll have to monitor for infection. Ring when he's out of surgery."

"Thanks." Hana yawned and followed her husband into the cool air outside. She shivered and he put his arm around her shoulders.

"You okay, babe?" he asked and Hana nodded.

"Yeah, just glad to be alive. It was worse for poor Caleb, but after he lost consciousness I started to convince myself nobody would ever come."

"Na. You knew I wouldn't stop until I found you." Logan's voice betrayed his sense of near loss and Hana leaned her head against his strong shoulder as they walked.

"I'm so tired." She yawned again.

"Yeah, me too. I thought we'd stay in town tonight, see the kid in hospital tomorrow and go home after that? What do you think? Or do you want to go home and see Phoe and Mac now?"

"I desperately want to see them but I won't wake them tonight. They love sleeping over with Leslie and Alfred so let's stay here and go home tomorrow." Hana hid her desire to hold her baby and kiss her daughter, seeing the exhaustion in Logan's face. "We're both shattered and a road accident is the last thing we need."

Logan parked under the hotel building in the heart of Hamilton and the couple walked into the posh reception, filthy, dirty and without luggage. Logan's credit card did the talking and he purchased washing powder and toiletries from the expensive hotel stock and led his exhausted wife to the third floor. "Get a hot shower," he told her. "Those dressings are waterproof. It'll help you recover."

"Come in with me?" Hana begged and he conceded. They washed in the hot town water and Logan shampooed his wife's hair to remove the remnants of the bush. A thin dust covered her whole body and he lovingly removed it, running his scarred fingers across her most sensitive places.

"I couldn't cope with losing you," he whispered against the hiss of the shower and Hana turned in the small space to kiss the black down on his chest.

"I love you, Logan Du Rose," she replied, caressing his name on her tongue. Logan's lips covered over hers and Hana tilted her head to feel his tongue begin its familiar dance. Her mouth filled with water and she choked and spluttered while her husband laughed and banged her on the back.

Logan settled Hana in the big bed and went back to the bathroom. "What're you doing?" she grumbled, tired but reluctant to let go of her consciousness without him.

"I'm washing our clothes," he called. "I bought washing powder. We can't wear them home like that; they're gross."

Hana sighed. "They won't dry in time."

Logan appeared in the doorway, naked but for a small towel around his waist. "Yeah they will. They're on the towel rail and I'll rotate stuff. I don't want your cuts infected by dirty clothes."

"You're so sweet. That's probably why I love you." She yawned and turned her back on him, snuggling down into the deep mattress. Logan's body felt smooth and hard as he slipped into the bed behind her, pulling the starchy sheets over them both. He moved Hana's damp hair from her neck and kissed the soft skin, nibbling gently with his teeth. She moaned and arched her back and Logan pushed his arm around her, pulling her in to his body with his fingers splayed across her stomach. He moved his hand so his index finger snaked up Hana's thigh, tracing her hip bone and tickling her stomach. She snuffed and twitched, enjoying the sensation of Logan's rough chin grazing her neck. Hana smelled the fragrance of washing powder bathing them in a floral haze as Logan moved over the top of her, flicking her bottom lip with his tongue. Hana shifted to take his weight, responding to his kisses and tensing when Logan's phone trilled loudly into the room.

"Ignore it," he begged, getting into his stride.

The phone danced off the dressing table and vibrated across the floor, sounding like an angry bumble bee. Hana wiggled under her husband and ended the kiss. "Loge, what if it's about the children?" Her green eyes widened in concern and she blinked in the lamplight, long lashes swishing against her fringe.

Logan exhaled and bit his lip, struggling to let go of the moment. "Okay." He kissed the end of Hana's nose and allowed the fingers of his right hand to brush her breast as he clambered from the bed and retrieved the phone. "Du Rose," he snapped. He produced an exaggerated eye roll for Hana's benefit and held the phone out to her, waiting until she gripped it securely in her sore hand.

"Hello?" Hana's voice betrayed the strain of her awful afternoon. "Oh, Mark, hi." She held her breath as her surgeon-brother ranted. Logan shook his head and got under the covers, lying next to his wife and wearing a pained expression. Hana shot him a look of apology and tried to placate Mark McIntyre. "Emergency is miles away from where you work. How on earth did you find out?"

Logan sighed at Mark's loud voice as he berated his sister. "The orthopedic surgeon operated on your friend's leg and I closed the wound. As I scrubbed in for the next emergency, a nurse came down asking about him and saying, 'Mrs Du Rose' wanted to know how it went. It *had* to be you. I pleaded with your doctor to hold onto you, but as usual they didn't bloody listen!" Mark's clipped English accent made the words sound sharper than he intended. Hurt laced his voice. "I would have stitched you up. You only needed to ask."

"I'm glad you dealt with Caleb instead," Hana said. "His leg looked a mess and I'm sure you did a good job."

"Of course I bloody did!" Mark spat. "Are you back at home now?"

"Not yet," Hana replied, Logan's wide eyed expression making her deliberately obtuse. Mark and Logan had locked horns before over Hana's welfare and she didn't have the energy for a repeat of their egotistical posturing. "I'm just in bed about to go to sleep. We'll head home in the morning. I'm keen to get back to the children."

Logan sighed as Hana disconnected, having overheard Mark's insistence on seeing her. She handed him the phone and ignored her husband's pout as he narrowed his eyes and placed it on the bedside table again. "Don't bother; I heard," he grumbled. "I suppose he thinks it's my fault you ignored my stockman, rushed into danger with no means of communicating and then slid down a gum tree to rescue a total stranger." Hana put her hand over his mouth, but Logan had more to say. "Then once down there, you realised you couldn't get him to safety and sat there with him and his gun."

"Fine! Say what you really think, Logan! I already feel an idiot."

"Good!" Logan turned on his side and pulled Hana's body on top of his. "The guy had a gun. didn't that occur to you?"

Hana shook her head. "No. He couldn't reach it but I didn't think about it. I'm sorry."

"Fine. Now make it up to me wahine."

Hana snorted and stuck her bottom lip out. "Sexist pig!" she muttered, as Logan's hand at the back of her neck snagged her and pulled her lips down onto his.

4

Mark McIntyre

"Oh, just for future reference," Logan said, letting the towel slide down his strong thighs as Hana sat up in bed. "You should've climbed down the kauri. It's got a better trunk for grip and the bark doesn't come off in shards like the gum. Gum bark strips easily, which is why we use it to start fires."

"Right." Hana hugged her raised knees, watching Logan's muscular body as he moved around the bedroom after his shower. Her eyes strayed from his defined pectorals to his ridged stomach, ogling the luscious olive skin covering his stunning physique. She knew every blemish and scar and drank in his loveliness.

"What're you staring at, wahine?" Logan asked and Hana saw his lip lift in a subtle smile.

"Just something nice," she whispered and Logan turned his grey eyes on her. To her sadness, he shook his head.

"Hardly, babe." His right hand strayed to the ugly scar which reached from under his armpit and snaked past his hip. The staple marks were like deep recesses in the fleshy watershed of ridged, damaged skin. Hana shook her head and slipped naked from the bed, taking the double sheet with her. She glided across the carpet like a ghost and placed gentle fingers over Logan's.

"Don't be silly, makau. It's part of you. All your battle scars are part of you and I love every single one of them."

Logan ran his hand over his face, hiding his eyes from his wife. Hana pressed her body into his and let go of the sheet, forcing eye contact with her husband as she felt his chest hair against her palms. "You're the most beautiful man I've ever met and I can't believe you're mine." She kissed his firm pectoral muscle and saw a flicker of desire spark in his grey irises.

Logan's response was instant and Hana smirked, pressing her lips against his hairy chest and blinking her eyelashes coyly up at him. He exhaled and his lips shivered against hers. Then he pulled away. "You're a worry, Mrs Du Rose! You know damn well your brother's due here soon."

"He can wait outside." Hana reached up and kissed the underside of her husband's rough chin.

Logan laughed. "Bad girl. He'll hear you screaming and break the door down."

"With his scalpel?" Hana's face was full of feigned innocence. "It'll take him a while."

"Get!" Logan slapped the porcelain skin of her bottom and sent a giggling Hana towards the bathroom. "And get a move on, wahine! I don't need his nagging. I'd like to be home by lunchtime."

Mark arrived while Hana was in the shower. He perched in an armchair, his regal grey head bowed and his elbows resting on his knees. "Will she be long?" he asked, without looking up.

"She's a woman; she'll take as long as she wants," Logan snorted, pulling his head through the neck of his tee shirt.

"Don't be rude!" Hana flicked Logan with her damp towel as she slipped from the bathroom, her hair hanging like a damp auburn curtain and touching the centre of her back. "Hey

Mark, how are you?" she asked, bending to kiss the top of the man's head.

"Worried about you, as per bloody usual!" he snapped, standing and grabbing her by the shoulders. "I need to check your stitches."

"No!" Hana pulled her arm away. "I'm fine. They covered the wounds up and said to leave them for a few days. They're only butterfly stitches; I don't want to mess with them." She pouted. "I thought you wanted to see me before I went home, not check your colleague's work."

"I do want to see you, foolish girl!" Mark sat down but his fingers beat an impatient tattoo on his knees.

Logan eyed him sideways as he pulled his cowboy boots over his socks, an air of warning shrouding his strong frame. "Don't talk to her like that." His voice sounded low and impassive but Mark's face twitched as he sensed the caution behind the statement.

Hana observed her brother's rigid body and panicked. "Is it Dad? Has the cancer come back?"

"No, not at all. Sorry." Mark stood up, took a step forward, thought better of it and sat down again. "Nothing like that. Dad's fine; I spoke to him yesterday. He sends his love."

Hana exhaled and observed the man she grew up believing was her brother. He was tall and thin, sharing the same green eyes as her but a different body shape. Hana closed her eyes and shook her head, wondering how she never guessed he was her Aunt Elaine's love child, given to her childless parents before Hana's birth.

"Hey?" Logan roused her with a gentle touch of his hand on her shoulder and Hana started. "You still look tired."

Hana's smirk betrayed her lack of sleep in the big bed with the virile farmer and Logan responded with a wink. "Perhaps you'll do better at home," he said with a smile and Hana read the double meaning and bit her lip.

"Anka's gone back to her husband," Mark blurted and the couple turned to face him. "I planned to ask her to marry me this coming weekend and she beat me to it. She's gone back to Ivan."

"I'm sorry," Hana breathed, relief mixing with sorrow for her brother. She fought the urge to say, *I told you so.*

"Don't say it!" Mark snapped but looked at Logan instead. The Māori shook his head and rolled his eyes.

"I don't give a rat's ass who you date, Mark. It's your business, not mine."

"Yeah, but I know you hated her," Mark spat. "I couldn't bring her to the hotel to see my own sister; I'm sure that didn't help!" The tall doctor stood up and postured, desperate for someone to blame.

"Oh, whatever!" Logan's patience sounded frayed. "Don't blame me for that stupid chick's behaviour! We warned you." He jerked his head towards Hana. "Anka was Hana's best friend when she screwed my eighteen-year-old nephew. She's lucky she didn't get locked up for it. The way she messed with Tama's head barred her from my home. Sorry and all that but *he's* my priority, not your sordid sex life!" Logan clapped his cowboy hat over glossy black hair and dipped his head to kiss Hana's lips. "Don't get into it, babe," he whispered. "I'll grab you some breakfast; I won't be long." With a look of disgust towards Mark, he strode from the room, pulling the door closed behind him.

Mark sank into the chair and put his hands over his face. Hana heard the stubble rasp across his palms. "Oh, Hana. What a bloody mess!"

Hana sat on the bed and sniffed the socks Logan washed for her. They smelled of washing powder and felt warm from the towel rail. She slipped them onto her cold feet and wiggled her toes inside. "I don't know how to help you." She pulled her tee shirt over the white pack on her arm and squirmed on the edge of the bed, feeling her jeans aggravating the cut on her calf. "I believed Anka to be a good friend, loyal and godly. Then when she had her affair with Tama she changed. I hoped she'd settled down with you, but obviously not."

"I know you warned me," Mark said, his voice low as he fixed his gaze on the carpet between his feet. "You must be desperate to say it."

"Not really." Hana pressed her toes into her boots, smelling the bush scents waft up into her face. Logan's efforts with the cleaning wipes left darker coloured streaks in the leather. She sighed. "There's no satisfaction in seeing you unhappy. Is there?" She fixed her green eyes on Mark and watched his face twitch with emotion. "Why don't you travel back with us today for a break?"

Mark shrugged. "I've taken a week off. But what about your husband? I got the distinct feeling I wasn't welcome on his mountain."

Hana chastised him with her eyes and shook her head. "Stop it, Mark; don't turn this back on Logan. I told you from the beginning that Anka wouldn't be welcome. The last time she visited our home, I caught her on my lounge floor with my nephew and she wasn't wearing knickers. I never want a repeat of that sight, thank you." Hana shuddered. "It made me feel bloody inferior for a start. I've never had such a nice ass. It's not fair."

Mark visibly winced and hung his head, his mind deviating to tempting thoughts of the lithe Anka with her underwear removed. He sighed. "You didn't tell me that."

"Why should I?" Hana replied. "You're big enough to make your own decisions and for the record, you could have visited alone. You put yourself in the middle and chose to stay away and that's your problem, not mine!"

"Fine then!" Mark sulked. "Please ask Logan if I can stay with you?"

"I don't need to ask him, idiot! He'll say it's fine. Do you want to stay at our place or in the hotel?"

"You've got a house full. Maybe I should stay at the hotel."

Hana pulled a face. "I'll put Wiri in with Phoe for a few days and you can have Tama's room. He isn't planning to visit for a few months."

"Who's Wiri?" Mark's head jerked up in surprise, his green eyes wide with enquiry. "Where do you find these people?"

"It's complicated." Hana slumped onto the bed, wincing as her jeans tightened against her bruises. She pushed her fingers through a gaping rip on the inner left thigh. "Wiri belongs to Logan's half-brother, Neville Du Rose. He's five and stays with us at the moment. His mother suffered a mental breakdown and can't seem to climb back out of the pit for long enough to take her son home."

Mark sighed and ran long fingers through his greying hair. "Yeah. It's like that sometimes. You hit rock bottom and can't get back up again."

"Are you speaking from experience?" Hana's voice sounded soft. "Because if you are, I hope you know you can talk to me."

Mark nodded. "After you left and then Mum died, my marriage broke up and I couldn't get access to the boys. Everything I ever strived for turned to ash in my hands and I got stuck in a dark ditch with no hope of digging my way out. It's as debilitating as any physical illness, sapping the life out of you."

"Mark," Hana whispered, "do you feel like that now?"

His head shot up quickly, already shaking in denial. "No, love. Not at all. I'm perfectly fine; just maudlin over having been taken for a fool. A few days at your place staring at the Tasman Sea and I'll be raring to go." He fixed Hana with an unconvincing smile and slapped his hands on his thighs. "I'll pack and head up sometime later today. That okay?"

"Course it is." Hana smiled and let Mark wrap his arms around her. She held onto the lean body and wished back the wasted twenty-six years of not having the stubborn man in her life.

"Hana," Mark mumbled, "I remember you telling me once that you suffered from depression. Was it because of me?"

Hana recalled the dark days of being a new mother at eighteen, robbed of family support because of Mark's disgust. He carried her father along in his rage and Hana ended up alone, fumbling through a tenuous fledgling marriage like a blind man on a cliff. She picked her words with care. "I think a spirit of misery hangs over everyone at points in our lives. It was hard when Mum died but I didn't go under then, no. It was after Vik died and I discovered he cheated. When the numbness wore off after the funeral it was replaced with excruciating pain."

"I'm so sorry." Mark's head sunk further into Hana's hair and she felt his body heave. She sat next to him on the bed and rubbed his back, saying nothing. Mark sniffed and wiped his eyes. "I behaved badly to you and I find it impossible to forgive myself. I've often wondered if the strain on Mum's heart killed her. You came to ask your parents for help and I denied you that. Everything which unfolded from that moment is my fault. I'm such a fool."

"We've done this, Mark. You've said sorry and I forgave you. Let's not go back over it? Vik's dead and I have Logan and two more beautiful children. I don't harbour some awful seed of blame anymore, I promise. I think you're trying too hard, love. You can't recreate everything you lost in your first marriage with a woman like Anka. You're snatching back things already long gone. Why don't you relax, enjoy life and see what happens? It could be amazing if you stop hounding yourself. God makes all things new but we seem to think we can do it ourselves. I should know, I spent years giving it my best shot and still failed."

Mark nodded and Hana fetched him a tissue for his weeping nose and he thanked her. "I thought Anka was sincere."

"Yeah well so did Logan's eighteen-year-old nephew when she introduced him to the hurts and marvels of an older woman. Poor Tama made a real mess of a year of his life because of her.

For Anka, it was purely about the sex and the thrill of feeling needed, but Tama believed she was in it for marriage."

"How's Tama doing now?" Mark used the distraction to blow his nose and clean himself up.

"Yeah, good." Pride crossed Hana's face and made her glow. "He loves the fire service. It fulfils his need to be a hot hero, so he's happy. He's still messed up in the relationship department." She frowned. "He broke up with his steady girlfriend at the end of last year and went off the rails again. He slept with six girls on a hen night at the hotel and got offside with Logan when they telephoned to book him again. I think he's been putting it about liberally ever since."

"Six girls on a hen night!" Mark looked in awe. "Half his luck! I don't think I could manage more than one anymore." He sighed and went back to his navel gazing.

"Pack it in!" Hana slapped his arm. "He's looking for love, same as you. But neither of you are going the right way about it."

"Maybe sleeping in his room will give me some ideas." Mark smirked and Hana glared at him.

"It better not!"

The sound of the hotel door unlocking disturbed them and Mark scrubbed at his face to hide his weakness in the face of intimidating masculine strength. Hana shook her head at his need to straighten his ego and pulled the door open to allow Logan entry, chastened by the memory of the one time he broke in front of her. The hideous image of her husband's tears left a lasting chill in Hana's heart and her smile faltered.

Logan's grey eyes sparkled as he handed Hana the brown paper bag filled with a warm bagel. He offered it like a sacrifice pulled from his soul and she smiled and reached up to kiss his cold lips. "Where did you go?"

"Bakery up the road. It's freezing out there." He looked around the room with eagerness and shifted on his boots with hyperactive impatience. "You ready to go?"

Mark cleared his throat and stood, taking a step towards Hana's husband. "Thanks for looking after my sister." He stretched out his hand and Logan looked at it in confusion before accepting the handshake, more as a reflex action than a decision. Suspicion weighed down any expression in Logan's eyes as he searched for sarcasm or double meaning.

Hana blew out a breath of exasperation. "Mark's got time on his hands. He wondered if he could come and stay with us for a few days."

Logan looked at his wife, knowing the invitation was already given but sensing she wanted his stamp of approval. "Yeah, it's fine," he conceded, seeing the relief in Hana's body language. She smiled at him and her green eyes sparkled with the promise of reward.

"I'll head back to my room and grab my gear," Mark said, sounding enthused. He kissed Hana on the top of her head and left, making little sound as he closed the heavy door behind him.

Logan observed Hana with interest as she exhibited familiar signs of stress, pressing the slender fingers of her right hand over the pacemaker under her left collarbone. He watched and waited as though she was a delicate filly he needed to understand before attempting to lay a saddle across her withers. Hana met his gaze with trepidation. "Anka really hurt him. He's sounding depressed."

Logan snorted and screwed up his face in disdain. "Don't talk about her! I warned him, but he's a sucker for a pretty face. I don't want to hear about it."

"Do you think she's got a pretty face?" Hana pouted as jealousy took root.

Logan cast his eye around the room for stray belongings before settling narrowed eyes on his wife. Amusement radiated out and he laughed. "Not prettier than yours. Why? You jealous, makau?"

"Yes." Hana smirked at Logan's use of the Māori word for favourite and hung her head. She often used it for him, pleasing him with her attempted mastery of his language.

Logan took two strides to reach her, forcing her to meet his eyes. He bent and kissed her on the cheek, his unshaven face tickling her soft skin with its bristles. His lips lingered and Hana smelled the hotel shampoo on his hair as it brushed against her neck. Desire shot through her stomach like an arrow and she inhaled. "I need to get back to the children," she whispered. "And we only have the room for another half an hour."

"I don't need half an hour." His soft lips on her skin made Hana swallow as they followed the roughness of his chin on her neck, arousing and soothing. Logan undressed her in the middle of the room, his fingers gentle on her cuts and scrapes as he removed her tee shirt and eased her out of her jeans. He picked up her slender frame and laid her on top of the expensive bedspread. Still fully dressed, he whispered, "You're my wahine matua." His lips moved down her body in a volley of sensuous kisses. "No other woman on Papa-tū-ā-nuku's earth measures up to you." He stripped his shirt and jeans off at speed, adding his boxer shorts to the pile on the floor.

Hana groaned as Logan's fingers joined his lips, roving across her body in arcs of pleasure. A sharp rap on the door heralded a call of, "Housekeeping!" The owner of the voice rattled a key in the lock and Hana's eyes widened in fear.

Logan swore and dived for the door, intercepting the uniformed maid in the gap. She squeaked at the sight of the tall, dark male oozing sex appeal and frustration in one confusing mix. The tiny Philippino woman cricked her neck to stare up at him, her face level with Logan's muscular chest. "There's no sign!" she said with indignation and Logan snatched the 'Do Not Disturb' notice from the hook and used it to cover his nakedness.

"Where would you like me to hang it?" he bit, barring her way.

The woman humphed and glared at him with irritation, noting the scars on his face and the unkempt dark hair and stubble. Her eyes wandered down his body and she took a step backwards. "Leave key at reception when you're done," she said, embarrassment colouring her olive skin.

Logan shut the door and leaned against it, trying to hold back the laughter bubbling in his chest. Hana groaned from under the sheet. "That was embarrassing." She popped her face out, cheeks flaring red in discomfort. She pointed a shaking hand at her husband's feet. "You would've got away with that if you didn't have a hole in your sock."

Logan glanced down and inspected his big toe through the torn fabric and his eyes crinkled at the corners. "You think she noticed my sock? Ah well, that's my modelling career over then."

Hana's eyes poked over the top of the sheet and Logan narrowed his sexy grey eyes and let her enjoy the view for a moment. "Well, wahine matua, I'll just have to start again."

Hana giggled and dived under the bedsheets. Her voice sounded muffled. "I'm not your head wife, I'm your *only* wife. I won't be sharing!"

Logan snorted as he slid beneath the bed covers, his nakedness radiating warm heat towards Hana. "Fine then," he conceded as he pushed his fingers through the swathes of fabric until he felt the soft skin of her hip, "then you'll just have to do twice as much work."

5

Conflict

"He's sleeping but I'll let him know you visited. What's your name?"

"Hana Du Rose." Hana's voice sounded flat with disappointment as she viewed the comatose teenager in the bed. His ash blonde hair spread out across the white pillow, his complexion waxen and sick. Logan eyed Caleb's face with a frown and then looked away, shifting impatiently on the soles of his cowboy boots. "When can he go home?" Hana asked and the nurse gave a bland smile.

"That's up to the doctor. Come back later. Visiting's from four until eight in the evening."

Hana shook her head. "I live above Rangiriri and I'm going home today." She glanced at Logan, who didn't offer to bring her back. "I need to get back to my children."

The nurse stopped shuffling paper on the desk and looked at Hana, her eyebrows raised in expectation. Having nothing left to say, Hana dropped her gaze and moved away. Logan remained silent as they faced the metal doors of the elevator and Hana shot nervous glances in her husband's direction. "You don't like him, do you?"

Logan's grey eyes narrowed and he shrugged. "I have no feelings about him. He trespassed; he got hurt. What do you want from me, Hana?"

"I don't know." She pressed the call button again, willing the lift to hurry. The sound of grating mechanisms filled the air as the elevator responded and then stopped at a floor above. Hana released an exaggerated sigh and closed her eyes.

The journey north felt painful, the atmosphere inside the ute strained. Logan concentrated on the road, tapping an annoying beat on the steering wheel with his fingers and Hana chewed her lip and stared through the passenger window, watching the northernmost reaches of the Waikato whip past her window. "This winter feels endless." Her voice sounded loud as she broke the silence and Logan nodded.

"It's like that sometimes. The weather's changed since we were kids."

"About Caleb," Hana began.

Logan shook his head. "I don't wanna talk about him." The impatience in his tone made Hana turn to face him.

"Why?"

"He's trouble!" Logan snapped. "He is trouble and he brought trouble with him. Once again, I'm driving you home from hospital and I'm sick of it!" He banged his palm on the steering wheel. "You've got a bloody death wish and him being around won't help. I give up with you sometimes, Hana."

"I did nothing wrong." Angry tears welled up behind Hana's eyes and she swallowed and fought them back.

"Didn't you?" Logan spat. The ute swerved as he took his eyes off the road to glare at her. "Don't you have two tamariki that need you?" His eyes blazed. "You're a whāereere. Behave like one!"

"You don't have to tell me I'm a wife and mother!" Hana hissed, translating Logan's Māori for herself. "Nothing I did in trying to help Caleb jeopardised that."

"Really?" Logan's eyes blazed, granite grey and hard. "So, you didn't need rescuing and you haven't just left my tamariki for a night with other people? I didn't spend a night away from my business and miss a meeting with the accountant yesterday? And you *didn't* nearly fall fifty metres or need medical care? No, I thought not; it's all in my head."

Hana's eyes widened and she turned away, chewing the inside of her cheek and staring through the window, unseeing. Logan's words seemed to squeeze her heart, constricting her breathing and bringing her to her senses. Hana's fingers writhed in her lap as she sank from the heights of heroism to idiocy. She took shallow breaths, exhaling through pursed lips to disguise the waiting sobs and fighting for control. Easing herself sideways in her seat, Hana brushed away the hot tears, hating her weakness and detesting herself.

Logan's hand on her shoulder was enough to drive her stupidity home and Hana gulped as he indicated and pulled into a layby, rolling to a stop. She heard him sigh as he removed his hand and put the gear lever into neutral. "I'm sorry," he said. "You're not a bad whāereere."

Hana sniffed and wiped her nose on the back of her wrist and Logan reached for her again. Insistent fingers pulled at her wooden body, cradling her head against his chest across the gear stick. "I am," she sniffed, her breath hitching in her chest. "You're right; I'm a rubbish wife and mother."

"You're not. I shouldn't have said it. You attract trouble and danger like flies around roke and it freaks me out, that's all."

Hana sobbed as Logan realised his error. "I didn't mean you were shit, Hana! I'll just shut up."

Hana wiped her nose on Logan's tee shirt and sniffed the unfamiliar hotel deodorant on his skin. The hot, angry tears subsided as guilt rose in her breast. "I knew I was in trouble when I got half way down the tree," she admitted. "It looked like miles to the bottom and I realised I'd overestimated my climbing ability. I prayed for you and the children and hoped you'd find someone nicer to marry."

Logan snorted. "You honestly think I'd bother looking for another woman?" He sighed and rubbed Hana's back. "Wahine, you've given me enough trouble to make up for the twenty-six years I spent looking for you. You're it, babe. If I can't have you, I'd rather be alone."

"Liar," Hana sniffed. "You'd castrate yourself out of frustration."

"Na, I'd get a hooker. Mindless sex and no grief."

Hana sat up, her fringe sticking up comically. Her green eyes widened with horror. "You wouldn't!"

Logan laughed and put the truck into gear. "You wouldn't be here to disapprove." He checked his mirror, indicated and pulled back onto the motorway, jerking his head back towards Hana. "Put your seatbelt back on, wahine." He hid a smirk as he checked over his right shoulder and pulled into the outside lane, overtaking a milk truck. By the time Hana clicked her belt back into place and faced him, Logan had tamed his teasing expression into his characteristic look of blank disinterest.

6

The Challenge

"Hey Macky, look at the horse. Wanna stroke her nose?" Hana shifted her son onto the other hip and turned so he could see Sacha's blue eye. The mare shifted her face and reached out towards the child, scenting his leggings and snuffing gently. Mac reached out a tiny finger and prodded the furry face. Sacha closed her eyes, responding to what she sensed of Logan in the small boy. "She's beautiful, hey Mac?" Hana crooned, watching the baby's face change as he concentrated, knitting his brow and looking serious.

"Excuse me!" The masculine voice sounded firm, coming so unexpectedly it made the humans and horse jump in equal measure. Sacha put her ears flat back on her head and snaked her neck. "What do you think you're doing? This is a private area." The male looked strong and imposing, striding towards Hana with bulging muscles and a threatening stance. "You can't just walk into my stable yard without permission!" he snapped and Hana saw frustration cross his face at her lack of response. Her first reaction was fear, closely followed by indignation.

"Pardon?"

"You heard!" he replied rudely. "And get away from that mare; she's unpredictable. She killed a man last year."

Hana took a step away from the approaching male, backing up into Sacha's space. The mare sensed danger and began to scrape her front hooves down the wooden door with a relentless grinding action. She snaked her neck around Hana's body, defending her and the baby against the intruder. The man swore.

"Get out of the way, you stupid woman!" he shouted into Hana's face and yanked on her arm, causing her to squeeze hold of Mac so as not to drop him. "That mare bites!"

Sacha went ballistic. She reared in the small space, banging her head on the lintel as she went up and pounding her dinner plate hooves into the wooden half door. Not content with the damage, she whirled and battered it with her back feet so the sound of splintering wood rent the air in the stable yard. Wood shards pelted Hana as the enraged horse wrecked her stable door. The stranger yanked Hana towards him and she toppled sideways before shrinking back from him in fear. She found her voice. "Get off me!"

As the half door crashed to the ground, the hinges groaned in protest and bent beyond recognition until they popped from the frame. Sacha whirled around, her eyes venting unbridled fury. Hana cuddled her son hard into her breast, anticipating bloodshed and putting her hand over Mac's eyes. Sacha's body glided past Hana in a blur of elegant white with grey dapples on a muscular rump, as she picked up speed and lurched towards the man in the tan cowboy hat. He swore and fled, narrowly barricading himself into an adjacent stable before Sacha attacked the door with her enormous hooves.

"Sacha!" Hana gathered herself enough to holler at the huge horse and draw her attention. "Stop that!"

The horse's eyes rolled back in her head and Hana sensed a pause in her equine enjoyment as the animal trotted over to her, shaking her magnificent mane and tossing her head in victory. "I'm fine!" Hana told her, reaching out to smooth the glossy white fringe from the mismatched eyes. "That was totally unnecessary!"

Sacha snorted and Hana held onto Mac and cast around her. "It's pointless putting you in any of these," she said. "You'll break out again. Come with me." Hana strode to the gate leading to open paddocks beyond and fiddled with the latch one handed, balancing the curious baby in her other arm. The catch snapped open and Hana pushed, creating a gap big enough for the large body to walk through. "Now, go find the others," Hana told the mare, jerking her head towards a group of Appaloosa females under the bush line. Some had foals at heel and Hana sensed their maternal irritation at the bossy white mare's entrance. They corralled their babies and turned their bums on the Sacha, communicating her unwelcome status.

Mac pointed a pale finger towards Sacha and made a popping sound with his lips. He clung to Hana's cardigan with the other hand, determined not to let go; ill at ease in the calming chaos. Phoenix would have sobbed in fear or anger with the furious passion of a Du Rose but not Mac. Hana stroked her son's cheek and he put his finger in his mouth and stared at her with huge green eyes. "Can you say, 'horsey' Mac?" Hana whispered, resting her forehead against his. He smiled and moved his lips and Hana felt the click in her heart. "You can't, can you?" Her voice wobbled. "You can't hear what I'm saying."

Worry clenched her chest and she struggled for control. Only she knew and it tore her soul in two. Sacha moved closer, thrusting her head over the gate and offering furry comfort from one mother to another. Hana's tears stuck to the white hairs on the soft, questing muzzle.

"Mrs Du Rose?" Toby's voice held an enquiry as he approached, alarm burgeoning in his face at seeing Hana's heaving shoulders. She wiped her sleeve across her face and turned to him with a false smile, dismayed to see he wasn't fooled. "What's going on?" His handsome face creased with concern. "I'll get Logan." He reached for the radio hooked on his belt and Hana gripped his wrist.

"Please don't. He'll go crazy."

"What happened? What's with the stable door?"

A bolt grated and the furious stranger appeared from inside his hiding place. Hana held her breath and turned away, feeling her heart rate hike. Her misery and sense of defeat channelled itself into anger and she gritted her teeth, her green eyes flashing with fury. Sacha snorted, blowing warm air over the baby's hand and he turned his head and smiled like a cherub. Hana gulped. "Toby, please hold Mac for a second?"

The stockman pulled a face filled with discomfort and shrugged. He pushed his Jackaroo hat further back on his head. "I'm not real good with little kids. They don't like me."

"Mac likes everyone." Hana watched her son's contented face as he reached out to touch Sacha's whiskery nose, exploring the contrast between the soft fur on her nostrils and the thick, prickly hairs underneath her lips. He concentrated on his experiment and Sacha waited with extreme patience for him to finish.

Hana shot a look behind her as the stranger went into the stable manager's office and slammed the door. "Please Toby?"

"What you gonna do? Don't leave me here for ages, will you? I've stuff to do."

Hana shook her head. "I promise. I need to do something."

Toby jerked his head towards the closed office door. "Stay away from that guy. Logan's got rocks in his head employing him; he's bad tempered, upoko mārō."

Hana's brow knitted in question at the Māori words as Toby hefted Mac onto his hip, smiling as the small boy tilted his body to look into the man's face. Mac studied Toby with concentration and then satisfied, sighed heavily and rubbed his eyes. "The man's stubborn and headstrong so don't go near him."

"Is that what it means?" Hana asked, pulling the baby boy's jacket over his back to keep him warm. "Upoko mārō," she repeated. "I don't intend to get too near him."

"Hana, no!" Toby hissed, dropping the formality of her married name in his anxiety. He stood up straighter as Hana strode across the stable yard and Sacha let out a worried snort and dragged her front hoof along the metal gate. "Stop!" Toby turned and chastised the mare and she glared at him and rolled her blue eye in warning. "Yeah, whatever!" Toby shook his head and went back to watching Hana.

She strode across the concrete, feeling the roughness of the surface through her boot soles. Everything built into a crescendo in Hana's chest as she remembered the man's malice towards Sacha and his painful grip on her arm. Her son's plight weighed heavily on her heart, his condition becoming more obvious with each new sunrise. Every day began with high hopes and ended in defeat. The tiny boy explored with his hands and made faces of extreme interest, but said nothing. Sometimes babbling sounds escaped his lips but Hana's desire to hear Mac speak real words became an obsession. She turned her life upside down thinking up new lures like the stables, knowing he loved Sacha's fur and believing he just needed the right encouragement. "Bloody man ruined it!" Hana raged as she picked up speed, convincing herself Mac would have spoken if the stranger hadn't spoiled the moment.

Hana crashed into the office with force, hearing the old wood groan as it slammed back against the wall. She stood in the gap, flame red hair and temper making an entrance even before her slender body followed. The stranger whipped around, caught staring at a picture on the exposed brick wall. Jack's face smiled through the dusty glass at her, mocking and defying Hana with its existence. Her remaining resolve snapped at the memory of the dead man's attack on her and her newborn son, fuelled by indignation that his image remained on the office wall. A much younger Jack mocked her with a tepid smile, his hat pushed back on his head. A teenage Logan stood next to him in ragged jeans and the hat he still wore. Her husband's face frowned in seriousness, his hands raised as the camera caught him signing something to the deaf man. Their familial secret hung between them, only seen with hindsight.

"Get the hell out!" the man snapped, surprise morphing into fury.

"*You* get out!" Hana shouted, rounding the table and prodding his chest. "Who do you think *you* are?"

The male took a step back and Hana felt the atmosphere change as he struggled to assess the situation. Cold blue eyes studied her and the ruggedly handsome face creased in confusion. "No. This is my stable yard. Who the hell do you think you are?"

Hana took another step forward, disappointment and anger stoking her fire into an inferno. "I know who I am, but clearly you don't!" Hana waved her arm around the office, pristinely tidy compared to the chaos Jack worked in for decades. "I'm Hana Du Rose and it's my husband's stable yard, *not yours!*" She gritted her teeth and heard her voice rise a few octaves, hating the screech it made. All control gone, she edged closer to the man whose colour paled from a healthy pink to deathly white. "How *dare* you put your hands on me!" she yelled. "And if you ever touch the white horse again, I'll..."

Hana finished her tirade and turned, sickened at herself as she listened to the uncharacteristic threat burst from her lips. Nerve endings in her head snapped as she lurched sideways and seized the photograph from the wall. The frame twisted as it hit the concrete floor and she stamped her foot into Jack's face, hearing the glass grind under her boot.

The stable manager stared at her, wide eyed as Hana marched from the office keeping her head high and slamming the door behind her as a final act of petulance. Shame and disgust crawled over her flesh as she strode back towards Toby. He cradled a sleeping Mac in his arms and Hana felt momentary relief her son didn't hear her disgusting words. The realisation he didn't hear her whispers of love either caused her heart to overflow and she struggled not to cry.

"Remind me not to get on the wrong side of you," Toby remarked, handing the sleeping child back. His eyes crinkled at the edges as he battled a smirk. "I thought you were gonna sit and have a nice chat, not yell him off the mountain."

"He pulled my arm!" Hana snapped through gritted teeth. "He shouldn't have done that!" She turned her wrist over, considering the ridged scar across the artery; a wound created defending herself from another madman.

Toby held his hands up and touched the brim of his hat in deference. "No, he shouldn't." His voice sounded soothing, offering comfort and solidarity. A smile curved his lips and he added his punch-line. "Logan's in the equipment shed. He wants to see you. Now."

Hana's eyes widened in horror. "No! Why?"

Toby laughed. "Beats me."

"He heard, didn't he?" Hana's contrition came quick and fast.

"I'm sayin' nothing," Toby laughed. He touched his hat again and strode towards the hotel gate, shaking his head and chuckling.

Hana rolled her head back on her neck and stared at the azure sky, searching for answers but finding none written there. The sleeping baby in her arms sucked on his thumb and Hana swaddled him up in her jacket, pulling the folds of material around him as though barricading herself against her husband's reproach. "I just threatened your daddy's new stable manager," she whispered. "And smashed up. Daddy's gonna kill me."

Hana sighed and steered her reluctant feet towards the large equipment shed, dawdling and delaying the inevitable. She heard clanking sounds at the furthest point from the roller doors and traipsed towards the noise, her steps getting smaller and smaller.

"Hey babe." Logan sounded calm and Hana dared to relax. *Please don't have heard. Please don't have heard.* Logan turned, wielding a long metal hinge and Hana's heart sank. She avoided the juvenile urge to wail and stamp her feet, waiting quietly for Logan's rebuke. When it didn't come, Hana realised she needed it as the antidote for her guilt.

"This should be okay for that stable door," he said, dropping another hinge on the floor at her feet. It clanged into the silence of the shed and Mac slept on without flinching. The absence of any reaction destroyed Hana.

She squeezed her nose to hold the sob in, balancing the baby in one arm and gripping her face. Her fingers spread over her mouth as she exhaled and felt misery bubble up in her chest. Oblivious, Logan searched in the metal cabinet for screws. "Did you put Sacha in the paddock?" he asked, his voice still calm. "I was gonna ride her." When Hana didn't answer, Logan shot a look in her direction and his brows knitted. He dropped the screws back into the long drawer. "Hana?"

Hana shoved her fist against her lips and closed her eyes, willing the desperation to go away. Logan's arms around her acted as a catalyst and she heard the groan come from her chest. His torso felt so strong against her face and Hana exploded into his shirt in an agony of heartbreaking sobs. Logan hoisted his son over his shoulder and used his free arm to crush Hana into him, rubbing her back with long, slow motions and kissing the top of her head. His soft Māori words offered soothing, lyrical speech which calmed her soul and laid a balm over her troubled heart. "Talk to me, babe," he whispered. "Whatever it is, we can sort it out."

We can't, Hana's desperation cried. *Nobody can.* She sobbed harder. Hana saw Logan's tan cowboy boots shuffle on the ground through a haze of tears and sensed his awkwardness. His chest felt rock hard against her cheek. He sniffed and she sensed his fear, remorse compounding her misery. "Hana?" He shook her shoulder. "Is it me? Did I do something?"

Hana smushed her face harder into his shirt and shook her head, her answer inaudible. Logan put his finger under her chin to tip her head back, his face questioning. "No." She sniffed. "It was me, I caused it. I took Macky to see Sacha and a man shouted at me and Sacha got upset and beat her way out of the stable. He was rude and angry, shouting it was his stable but it's not; it's yours. I went into the office and picked a fight with him and I'm so ashamed."

"But *we're* good?" Logan ran his thumb through the tears under Hana's chin, his grey eyes narrowed in fear. She sighed and caught hold of his hand, pressing it against her cheek.

"We're fine," she breathed, their awful separation before Mac's birth acting like a barb in their marriage.

"Did the new guy touch you?"

Hana saw anger cross Logan's face and gulped. She shook her head. "He thought I was in danger and pulled my arm, so Sacha chased him into a stall."

Logan swore and laughed. "She did what? I saw her looking guilty, stupid mare. I'll have to brace that bloody door again. Toby wouldn't tell me what happened. He said I had to ask you."

Hana exhaled and ran a hand through her red hair. "Did you hear me shouting?"

Logan nodded and smirked. He leaned forward and pressed his full lips over hers. "I wish I'd seen you. You've no idea how gorgeous you are when you're angry; I can never resist you." His forehead rested against hers and the squished baby grunted in his arms.

"I'm so embarrassed," Hana whispered. "I can't remember the last time I lost my temper."

"Hey," Logan stroked Hana's cheek and smiled. "It's fine. It sounds like he was out of line. I'll have a chat with him." Logan's jaw squared as he gritted his teeth and Hana wondered if the chat might get physical.

She groaned. "He's horrid. How can you employ someone so nasty? He'll make the hotel and campsite guests too scared to visit the stables. Can't he see his wages come from paid treks?"

Logan shrugged. "Not entirely. He's running the bloodstock business as well but I'll talk to him. He's taken over...he's doing..." Logan faltered and Hana licked her lips.

"Just say it, Logan. He's doing Jack's job." She gulped. "There was a picture on the wall of you and Jack." Hana raised her eyes, tears welling into their corners. "I smashed it. I'm sorry." Her face crumpled. "It's your history and I smashed it. I should've given it to Will to keep in the museum where I never had to see it again but I wrecked it."

"Oh, Hana." Logan's soft sigh was a caress, washing over her soul in understanding.

"But he was your grandfather and I just smashed it." Hana swallowed mid sentence, hating how pathetic she sounded.

"He tried to kill you and Mac." Logan's voice contained a granite hardness and his jaw worked with emotion. "It doesn't matter what he was to me, babe, or what he thought he knew, he nearly took you both away from me." Logan exhaled and his pupils contracted as he stared through the open roller door into the brightness outside. "Sacha did me a favour." His voice sounded wistful, as though he didn't mean it and Hana watched a momentary trail of grief flash across his face. Then it was gone.

Hana shivered and closed her eyes, waiting for the disturbing visions to pass.

"Hana, I'll sort it." Logan's voice held softness as he turned his attention back to her, dragging them both into the present. "I'll make him apologise."

"The stable manager?" she asked, Jack's face still not banished. When Logan nodded she shook her head. "Don't. Tell him to leave me alone. I'll replace the glass in the picture if you fetch it for me and then I'll take it to Will. But I don't want that arrogant stable manager near me; I can't cope with him at the moment."

"Okay." Logan's smile had a sad, down turned quality. "But don't hate him because he does Jack's job; it's not fair."

Hana opened her mouth to object and then closed it, recognising the origin of her irrational, overwhelming fury. She nodded. "I'll try."

"Ā kāti, ko tēnā, tēnā!" Logan pressed his lips against her forehead. *Well then, that's done.* "Shall I ask Leslie and Dad to babysit the kids tonight? I'd love to take you out to dinner. I've got things we need to discuss."

Hana nodded and smiled, wiping her face on her sleeve. "I'd love that." Worry crossed her green eyes. "What things do we need to discuss?"

"Nothing bad, pōhauhau!" Logan laughed and squeezed her in his strong arms. "Just interesting."

Hana sniffed and straightened her blouse. "I am an idiot, you're right. Do I look like I've been crying?"

Logan used his free hand to wipe the skin under her eyes with such gentleness it unpicked Hana's false courage. "Na, you're beautiful, wahine." He smiled at her and she felt a dart of desire shoot downwards from her stomach. Logan wrinkled his nose as he handed the baby back. "Hana?" he said, his tone gentle. "I'm happy for you to use your authority with the staff when they mess up, but you need to think before you speak."

Hana gulped and chewed her lip. "You heard."

Logan snorted. "Yeah. Picture the employment tribunal, babe, when my new stable manager stands up and repeats what you said to him."

Hana coloured a rosy shade and stared at the floor. When she glanced up, Logan's amusement mocked her. "Sorry," she mumbled. "I'll apologise."

"No, don't," Logan said, his hand snaking around her waist and drawing her in. "Stay away from him like you said you would. It's sometimes good for the staff to see you're not a pushover on the mountain. You're mostly the buffer between them and me and it's not always a good place to be. This new guy's got major issues, babe, but he's still a good man, deep down."

"He hated on Sacha," Hana began and Logan raised his hand to stop her launching back into ugly territory.

"Yeah, I believe you. But yelling at the top of your voice, '*Touch the white horse again and I'll shoot you in the balls,*' is probably not an appropriate form of discipline." Logan's grey eyes twinkled. "And anyway, I've seen you shoot."

7

The Proposal

"This is nice." Hana sipped a glass of merlot and looked around the restaurant. "I'm glad it's not too busy." She raised a hand to acknowledge Logan's cousin through the serving hatch as he smiled and waved.

"Yeah, this place is a gold mine." Logan sipped his glass of cola and nodded to Alex. "There's nothing similar nearby so it gets trade from passing tourists."

"Those don't look like either," Hana whispered, jerking her head towards a large group enjoying the French cuisine. Business suits and expensively tailored shirts set them apart from locals and tourists.

"Oh, yeah. I recommended this restaurant to them. They're a group of surgeons staying at the hotel and using the conference facilities. They fancied something different tonight." Logan swilled the liquid in his glass, his brow furrowed as he processed an internal wrangle.

"Mark seems settled at our place," Hana said with a smile. "I forgot how messy he is though. He's driving Wiri mad."

"Wiri?" Logan's confusion raised a smile to Hana's lips. He showed no clue that his obsessive tidiness and compulsive behaviour was reflected in his nephew.

Hana nodded. "Yeah, Mark's leaving things out and Wiri's putting them away. I'm watching a mini version of you walking around the house tutting."

"I don't tut!" Logan looked offended and Hana snorted.

"Yes, you do; you think we don't notice."

Logan shrugged and pursed his lips. Hana watched him plan his next sentence and dodged the subject, cutting back to the reason for their meeting. "So what's wrong?" she asked, fixing her eyes on her gorgeous husband. "You're looking very serious." She tried to smile but gave up, nerves making her face muscles twitch.

Logan's grey eyes held a sheen of amusement as his gaze rested on Hana's face and he shook his head. "You always expect the worst," he said, his lips turning upwards. Hana grimaced, irritation snapping at her sensibility. Perceptive, Logan reached for her hand, clamping her writhing fingers in his and forcing them to be still. "There's nothing to worry about," he began.

Hana interrupted. "Those words make me worry."

"Yeah, but don't. No secrets; we promised, remember?"

Hana nodded. "Just put me out of my misery."

Logan pulled her hand to his lips and kissed her tense fingers with seductive flare, making Hana squirm in her seat. "Someone's offered me a job."

Her expression became stony and she froze in place. Fear danced across her eyes. "I don't want to leave Mātakitaki!" Her use of the Māori name for the mountain softened her husband's intense grey eyes and drew a firm squeeze of his hand on her fingers.

"I love you so much," he breathed, appreciation oozing from every pore. "You're my perfect wahine, you know?"

Hana's features morphed from blank to miserable. "Then leave things as they are, Logan. I'm happy, the children are happy; please don't make us move."

Logan dipped his head. "Fine, I'll say no thanks." Sadness leaked through his tone and Hana's brow knitted. Guilt tugged at her heartstrings.

"Tell me about it," she ventured, unable to hide the dread in her voice.

Logan shrugged. "It's back at the school, teaching English. The principal rang me last week and I said I'd consider it."

"Angus rang you?" Hana screwed up her face and looked surprised.

"No. Angus retired after Dobbs died." Logan's eyes took on a flint like quality and Hana knew not to probe for answers. Her husband smoothed his scarred thumb over the back of her hand and chose his words with care. "The new principal started two years ago and it sounds as if they made some decent changes. Malcolm Levine's sick, so is retiring early. Someone recommended me to cover his classes."

"What's wrong with him?"

"Cancer." Logan wrinkled his nose. "Unfair, hey?"

"Yes. That's terrible. How long would you be there?" Hana's mind wandered to thoughts of the cramped staff accommodation and Logan's endless work duties at the boarding house. The sigh escaped her without warning.

"A term," Logan said. "The Gatehouse is still empty and they've offered it to us until December. It's still furnished after our last stay, so we only need a few suitcases and ourselves. It doesn't matter now." Logan smiled politely at the waitress who brought their dinner, terminating the conversation while she grated the pepper mill over his food. Hana gritted her teeth as the woman simpered far too long over him, feeling the sexual attraction coming off her in waves as she wiggled her young hips and made grinding pepper into a pole dancing routine.

"Let me pull the blind for you," the woman said, leaning over Logan to twitch the curtains. He leaned back as her breasts thrust into his face.

Defensiveness rose in Hana, fuelled by an overwhelming sense of inadequacy which told her she was an average looking woman married to a demi-god. She stood and slammed her napkin on the table. "I'll get out of your way if you want," she stated, squeezing out of her seat in the corner. Logan's expression channelled pained awkwardness as Hana stalked towards the bathrooms. She heard his quiet rebuke to the waitress as the door closed behind her, but rejection drove her into a cubicle to sit on the toilet lid and release her tears.

Five minutes later the outer door clicked and Hana heard soft footsteps in the bathroom. Their early sitting meant the restaurant was quieter than usual and she'd cried undisturbed in her three square metres of peace. Dread snaked a hand around her heart as she saw Logan's black cowboy boots in the gap under the door. He knocked with his knuckles, the sound jarring in the silence. "Hana, come out," he said.

"No!" She resented the sullenness in her voice, hating the petulance she heard. It smacked of a pure Phoenix meltdown at bedtime when separation from Wiri became inevitable.

"Fine!" Logan did his mysterious thing with the lock and the door sprang open, revealing a dishevelled Hana sitting on the toilet seat. Her auburn hair hung from its clip like a curtain and her makeup had defected to her chin.

"Go away!" Hana insisted. "I can't come out because I look a mess. Leave me; I'll climb through the window."

Logan snorted and squatted next to her. He rested his forearm on her thigh for balance. "I told her off," he said. "She was out of line."

Hana shook her head. "The wiggling and flirting reminded me of Sylvia. She pulled out all the stops to get to you and if Jack hadn't killed her, she'd have succeeded." She sniffed and wiped her nose on the sleeve of her cardigan.

"No, she wouldn't," Logan said, his voice controlled. "It takes two and I wasn't interested in Sylvia any more than I'm attracted to the waitress."

"Tell *her* that, then!" Hana raised her voice and Logan dried her tears on the neatly creased handkerchief from his breast pocket.

"I did, but you walked away just as I opened my mouth. She apologised."

Hana grunted and blew her nose into the handkerchief. Logan's eyes smiled up at her, making her feel even more of a fool. "Stop looking at me," she bit and then hiccoughed, ruining the illusion of anger.

"I can't." He reached up and touched her cheek, smoothing away damp tears. "You're beautiful and you're mine," he soothed. "I want no one else, only you."

"I bet everyone out there thinks I'm an idiot now," Hana sniffed, regretting her dramatic exit.

"Nobody knows," Logan replied. "I told her to stop being inappropriate and she scuttled away after apologising. I'll phone Alex tomorrow."

"Does she know you own the restaurant? Is that why she did it?" Hana asked, mopping her eyes.

"Part own and no, I don't think she knows."

"That means she'll do it to any good looking customer," Hana sighed. "Ugly wives won't dine here anymore."

Logan snorted with laughter. "You're not ugly, Hana! But yes, it's a fair point and I'll sort it out." He smoothed tears from underneath her eyes again, his expression attentive. "Come out and eat. It's going cold."

"No thanks." Hana shook her head. "I'm not hungry anymore. I want to go home to Mātakitaki and my children."

"Okay." Logan stood and held out his hand. "You sneak out the front and I'll pay."

Hana stood and pulled her dress straight, self-consciousness robbing her last vestiges of dignity. "Sorry," she said, her voice subdued.

"It's fine." Logan cradled her face in his palms and kissed her salty lips. "Jealous wahine are the hottest." His eyes glinted with mischief and he covered Hana's lips with his to still the next question. "No, I didn't pay her to do it either."

Logan fished the ute keys from his inside pocket and Hana took them with a last wipe of her nose on the handkerchief. He kissed her nose and strode from the bathroom, ducking to avoid banging his head on the lintel. Hana ventured to the mirror and examined her ruined attempt at finesse, the eyeshadow long gone and a streak of red lipstick smeared across her cheek. "You're a worry, Hana Du Rose," she sighed, dabbing at it with Logan's handkerchief. "The whole township will know about this by tomorrow." She pondered on imaginary headlines and sighed, hating the small-town-goldfish-bowl mentality of the community surrounding the foot of Logan's mountain. Hana leaned over the hand basin and stared at her reflection. "Maybe a break from here would be good," she mused. "Just a little one."

8

Mātakitaki, Du Rose Mountain

"The hospital rang; they're releasing Caleb tomorrow." Hana pursed her lips and stared at Logan with expectation in her green eyes.

"So?" He flexed his biceps and loaded the bale of hay into the back of the ute without puffing.

"I'm just saying," Hana said, the pout making her face sour. Busy working her spoilt brat act, she missed Logan's smirk as he hefted another bale and dumped it on top of the first. "Where are you taking that?" She pointed a finger at the sweet grass mixture from last year's bumper harvest, the distinctive scent reminding her of the final throes of her pregnancy with Mac.

"Twenty third paddock," he said, raising the tailgate and slamming it shut. "The Friesian cross herd need bales. Spring's around the corner but we're still topping them up."

"Hey, Logan!" Toby's booming voice cut across the yard, echoing inside the hay barn. Logan turned and pushed his hat back, greeting his head stockman with an upward tilt of his head. "Can you take extra bales and drop three off in the Nineteenth? I've moved the mares into there for now. There's a storm brewing and I don't want them near the bush line."

Logan's face remained impassive but his remark sounded biting. "Your timing sucks, man."

Toby smirked. "Oh, sorry, boss." He eyed the flat bed of the ute and winked at Hana. "Cheers bro' that saves me a trip. See yas later." He waved over his shoulder and Hana watched his neat butt filling his jeans as he stalked away. When he glanced back she averted her gaze, fixing it on her husband's annoyed expression instead.

"What's wrong?" Hana asked, watching his temper flare and calm in the blink of an eye. "Don't you want to feed the mares?"

"Not really," Logan sighed, punctuating his sentence with a swear word. "I wanted to finish for the day and he knows that. Asshole."

"So tell him." Hana watched Toby climb onto the quad bike and drive away. "You own the place; he works for you."

"Whatever gave you that impression?" Logan's smile betrayed his teasing. Hana dropped her indignant glare from Toby's arrogant back as he wound his way up the mountain track and disappeared into the native bush.

"What's the joke?" she asked. Her finger stroked the dusting of dark hair peeking over the top of Logan's tee shirt.

"Do you really wanna know?" he asked, his voice soft. Hana nodded, hating being left out. "Come in here for a minute." Logan jerked his head towards the hay barn and set off at a brisk walk. Confused, Hana followed.

"Couldn't you tell me out there?" she asked, irritated as Logan led her to the back of the barn. "I asked Leslie to watch the children while I nipped out to talk to you." Logan disappeared behind a wall of bales piled so high they touched the rafters. "I can't be hours, Logan!"

Hana squealed as her husband's strong hand reached out and dragged her into the tight space between the bales and the wall.

He pressed his lips over hers. "I couldn't tell you this outside," he whispered, teasing Hana's shirt from her jeans. His fingers contacted the thermal shirt beneath and he stopped and peered at the cream fabric. "Does this go all the way down, wahine?"

"Might do!" Hana pushed at Logan's chest and slapped his hand away. "It's freezing on this damn mountain."

Hana's reticence fuelled Logan's curiosity and he unfastened her jeans and tugged them down, wrinkling his nose at the creamy coloured long johns. "They're not sexy, are they?" he commented, fingering the ribbing.

The look of offence pulled Hana's pretty lips back in a sneer. "They're not supposed to be! They're practical."

"How do they come off?" Logan pushed his hat back on his head and tucked his fingers into the waistband. His eyes sparkled and danced as he worked it out. "Ah, I get it. For a horrible moment I thought they were a one-piece."

"Why do you never take me seriously?" Hana pouted and grappled with her jeans, cursing as they slithered to her knees, exposing her long johns to further scrutiny.

"Babe, I take you dead seriously." Logan pressed his body against hers and reached his hands into the thermal underwear, disappointed to discover knickers beneath. He sighed, fumbling with layers of material until his palms rested over Hana's soft buttocks. "You're gorgeous," he whispered, his voice husky with desire.

"In my thermals?" Hana sounded doubtful and Logan silenced her with a kiss.

"In them. Out of them; I'm not bothered." He smirked. "I don't mind a challenge."

Hana held her breath and tensed at the sound of skittering in the bales and her green eyes widened. "There's creatures in here!" she hissed.

Logan smiled. "Yep, and I own them too." His expression creased in determination as he lifted Hana under the thighs and pressed her spine against the prickly hay.

Their muted cries of pleasure went undisturbed as Logan made love to his wife in the hay barn. Hana found grass seed in her underwear as she hopped into her clothing, wincing at the discomfort. "Someone might have walked in," she complained, pulling her shirt over her head.

Logan shrugged. "I think we made enough noise for them to work it out, Hana. Nobody's that desperate for a bale of hay."

She pouted and yanked her thermals back into place. "This isn't why I came here."

Logan grinned. "It's a bonus then."

Hana turned to leave and he snagged her wrist in his strong fingers, keeping a firm grip on her while he pulled his zipper up one handed. "I need to go back to the children," she grumbled and Logan shook his head and kissed her neck, burying his face in her hair.

"Not yet," he whispered. "Come up to the paddocks with me. I want to spend time with you."

"Do you?" Hana searched Logan's face, thwarted by his butterfly kisses on her lips and cheeks. She giggled as his fingers probed the thermals again, alarmed as she sensed him working up to another round of seduction. Hana pushed at Logan's chest. "Lend me your phone and I'll call Leslie and ask if it's okay." She watched him bite his lip as she eased it from the front pocket of his jeans and turned her back on him. Big mistake. He lifted her clothing and fumbled with the catch on her bra. "Stop!" Hana held up a warning finger. "Behave or I'm not coming with you."

Logan sighed and wrapped his arms around Hana's waist as she called his stepmother, hearing the pleasure in Leslie's voice at the thought of an extra few hours with the children. Hana disconnected and turned in the tiny space, finding Logan's chest near her chin. "I'm all yours," she said with a grin, squeaking as her husband undressed her for a second time.

The mountain put on its best show as Logan bumped the elderly farm vehicle over the rutted terrain. Exhaust fumes left a white trail in the chill air and it grew colder the higher they climbed. The rugged tracks contained pot holes and washouts which appeared without warning and the ute creaked and groaned around the hazards. Hana pointed to a hole next to the track and Logan stopped and peered at it from the driver's seat. "What's the correct name for those?" she asked, stroking his face as he leaned across.

"A tomo," he replied. "Like Waitomo Caves. That looks nasty." He reached for the radio on the dashboard and relayed a message to the hotel receptionist. "Tell Toby there's a hole opened up in the Fourteenth paddock, please Marla. It needs fencing before dark. It's sheer and I don't want stock to fall into it."

Hana's eyes widened as the other stockmen commented on the same frequency, calling from their various duties on the mountain. She registered the devious smirk on Logan's face and shook her head. "It doesn't need doing tonight does it?"

"Course it does," he replied, his grin producing dimples in both cheeks. "It's perfect timing."

"You're mean," Hana commented. "You know Toby's got a date with Leslie's daughter tonight."

Logan pulled a face. "No, I didn't know that. How come you're the fount of local gossip?"

"They trust me enough to tell me stuff. And I like her. Isla was brilliant the night Phoe was born."

"True, true." Logan relented. "I might let him delegate." He ran his hand along Hana's thigh and she narrowed her eyes.

"Do I need to drug you?" she joked. "Is it bromide they gave the poor soldiers in the war to control their sexual frustrations?"

"I think that's a myth, isn't it?" Logan asked with a grin, withdrawing his hand.

The ute struggled up the track, labouring as the incline increased to greet a frightening landscape of scarred rock face and boulders the size of the vehicle. Hana got out and closed the gate, latching it behind her. "Where are the mares?" she asked, searching the bleak view. "There isn't much grass left."

Logan hefted a bale onto the ground and cut the twine with his penknife. "No, but there's shelter. There's more grass on the upper slopes but the storm will be miserable up there." He eyed the sky through experienced, bushman's eyes, understanding the up draughts and warnings he read in the cloud formations. As Hana watched, he spread the hay under an outcrop of stone and put two fingers into his mouth. A piercing whistle split the air molecules and disturbed the silent birds, who flew upwards in a frightened arc and settled back in the tree tops.

"Come on." Logan turned back to the ute. "They'll be happier if we're away from the feed when they get here." He climbed into the driver's seat and spun the ute in the tiny space at the end of the track, negotiating the ruts as he pointed the vehicle downwards. Hana opened the gate and closed it after him, hearing the clopping of bare hooves and feeling the vibrations through the soles of her boots.

The mares were Appaloosa, white with grey dapples on their flanks and shoulders. The characteristic stumpy tails and scrubby manes marred the beauty in their conformation as they picked their way over the landscape and gathered around the hay bales Logan spread out for them like a poor man's alfresco lunch. Tiny foals appeared at heel, spindly legs on bodies which would grow to the size of their mothers' and heads like toys nodding on skinny necks. Hana watched in fascination as the babies nosed the hay, tugging at it and getting underfoot. She counted sixteen mares and four foals; identical peas in a pod. Logan left the ute running and joined her, resting his chin on the top of her head.

"Neat little herd, aren't they?" he said, pride in the question.

"Gorgeous," Hana breathed. "The babies are so cute."

The tiny replicas gave up on the grass and nosed at the mares' stomachs searching for milk. They suckled greedily, their hooves moving in time with the adults' legs, avoiding being trodden on as the mothers replenished their own stores.

A muscular Appaloosa trotted between the tight rock formations, nipping at the heels of a heavy, reluctant mare. Hana's lips parted and she pointed. "Methuselah?"

"Yep," Logan replied, running his hands up and down Hana's shivering shoulders. He kissed her neck. "This is his herd. The foals belong to him. Old boy started early this year but Dad used him for work over the autumn, so I figured he felt glad to be home."

"I've never seen this herd."

Logan nipped the soft flesh beneath Hana's ear. "They're my mares and most of them aren't broken. I keep them for breeding and sell the foals or train them to drive the cattle."

"They look like Sacha," Hana mused and Logan nodded, his stubble grazing her ear.

"Yep, she's out of Methuselah and Rahab." He pointed to the mare kicking out at the stallion's ministrations. "She can't have much longer to go before she gives birth." Logan examined the mare with his eyes, observing the swollen belly and ears flat back against her head. He snorted. "She's a bitch; I shouldn't breed from her."

"Do all the foals end up with Sacha's temperament?"

"Na. She's a real one off. Even Rahab's not that difficult." He sighed and turned back to the idling ute, aiming a casual slap to Hana's backside. "Come on, Mrs Du Rose. We've still got the Friesians to feed."

"Have you phoned the principal about the job yet?" Hana asked, clinging to the door handle as the ute lurched downhill.

"Haven't had time." Logan jerked the steering wheel to the right and the ute fishtailed. Hana cringed but her husband let out a whoop of victory as he countered the skid and pulled it straight. "I will though." He dodged the washout with years of practice guiding his movements and Hana watched the ground disappear to the left of her, the remaining road scarred by a giant's hungry bite. She shivered and looked away.

"Don't."

"Don't what?" Logan skidded to a halt in front of the next gate and looked at Hana expectantly.

"Don't tell him you won't take the job." Hana slammed the ute door behind her and unlatched the heavy wooden gate. It warped on its hinges as she pushed it open to allow Logan to drive down the hill into a paddock containing black and white yearlings. The calves headed towards her at speed, kicking their heels and lowing in deep, throaty voices. She heard Logan yank the handbrake on and exit the vehicle, dishing out the hay to a disinterested audience.

Hana stroked the eager faces which pushed into her body. The excited calves licked her fingers and butted her thighs, clamouring to get as close as possible. "Hey babies," she crooned, stroking each face as the calves fought for her attention. "How are you settling into your new home?" She smoothed fluffy ears and and admired their black eyelashes as one by one, they turned their attention to their stomachs. Hana stroked the last black and white body as the heifer rubbed her forehead on the woman's jeans, reluctant to join the throng of chewing faces. "You can't live in my garden forever, Daisy," Hana said, using her sleeve to wipe the dribbly nose. "One day you'll be a giant cow and there won't be enough grass for you on my lawn. Besides, your brothers and sisters are here."

The heifer hung back as though unhappy, shifting on her cloven hooves in nervousness. She still sported the remains of Phoe's pink ribbon dangling from her ear tag, faded and shredded in places. "Come on, Daisy." Hana tugged at the fleshy ruff around her neck and led the calf towards the group of excited, chewing bovine. She grabbed a handful of hay and offered it to her, waiting while she took a few tentative mouthfuls and chewed with the stalks sticking from her lips. "Good girl," Hana said, stroking a fluffy ear. She glanced behind her, seeing Logan's muscles stretch the fabric of his shirt sleeves taut as he hefted the last bale. Wrapping her arms around the large, furry face, she kissed the top of Daisy's head. "Be good," she whispered. "I'll come again and bring the children."

Daisy flicked her rope-like tail and bent her head to the hay. Hana slipped away while she was busy, climbing into the ute and slouching below the level of the window. Logan got into the driver's seat and looked at her with narrowed eyes. "What're you doing?"

"Hiding from Daisy," Hana whispered. "Can we go while she's busy?"

Logan bit his lip and stifled a snort. "Open the gate for me?"

"No," Hana hissed. "Don't make me."

Logan spun the ute and climbed out to open the gate. He sighed in annoyance as he drove the vehicle through and then got out again to close it behind him. "You're kinda not getting the point of this farming thing," he snorted as he put the ute into gear and pointed it up the steep track toward home. "The calves weren't supposed to exist, remember, Hana. They're the result of Asher's sabotage. I should have shot them the day they were born. I run a damn Charolaise herd, not Friesian." He cranked the gear stick back into first as the ute shuddered against the incline in second gear.

"You wouldn't!" Hana sat up, glaring at her husband in indignation. "That's cruel!"

"Yeah, but I'm not keeping them or breeding from them. They're destined for the market as soon as they're fat enough; that's what beef farming's about."

Hana screwed her face up. "I'm becoming a vegetarian," she grumbled.

"You might as well! You've turned those damn cattle into idiots with bows in their ears and bloody scarves around their necks!"

"That was Phoenix, not me." Hana leaned forward and peered in the side mirror. "Oh, phew. She's still eating."

Logan laughed and Hana slapped his thigh. "You're mean!"

He shrugged. "I had a calf when I was ten. I called him Ice Man because he looked pure white and I taught him to follow me, lie down and come when I whistled."

"You ate him, didn't you? Miriam made burgers out of him and you lost your compassion for farm animals."

Logan put his head back and laughed. "No. I keep him on the other side of the mountain in the bull pen. Ice Man's sired most of the last two generations of the Charolaise herd." He pulled up at the next gate and pulled the handbrake up. "He still comes when I whistle too, only now he's two tonnes of bull and when I give him the hand signal to lie down, he looks at me like, 'are you freakin' kidding me?' I'll take you to see him tomorrow."

"Okay." Hana left the vehicle and dealt with the gate, settling herself back into the passenger seat and fastening her belt for the long trek home.

"So, why shouldn't I say no to the Hamilton job?" Logan asked, keeping his tone light as he jolted the ute over rough terrain.

Hana sighed. "It might be good to be in town for a few months. I can catch up with Bo and his family and Mark's lonely. He doesn't know whether to stay in New Zealand or go back to England now."

Logan braked and turned to his wife. He stretched out a hand and stroked her cheek. Hana smelled the scent of hay and twine on his fingers and closed her eyes, remembering the warm sunshine of six months ago. "What does my wife want?" he asked, his voice soft. "Because she's all I care about in this."

Hana sighed. "I know you miss teaching and you must get the hours in to continue your teacher registration. I sense you want to do it and I need to support you."

"You don't need to do anything, babe. I'm happy here; it's fine."

"I'll come back with you." Hana's decisiveness faltered and she narrowed her eyes. "But promise it's only for one term. I can't cope if it's like the boarding house job. That was a month which turned into a year."

"It's definitely a term," Logan confirmed. "After that, they'll want someone more permanent. You're right, I need the hours." He bit his lip. "I wondered about covering a few classes at one of the South Auckland schools next year; it's only half an hour up the road across country. What do you think? I could teach a few periods a week and give something back to the local community."

Hana smiled and nodded. "That's a great idea and they'd snap you up. Teachers of your calibre don't come along every day. Fine, we'll go south but only for a term." She sighed and watched the light dim on the horizon as the sun sank behind the highest ridge in the west. "Logan?" Hana's tone held a question. "What's really going on with Toby?"

Logan rolled his eyes and shook his head. "It's a bet. He said you'd ask if that kid from the hospital could come and stay with us and I said you wouldn't dare."

"But you knew I would, so why did you say that?" Hana frowned in confusion.

Logan winked at her. "Because sometimes you gotta let them win if you want the best out of people. He'll enjoy himself for a few days thinking he got the better of me but eventually he'll wise up."

"How?" Hana asked. "He can't know what you're thinking."

Logan grinned. "Yeah, he can. I asked David Allen to fetch the kid when the hospital discharged him."

"Really?" Hana's face creased in pleasure, her smile fading as she failed to grasp Logan's point. "I still don't get it."

Logan dragged her into him and pressed his lips against hers. "Toby was real insistent and loud, claiming he knew you better than I did so I let him run with it. I accepted his bet and I've just fulfilled my part of the bargain. But I asked David Allen to check when the kid was due for discharge days ago, so our mate Toby's gonna look a right dick."

"You're evil," Hana breathed. "He'll be so angry."

Logan kissed her again, stilling her words. "No," he whispered. "He'll be contrite and do as he's told for a while until he thinks of another way to get one over on me. And he'll fail that time too. It never hurts to let your staff see you've got class, Hana. I've let him push me around today and I didn't need to."

"You're a wise old bird, Logan Du Rose," Hana sighed, wrapping her arms around her husband's neck. "I don't deserve you."

"Yeah, you do," Logan replied, parting her lips and drawing her closer. His foot slipped off the clutch and the ute lurched forward, slamming his arm into the steering wheel as Hana banged her head against his.

"You're just a rubbish driver," she groaned, alarmed to see the blue egg appear on Logan's temple.

"I'm fine, I'm fine," he insisted, rubbing at the instant bruise exacerbated by the haemophilia. "It's your fault." He smiled and winced. "You screw my concentration."

9

The Burden

"Dr Haines will see you now, Mrs Du Rose." The receptionist smiled and nodded her head towards the corridor.

Hana rose, balancing Mac on her hip. "There's been a mistake," she said, licking her lips. "I booked for Dr Francis."

"He's not here." The girl behind the counter blinked in rapid succession. "Dr Haines is taking over his appointments this week but you can wait for Dr Seuli instead."

Hana's eyes widened and she shook her head in a frenzied action of denial. "No. Thanks." She scurried towards the corridor, wishing she'd asked which room the new doctor occupied. She spun in a circle, her eyes raking the name plates until the door belonging to Dr Francis swung open and a stunning brunette stepped towards her. Grey-blue eyes surrounded by thick lashes narrowed in a smile and she held her hand out.

"Mrs Du Rose?"

Hana nodded. "Yes. I expected Dr Francis and then didn't know if you were in his office or somewhere else." She clasped the offered hand, her own sticky with sweat. "Sorry," she said, withdrawing it and wiping her palm on her skirt.

"Come in." The doctor stood back and allowed Hana to pass. Mac studied the woman with interest, sucking on his fat thumb and winding his other hand through Hana's red curls. Hana dived into the nearest seat and settled her son on her knee, casting around the familiar room with anxiety in her face.

"Gorgeous baby." The doctor leaned forward and tickled Mac's tiny foot through his sock and he kicked his leg and beamed around his thumb. He pressed his face into Hana's chest and then spun again, a wide smile on his face as he engaged in a game of hidey boo.

"How can I help you?" the doctor asked, cocking her head to one side.

Hana floundered. "Pills!" she exclaimed with relief. "Yes, I need pills."

"What sort of pills?" Dr Haines knitted her brow.

"Contraceptive pills," Hana said, trying to sound convincing as her head nodded in an exaggerated motion. "Yes, that's what I need."

The woman turned towards her computer and tapped on the keyboard with long, manicured nails. Hana squeezed her baby into her body and he sighed and laid his head on her breast. "Are you breastfeeding?" the doctor asked and Hana nodded.

"Yes, but only in the night. He's weaning himself." She ran her fingers over the downy orange hair and kissed the top of his head.

The doctor turned back to face her. "Mrs Du Rose, Dr Francis gave you suitable pills when you came a month ago. What happened to those?"

"He didn't give me enough." Hana's palms sweated more. "I ran out."

The woman stared at her and her brow creased. "Mrs Du Rose, would you rather see Dr Seuli? You're obviously not here for contraceptives because Dr Francis gave you a prescription for six months' worth. It's fine if you don't want to talk to me, but at least talk to someone. I'll ask if he's free." She stood up and took a step towards the closed door.

"No!" Hana cried. "Please don't! I'll tell you but don't make me see him."

"Why ever not?" Dr Haines sat heavily in her chair. "He's nice."

Hana rolled her eyes. "The last time he treated me, I said some things in private and he repeated them to the police. They found a body behind my brother-in-law's house and arrested my husband because of what he said. I'm not talking to Dr Seuli!"

"Will you talk to me?" the doctor asked, leaning forward, her sweet face kind and endearing. Hana nodded, sensing the other woman's compassion reaching out to her across the gap and it was enough to unpick her fragile resolve.

Mac frowned as the dripping sensation began on his head. He looked up, squinting as another of Hana's tears went into his eye. Putting both of his fat arms up to his face, he scrubbed at his eyes with little fists and yawned. "I don't know where to start," Hana sobbed as the flood gates opened and gulped breaths choked her.

"Is it you or your baby?" the perceptive doctor asked, handing Hana a fistful of tissues. Mac made a grab for the fluffy white bunch and thrust one in his mouth, pulling a nasty face at the taste and pushing the bits out of his mouth with his tongue.

Hana sighed and collected the white shards, balling them up and dumping them in the dustbin the doctor offered. "It's Mac," she confessed, lowering her voice. "I think he's deaf. I know he's deaf."

She tensed awaiting either rebuke or dismissal, surprised when neither came. Instead, the doctor smiled at her. "Okay, sweetheart," she said. "Let's talk about why you think that and then I'll organise tests."

Hana's lips parted and she mopped at her eyes with the remains of the tissue. "You believe me?" Her chest heaved and the baby sighed and snuggled closer.

"Definitely!" the doctor answered. "Mums always know best so I'd be stupid not to listen to your instincts. Talk me through it so I can make notes and start the referral."

Hana nodded. "Okay. But can you stop calling me Mrs Du Rose? It makes me feel a hundred."

"Nice to meet you, Hana." The doctor offered her hand again. "I'm Fiona."

Hana explained her observations and Fiona tapped away on her keyboard. "So, your mother is profoundly deaf?" she asked, correcting a typing error.

"Was," Hana said, her voice flat. "She died."

"Aw, I'm sorry," Fiona said, shooting her a sympathetic glance. "Any other deafness in your family?" At Hana's silence she turned to find her patient ashen faced and chewing her lip. "Hana?"

"I don't know. Yes. No. Yes." Hana agonised with her answer, standing up and putting her son over her shoulder. "Logan's gonna freak out," she whimpered.

"Why?" Fiona asked, her fingers ceasing their activity.

Hana squeezed the bridge of her nose between finger and thumb and resumed patting her son's back. "His grandfather was deaf from birth."

"Your husband's?" The doctor looked confused. "Or your son's?"

"Logan's," Hana replied. She paced the room like a maniac. "Logan's grandfather was deaf. He delivered Mac, just me and him." She stared at the doctor, her eyes wild. "Then he tried to kill us both."

"Oh." The doctor put her hands in her lap. "I can understand why you're distressed. If it's genetic, it might be a constant reminder."

"Yes!" Hana nodded her head in gratitude. "That's it. But also," she gulped, "Logan detests weakness. What if he sees this as Mac being weak?" She groaned as the trusting infant settled his arms around her neck and turned his face to the side over her shoulder. His eyelids fluttered.

"How about we cross those bridges as we come to them?" Fiona suggested, standing and putting a steadying hand on Hana's forearm. "Now, before this little man nods off, let me take a look at him and work out what's going on."

Mac's bottom lip protruded as he stuck it out for the doctor's benefit, showing his disgust at being interfered with during nap time. He grumbled in protest at the instrument in his ear, flinging his arms and legs around and turning his head to watch it. He followed the doctor with his eyes as she moved around him, but as she sneaked behind and he couldn't see her, he lost interest. The noises she made behind Hana's shoulder to attract his attention went unnoticed.

More for her own comfort than his, Hana fed her son under her blouse until he slept, his delicate chest rising and falling in a regular motion. The doctor typed the referral. "Auckland or Hamilton?" she asked. "We're far enough north to come under Franklin and south enough to be Waikato. You choose."

"Hamilton," Hana answered, watching her sleeping son. "What will they do to him?"

"Nothing terrible," the doctor said, smiling. "The specialist will run tests to determine what kind of deafness he suffers from and decide how to treat it. Deafness isn't always final nowadays; there's so much helpful technology out there. It could be glue ear which requires a simple surgical procedure, or he could need implants. There's heaps of possibilities. Don't worry." She smiled at Hana again. "We'll journey it together, Hana," she said. "This was the hardest part, saying it out loud."

Hana nodded. "I guess so."

"Now, do you want me to write anything down for your husband?" Fiona asked, alarmed by Hana's frantic expression.

"No!" she cried. "I can't tell Logan!"

"Yes, you can." Fiona squeezed her shoulder, offering solidarity. "You must. I'm happy to be there if it helps, but he needs to know."

Hana blew out a ragged sigh and nodded. She pressed her palm against her sleeping son's back and dragged the car keys from her cardigan pocket. "I'll be fine," she replied.

She turned to leave, nodding in thanks as the doctor held the office door open. "Do you think a shotgun blast very close to Macky could've caused his deafness?" Hana whispered, guilt running riot across her devastated features.

The doctor shrugged. "I don't know. Is that what's worrying you?"

Hana nodded, fighting the ready tears with a valiant effort. "Yes. I put cotton wool in his ears and made a nest of towels, but could it still cause this?"

The doctor's eyes widened at the terror in Hana's face, seeing the hatchet of blame already falling. She laid a gentle hand over Hana's as it writhed on the sleeping child's back. "Who fired the gun, Hana?" she asked.

"Me!" Hana's voice broke and she squirmed under the weight of the heavy sob which escaped her breast. "Me. I fired it."

"Okay." Understanding flitted across the doctor's pretty face. "I get it. Only the experts can answer that but Hana, there's deafness on both sides of Mac's family so I'm putting my money on genetics for now and I want you to do that too. We'll deal with whatever comes up together, okay? We can do this." The doctor's fingers felt soft over Hana's sweating hand and the stricken mother nodded, keen to escape kindness she didn't deserve.

"Thank you," Hana breathed, eyeing the gap in the doorway with hungry desperation.

"It's funny," Fiona remarked as Hana placed her left foot in the white, clinical corridor. "I never realised Henri Du Rose was deaf." Her brow knitted in confusion and Hana's heart quailed at her mistake.

Her green eyes glinted like emeralds in the face of a pursued fox and her voice came through the hitch in her chest. "You know the Du Roses?" she breathed.

Fiona smiled and nodded, opening her mouth to explain. Hana bolted, burying her face in Mac's cardigan as she shot through the waiting room in an ungainly rush. Her world crumbled around her as she stumbled through the car park, wishing she'd brought Phoenix so she could run far away and start again, reinventing herself as a calm, capable woman who rode life's problems like a pro surfer.

10

The Visitor

Hana arrived home to find David Allen knocking on the front door, his body stiff and impatience marring his pleasant face. She plastered a fake smile onto her lips and parked on the driveway, exiting her vehicle with suitable aplomb and appreciation. "Thanks, David," she said with enthusiasm, ignoring the immaturity of the tongue he stuck out in response.

Caleb emerged from the ute on crutches, his face screwed up in pain. "How do you feel?" Hana asked, realising the futility of the question as he forced a watery smile in her direction and lied.

"Great," he said and David rolled his eyes.

"Here's his medication," David said, his tone grumpy as he handed over a paper bag filled with packets and boxes. "Kid had no money."

"All right," Hana said, feeling the stockman's animosity oozing out of him like syrup. "I've got cash inside the house. Let me get Mac out of the car and I'll open the door."

"I'll fetch the baby," David said, jerking his head towards Hana's vehicle. "You deal with yer mate."

Hana smiled at Caleb and ground her teeth, helping him up the porch steps. She fumbled her keys and was still fiddling around as David appeared with a sleeping Mac still encased in his car seat. "Sorry," Hana exclaimed, grinding the key in the lock and pushing the door open. She deactivated the burglar alarm and turned to help Caleb inside. David put the car seat on the hall floor but continued to rock it with his foot.

"I'll just get your cash. How much do I owe you?" Hana asked.

"Twenty-eight bucks and fifty cents," David chimed, never taking his eyes from her face. Hana nodded and raided Logan's change jar, handing it to the man in enough coinage to make his trousers fall down from the weight in his pockets.

David's top lip pulled back in disgust. "I could've waited for notes!" he bit.

"Well, now you don't need to." Hana smiled to make her point and David ran a large hand through his blonde curls.

"Watch him!" he stressed, cupping his hands and leaning forward to catch the coins pouring from Hana's fingers. "He's bad news but you won't listen."

Hana's lips parted in a sigh of annoyance and she shook her head. "You need to forgive me for the other day. I know Logan was cross with you."

"Cross!" David gritted his teeth and his blue eyes flashed. "He was bloody ropeable!"

"I've said I'm sorry!" Hana hissed, glancing at her house guest who balanced on one leg against the wall and pretended not to listen. "He would've died."

David shook his head and huffed out in frustration. "There's ways of doing things and then there's the Hana Du Rose way. Next time you almost get yerself killed, make sure you warn me first so I can take the day off." He turned and let himself out, closing the front door behind him with a click. Hana heard his footsteps tap down the porch steps and crunch across the gravel.

"Sorry," Caleb whispered, his voice a low hiss. "It's my fault."

"No, it's not." Hana looked crestfallen as she indicated the lounge with her outstretched hand. "Why don't you go in there for a lie down? I can bring you something to drink. Did you get food at the hospital?"

Caleb shook his head. "No, miss. They put me in the day room once the doctor signed my papers and I waited there for the man you sent."

Hana nodded. "Was David nice to you?"

The teenager shrugged and looked nervous. "Fine, thanks."

Hana narrowed her eyes, unconvinced by the boy's fake smile. She accepted his lie and helped him into the lounge, directing him to an easy chair which reclined flat. "I'll put the TV on for you and sort out things in the kitchen. What would you like to eat and drink?"

"I don't know." Caleb's blue eyes opened wide against his pale, sickly complexion. "I don't want you to go to heaps of trouble." He gulped and looked around at the opulence of the room. "I probably won't stay too long."

"Just relax," Hana said, keeping her voice light. "You don't have to stay here with us. Logan's put aside a motel unit for you next door to our museum curator. You can eat at the hotel restaurant until your cast comes off and then we'll give you a lift to wherever you want to go."

"Why're you being so nice?" Caleb muttered. "Rescuing me was more than enough."

"Because they're nice people." Mark's English accent cut Caleb's miserable monotone off in its prime. He ran a hand through his thick, grey hair and sat in the seat next to Caleb's. "Tell me what the doctor said about your leg and my sister can sort out her baby?"

Caleb nodded and Hana knitted her brow, offended by Mark's easy dismissal. Mac slept soundly and Hana moved his seat into the kitchen where she prepared cheese sandwiches and made a pot of coffee.

"Here you go," she said, placing the tray on the coffee table and dumping coasters near the men. "I just guessed what you might want."

Caleb smiled, his blue eyes huge in his pale face. "Thanks, I need to take my medication before I eat."

Hana frowned. "You didn't take it on the way up here?"

"The guy didn't want to stop. He seemed angry." Caleb stared at his hands and Hana sighed and shook her head at Mark.

"It's not you," she reassured the boy as Mark narrowed his eyes in question.

"I always thought David an amiable soul," he mused.

Hana rolled her eyes and looked like a sulky teenager. "I'm guessing Logan bawled him out for letting me ride away. But to be fair to David, he got little choice." Hana chewed her lip. "I always tell the children how actions lead to consequences and then don't take my own advice."

"I'm glad you ignored them," Caleb said, his voice a whisper and fear in his blue eyes. "I'd still be there." A shudder rocked his body and Mark put a cool hand to the teenager's forehead.

"You look knackered and you've got an elevated temperature." He grabbed the paper bag of pills from the coffee table and ripped it open, examining the boxes and labels inside. He tipped them into his lap and held up a white box. "Take these. I'd increase the dose just to get some into your bloodstream." He pressed two pills into Caleb's outstretched palm and added ones from a different box. Mark shook his head as Hana reached for the coffee pot. "He needs to take them with water, love. Have them with food Caleb, or they'll damage your stomach lining. Those are antibiotics, painkillers and anti-nausea tablets."

Mark smiled at Hana as she returned with a glass of water, watching while the young man swallowed the concoction. He reached for a plate and piled two triangular sandwiches on it. "Eat these and then you can settle in my room for a couple of hours. I'm going for a long walk in the bush with Hana's father-in-law so you can rest." Mark nodded with satisfaction as Caleb bit into the sandwich. He stood and poured coffee for himself, moving over to the wall of glass facing the seascape to drink it. "I love it up here," he mused.

"You feeling any better?" Hana asked, moving alongside him to give Caleb space to eat. "Made any decisions?"

Mark shrugged and shook his head. "I don't know, Hana. My head wants to stay in New Zealand but my heart doesn't want me to settle."

Hana nodded and linked her arm through his, feeling indecision shrouding him like a veil of confusion. "Because of your boys?" she whispered.

"Maybe. Maybe."

"Have you tried to find them?" Hana asked, remembering the small tow haired boys with the serious faces.

"Yeah." Mark's eyes narrowed as he struggled with emotion. "I paid a private detective twenty years ago. Their mother moved them to London. He tracked her down through employment records and I secured the documentation to summon her to a custody hearing, hoping I could at least see the boys and let them know I never stopped thinking about them. He handed her the paperwork and she tore it up in his face and scattered it on the carpet of a posh accountancy firm. I visited a week later and she refused to see me. Security guards forcibly removed me and the police weren't interested in my desire to see the boys."

"What happened then?" Hana asked, her eyes widening at Mark's flexing jaw and the signs of tears in his eyes.

"Nothing!" he spat, his face hard and unyielding. "I did nothing! I let my boys go because I was ashamed of myself." Mark shook his head and squeezed his eyes tight shut. "I got what I deserved, Hana. I hurt her. She didn't deserve the awful man I'd become and her punishment of me was justified."

"You hit her?" Hana whispered her question, aware of Caleb's presence but seeing a confessional side of Mark McIntyre he'd kept hidden.

He nodded. "I'm a monster, Hana. I made everything her fault. When they treated me like shit on the wards or my professors marked my grades down, I blamed her. There's no excuse for who I became. Rage consumed me and I lashed out enough times to justify her leaving. I arrived home after a night shift to find her and the boys gone; no note, just gone." Mark gulped and took a deep breath inwards. "They left everything; toys, bikes, clothes. Everything. We shared a housekeeping bank account and for years I put money into it and watched it disappear. It was the only activity on the account; money in, money out. On Florian's eighteenth birthday she closed the account and my bank transfer returned unclaimed."

"Couldn't you see where she spent the money each month?" Hana asked. "You could track her movements."

Mark shook his head. "No. She drew it out from different cash machines around London. The statements still came to me and I relied on them to show she was still alive." Mark swallowed. "I stayed in the same house for ten years and kept it exactly the same so they could walk back in and turn on the TV as usual. I looked at Brewster's bike one day and realised I'd spent a decade kidding myself. They weren't coming back and even if they did, Brew couldn't ride the bloody bike anymore. I did a house clearance, put the money into the account and sold the property. I put half of that there too. It all disappeared and I persuaded myself to get on with my life."

"And now?" Hana said. "Brewster must be thirty-five and Florian thirty-two."

"Yep." Mark forced a smile on his face. "They won't be needing those bikes now, will they?"

He physically disconnected from the conversation and emotionally from Hana, turning away from the window. "Alfred will be waiting for me at the hotel," he said, the crow's feet in the corners of his eyes visible as tracks of pain instead of pleasure.

"Okay." Hana reached for his forearm but Mark strode from the room, taking his agony with him and leaving only a drifting after burn in the air.

"He left his kids." Caleb's voice sounded flat as he stared at the sandwich on his plate and Hana walked around the sofa to face him. A single bite scarred the soft surface of the bread. "And he beat his wife."

"He sounds pretty sorry to me," Hana said, slumping onto Mark's vacated seat. "We all make mistakes, Caleb. I know I have." She picked at a thread on her sweater and watched as the teenager swallowed, his jawline moving as he clenched his teeth.

"Yeah," he breathed. "Doesn't give me much hope for finding my dad though, does it? Maybe he doesn't want to be found like that man's wife. What do I do then?"

"I dunno," Hana replied. "They're both awful situations." She leaned across and removed the plate from Caleb's lap. "You don't want this, do you?"

He shrugged. "The man said I had to eat it."

"Mark. Mark's a doctor." Hana kept her voice light. "He's my brother."

"Ohhhh!" Caleb turned sideways to face her. "You talked about him in the gully! You found out he's really your cousin?"

"Yeah, that's right. So maybe don't be so hard on him. He's had his own troubles. I'm not gonna make excuses for him because he's not making them for himself. Live and let live, Caleb. Life's a journey for us all." Hana pressed the sandwich plate back into the boy's fingers. "The doctor said eat, so eat. I'll check on Mac and come back."

Hana leaned against the kitchen doorframe and watched her son in his car seat. Small, vibrant green eyes watched shadows move across the ceiling as the trees swayed in the breeze outside the kitchen window. He flapped his arms and opened his mouth as though intrigued. Hana squeezed the bridge of her nose and the baby's sharp eyes caught the moment, drawing a smile of glee from his pink face. He made popping sounds with his lips and knitted his brow in a pretence of irritation.

Hana bent to undo the straps of the car seat and lifted the child onto her hip. "I love you so much, little boy," she mouthed and kissed his forehead. She smoothed down the unruly auburn locks and smelled his clean, baby scent. Lurching for a long strand of Hana's red hair, Mac clutched it in his hand and balled his fist, poking his thumb into his mouth and resting his temple against her shoulder. "You don't want much out of life, do you baby?" she cooed, enjoying the weight of his head against her. He sighed, a peaceable soul in a tortured world and closed his eyes. Hana patted his nappy. "Don't go back to sleep, Mr Sloth. Let's show Caleb where he can take a nap and then we'll ask Nonie Leslie to bring Phoenix and Wiri home, shall we?" Hana felt the familiar sinking in her breast, hearing herself asking questions like someone with verbal diarrhoea and receiving only silence in return.

11

The Inconvenient Du Rose

Leslie headed up the mountain in the old red Jeep which Jack ran on the farm for over twenty years. She waved her wrinkled hand at Hana as she met them at the front door. "I know, I know," she soothed. "I didn't wanna bring it up here and upset youse but Alfie took ours out to the reserve with that brother of yours." She opened the rear door and Phoenix and Wiremu spilled out of the same seat.

Hana cringed and bit her lip at the realisation they shared a seat belt past washouts and sheer cliffs. "You should have called," she said, cradling Mac. "I would've come for them."

"Look what I did, Ma," Wiri said, waving a picture at her stomach. "It's our fambly."

"Beautiful," Hana intoned, biting back the cringe of dismay at how the child's drawing depicted him at the centre of her family.

Leslie rolled her eyes, sharing Hana's concerns. The children pattered towards the house and kicked their shoes off under the porch. Hana spun round but was too late to warn them. "What's up?" the elderly woman asked, puffing up the porch steps into the hall.

"I wanted to ask them to be quiet because Caleb's gone for a sleep in Mark's room. I didn't say it fast enough."

"Hmmmn!" Leslie humphed. "Least said about that, the better."

"Not you too," Hana sighed. "I've already had David's opinion on the matter. He's just a homeless kid, Leslie. What else could I do?"

"And that's why we loves ya," the old woman said with a smile. She hefted the gurgling baby from Hana's arms and pushed the front door closed with her foot. "What's happening with the other wee cuckoo? I hear you're heading back to Hamilton in a few weeks." Leslie's smile lost its sheen. "I'm gonna miss youse."

"It's only for a term," Hana said, flicking the switch on the kettle. "Logan wants to re-register for teaching and I've good reasons for needing to be in town for a little while." She glanced across at her son as he lurched for the jade necklace around Leslie's neck, staring at it before pressing it between his lips.

"So, will Wiremu go home to Nev then?" Leslie asked, jerking her head towards the lounge and the sound of Lego being tipped onto the floorboards.

"I don't know what to do." Hana slumped into a kitchen chair and put her head in her hands. "He came to us because Nev couldn't cope and it's meant to be temporary. I saw what he drew on his picture and his attachment to us gets harder to break the longer this goes on. What should I do, Leslie?"

"Well, this is one calamity youse didn't put yerself in, kōtiro. Nev don't talk about Anahera much but I heard him tell Logan she wasn't improving. Can't be much fun being sent to the mental hospital. Nev said them clever doctors diagnosed her with a mate hinengaro." She put a gnarled hand up to her mouth and covered it when she said the Māori word, leaving Hana sighing in frustration.

"What's that?"

Leslie flapped her hand and then used it to cover Mac's ear. Hana tried not to dwell on the irony. "She's a porowairangi, a lunatic. She's not coming out soon."

"Mama! Peese m'av bissit?" Phoenix stood in the doorway, extracting her thumb long enough to utter the request. The fingers of her other hand writhed through her cousin's and Wiri pursed his lips, attempting an angelic face.

"Playing's quite tiring," he said, affecting a perfect yawn and rubbing his stomach with his free hand to add to the prompt.

Hana stood. "Wash your hands in the bathroom first and you may have a drink and one biscuit each. It'll be dinner time soon." The children turned to leave and Hana halted them. "Guys, I need you to be quiet. There's a poorly person in Uncle Mark's room."

"Tama's room!" Wiri insisted with a frown. "Not Uncle Mark's." Hana saw a flash of jealousy cross the sparkling grey eyes. The little boy floundered in a sea of adult mistakes and had thrown his energies into anchoring himself in this branch of the Du Roses. Wiri lessened the impact of his statement with an endearing smile and led Phoenix along the hallway towards the family bathroom. Hana heard him telling her to be quiet as she chattered away.

"He's becoming very emotionally involved," Hana mused, frowning as Leslie remained quiet while dandling Mac on her knee and bouncing him until he burped. "Help me out here," Hana demanded. "What can I do? He's stopped asking for his parents and calls me Ma. I've told him to call me Aunty Hana or just Hana but he slips it in there when he thinks I don't notice. Give me a clue, please?"

"Tama calls you Ma and he's not your boy," Leslie said, raising a dark eyebrow.

"That's different," Hana protested. "His parents abandoned him; he has no relationship with Michael and doesn't want one."

"Obviously Wiri feels the same way." Leslie grinned at Mac and delighted in his beamed response.

Hana shook her head. "It's completely different! Anahera's suffered a breakdown and Nev works full time. I offered to take Wiri to school and then it was, 'Could you have him overnight while I help with the foaling?' Then it was, 'Can he stay with you a bit longer while I go to the cattle market because I'll be late home?' That was months ago and Nev shows no signs of wanting his son back."

"Get Logan to talk to him," Leslie suggested, a smirk lifting a corner of her mouth.

"Been there; done that!" Hana grumbled. "His honest opinion was that Wiri wouldn't be taken care of properly if Nev took him home. He's got massive concerns, which is why Wiri's still here." Hana chewed her lip and shrugged. "I'll talk to Logan again tonight but I'm assuming nothing's changed."

"That settles it then." Leslie pressed her lips against Mac's crown as he sat facing the table, patting the scarred wood with his hands. "Youse got seven children." She chuckled. "You taking Ryan to Hamilton with yas? Youse got one of Michael's meamea, youse might as well have the other."

Hana's eyes widened in horror at Leslie's tactless use of the expletive. Logan's status within the Du Rose family as Reuben's bastard made her sensitive to such slurs on his behalf. She glanced around nervously, relaxing at the sound of Phoenix singing amidst running water.

"I left her there," Wiremu announced, flouncing into the kitchen. "She won't turn it off."

"Oh." Hana eyed the empty table which should have contained warm milk and biscuits. "I'll be back in a minute."

She reappeared with her two-year-old under her arm, Phoenix giggling as she hung like a limp rag doll. "She turned it off,"

Hana told Wiri in response to the worried look on his face. "I checked."

Phoenix clambered onto the seat next to her cousin and poked her face into his. "I gettin' paint off," she said, her voice insistent as she jabbed at her stained palm with an olive finger. "It dirty wiv Nonie's paintin'." She kissed Wiri in the eye and sat on her seat, only her eyes and forehead visible over the table top.

All eyes turned to Hana as she heated milk in a saucepan and she felt the pressure of provision like a weight around her shoulders. Phoenix's clear voice cut through the leaden atmosphere like a knife. "I 'ave brandy in mine, fanks," she said.

Hana's jaw dropped and she narrowed her eyes at Leslie. "I don't think so," she said, keeping her voice light.

Leslie rolled her eyes. "Poppa Alfie has brandy with his milk, don't he mokopuna?"

"Yes," the children agreed in a well-rehearsed chorus.

"We never has brandy in it does we Nonie? Nope, never, we don't." Wiremu's insistence only strengthened Hana's concerns. She shook her head and poured the milk into two mugs and two beakers. "Is that with his wacky baccy or instead?"

"Shhhh!" Leslie flapped her arms in horror and the children laughed at her duck impression.

Hana's eyes widened. "Please tell me he's not driving my brother round the property unlicensed?"

Leslie shook her head. "Na, kōtiro! He's got my licence with him, just in case."

"It doesn't work like that and you know it. I hope they don't go on public roads or the cops will throw the book at him."

Wiri sniggered. "Throw the book at him," he repeated. "How big's the book?"

"Very big." Hana glared at Leslie and laid tea plates on the table and gave each child two biscuits each. Leslie looked at the packet with the hopefulness of a Labrador and Hana gave in and put two on a plate for her, rolling her eyes and wondering which of them was meant to be the adult.

"I saw somebody's dad who we can't mention right now, but were talking about before." Leslie shoved a cookie into her mouth whole, widening her eyes at Hana's lack of comprehension and jerked her head towards Wiri.

Hana nodded in recognition. She'd seen Nev. "Ah yeah?"

"He's heard from his brother. Kane's making good money building in Christchurch. There's lots to repair after the earthquake. He mentioned something about that blonde woman whose name I won't mention either."

Hana winced, not wanting to hear news of Caroline Marsh, her rival for Logan's affections. Something told her the woman would never give up and even thinking her name felt like poking a wasps' nest and anticipating trouble. "I don't want to know," Hana sighed with sincerity but Leslie never kept gossip to herself. She told Hana the latest news and left her poleaxed.

"You're not serious?" Hana said, her porcelain skin paling further and her red hair standing out like a fiery halo. "It's not true."

"Is true," Leslie said, reaching for another biscuit, unaware of the devastation those two small words had wrought.

12

Caleb

Hana waited as Caleb dragged himself up the ramp to his motel room, situated along a lane next to the main hotel. The museum curator followed in his wheelchair, watching as the teenager coped with his crutches on the wooden deck.

"Youse more pathetic than me," Will grunted, holding the wheelchair halfway up the ramp using the strength in his rippling biceps and Hana shot him a look of rebuke.

"I offered you to go up first!" she hissed. "He can't help it."

"Didn't know youse'd be all day," Will grumbled, his face scowling so that the dark eyes became obscured by the drooping grey eyebrows. Phoenix sat on Will's knee in the chair, adding to the ballast.

"I'll push you," Hana offered, switching Mac to her left hip and reaching out for the wheelchair handle with her right hand.

"Don't!" Will snapped. "I got no legs. Me brain works fine. Last time I let you push me anywhere we ended up in the bushes."

Hana withdrew the proffered hand. "That wasn't my fault. I didn't know the ramp would be icy."

A ranch slider hissed on its runner as it drew back, disgorging the guest in the far room. The man strode out and seeing the ramp filled with people, changed direction and leapt the low railing enclosing the widow's walk in a single fluid leap. He landed on the gravel below and moved towards the knot of bodies with a blank look on his angular face. "What's up?" he asked, directing his question at Will.

Hana pursed her lips and ignored Logan's new stable manager, still seething and embarrassed by their last encounter.

"Kid's moving in next door to you," Will grunted, smiling to reveal neat, pink gums. "The missus likes her staff all broken."

Hana glared at him, resenting his reference to her tendency to ally with those whom the rest of society wrote off without a second glance. "You'd know," she muttered, avoiding the sight of his trouser legs tucked beneath his stumps. The low chuckle Will emitted shook his body and Phoenix perched on his knee, joining in the merriment without understanding. Will reached out an arm and spanked Hana's thigh, realising the stupidity of the movement as the released wheel slewed backwards, arcing him towards the safety rail and bushes beyond. Phoenix's eyes opened wide in horror and she gripped Will's thighs in a pinch which made him roar.

The stable manager moved with incredible speed, leaping the rail and snatching up the wheelchair handle just in time to yank it back into line. The chair stopped its horrible backwards descent and Phoenix let out a peal of laughter which sounded maniacal on the quiet terrace. Will gave the tall man a look of gratitude and then yelled at Caleb as the teenager made his tortoise maneuver. "Get a bloody shifty on, boy!" he shouted. "I got no legs and I get on better with crutches than you! I could've got to Auckland by now!"

"When can it be my turn on your knee?" Wiri asked with a whine in his voice.

"Sorry!" Caleb exclaimed. He leaned against the side of the building, his face pale and sweat beading on his forehead. "It hurts."

"Just stand there," Hana said, pressing her hand against his chest. "Let Will go past before he bursts a blood vessel."

With the stable manager's help, Will hauled himself up the rest of the ramp and wheeled to his motel room, stopping half way along the deck. He retrieved the key from his breast pocket and ignored Hana's presence, speaking to Phoenix and Wiri, as the little boy bounced up and down next to him. "Let's get inside and see what old Will's got for you in his fruit bowl."

Hana glared at the curator's back, a look which also took in the new stable manager, his spine ramrod straight as he pushed the chair into the room and disappeared. She looked at the teenager as he let out a sigh. "Sorry," Caleb said. "I don't mean to be a pain in the ass."

"You're not." Hana transferred her hand from his chest to his upper arm, fearful he might plummet south onto the wooden surface. His hands shook on the crutches and a greyness entered his pallor. As the first of the crutches went out from beneath his trembling body and he began to slide down the wall, Hana screamed for help. "I can't hold him," she shouted, balancing Mac and trying to hold Caleb upright. His slender body felt like a dead weight slumping against her, dragging her down with him. Hana's brain took in the sharp edges of the weatherboard and the deck rail, knowing she'd hurt Mac if she fell sideways. "Help me!" she wailed, feeling Caleb become weightless as strong hands pushed between them, alleviating her burden.

The stable manager dipped his tall body and shoved his head under Caleb's arm, lifting him over his shoulder like a fireman. Out cold, the boy grunted and the crutches fell away with a clatter. "Where's he going?" the stable manager demanded and Hana forced her shocked self to react. She reseated Mac on her hip and darted past Will's open door to unlock the ranch slider of the next room.

"In here," she said, shoving the door aside and watching as the man carried Caleb over the threshold.

The stable manager spun on his feet for a second, rejecting the lounge and its two seater sofa in favour of the double bed in the room behind. An expanse of white cast dangled from Caleb's knee like a millstone, pulling one leg longer than the other. The man lay Caleb down with surprising care and stood back. "Not good," he muttered, He put his hands up to the teenager's throat and Hana tensed, watching as he undid the zipper on Caleb's jacket and rested a hand over his chest. "He's still breathing," he said. "But he's unconscious." Worried eyes darted back towards Hana. "An ambulance will take ages. Call the local doctors and get one of them to come out here."

Hana looked down at her mobile phone and her heart sank at the lack of signal. The motel unit telephone sat on a sideboard and she reached for it and dialled zero for reception. She tapped the carpet with the toe of her boot, waiting for the receptionist to answer. Will's wheels made a steady rumble along the deck as he travelled down to investigate and Wiri's anxious face appeared in the doorway. "Hey, Marla." Hana exhaled with relief as the phone gave a click and the receptionist's voice came through the handset. "Could you find my brother, Mark?" Her shoulders slumped. "Oh, he's still out? Then call Dr Seuli's surgery please?" She gave a brief explanation and one last instruction. "Ask for Dr Francis."

Hana disconnected and placed the phone back on its charger. Her mind raced, hoping the gentle elderly doctor made the home visit priority. She winced at the thought of him pootling through the mountains in his tiny shoebox of a car, counting down the days to retirement and arriving confused about why he was there. A moment of panic visited at the same time she realised perhaps Dr Seuli might visit instead; Dr Seuli who made a statement to the cops which inferred she was crazy and implicated Logan in a murder. Hana closed her eyes and prayed for Dr Francis and his octogenarian bedside manner.

"What's up, Linc?" Will's face peered through the door, Phoenix still riding in his lap like the queen with her legs crossed and arms folded. Wiri held two bananas, one in each hand.

The stable manager glanced back at the door and shook his head. "Take the kids away," he said. "He might throw up when he wakes."

Will nodded and nudged Phoenix. "Hop off kōtiro," he said. "It's Macky's turn." As Phoenix rolled down the front of the chair grumbling, Will ignored Wiri's protestations of fairness and held his arms out for Hana's baby. "We'll go to the swings," he stated, brooking no argument and the objections halted, replaced by childish whoops of excitement.

Hana handed Mac over, settling him on the old man's knee. He got eye contact with her, promising he'd be careful. She held her breath until she heard his chair grinding over the gravel, the ramp safely navigated.

"Won't that baby fall out of his wheelchair?" the stable manager asked as he stripped Caleb's body out of his jacket and lifted his scruffy tee shirt.

Hana shook her head and rushed over to help. "No, Mac's ridden with him since he was born. He knows to hold on." Together they pulled the tee shirt over the boy's head. Caleb groaned and Hana stroked his cheek. "It's all right, love. Help's coming." She squatted next to the bed and glanced over at the imposing man in the process of running water onto a cold flannel in the ensuite bathroom. "What's wrong with him?"

"I think he's reacting to the antibiotics," the stable manager said. He bathed Caleb's hot forehead with the flannel, a frown on his face. "How long does it take to get here from the surgery?"

"It depends who's coming," Hana said, chewing her lip. "Dr Francis could be ages. I thought my brother, Mark might help but apparently he's still out with Alfred."

"Where's the medication he's on?" the man said.

"In the car. I'll get it." Hana's boot heels clicked as she ran along the deck and down the ramp. The gravel scrunched underfoot and she sped along the lane to the main car park and unlocked the passenger door. The white pharmacy bag lay in the foot well where Caleb dropped it and she snatched it up and locked her car before powering back to the motel room. Her companion spewed the contents onto the bed next to Caleb, an array of boxes and bottles bouncing on the comforter. He sorted through them with deft hands, throwing the pain killers aside and examining the antibiotics.

"Could he be on something else?" he demanded, squinting to read the tiny writing ordering Caleb to take two tablets every six hours with food. "A drug you don't know about?"

"I don't know," Hana said. "I only met him the other day and that wasn't conducive to questions about addictions." She hissed with annoyance at herself, wondering if she'd bitten off way more than she could chew. "Look, he's been in hospital for days, so anything he's got on him came from there. I doubt he's got other drugs or the energy to take them."

"Bloody stupid bringing someone you don't know around your kids," the man bit, his tone barbed.

Hana swallowed, feeling his chastisement and turning the guilt into defensive anger. "I don't know you!" she spat. "Maybe you should leave."

The brown eyes turned in her direction, sparkling in challenge with lighter flecks gathered around the irises. "Your husband knows me just fine," he replied.

"Lucky him," Hana muttered. "But I didn't think he employed assholes."

"Equal opportunities," he said, his tone lighter. "I'm in a minority group."

"Whatever!" Hana stroked Caleb's hot forehead and felt the dampness left from the flannel as the stable manager went to soak it again.

"Lincoln," the man said, placing it on Caleb's forehead with care. He stepped back and wiped his hands on his jeans.

"What?" Hana's brow furrowed in confusion as she reached for Caleb's floppy hand, wondering what a South Island city had to do with her current predicament.

"My name." The stable manager stuck out a damp hand and Hana stared at it. Big knuckles and a bent index finger moved closer and she let go of Caleb and stood. "Lincoln. It's my name. I'm not an asshole and I'd like to start again with you." His lips twitched with a nervousness he managed to keep hidden most of the time and he jerked his hand. "Come on, put me out of my misery. Please."

Hana stared at the giant hand and then raised her own, allowing it to be enclosed in the warm, damp palm. "Hana," she said. "I'm the spokesperson for the asshole jury and I'm afraid they're still out."

The tanned skin around the brown eyes crinkled in amusement. "Nice to meet you, Hana."

"I'm gonna chuck!" Caleb's slurred speech caused them to leap apart and Lincoln dragged the limp teenager to the ensuite, holding him up over the toilet as he threw up for the best part of twenty minutes.

13

Lincoln

"Dr Haines." Hana let go of Caleb's hand and took a step back as though guilty of making him sick. Lincoln sat in the armchair nearest the door and Hana watched as his body stiffened, his face channelling pure dismay.

"Hi, Hana." Fiona Haines breezed through the ranch slider and nodded her thanks to the retreating receptionist. The room remained silent as the sound of Marla's high heels clopped along the deck and scrunched through the gravel back to her post. Fiona looked from Hana to Lincoln and back again, her face maintaining a cool mask of capability and calm. "Is this the patient?"

Hana nodded and stared at Lincoln, noting his sudden discomfort and the way he squirmed in the armchair. "I'll head off," he said and Hana held up her hand.

"No. Stay. We might need help to move him and you went through his pills. You thought it might be a reaction to the antibiotics."

Fiona raised her eyebrows but kept her inner thoughts private.

"We didn't Google it or anything," Hana added, her green eyes wide. "I did that once for a cold sore and convinced myself I had all sorts of things wrong with me." Her laugh sounded false in the awkward silence, the atmosphere hanging like a heavy curtain. Nervous hands fluttered by her side as Hana missed the weight of her quiet son in her arms, realising how often she hid her outward signs of distress by fiddling with his cardigan or patting his back. She wondered if she needed him more than he needed her.

"Where's his paperwork from the hospital?" Fiona's lips moved and Hana saw Lincoln's eyes flick to her face.

"What?"

"His discharge papers. Where are they?"

"I don't know." Hana lurched for the paper bag. "Weren't they in here?" She upended it and a receipt for the prescription fluttered down alone. "I don't know then." She waved her arms towards the stable manager. "Lincoln, check Caleb's jacket."

The tall man lumbered across to the chair onto which he'd slung Caleb's outer layers. He shook his head after rifling through the pockets. "Nothing here except an old photo."

Hana watched as large fingers unfolded the shiny paper and Lincoln grunted disinterest. He refolded it and shoved it back into an inside pocket, dropping the scruffy jacket onto the chair. His eyes strayed towards the door and then back to Hana, his expression appealing for release. She shook her head, needing him to stay as a buffer between the doctor and her. Mac's obvious deafness created a knot in Hana's chest and made her want to sob with abandon outside on the gravel. If Lincoln left her alone with Fiona, she might ask how it was going and Hana knew she'd cry.

"Sick!" Caleb lurched upright again on the bed and Lincoln hauled the boy back over to the toilet. Hana closed her eyes and droned out the sounds of dry retching with noises from inside her own head as she recited her schedule for the day. Feed the kids; put the washing on the line; ring her other children; start packing for Hamilton and talk to Wiri's father; the job's list ran like a chant.

"Are you all right, Hana?" Fiona's voice cut through the list and Hana jumped.

"Fine. Just busy." She exhaled in a rush. "I haven't heard from the hospital and I don't want to talk about it."

Fiona Haines cocked her head to one side and observed Hana. "I wouldn't dream of discussing your private medical concerns with other people present." Glancing around the room, she oozed professionalism and control. "That would make me a terrible doctor, Hana."

"Sorry." Hana wrung her hands and wished Caleb would finish his extended barf so she could escape. "Does he need to go to hospital?"

"I don't believe so." Fiona shook her head. "I'm sure he's reacting to one of the pain killers. It's a known side effect. I'll take him off that and prescribe something else."

Hana nodded and watched her children on the play park in the distance. The green lawn stretched out on the other side of the motel units like a glossy carpet. Mac sat on Will's knee and let himself be wheeled around the swings. Hana saw the baby's auburn fluff disturbing in the breeze and her fingers itched to stroke it back from his soft forehead.

Hana felt Logan's presence before she heard or saw him, knowing he'd entered her air space through some peculiar connection between their souls. As he skipped up the ramp and trod the boards to the ranch slider, he found Hana already turned towards the door, gnawing on her lower lip in distress. "What's going on?" He occupied the room from the entrance, his personality filling the space around him and sucking out the oxygen.

"Caleb's sick." Hana's brow creased with concern, more for Logan's reaction than Caleb's discomfort. "I'll pay for the doctor," she added, watching as Logan's eyes flashed with danger at her presumption.

"No need." Fiona turned a dazzling smile on Hana. "I'll follow the paper trail back to the original ACC claim at the hospital and add it to that."

Logan's gaze grazed the doctor's attractive face and then returned to Hana. "A word," he said, jerking his head towards the door and retreating outside. Hana gulped and followed, feeling chastened and foolish. Logan didn't want the responsibility of Caleb and as another bout of dry retching filled the air, Hana sensed her husband's frustration. She covered the space with fairy footsteps like a child delaying punishment.

"I know, I know." She raised her hands palm upwards in supplication, detesting the whine in her voice. "I said he'd be no trouble and already he's barfing up his guts. I'm sorry. You were right and I was wrong." Hana took a breath and opened her mouth to continue, prevented by the soft lips which covered hers.

Logan's eyes narrowed in a lazy grin as he smoothed her chin with his thumb and kissed her again, stoking his desire at the same time as silencing her. "Anyone ever tell you that you'd be crap under torture?" He smirked, pulling her into line with his body and ran large hands into the small of her back and down over her buttocks. "I haven't said anything yet and already you're confessing like a nark."

"I thought you seemed cross." Hana sulked, pushing her face into Logan's broad chest. "It's called mitigation."

Logan's short laugh irritated her more. "It's called verbal diarrhoea, babe. And it changes nothing. He's trouble and you know it."

Hana shrugged, reluctant to concede his point. "Is that what you came to say? I told you so." She pulled away, tugging against the strength in her husband's fingers as he snaked them around her wrists.

"No." His grey eyes held mischief and he poked his tongue into a corner of his mouth. Hana watched its lazy trail along his bottom lip and sighed.

"What then?"

"I spoke to the new headmaster of The Waikato Presbyterian School for Boys earlier today. I need to travel down to Hamilton ready to start next Monday, but you can follow when you're ready."

"Next Monday?" Hana swallowed and the colour drained from her face. "But what about Wiri? Did you speak to Nev?"

"He's coming with us."

"Nev?" Hana pulled a face laced with horror and Logan smiled.

"No babe. Wiri."

"How? What about school and stuff? We can't just kidnap him for a term and hope nobody notices."

"We'll take him to the primary up the road from the boys' school and Phoe can join the kindy next door. Then you'll just have Mac to worry about."

Hana swallowed. "Yeah. Only Mac to worry about," she repeated, giving more of herself away than she wanted. She closed her eyes against the sound of Caleb retching again. "That kid's gonna burst something."

"Why did you call the lady doctor?" Logan asked, pulling Hana close and running his hands over her back.

"I didn't. I asked Marla to call Dr Francis, but she turned up. Why?"

Logan shrugged. "No reason. I just assumed she'd avoid all contact with us."

"Why?" Hana leaned back and narrowed her eyes. "Is she yet another adoring female of the Du Rose whānau?" She shook her head, resenting her husband's peculiar magnetism and the way women flocked around him like flies. Feeling insecure, Hana snaked her fingers under Logan's shirt and found his soft, olive skin. Despite his limited clothing he felt toasty warm and she made him jump with her cool fingers. Her palm caressed the rugged skin over the scar which ran from hip to armpit on his right side, not daunted by its ugliness, but content with its attachment to him.

"Mrs Du Rose?" The doctor's voice sounded soft as she broke into Hana's moment and she experienced a flash of resentment. Turning to meet the enquiring eyes, Hana fixed a fake smile onto her face. Fiona Haines glanced back into the motel room and then addressed her as though Logan didn't exist. "Caleb should stop vomiting soon. I've swapped the Tramadol for something less damaging to his stomach and given him an injection. Get more antibiotics down him as soon as he's able to sip water and monitor him."

"Thanks," Hana replied, irritated when Fiona's eyes strayed to Logan.

"I'm surprised at you," the doctor said, a bite in her tone. "I thought whānau stuck together."

Confused, Hana looked from the doctor to her husband and back, knowing she'd missed something important in the leaden atmosphere. Logan shrugged off the rebuke with his usual brand of casual disdain. "And that's what is happening here. I'm taking care of my family."

"Leave it, Fi." Lincoln appeared at the ranch slider and shot a nervous glance at Logan. "I'm grateful for a job and a roof over my head. Please leave it. I'll stay out of your way, I promise, wahine."

The doctor snatched up her medical bag from just inside the doorway, bashing Linc's legs with it as she yanked it through the gap. "Goodbye, Mrs Du Rose," she said, forcing seriousness into her expression. "Call me if you need to, or bring Caleb to the surgery and I'll see him there."

"Thanks." Hana shrugged Logan's arm off her shoulder. "I'll walk you to your car."

Logan's grip around her upper arm shocked her and she stared at her husband aghast. The slight shake of his head warned her not to disobey him and she relented. "Sorry, I'm sure you know your way back. Thanks for coming out here. I'll call you if there's any change."

Fiona Haines gave a curt nod and set off along the deck in her heels, watched by two brooding males and one confused female. As soon as she left earshot, Hana rounded on the men and fixed her hands on her hips. "What was that about?" she demanded. Logan looked smug but Linc cringed, his huge body seeming to knot up and shrink. The sound of wailing from the play park halted the need for an immediate answer and Hana glared at the men. "One of you can stay with Caleb while I sort that out!" She jerked a pointed index finger in the direction of her daughter who lay flat on her face under the swing.

Hana stomped down the ramp and headed towards the rising volume and heard Logan retort with a laugh in his voice, "That will be your job then, mate." She heard his familiar footfall on the deck and turned as she scooped Phoenix off the floor, seeing him stride away. Logan Du Rose ran his hands through his dark hair before shoving his cowboy hat back on his head. She felt his amusement from across the lawn. Just as well he didn't see the abusive hand gesture which his new stable manager jabbed towards his retreating back. Linc saw Hana's gaze fixed on him and let the hand fall to his side, walking back into the motel room and closing the door behind him.

14

The Haines Dilemma

"**S**orry for this." Caleb sat in an armchair with his leg raised on a coffee table. A pillow softened the surface and he looked sorry for himself, his hair mussed and a downy stubble growth gracing his chin. "I didn't know it would be so bad."

"It's fine." Hana winced as Phoenix gripped her neck and shifted her weight to look at Caleb's plaster cast.

"I draw on it?" Phoenix asked, pushing her face into her mother's, her little chest hitching. Hana kissed her nose and shook her head, reaching down to stop the oozing graze on the child's knee from touching her sweater and setting off another bout of painful tears.

"It's too sore, baby. Ask again when Mr Caleb feels better."

"Okay." Phoenix pushed her small thumb between her lips and laid her head on Hana's shoulder, closing her eyes against the world.

"I need to feed the children." Hana chewed her lower lip. "But the doctor said to monitor you. I'm not sure how that's gonna work." She cast around the motel room for a solution and her gaze rested on Lincoln. He put his hands up in self-defense.

"No way! I'm employed to run the stables and elite equine breeding programme." Lincoln quoted straight from his job contract. "There's nothing in there about babysitting morons who get hurt in the bush."

"I don't need babysitting." Caleb looked hurt, slapping the cold flannel over his damp forehead, his face pinched with pain. "And I'm not a moron. I'd be doing it tough on the streets if it wasn't for Mrs Du Rose. That means I can manage by myself in a flash motel room."

Hana placed the telephone by Caleb's hand and fetched a glass of water from the small kitchenette. "I'll pop back with some afternoon tea," she promised, hitching Phoenix above her hip as the child dozed. "Dial zero for reception and Marla or Kevin will fetch me if you need something." She added the remote for the TV and another pillow.

Lincoln snorted over her fussing and Hana suppressed the urge to kick his shin. He was close enough for a backwards jab, but it would overbalance her and Phoenix's head lolled sideways as Hana contemplated the maneuver.

Lincoln pulled the ranch slider closed and faced Hana on the deck as she propped her snoozing daughter's head up with her hand. "What's your problem?" she demanded. "What's Caleb ever done to you?"

Lincoln shrugged. "Nothing, miss." He narrowed his eyes to slits and a mask crashed down over his expression. "Is it okay if I go back to doing my proper job now?"

"No." Hana shook her head. "What's the deal between you and my husband? Why are you here and why does the local doctor object?"

The tall male heaved out a sigh and looked towards the rising turret of the main house above the trees. He pondered his answer for a moment, ordering the words and anticipating their effect. "If you were anyone else, I'd tell you to mind your own business." He glared at Hana. "I'm also wondering why your husband didn't think to mention it. Maybe I should leave him to fill in the gaps."

Hana felt the sting of his words as he hit the bulls-eye. Logan promised to share details of the business with her as an equal, whilst leaving out salient parts which often came back to bite her. The realisation he'd done it again lit a fire in her heart and she took a threatening step forward. Her chin barely reached Linc's collar bone. "Why are you here?" she repeated, her tone angry.

"I took over from the previous stable manager, who died last year. My role is to..."

"I don't need the sanitised version!" Hana snapped. Inside her brain she dreaded the sound of Jack's name; his crime against her still fresh in all its dismay and horror. "Why are you here?"

For a moment, Linc's mask failed him and Hana saw his vulnerability. His mouth opened and closed and she seized on the loose thread which instinct directed her to. "What's your last name?"

Linc swallowed. "Haines."

"So the new doctor's your wife?"

"Ex-wife." He closed dark eyes against an inner pain which threatened to eat him from the inside out.

"You're not a Du Rose?"

He shook his head. "Fiona is. Was. She's Logan's cousin. We both grew up here in the township." Hana watched the huge fists ball at his side, unable to imagine the pretty, slender doctor in the giant's embrace without breaking bones. Her eyes widened.

"Did you hit her?"

Linc's mouth dropped open in horror. "No! Never. Why would you jump to that conclusion?" Shock dropped the mask and Hana saw a man who'd suffered unimaginable emotional trauma. His eyes held the same haunted look which used to drive Logan and she saw a glimpse of how far her husband had journeyed since the start of their marriage.

"Because you're so bloody aggressive!" Hana retorted. "You behave like a dick!"

Linc's pupils dilated and he took a step back, seeing himself through another's eyes. He glanced at the sleeping child on Hana's shoulder and whirled away, striding along the deck and down to the gravel, crunching away with footsteps which slammed into the earth. "Nice one, Hana," she rebuked herself with a sigh. "How to make friends and influence people."

Will approached in his wheelchair, shunting across the grass in a series of lurches over the uneven surface. Mac lounged on his knee with tiny fingers clasped around the chair arms either side of him, examining the sky with intense interest. Wiri trailed behind, his face set in a sulk at being yanked away from play. "Yer don't wanna be poking that wasps' nest," Will advised, when he got close enough for Hana to hear his hushed warning. "Yer'll get stung."

"I just did," Hana sighed, watching as Linc rounded the end of the lane and set off towards the main house. "Why would Logan employ someone so rude?"

"Appen youse best ask him." Something in Will's answer alerted Hana's suspicious mind and she smiled a slow, fake smile.

"I'm asking you, my friend."

"Aw, darn!" Will complained. "Bloody women!"

They wandered to the hotel and used a side entrance with a purpose built ramp for the wheelchair. Hana carried Phoenix and held Wiri's hand. "I didn't mean to make her fall," the little boy muttered. He caressed Phoe's dangling toes and stared up at her with doe eyes. "I thought she wanted to swing high."

"It's fine." Hana stroked the downy head. "She knows you didn't do it on purpose."

"I didn't, Ma," he reiterated and Hana's heart quailed at his use of the maternal tag, not knowing how to point out his error.

The small boy had latched onto her like a life raft and correcting him resulted in tears and then painful silence as his fragile world tipped on its axis again. He resumed the grip on her fingers as though terrified she might disappear like his own mother and Hana felt a lump in her throat at his agony.

"Your new wheelchair should arrive soon." She changed the subject and Will grunted back at her, his sparse hair sticking upwards like antennae.

"Youse didn't have to buy that," he protested, navigating the corridor to the kitchen on the west side of the house.

"I know I didn't." Hana sighed. "But I wanted to."

"But what if the electrics pack up and I'm stuck in the middle of the car park like a bloody bollard?" he said, waiting for Hana to push on the heavy door.

"Keep it charged at night and that won't happen," Hana promised. "And it comes with a warranty. You worry too much."

"Said the prostitute to the vicar," Will retorted with a dirty chuckle. Wiri laughed too, which was even more worrying and the old man licked his lips and looked ashamed.

Leslie sat at the dining table in the family room, reading the newspaper with a large scone between her fingers. Alfred tucked in to a chocolate muffin, spreading icing on his long nose.

"Poppa!" Wiri exclaimed with pleasure and bounced across to the old man. Leslie raised an eyebrow at Hana and rolled her eyes.

"There's nothing I can do!" she hissed at her mother-in-law. "His mum's on a mental ward, his father's clueless and his grandfather's dead. Just give the kid a break."

Alfred accepted the child's hongi, pressing his forehead to Wiri's in an affectionate Māori greeting. He settled his brother's kin on his knee and fed the little boy chocolate muffin; the heart cry of all males. Food. Hana settled her children and sat with a mug of tea in front of her. She waited until the kitchen girl retreated back to the clattering of pots and pans next door.

"Right then, who's gonna tell me what's going on with Lincoln Haines?"

Alfred inhaled through his nose, Leslie shifted on her large bottom and Will found the chocolate chips in his muffin worthy of great concentration. Phoenix limped over to the sofa in the corner and snuggled down, choosing sleep over nourishment. Hana observed her whilst watching the others through her peripheral vision.

"What about him?" Leslie ventured, feigning disinterest. "Hasn't he just replaced...himself who's not here anymore?"

Hana sighed, waiting for the punch line. She heard the men clear their throats in discomfort. "I want to know what Lincoln's done? I figured it must be along the usual lines; an illicit affair, drug taking or a mixture of both. Aren't those the most common Du Rose vices?"

Alfred squirmed in his seat and Hana caught a faint whiff of marijuana. Her eyes flickered at the memory of the series of lies she told her husband to protect the foolish old man's secret and resentment bubbled in her chest.

"That's harsh, Hana," Leslie complained, darting a sideways look at her husband. "We're not all shaggin' and draggin'!"

Wiri let out a peal of laughter and repeated the phrase like a rhyme. Alfred sank lower in his chair, possibly guilty of both since breakfast. "Shaggin' and draggin'," Wiri sang, continuing with a full mouth until Hana gave him the evil eye.

"He got out of the big house after Christmas," Leslie said, ignoring the collective groan of the men either side of her.

"Now you've done it!" Will jibed, buttering a scone and adding an artery clogging blob of jam.

"Prison?" Hana slopped tea up her wrist and put the mug on the table, her hand shaking. "What for?"

"Man's served his time," Alfred chided her. "It don't matter no more."

"What did he do?" Hana knew the answer before anyone uttered it, certain it would be something her husband thought best not to tell her. "He killed someone, didn't he?"

Leslie nodded. "Yeah. A woman."

The memory of Jack's face as he held the gun on her tiny newborn shuddered into Hana's inner vision. She saw his lips move in gibberish as he accused her of bearing another man's child; a baby he helped to slide blood soaked into the world. Her heart quickened as she remembered Mac's red hair glinting beneath the sunlight, condemning him as not a Du Rose. She saw Jack pointing the pistol at the baby's delicate, fine-boned face, wishing the newborn dead with every fibre of his bitter old body.

Hana's chair scraped backwards as she stood. Her hands shook and she looked sick. "I need some air," she gasped and fled the room, leaving Mac gumming pieces of scone from Will's gnarled fingers and her daughter asleep on the sofa. She stopped at the end of the corridor, knowing she shouldn't abandon her babies but panic drove her on. She sought the cool air outside the hotel and the sense of calm the bush offered. Lincoln Haines killed a woman. Hana shook her head. Logan knew about the night terrors which woke her in the darkness, panicked and gasping as she screamed for her son and tried to shield his fragile body from a madman. "How could you, Logan?" she groaned, pitching forward on the steps and hugging her knees. "How could you?"

15
Du Rose Future

Sacha grazed with easy grace, lipping sweet blades of grass with her ears flicking forwards and back. Her dinner plate hooves lifted and fell as she strolled and her tail flicked at imaginary flies. Hana leaned her chin on her forearms and sighed. She repeated the sound louder, wanting the mare to notice and comfort her with soothing snuffs of air and bristly kisses. But Sacha only mirrored the noise, blowing out warm puffs into the coolness of the mountain.

Hana clambered over the post and rail fence, sitting on top for a moment to absorb the silence of the bush. A mist descended from the highest points of the mountain, drifting down to cover the landscape with a hazy blanket. A native tui fluttered from tree to tree, clothed in his feathery dinner jacket and white bow tie. He tilted his head to get a better view of the woman and cackled like a lunatic, fleeing to the lacy heights of a silver fern in the canopy.

The grass felt lush underfoot and Hana's boots swished through Sacha's feast as she approached the mare with caution, remembering the rules of the game. The white horse lifted her head in a swift action, feigning surprise although her different coloured eyes channelled amusement. "Yeah, very funny," Hana grumbled, moving with slow deliberation to the biting front end and avoiding the murderous back feet. "I'm not really in the mood to play."

Sacha lowered her head and peered through the tops of her eyes as though Hana played the part of naughty schoolgirl approaching the head teacher for a growling over a minor misdemeanor. She snorted, appreciating Hana's deference but sensing the play act.

"Hey, don't make me beg." Hana reached for Sacha's broad cheekbone and ran a hand along the coarse fur, closing her eyes to savour the sensation. Acknowledging the blue wall-eye she turned the noble head with gentle fingers, making sure Sacha saw her through the brown eye too, uniting both halves of the equine brain in a realisation of her presence so there would be no surprises. "I wish I was a horse," Hana declared, wondering if the calm of the mountain and the lure of mineral rich grass would be a fair swap for her crazy, tumultuous world as a prosperous farmer's wife. Sacha snorted, coating Hana's fleecy jacket with a fine, grassy spray. She lifted her huge head and nuzzled into Hana's neck, pushing her whiskery nostrils beneath the long, curly tresses. "You say that," Hana continued, as though Sacha had spoken words of great wisdom and contradiction, "but I have no more control over my life than you do. Logan makes the big decisions and I'm meant to smile and go along with them." Sacha's tail went flick, flick, swish in reply.

"I can't get it out of my head." Hana sighed and kissed the leathery lips close to her face. "Is this how it must be? Every year on Mac's birthday instead of celebrating my son's safe arrival, I'm reminded of the deaf man who helped me deliver him and then held a gun on us." She shuddered, unable to say Jack's name and Sacha breathed warm air onto the side of her face. "I shouldn't be glad he's dead. It makes me sick to think of how he died, but my heart feels relief because he'll never come after us again." Hana released a sob into the silent paddock. "And then I remember how sweet he was to me in the early days. All those years playing the role of stable manager just to make sure Logan grew up safe in the Du Rose wasps' nest. That's the action of a loving grandfather; not a killer. I'll never understand what happened."

The white mare shifted closer, rubbing her hard forehead against Hana's shoulder. She braced her feet against the steady pressure of half a ton of horseflesh. It grazed her tender skin and fragile bones and she grounded herself in Mātakitaki Mountain's unshakeable foundation, feeling the earth hum beneath her feet. Hana smelled the familiar Sacha-scent and her body relaxed under the mare's maternal safeguard. "Logan's replaced one murderer with another. Why wouldn't he warn me? It's cruel."

Sacha's head rose at the sound of the quad bike and she gave a whinny which came from her chest. It spelled excitement and thrill and heralded Logan's arrival. Without a backward glance she turned her huge body and clopped to the fence, pushing her face over the top rail and whickering to the tall male delivering hay and chaff. Logan leaned his sinewy forearms on the top rung and let the mare scold him for his absence. She tugged at his shirt and lipped his face, scenting his hair and rubbing her whiskers against his stubbly cheek. Hana stood alone in the centre of the paddock, isolated and forgotten. She felt a flicker of jealousy at Sacha's abandonment but resigned herself to the mare's affection for her husband being greater.

"Leave me alone and get on with your business," Logan crooned, pushing the mare's face away from his. She returned like an irritating wasp until he relinquished the apple hidden in his jeans pocket, crunching the delicacy in huge molars and dribbling juice like a baby.

Hana turned away from the happy scene and strolled towards the bush line, meaning to escape into the dense canopy and return to the hotel another way. She heard Logan's long stride catching her up and squeaked, breaking into an ungainly run. He laughed as he seized her from behind and lifted her into the air. "Oh no, you don't!" he exclaimed, holding her around the waist and breathing soft kisses onto the back of her neck. "Leslie's worried about you."

Hana groaned. "I just wanted some peace!"

Logan spun her around and crushed her into his chest. "Did you find any?" He kissed the top of her head.

"No!" she grumbled into his shirt.

Logan held her close, rubbing her rigid back and soothing her with his strength. He said nothing, offering no explanation for his omission and her rational self agreed with him, seeing how irritating her flash of self-pity might seem from the outside.

"Come for a walk with me?" Logan's voice rumbled through his chest and Hana fought the smirk which rose to her lips.

"You mean a lie down."

Logan snorted. "Only if you insist, babe. But the mist is closing and I meant a short walk. There's something I wanna show you."

"I've seen it." Hana's sarcasm made her husband throw back his head and laugh.

"One track mind, wahine. No wonder you're always pregnant." He dodged the slap she aimed at his bicep. "Come on; humour me."

Logan seized Hana's tiny fingers in his big paw and pulled her towards the far end of the paddock, opening the gate and waiting as she passed through. Hana glanced back to see Sacha tossing her head and dancing towards them, her round hooves slapping the ground in a series of excited steps and leaving clods of soil in her wake. "Come on then!" Logan yelled and she picked up speed, crossing the ground with effortless grace, blurred legs and white mane and tail streaming behind her like sails.

"Where are we going?" Hana asked, stepping back as the white mare squeezed through the closing gate with a snort of warning.

"Not far." Logan gave her a sexy grin and Hana felt her heart lurch in her breast.

"Then can we discuss the new stable manager?" she asked, her voice tight.

"Yeah. Reckon so." Logan held out his hand and she took it, hoping he kept his promise.

They clambered up a steep side and onto a ridge. Sacha climbed next to them, bracing herself against outcrops and tufty hillocks, digging in with her front hooves and shifting her weight with jerky, awkward movements. Rugged bush spread out either side of them, the uppermost parts of the canopy shrouded in drifting white mist. The tui bird followed, alighting in overhead pungas and mimicking Sacha's snorts and grunts.

At the top of a rise, the white mare stopped dead, her body becoming rigid as a statue's and Hana halted in concern. The majestic head lifted, eyes burning bright and ears pointing forward. She'd never looked more beautiful and Hana felt a lump rise into her throat. Logan chuckled. "She's been desperate to get up here; I'm surprised she didn't jump the fence before now."

The ridge opened out before them and Hana gasped at the splendor of the mountain as it spread before her. Dense bush huddled on both sides of a lush green valley, the colours spectacular in the mist. Nature had created the perfect fairway and a divine paintbrush had dabbed a group of horses into the centre, spread out and grazing. Hana felt Sacha's breath on her arm as the mare clattered onto the ridge, exuding power in the bunched muscles. She reached out and touched the corded tendons across the furry shoulder and felt the electrical pulse go through the horse as she spotted the group. Sacha lifted her head and emitted an ear splitting whinny which echoed out across the landscape. Twelve white heads rose in reply and the answering call came back, loud and challenging.

Sacha repeated her deafening introduction and Hana heard a series of angry snorts from the valley floor. A powerful body pushed through the gathering throng and faced the ridge, head high and feet planted in a perfect square. Hana's brow knitted in confusion at the charcoal markings on the creamy white body and she looked to Logan for confirmation. "That's not the little foal I named a few years ago, is it?" The spidery body and too-long legs had formed into tree trunk proportions and the shoulder muscles on the animal bore testament to the rough terrain he roamed. The dappled patches spotted his legs and stomach like dark dabs of a paint brush.

Logan's face lit up in pleasure. "Yeah. That's Du Rose le Prochain. Remember? Du Rose Future. He's got enough Appaloosa to be decent natured and the Station Bred in him makes him hardy."

"Sacha's tiny foal. I remember. He's stunning."

"Sure is. By pure accident we've bred one of the best sires we'll ever have, I reckon. Toby split that group of colts from Methuselah's last spring and we're running this bachelor herd for a year or so. They'll work out how to behave between them." Logan laughed and Hana imagined the bawdy conversations on the subject back at the stable yard. Her husband fixed his arm over her shoulder and pulled her into his armpit. "I trained him enough to manage him when he's brought back to the stables for checks. He's worth more as a stallion than a work horse, although he could be either. I've ridden him and I'd trust him to an extent. I thought you'd like to see him; seeing as you gave him the cool name." Logan blinked, dark lashes stroking his cheeks. "Must've been prophetic because his future is brilliant and ours too. That foal's smart, pretty and already better than any we've had out of Methuselah. I'll take orders from other breeders once we've picked mares for him and worked the first lot through our own system."

Hana turned and placed a cool hand against the hard equine shoulder next to her. "Hear that, Sacha? Your boy's a winner."

The mare turned glassy eyes towards her and snorted, her movements jerky with excitement. Logan reached around and patted the white rump, his fingers lingering on a lighter grey patch. "Say goodbye, Hana," he said, his smile sad.

"What do you mean?" Hana heard the panic in her voice and Logan gripped her shoulders.

"I'm putting her out to grass with Methuselah's herd, babe."

"You can't!" Her eyes widened in horror and she put out a hand and wrapped her fingers through the wiry mane. Her lip curled back in horror, seeing the flash of irritation in Logan's eyes.

"Nobody trusts her after she killed Jack. We know she's fine but I can't get anyone else to go near her. Superstitions are flying around like confetti and I think a break would be good; for her and everyone else in the stable yard."

"It's because of Lincoln Haines, isn't it?" Hana spat, balling her hands in temper. "He hates her."

"Yeah, he doesn't like her, that's true. But she doesn't do herself any favours either." Logan's fingers scratched the dappled rump and Sacha's ears twitched, her body fixated on the approaching group as they edged towards the bottom of the ridge.

"It's your business, not his!" Hana raged, her eyes filling with hot, angry tears. "You make the decisions!"

"And I have." Logan turned Hana to face him and lifted her head with his finger beneath her chin. "I decided now was a good time to repeat the happy accident and I borrowed Nev's stallion and put them together again." His lips quirked upwards as he teased her. "She's like you; needs a strong male to control her and she likes him. Must've been in season within about five minutes and it worked; she's in foal."

Hana's brow furrowed with her own selfish sense of loss. "Who will I ride now? I can't trust the others not to dump me off."

Logan reached down and brushed her cheek with soft lips. "I'll sort it out," he promised. "But we're going to Hamilton for three months, anyway. By the time we get back you'll see she's pregnant and you won't wanna ride her. It's exciting, babe. If I get another foal like her last, I'll be ecstatic." He glanced back at the mare with fondness. "Reuben owned that old hack of Nev's for years; he took it off some dude as payment of a debt. It used to take him home across country when he got too drunk to find his way back from the tavern and I assumed it was gelded."

"Apparently not," Hana mused.

"Yep. Looks like shit but mix its genetics with Sacha's and you get something spectacular." Logan stared down at the majestic horse pushing out from the tight herd below, curiosity budding in its mismatched eyes; Sacha's eyes.

"Reuben's horse?" Hana cocked her head, feeling the old misery surface and the memory of the house fire which killed Logan's mother and birth father licking at her inner vision.

Logan nodded. "I knew his horse sired the foal, but I didn't know back then Reuben fathered me. The name you gave the foal stuck in my head. When you think what we've achieved since the fire, it's incredible. The Du Roses do have a future now. The mountain's reunited and the two halves of the family interact like we haven't been able to for over forty years. I've gained half-brothers, nephews and a sense of peace I never knew possible. We've got Phoe, Mac and Tama. Du Rose le Prochain. I don't think there was a better name."

Hana nodded in acknowledgement of her husband's success. Her fingers strayed to Sacha's furry coat next to her. "Where's Methuselah?" she asked, peering down at the furry band of brothers below the supplejack covered ridge. Sacha whinnied again.

"This way." Logan took her hand and led her to the left, navigating punga and following a well-trodden path as the bush area began as low-lying supplejack and increased in density either side. Sacha whinnied to the boys again and Hana stopped at the answering call. Logan tugged on her fingers, whistling to his mare. Snorting in a sharp sound of irritation she followed, picking her way behind on heavy footsteps. Fifteen minutes later, the ground opened out before them in a lush green landscape dotted with craggy rocks thrown from the mountain by a giant hand. Hana recognised the view from her visit with Logan when he delivered hay to the small herd and she raked the area for a glimpse of Alfred's favoured horse.

Sacha scented them even before they moved into view, grazing in a spread out group on the other side of a low outcrop. The post and rail fences looked higher than elsewhere on the property, designed to keep the bachelor stallions separate from established herds and prevent fighting. Dense bush and double height fencing contained the colts, their position downwind blinding them to the presence of the group of luscious mares. Hana spied Methuselah as he grazed into view, nibbling the grass shoots and tearing them in short, jerky movements. "He's getting old," she said with a sigh. *Like Alfred*, her mind told her.

"He's good for a few more seasons," Logan said, resting his forearm on the top of the sturdy gate. He sniffed the air. "Spring's coming. Can you smell it?"

"No." Hana sniffed and shook her head, cringing with a sense of foolishness and displacement. "Will Sacha be safe with Methuselah?"

Logan snorted. "Sacha will be safe anywhere. She'll take charge, like she always does. He'll be doing as he's told soon enough."

Sacha sent out a deafening call and the grazing heads rose. The tiniest members of the herd gathered into a tight knot and circled the nearest of the females like surging water. Methuselah's giant head rose, his shoulders bunching in challenge. Logan put his fingers into his mouth and mimicked the whistle Alfred made to summon his mount. Fooled, the old stallion flicked his ears and trotted forward. The mares walked behind him, keeping their distance but their heads moved as they searched the occupants at the high gate. "Going back home to Mum and Dad," Logan said, slapping Sacha's muscular neck. She let out a low whicker as her sire whirled in the dust before the gate. He tossed his head and sniffed the air, seeking confirmation of her identity before deciding if he would permit her reentry into his family.

"Do they remember each other?" Hana asked and Logan shrugged.

"Some definitely do and there's a real sense of reunion. Others don't seem to care."

"What about people? Do they remember us from one year to the next?"

Logan wrinkled his nose. "Harder to say. Again, some do. Sacha remembers me no matter how long I stay away. Methuselah knows me and Alfred, but the biggest recognition comes when you mount up. They'll recognise a rider based on how they interact; whether they yank their reins or kick too hard. They respond to confidence and I figure that's what they remember most; feeling safe with a rider. Riding's like plugging into a horse and creating a continuous current. I think that's where the communication and the relationship happens best."

"Sacha's special, isn't she?" Hana chewed her lip as Logan used a numbered code to open the gate. Sacha's eyes grew wide and Hana stepped back as the mare pushed through the gap and into the paddock, meeting her sire with an arrogant snort. Logan grinned.

"Yeah, she is. Le Prochain's just like her too. He's the male version of pissy and difficult but like his dam, he does it with a twinkle in his eye. Toby couldn't break him in; he gave up." A sense of victory played in Logan's grey eyes. "Fantastic to watch."

They quieted as Methuselah approached Sacha. Hana gripped Logan's fingers and tensed, knowing the old stallion could damage the mare if he decided he didn't want her back in his herd. Logan appeared calm and unworried, licking his lips and watching the scene with curiosity. Sacha raked the ground with an unshod front hoof and tossed her mane in defiance. Methuselah snorted and his brown eyes held intensity as he edged towards her, scenting the air from her nostrils with a series of short sniffs. He filled his lungs with the newcomer's essence. Both horses appeared on edge, jerking and dancing on light feet, ready to run or attack if some unseen thing changed. Their movements were defensive and anticipatory as the horses checked each other out. Methuselah kept his head down in a peculiar equine hongi as his eyes raked the mare's and he sniffed the puffs of air escaping her nostrils.

Sacha let out a high pitched squeal as the old horse lipped at her cheek and Hana panicked, fearful he might bite. Logan laughed and closed the gate, connecting the metal parts of the lock together and turning his back on the dancing hooves and tossing manes. Hana peered around him as he tried to steer her away from the gate. "But what if he hurts her?"

"They'll sort it out."

"But she's pregnant." Hana braced herself against Logan's imposing chest, feeling the muscle resist her palms. He caught her wrists and pulled her arms around his waist, pinning her in an embrace.

"And she'll be fine, Hana. She's from this group. They'll stamp and fuss and by tonight it'll be like she never left. Don't worry about her." He glanced back at the two prized horses. Sacha put her nose in the air and her tail rose like a flag behind her. She resembled a snooty teenager as she shook her head and set off towards the mares at a lazy trot. They shuffled position amongst themselves, eager and afraid. With an indignant snort, Methuselah set off behind her. "Watch yer face, man!" Logan called out in warning. The old stallion bent his majestic neck and bared his teeth, ears flat to his head as he attempted to nip at Sacha's hocks. She felt his breath on her flesh and Hana's chest froze mid-inhale as she watched the powerful muscles bunch in the thighs and flank of the white horse.

With a quick flick of her back feet, Sacha lashed out in a cow-like movement, missing the stallion's muzzle by a whisker. The old male shrieked in protest and his daughter gave another smaller buck as though to let him know she didn't care for his rebuke. The other mares received her entrance as she slipped and slid down the rocky path, gathering with a mix of fear and curiosity. Hana winced and exhaled, seeing Methuselah sulk and snake his neck in spite towards another mare on the herd's periphery before making his way back to the unpredictable Rahab.

"Come." Logan turned Hana before him and pushed her along the bush track towards the bachelor herd further down the mountain and the quad bike beyond that. "My stomach thinks my throat's been cut," he complained. "My wife didn't bring me lunch."

"I'm raising three children! I can't always get away." Hana pursed her lips and blew out warm breaths, desperate to smell the tempting scent of approaching spring which Logan described so often. Spores and pollens rose from the bush as though the foliage appealed to the sunshine to stay high and lit for longer each day. Hana regretted how far away her God felt of late. She wondered if he took part in the smallest details of every change of season still and if the action of nursing winter into spring got old and dull with repetition.

She dug her heels in and locked her calves, surprising herself with the suddenness of her rebellion. "No!" She spun to face Logan, almost bowled over by his mass on the downhill. "I want to discuss why you lied about Lincoln Haines!"

16

Lies by Omission

"Ah yep." Logan didn't bother defending himself. He lifted his chin and straightened his torso, dwarfing Hana with intention and fixing calm grey eyes on her face. "Can we keep walking?"

Hana turned with gritted teeth, gravity giving her little choice as it pulled her towards the hotel in the valley. She stumbled ahead of her husband, wondering if he grappled behind her with ready excuses. She paused at the ridge above Le Prochain's bachelor herd and watched them at play. Excited by the momentary visit of a mare, they skipped and flitted like foals, mounting one another and squealing in angry protest. Bucking and kicking they dodged flailing hooves with exceptional skill, learning the life lessons they'd need to coexist with temperamental females. Logan's lips quirked upward in a sad smile and Hana remembered his childhood stories of the formidable female Māori elders. They terrified their male kin; when his mother yelled they all ran, including his father. The colts seemed to mimic that sentiment with their high jinks.

"I want to know now!" Hana demanded as her boot heels touched the soft grass in Sacha's former paddock. She rounded on her husband and body blocked him as he finished closing the gate; a tiny twig in the way of a gathering tornado.

"Yeah," he replied, sighing as though being pestered by an irritating child. "Who's the big mouth?"

Hana opened her lips and then closed them again, halting her instinctive betrayal of Leslie. "Just tell me!" she snapped.

Logan walked across the paddock, heading for the quad bike outside the gate. He didn't slow his lengthy stride and forced Hana to trot to keep up. "It's no big deal," he began and Hana let the angry snarl escape.

"Then why not be honest? Why keep it a secret if it's no big deal? Or am I reduced to the level of an employee again?"

"You were never just an employee!" Logan exploded. "Don't start the hard-done-by thing with me, Hana. I thought we'd got through that."

"Yeah, well, I thought secrets were a thing of the past too. Stupid of me, hey?"

"It wasn't a secret." Logan's hands felt warm on Hana's shoulders, pinning her in place. "And it's no big deal. Trust me."

"No!" Hana's lips turned down into a grimace. "Whenever you say I have to trust you; I know there's reason for me not to."

Logan put his head back and laughed. "Yeah. I deserved that." He pulled her into his armpit and turned them both to walk downhill, not letting her go despite her futile wriggles.

"Are you going to tell me or will I ask Leslie the whole story and just not speak to you again?" Hana demanded as Logan closed the final gate.

"Leslie!" He snuffed out his mother-in-law's name with an air of disgust. "Should've guessed."

Hana chewed her lip, green eyes widening with guilt. "Don't you blame her!" She glared at her husband. "If you can't be bothered to tell me the truth, I'll have to get it elsewhere. You leave me no choice."

Logan's lips twitched and he fought an inappropriate smile. "Even if what you get bears no resemblance to the truth?"

Hana huffed and puffed but couldn't refute his claim, left with the dregs of half-truth and gossip in place of hard facts. "I heard Linc got out of prison a few months ago after serving a jail term for killing a woman. It made me think of what happened with the old stable manager."

"Jack," Logan said, his voice soft. "My grandfather. He was in his nineties, Hana and lost the plot. His mind took him back in time to some other circumstance and I believe he thought you were Antoinette, messing with the blonde drover my grandmother wrote about in her diary. He'd started calling me Reuben towards the end and I assumed it was forgetfulness. It's possible he really believed I was my father."

Hana shuddered and put her hands over her ears. "Don't make excuses!" she hissed. "You weren't there!" She removed her hands and screamed at Logan, thumping her fists on his chest. "You weren't there! I swaddled my newborn son in towels and put cotton balls in his ears and then I discharged a shot gun through a wall to protect us." Tears of fury pricked at the corners of her eyes, enraging her further. "I'm not the only one still paying for it, Logan! I'm not the only one!"

She left him standing next to the quad, a look of pure confusion on his angular face. Hana heard him shout her name but couldn't look back, couldn't go back, wishing she could turn time back, though. She took a shortcut through a bush walk and another paddock, knowing Logan couldn't follow on the quad. "He hides his identity as your grandfather for forty years and then tries to kill your son and wife." She punched the air with her fists in temper, feeling sweat gather in the small of her back and under her arms. "You just keep making excuses for him, Logan Du Rose. But don't expect me to worship at the feet of yet another bloody twisted Du Rose male!"

Hana found her in-laws and her babies in the apartment on the top floor of the hotel. Leslie knitted a round beanie hat while Alfred made a pom-pom by poking wool through a cardboard donut. His pink tongue poked from between his gums. Hana knocked and walked through the open doorway, looking around for her children. Leslie put a finger up to her lips. "Macky's in the bean bag." She jerked her head towards the sleeping child at her side. "Phoe and Wiri fell asleep in the guest room after we came up here."

"Damn!" Hana groaned. "I promised to take Caleb some food and check on him. I'm such a drop-kick!" She turned back to the door.

"Dude's all good," Alfred wheezed. "I took him muffins and hot coffee. Says he feels much better and I sat with him while he ate. He's stopped the pills what caused it so he's lookin' perky now and the doc gave him a jab up the ass so he's not keen to repeat that experience."

Hana felt her bottom lip wobble and begged her body not to let her down. Failure crowded in on her for leaving her own children and forgetting Caleb. Leslie's voice broke into her private self-bashing. "Sit down, kōtiro. I can see youse brain whirring. Ya didn't abandon yer babies; youse left them with us. And that Caleb isn't your responsibility to be worrying over. I told that big husband of yours that too when he came in throwing his weight around."

Hana rolled her eyes. "He came to find me and we had a fight. He let Sacha go and I didn't want him to." Hana winced. "She listens to me."

"Does she help much?" Alfred joked and earned himself a glare of rebuke from Leslie. "Well, wahine! You ladies talk too much about nothing and it gets ya nowhere. I just wondered if the beast gave better advice than the men in this place." He snatched up his craft like a guilty puppy going back to its bone instead of chewing the skirting board. "I'll just make this here bobble then, will I?"

Hana's eyes strayed from Alfred to Leslie. "Don't fall out because of me. It's my mess and I'll fix it."

"He should've told ya," Leslie remarked, turning her knitting to begin another row, her wooden needles clacking together in the silence. "Lincoln Haines drags trouble wherever he goes. He married that nice doctor lady and got mixed up in a messy affair. The woman died and he went to jail for killing her. Logan never believed he did it and paid for a flash lawyer, even though he'd just arrived home from England. The judge told the jury to find him guilty of manslaughter and then locked him up. Never expected Logan to bring him here though. Not after what happened." Leslie contorted her face into a grimace to stop her continuing and Alfred raised a bushy eyebrow.

"Shut up now, wahine," he murmured and Leslie knitted her brow and acknowledged his rebuke with a short nod.

"It's fine." Hana settled into an armchair opposite and studied the rise and fall of her son's chest as he slept, his cheeks flaming pink from the teeth which pressed through his tender gums and made him grumpy. "I've just enjoyed a lecture about how it wasn't Jack's fault; he was suffering from dementia or some out-of-body experience which caused him to cut Mac's umbilical cord and then point a pistol in his face." Hana swallowed. She'd said his name and the earth hadn't cracked open, but the yawning void of misery still remained in her heart.

Leslie tutted but Alfred put down his cardboard circle, shoving his thumb in the centre hole like the ring of Saturn orbiting a gnarled, arthritic joint with a trail of blue wool hanging loose. "We think it likely, kōtiro. Old men suffer brain farts sometimes." His smile was wistful. "He lost his way and did a bad thing."

"A bad thing." Hana rolled her eyes at the understatement.

Alfred raised his hand. "I do know, girly. I was there remember and I seen your face, sweetheart. Covered in blood from the birth and exhausted as I've ever seen anyone look. I don't think I'll forget the haunted expression in your eyes, Hana. I'll take it to my grave and that's even after the kaumatua prayed a karakia for me to rid me of the taste of terror. You nearly blew my bloody head off when I looked in that door but I couldn't have blamed ya. It went down as one of the worst days of my life and I've endured some terrible ones in my time." Alfred dipped his head and Hana felt her chest swell with tears she couldn't allow to fall. Ten months after Jack's death she knew if she let anything out, it'd bring everything else with it and she wouldn't be able to stop.

17

Flick

Logan arrived home long after Hana put the children to bed. She read them a story and tucked them into their covers like sausage rolls. They giggled and fought the process, but routine won through and they slept within minutes of the lights clicking off. Mark arrived home and then went out again after a shower and a mysterious dousing in aftershave. Hana caught him at the front door, detaining him as he slid his feet into expensive loafers. "Mark, where are you going?"

"Just out." His face coloured and Hana's heart sank.

"You've met a woman, haven't you?"

Mark shrugged and pursed his lips. "Don't worry about me, Hana. I won't get caught up in something lurid again; I'm not stupid."

"No, you're on the rebound and vulnerable." Hana put her hands on her hips and observed him. "When will you be home?"

"Not sure." He planted a kiss on the side of Hana's head and avoided her eyes. "I'm due back at the hospital tomorrow so I'll probably head off around lunchtime."

"I've hardly seen you." She knew her voice betrayed her sadness. "I'm sorry if that's my fault. I seem to be acquiring children all over the place at the moment."

"Don't apologise, Hana." Mark's strong arms enfolded her and he rested his chin on the top of her head. "It's been great staying here. I love how you let me do my own thing and leave me to my devices. You haven't hassled me for answers and I'm grateful."

"Can I bug you for answers now?" Hana lifted her face, green eyes boring into Mark's identical irises. He grinned.

"It's possible that I'll stay in New Zealand a while longer. I haven't met a woman so don't worry. I've met a bunch of excellent bedfellows."

Hana's eyes widened and she opened her mouth in horror. "It must be Tama's damn bed! Last year he ended up as the pornographic addition to a hens' night at the hotel. It's the bed. I'll burn the mattress."

"It's not the bed." Mark laughed. "There's a conference at the hotel for surgical registrars and I met a few of them at dinner the other night. They're a decent group of surgeons. Some of them are from Auckland General Hospital. They've altered my perspective on a few things and convinced me to stay." He kissed Hana's forehead. "So, I'll stay. Tonight's their last night so we're meeting for a drink in the hotel bar. It may go on a while. I might grab a room down there so I don't have to navigate the skinny driveway in an inebriated state or wake you all with my rowdy singing."

Hana narrowed her eyes and watched her brother bluff his way through the excuses. Then she popped his well-crafted balloon. "Right, Casanova. Be good. And if you can't be good, be careful."

"Trust me, I'm quite safe. The ladies are married and not my type." Mark gave her a wink and left, closing the front door behind him with a click. As she stood watching through the leaded lights alongside the front door, Hana saw Mark's brake lights flicker as he pulled to the side of the driveway. Logan's ute rumbled past and the headlights flashed in thanks. Hana turned from the lobby and padded to the kitchen, keen to avoid another argument with her husband.

"I'm sorry." Logan's instant apology sounded crestfallen and his words genuine. Hana wondered if Alfred had ripped him a new one after their conversation. "Dad ripped me a new asshole," he conceded and Hana hid her smirk in the front of his shirt as he gathered her into him. "He said I should explain. So, aside from everything else, I feel I need to help Linc just like you want to rescue Caleb. They're both broken, Hana. Linc's innocent and he served jail time for something he didn't do. He won't hurt you, babe; I need you to trust me on that. He was Jack's apprentice before all the bad stuff happened so he knows the business." He lifted her chin with his finger and she smelled the scent of hay and horse. "Wait here." He kissed the end of her nose and Hana's brow crinkled as she watched him dash into the hallway in his socks.

When he returned, she let out a gasp of pleasure and he smiled. "Thought that might make amends." He held the precious diary aloft as Hana reached for it, bouncing on the balls of her feet in eagerness. "But it comes with conditions!" he stressed. "You do not go poking into old crimes, rumours or mysteries. You do not search for dead bodies, uncover problems which might come back to bite me or discuss anything you read in here with anyone else but me. My feisty old grandmother's words stay inside this book. Got it?"

Hana's head nodded with renewed vigor, her eyes alight and filled with excitement. "I promise!" She reached for the diary, gratified as Logan's arm lowered enough for her to seize the leather binding.

"Will said it's fragile and you need to wear gloves at all times." Logan's eyes narrowed. "He also said he's not interested in an old wahine's ramblings and he doesn't want to hear them."

Hana's head nodded, her attention already on the treasured book. "I thought you threw them away." She glanced up at Logan. "You said you'd destroy them."

"If they cause any more strife, I will." His look of determination made her want to hide the addictive tome behind her back.

"Thank you," she said instead, wrapping an arm around Logan's neck and forcing his head down for a kiss. "It will take my mind off things."

"Hmmmn!" He looked dubious, figuring his grandmother's diary entries had caused nothing but trouble so far. "I know you're struggling," he said, grey eyes staring into Hana's. She swallowed and nodded.

"I am."

"Do you wanna talk to someone?" Logan asked and Hana knew it cost him to offer counselling. The Du Rose men neither admitted weakness nor accepted help for any.

Hana shook her head. "No, thanks. Going to Hamilton for a while might help me shake off the nightmare and the book will give me another focus." She smiled, order restored on the outside and buried within. "I promise to read it and behave."

"Okay." Logan leaned in for a kiss and wrinkled his nose at the smell of his shirt. "I'll take this off and then hunt up some dinner."

"It's in the oven." Hana laid the book on a clean counter with care and watched as Logan attacked his buttons and let the shirt slide down his arms. He stripped the white tee shirt over his head and she chewed her bottom lip and checked him out through narrowed eyes. His muscles bulged, decorated by scar tissue and tattoos and she sighed, craving the feel of his skin under her fingers. She took a step forward as he spoke, watching him undo his belt and slip his jeans down, taking his socks with them and piling the dirty clothes by the laundry door. His boxer shorts clung to his neat bum and Hana almost missed what he said as he turned to the sink and ran the tap.

"What?" She stared at Logan with surprise in her face, sure she'd misheard. "He what?" she repeated, attempting to keep her tone bland.

"Flick's got a girlfriend," Logan repeated, washing his hands under hot running water and lathering soap onto his wrists. "It'll be good not to have dirty hands for a while," he mused. "Teaching's cleaner than farming." He reached for the towel and dried his fingers.

A peculiar emotion flitted across Hana's heart and with horror, she recognised the snakelike tendrils of jealousy. "Who is she?" Her eyes studied her husband's hands as they moved in slow, deliberate movements under the towel.

"Pardon?" He glanced up, his face blank.

"The girlfriend. What's her name?"

Logan shrugged. "What does it matter? You'll never get to meet her. He rang Alfred and seemed real keen for me to know, so now I've told you too."

Irritation blossomed in Hana's chest, knotting up her lungs until it became difficult to breathe. "I'm just asking!" she snapped. "Sorry for taking an interest."

Logan laid the towel on the bench and turned, resting his bum against the dishwasher. A flash of darkness crossed his eyes and Hana sensed the gathering storm, but chose to ignore it. "What's the problem, wahine?" He folded his arms and settled his gaze on Hana's reddening face.

"There's no problem." She punctuated the rebuke with a sigh and raked a damp cloth across the table. The breadcrumbs from Mac's dinner stuck to the fabric and frustration built like a tornado in her head. Bobby's new life seemed attractive and fresh compared to hers. A spiteful slither of regret felt like a shard of glass in her brain. The stockman sat on her bed in the months before Mac's birth and offered Hana an escape route during the most awful moments of her marriage. He made no secret of his adoration. Despite believing the very worst of her husband, Hana refused, a decision which almost cost her life and Mac's.

"There clearly is a problem." Logan contradicted her, uncrossing his ankles and staring at Hana with an intensity which caused her heart to flutter.

"No. There. Isn't." She gritted her teeth and spewed out the answer, chastising herself for the foolish reaction. Bobby loved her from afar but she didn't love him. She loved Logan, despite the acid stare he fixed on her face from across the room. The cloth shook in her hand and the crumbs tumbled back out onto the scarred wood. Hana chased them again, swiping the damp fabric over tiny teeth marks in the edge of the table. All four of her babies had used the table to teethe, champing down on the wood seeking to quench the pain of aching gums. Hana traced the newest mark with her fingertip, wondering if Mac did it at lunchtime when she turned away for a second. She remembered his sorry little face, cheeks pink as he cried a sad, pitiful wail. The teething cream she reached for left a minty jelly on his gums but her words of comfort went unacknowledged. Hana's finger froze over the dent and she swallowed, Logan's grey eyes burning a hole in her temple.

"Talk to me, Hana." His voice sounded calm, but she sensed the underlying tension, biting back a retort which would send him sky rocketing into anger and dismay. "Do you love Flick? Is that what this is?"

Logan's question floored her, removing her ability to find a coherent answer. She shook her head, surprise etched on her face.

"He told me." Logan's jaw tensed, the bone showing through his cheek as a sharp line. His hands balled into fists at his side. "At the airport. He told me I didn't deserve you and if I ever gave him cause, he'd come back and take you away." Logan's nostrils flared like one of his horses and Hana's body stilled in shock.

"I didn't realise how he felt." Hana's voice sounded tinny and wavered as she struggled to finish her explanation. "I never encouraged him. When we all thought you were sleeping with Sylvia, he offered to take me away but when he defended me and Macky against Jack, I knew for sure he was serious."

"Do you wish you'd gone with him?" Logan asked. "Do you still want to?" His eyes flashed storm water grey and his complexion paled to a deathly hue.

Hana's jaw dropped and she pushed her finger along the tiny teeth marks, remembering Mac's huge green eyes imploring her for help as he gnawed on his hand. A fire lit her from inside and she detonated like a bomb at Logan's question. "Really?" She heaved in a breath and repeated the word, loading it with scorn. "Really? You think that's my biggest problem right now?" Hana balled the cloth into her hand and flung it across the room where it missed the sink, scattering crumbs over the floor tiles before landing over them with a plop. She felt a lump push up from her stomach into her chest as anger possessed her brain and mouth in one fluid movement. Hana grasped the plastic bowl Mac ate from in one hand, her fingers still sympathising with his pain through the grooves in the table.

She threw it like a Frisbee, enjoying the satisfying smack it made against the side of the Belfast sink. It lifted her spirits enough to make her want more and her fingers alighted on her own plate, not plastic but crockery. Hana gritted her teeth and sent it after the bowl, hearing it smash against the cupboard and then shatter on the tiles. Exhaling in a rush from the influx of adrenaline, she sought the momentary distraction like a drug and fixed her fingers around the tea mug on the table.

"Hana!" Logan's shout broke through the mist and she resisted the authority in his voice, hurling the mug towards the wall and watching a tea stain dribble down the paintwork as the mug smashed. Her mug. Her favourite mug with the cheerful strawberries on its delicate sides. The roar of anger escaped without control and Hana let go, releasing all her anxiety and distress as she snatched up the other crockery on the table and pelted the wall with it.

Logan seized her wrist as she ran around the table in search of more of the same rush, yanking her backwards until her spine hit his chest and his arms formed a cage around her. "Stop!" he told her, his tone commanding. Hana swore and struggled, reaching for the fruit bowl in the centre of the table and imagining the noise it would make against the tiles. And the mess. The mess made the pain hurt less for a fraction of a second. "Geez, Hana!" Logan pleaded, pinning her upper arms tighter to her sides, working his hands forwards and clasping her harder around the chest. Hana screamed and kicked, no longer sure where the tantrum began or ended in the runaway expression of her misery.

The fleeting thought that Logan had done this before with his Bi-polar mother introduced a wave of guilt which added to the anxiety and Hana's rage turned to tears. Her body sagged and she resented every sob that wrenched itself free from her throat. Logan's biceps felt rigid around her chest, his arms crossed over like a strait jacket. Hana groaned as her brain made the mental leap and shame flexed its influence. "Oh, God!" she wailed, the plea heartfelt, a woman at the end of her rope. "I can't do this," she sobbed, her words slurred and nonsensical.

"Sshhh, baby, I've got you." Logan's hushed response stilled the panic which flowed in to replace Hana's fury and grief washed in after.

"I can't do it, Logan," Hana cried. "I can't keep all these secrets anymore."

His breath caressed her left ear, his mouth near her cheek. "It's fine," he whispered. "We'll sort it out."

Hana shook her head, feeling Logan's stubble graze her cheek. "Can't," she sniffed. "I can't, you can't, nobody can."

Sensing her submission, Logan relaxed his grasp and turned Hana in his arms. His hold tightened again as her breasts rested against his tight stomach and his fingers stroked her back in slow, comforting movements. "Do you want me to help you find him?" he asked, his voice wavering and his eyes glittering like diamonds in a pale, distressed face.

"Find who?" Hana freed her right hand and used her sweatshirt to wipe her nose, irritated by the prickling of the tears and snot on her skin. Her chest heaved and bucked with every breath and she wriggled inside the cage of Logan's arms.

"Flick." He spat the word and his arms tightened, trapping Hana's wrist against his armpit.

Hana's chest shuddered and she resorted to wiping her face on his chest, feeling the hard muscle beneath. "Why?" she asked, her tone flat.

"So you can be with him," Logan answered, eyes glittering as he looked down on her and his teeth grinding.

"What?" Hana's eyes widened in shock and she struggled against Logan's grip, feeling his arms tense more instead of less. "That's not what's wrong with me!" Her voice rose as hysteria made its triumphant rise to the surface again. "Is that what you think?" She pushed against Logan's chest and finding him immovable, kicked his shins with her feet encased in fluffy socks. His body shook, but he held on, his face blank and impassive as he fought the mask of indifference back into place.

"Get off me!" Hana screamed, growing afraid as her tussle proved ineffective.

"Tell me you want him instead of me and I'll let you go." Logan swallowed and Hana saw his Adam's apple bob in his throat.

"I don't want him!" she screamed, jumping up to shout at his chin.

Logan's face registered surprise and his arms relaxed. Hana morphed back into the angry pixie and she lifted her knee in the increased space, tipping her body backwards enough to knee Logan in the privates. He gave a roar and dropped his arms, his hands seeking to take the pain away. He swore and let out a stream of unintelligible Māori while Hana backed away, finding her bum against the side of the table. Logan stood up, one hand covering his groin and his face creased in pain. "Bloody hell, Hana!" he gasped.

Remembering her husband's haemophilia, Hana looked ashamed, growing quiet and still as her hands sought the marks from her son's baby teeth around the table's edge. "Sorry," she conceded. "Sorry."

Logan shook his head, the colour returning to his olive cheeks. "Why the balls, wahine?" he asked, his voice husky.

Hana shrugged, her heart pounding in her chest. "Couldn't reach your head," she replied honestly. She swallowed and glared at her husband. "You really think I'd leave you for Bobby?" Her voice sounded strained.

"I don't want you to," he said, his eyes calmer than before. "But you scared me."

Hana sighed and used the bottom of her sweatshirt to dry her eyes. "You're an idiot," she said. "I don't know why I love you."

Logan glanced towards the baby monitor on the bread board as Mac snuffled in his sleep. "We've woken him up," he said, rubbing at his sore groin.

Hana sniffed and covered her mouth with her hand. Tears bubbled from her eyes and ran over her fingers. "You don't get it," she sobbed. "You just don't get it."

"Then bloody tell me!" Logan hissed, reaching Hana in one stride and pressing her face into his chest. "Stop trying to be a hero and level with me." He kissed the top of her head and stroked the red curls which stretched down her back. "We're meant to be a team."

"I don't want to upset you," Hana sniffed. "But this will."

"Just say it." Logan cradled her to him, resting his cheek on the top of her head. "It can't be worse than what I imagined. I believed you loved another man and it's eaten me up. He was there and I wasn't. He defended you, him and Sasha. It should've been me."

Hana took a deep breath, feeling Logan's muscles tense in his chest and biceps. His head seemed to weigh heavily against hers, bowing her under the pressure. She disconnected, needing to see his eyes and read his reaction. Taking a step back, Hana faced her husband, watching curiosity and dread turn into an emotion she didn't expect. She swallowed. "Mac's deaf," she said.

Logan's eyelashes fluttered and he dropped his gaze to the floor. His exhale seemed to come from the soles of his feet and he ran shaking fingers through his hair. "Like Jack?" he asked.

Hana nodded, her eyes refilling with tears. "Maybe. The doctor doesn't know yet."

Logan turned away and Hana resented him shrouding his reaction. The set of his shoulders helped her translate the cry of his heart. "You guessed," she said, relief in her voice.

When he looked at her, his grey eyes narrowed in pain. His shallow nod caused a flash of anger to erupt in Hana's breast. "You knew and you let me bear it alone?" Her voice channelled betrayal.

Logan nodded. "My deaf grandfather tried to kill you both and neither of us wanted the reminder, did we?" He chewed his lip and slumped into a kitchen chair. "What a mess."

Hana paused and then crossed the floor between them and dumped herself onto his knees. Logan wrapped his arms around her and pushed his face into her shoulder. "The hospital will send for us when they make an appointment," Hana said, breathing in her husband's familiar scent. "Being in Hamilton will help."

Logan nodded, his hair brushing against her sleeve. "We'll be fine, Hana. If we stick together, it'll be all right."

"Yeah," Hana conceded. "I'm sorry I didn't talk to you about it."

Logan sighed. "I'm sorry too." He ran his hand up her thigh and let his fingers rove under her sweatshirt until they touched the smooth porcelain flesh. Hana shivered, her lungs still shaken from her crying and she held her breath, confused when he stopped with his fingers grazing her ribs. "Hana?" He raised his head, framing her face in his piercing grey eyes. She gulped, sensing trouble. "You said 'secrets' babe." Logan's eyelashes fluttered as he narrowed his gaze, his focus intense. "You can't keep all these secrets anymore. So what else is there, Hana Du Rose?"

18

Other People's Dirty Washing

Hana's body froze on Logan's legs and her brain worked like a windmill, sifting through ready answers and discarding them. She shook her head, damning the pink flush which speckled her cheeks and neck. "I said secret," she lied, struggling to remember. "That was all. The possibility our son is deaf should be enough for you." She shifted on his knees and felt his arms react, winding around her waist like supplejack vine and pinning her in place. Hana sighed. "You believed I had an affair with your stockman and wanted to run away with him. I didn't. I don't. There's nothing else."

Logan's expression remained intense and Hana cringed. "Why wait for ten months to broach it, anyway? Bobby left age ago."

He shrugged. "Didn't want to face the truth, I guess." His nose wrinkled at the sides as he pulled a face. "I knew you wouldn't do anything wrong. He admitted at the airport you'd given him no reason to believe you felt the same. But lately you seemed more distant and I wondered if you missed him. Your reaction when I told you he got a girlfriend made me read into it."

Hana cursed her overreaction and she shook her head. "I suppose when someone's hero worshipped you for years, you kinda get used to it and take it for granted. I should be happy for him but I actually feel displaced. Is that stupid?"

"Na. Guess not." Logan's gaze wandered to the broken crockery littering the kitchen floor. He sighed. "But if he ever comes back here, I'll break his face, just like I promised." Logan's jaw worked under the skin and Hana snorted.

"You threatened him?"

"No." Logan's eyes flashed with dark danger. "I promised him what I'd do and I will. I don't intend to lose you Hana so get used to it."

She nodded, her face shrouded with a careful mask and she dipped her head to nestle in the crook of his neck. Logan's intensity terrified her, but she knew what she'd gotten into the moment he snagged her ring finger with the simple gold band. He would be her salvation and her gatekeeper, the Du Rose name pinning her to him like an invisible chain. Her nose touched the soft skin of Logan's neck but he forced her backwards, strong fingers pressing against her shoulders. She slapped at his right hand, shoving it away. "Be careful of my pacemaker wires!" she complained, her eyes wide with fear as her hand sought the ridge beneath her collar bone. The old panic rose into her breast and she felt her heart race with anticipation.

"Sorry." Logan soothed her, pulling her fingers away and caressing them. "It's fine, Hana. I'm sorry."

"I need to clean up the mess." She sighed, hearing the tiredness in her voice.

Logan shook his head. "No, Hana. What other secrets are there?"

"Please don't make me tell," she begged, twisting her hands together in a dance of agitation. "They're not mine to share."

"So there's more than one." It was a statement, not a question.

Hana stood and picked her way through the broken crockery, snatching a broom from behind the laundry door. She swished the bristles until the shards obeyed, forming into a neat line. Logan found a dustpan and brush in the laundry and helped, sweeping up the debris and tipping it into the dustbin. When the floor looked clean Hana dealt with the remains of dinner, washing up, loading the dishwasher and clearing the table.

Logan watched, arms folded across his broad chest and his bum leaned against the kitchen counter. Hana felt his gaze burning a hole in the back of her head. As the baby monitor registered a snuffle from her son, she seized the reprieve and edged towards the door on a pretense of putting a clean dinner plate back in the tall cupboard next to it. She turned ready to make a run for it and lock herself in the bathroom but contacted her husband's chest with a grunt of pain. Logan caught her as she pitched sideways. "Do you think I was born yesterday?" he asked, picking her up in a fireman's lift and dumping her over his shoulder.

"Logan!" Hana hissed, thumping his back with her fists. "Put me down!"

She watched his heels lift and fall as he walked through the lounge doors and closed them behind him. He selected the wide sofa and manhandled her into a sitting position, parking his bum on the solid coffee table and pinning her in place with his arms either side of her thighs. "Now," he began, blinking with irritating slowness as he fixed his facial muscles into hard lines. "What secrets are there under my roof, Hana?"

She relaxed on the seat cushion as Logan overplayed his hand. "None." Her confident reply made him narrow his eyes and a smirk twitched at his lips.

"You do realise my roof extends across the whole of Mātakitaki Mountain, don't you?"

"I thought you said I was an equal partner," Hana sulked, pouting.

Logan snorted a laugh. "Fine. What secrets are there under our roof, Hana?"

Hana groaned. "Don't make me, Logan. Please? It's not mine to tell."

Logan leaned back, his brain working hard to decipher the source of her guilt. He lifted his hands and said the names of those she loved, counting them off on his fingers. "Will, Ryan, Tama's not here." He studied her face, finding her unflinching. Hana allowed a smug expression to slide into place, impressed with her poker face. "Alfred, Leslie," Logan continued, halting as Hana's pupils dilated and she blinked. She saw her husband taste victory and his lips widened in a smile. "What did they do, Hana?"

"No!" She squirmed in the seat and Logan enjoyed her discomfort, replacing his sinewy arms either side of her legs.

"What could they do to annoy me?" he mused, watching Hana's distress. "It would need to be something that jeopardized the hotel, but was a secret due to its, what? Illegality?"

Hana exhaled and Logan's face changed to one of extreme alertness. "What's happened, Hana? I need to know."

"He'll never speak to me again; he'll know I told you. Please Logan. Let's deal with Macky and then I'll tell you everything."

"No." Logan sat up and Hana felt his disconnection like a physical pain. "I'm worried now. Just tell me."

Hana slumped in the seat and closed her eyes against his piercing grey eyes. "Alfred's growing marijuana on the roof to control the effects of his arthritis." She put her head in her hands and let bitterness seed her tone. "He'll never forgive me now. He trusted me."

Logan snorted. "But not me."

Unable to answer that, Hana felt exhaustion bite at the outer edges of her psyche. Bone-tired, she ached for bed. Hazarding a glimpse at Logan's face through her fingers she saw him deep in thought, his brow furrowed and his eyes glassy. "I hated lying to you," she whispered and felt some of the weight lift from her shoulders. Logan's complicity brought release. "I'll tell you the other thing too. You'll know what to do about it."

"What?" Logan licked his lips and his face showed curiosity.

"It's about Caroline Marsh," Hana began. "I know something and it's important..."

Logan stood, his face screwed into a look of pure hatred. "I don't care!" he bit. "Don't mention her? I don't want to hear her bloody name!"

"But it's the other secret," Hana said, wounded by Logan's reaction to the truth. "You wanted to know and now you don't. That's not fair. You started this."

Logan shook his head. "No thanks. If it's to do with her, I'm not interested." He backed away, catching his heel against the coffee table leg and stumbling. He raised his hand as Hana opened her mouth again, wincing as if she'd struck him a physical blow. "I'm surprised at you!" he snapped, disgust in his tone. Before Hana could speak again he'd gone and she heard the bedroom door close. She gave him time to cool off but after a few minutes she heard the front door slam. Dismayed, she ran to the hallway and saw the tail-lights of the ute dance like red demons in the darkness. Logan crested the rise at a dangerous speed and plunged down the narrow cliff road towards the hotel.

"Bloody marvellous!" Hana shouted into the darkness. "Thanks for that! Honesty's so overrated!"

Hana checked on the sleeping children and covered up Wiri's bare legs. He'd retreated to Tama's empty bedroom and forced her to leave Mark a note warning him he had company. Her life felt cluttered with other people's troubles and concerns and she put herself to bed with a half-finished novel. As the story failed to progress, she realised she'd reread the same page four times. Caroline's elfin face pushed itself into her inner vision, smug, self-satisfied and dangerous. She'd lost Logan to Hana and settled on his half-brother, Kane, disappearing to Christchurch with him for a fresh start. Logan's grandmother's diaries betrayed a sickening legacy; one in which the older generation conspired to keep Caroline from ever gaining the Du Rose name. She'd jilted Logan at the altar at the behest of her foster father, Reuben. In Hana's mind she dug a confident hand through her cropped blonde hair and laughed, a cruel sound.

Hana sat up in bed. "Oh Logan! Why wouldn't you let me tell you?" Remembering the diary, she padded back to the dark kitchen and seized it from its resting place. "What trouble do you want to uncover now, kuia?" she whispered, stroking the soft cover with her fingertips and wincing at Will's warning. "I don't have gloves up here. Do you mind?"

The book gave no answer, lying placid and heavy in her palms and Hana felt a sense of peace and satisfaction mixed with a frisson of fear and anticipation. What other damage could Phoenix Du Rose Senior do? Hana sighed. "I nearly told him, kuia," she breathed. "I nearly told him what you set in motion. This is your fault." Hana shivered in the cool air, a draught licking her bare toes and her heart drowning in regret. "And now I don't know what to do." She cradled the book of secrets to her breast and retraced her steps back to bed, praying it contained nothing more than a list of cattle prices and auction stories. But she'd read enough of Phoenix's diaries to know her style and wished she could hand it back to Logan without reading it. Natural curiosity and loneliness won through and when Logan crawled into bed after a dreadful argument with Alfred, he eased the open book from her fingers and laid it on the bedside table.

19

Guardianship

"How could you, kōtiro?" Leslie ran down the hotel steps as Hana clambered from the car with Wiri and Phoenix tumbling out behind her. "How could you tell him?"

"He got it out of me!" Hana insisted, heaving Mac's car seat onto the gravel. "Have you ever tried to keep a secret from Logan Du Rose?"

"He keeps enough from you!" Leslie retorted and Hana felt the sting of truth.

"I didn't come here to fight," Hana said, lifting the handle of the seat into the crook of her right arm. "I wanted to talk to Will."

"Your damn husband wants it gone!" Leslie threw her arms in the air. "What will my Alfie do now?"

"Go to the doctor like normal people." Hana felt her energy ebb away. "Take pills, go to clinics, get proper help."

"I can't believe you did this." Leslie's breasts wobbled in her dress, clanking together like bowling balls and Wiri sniggered and pointed at them.

"Kuia Leslie, your boobies are dancing," he chortled and Phoenix put her hand over her mouth and giggled; not understanding but joining in anyway.

"Stand here!" Hana ordered, her tone offering no chance of disagreement or rebellion. "Behave and stop being rude."

Wiri lowered his eyes and reached for Phoe's hand, his lips curved upwards in a resistant smirk. Phoenix's eyes twinkled and she bit her lip in recognition of some shared joke which was beyond her comprehension, but not her enjoyment.

"Leave them with me!" Leslie demanded but Hana shook her head.

"We're not staying. I need to collect something and then we're leaving." She glared at the protesting children and they silenced, picking up on her taut nerves and fraying patience. "I'm here to see Will and then I need to find my brother before he leaves."

"Tell that husband of yours it's none of his business!" Leslie shouted after Hana and she nodded but didn't look back, grateful the children were too young to understand the dispute. Logan left the house before dawn and hadn't spoken to Hana, but Leslie's reaction told her exactly what he'd done.

"Nice one, Logan," she breathed through clenched teeth, chiding herself as two sets of eyes looked up at her with enquiry.

"What did Pa do?" Wiri demanded and Hana shook her head, losing the energy to correct his noun usage.

"Nothing."

In the museum the children fought over Will's knees, desperate to sit on his severed legs and ride the chair. Their selfish enjoyment dismissed the adult qualms of squeamishness or distaste. Will was Will and his thick biceps whipped the chair into noisy spins on the polished floorboards and break neck rides down the ramp. Such was childish simplicity and juvenile egotistical desires. They loved Will; they coveted the wheelchair more than sugar.

"You can both fit!" he bellowed, silencing the sniped roots of bickering. "One on each stump. Hop up."

Wiri sprang up first, all selfishness forgotten as he hauled Phoenix up by her slender, delicate wrist. They clung together, bodies tensed in excitement as the old man pushed the chair towards the furthest corner and then spun it on one wheel. Hana stared at her baby son and saw his eyes alight with feverish giggles, wanting to join in but afraid. "I love you," she mouthed to him, squatting in front of the car seat and smiling with her eyes. He responded, rosebud lips moving in words of his own response, but no sound emerged. Mac's arms and legs flapped like tiny windmill sails as he expressed his pleasure in Hana's attention and she enjoyed a connection in which sound took no part. The delight in his eyes at the sight of her face in his vision and his appreciation of her comforting arms seemed reward enough in the cold light of day. "My perfect boy," Hana crooned, stroking the delicate alabaster cheek and receiving his smiles with gratitude.

"Cookie time!" Will sang, wheeling towards his work room behind the museum. He skidded in the doorway and the tyres squeaked on the boards, accompanying the children's howls of pleasure.

"Come on Macky." Hana hoisted the car seat back onto her arm and followed the giggling group through the doorway.

Will doled out chocolate cookies to the children, warning them not to touch anything with their sticky fingers. "Use the sink at the end," he stressed, eyeing the precious family artifacts spread around them.

"I've lost my cotton gloves," Hana confessed, propping Mac's car seat on the counter and watching as he pressed the cookie between his pink lips.

"I didn't want youse to have that diary." Will spoke with honesty, reaching into a low drawer and yanking white gloves from a rustling packet. Wiri craned his neck to see and Phoenix followed suit, like vultures. "Nothing for noseys!" the old man rebuked them and as one, they resumed cookie eating, sucking the succulent chocolate chips out whole.

"Caroline's pregnant." Hana eyed the children and mouthed the words to her friend, watching his reaction of distaste. He exacerbated her discomfort by raising his finger at her.

"I told youse to say something last year!" he hissed. "Youse coulda stopped that."

"Oh, gosh." Hana put her hands over her face. "How could I? If she's in Christchurch with Kane then she's leaving my husband alone. Why would I risk that?"

"Because she's now pregnant to her half-brother," Will hissed. "It's not just immoral, it's illegal."

"Only on the say-so of an old woman's diaries. It's not proven."

Will cocked his head as though he thought Hana thick. "DNA proves stuff like that, Hana. All the damn time. That's a right can of worms about to blow up in our faces."

"Not mine!" Hana held her hands out, palms facing Will. "It's nothing to do with me."

"What did Logan say?" Will delivered another round of cookies to prolong the silence and spirit of cooperation. "You did tell him?"

"He doesn't want to know." Hana's voice sounded leaden. "I tried."

"Then just leave it." Will rolled forwards and patted her knee. Mac wiggled his legs and beamed when his booties ruffled Will's sideburns. "Just leave it."

"I feel buried in other people's problems at the moment." Hana watched Phoenix take a bite out of Wiri's cookie whilst keeping hers in her tight little fingers. "Phoe! Eat your own."

"It's okay." Wiri beamed at his partner in crime and Mac gummed his own half-cookie and grinned, green eyes narrowed in silent conspiracy.

"Whose problems?" Will pushed a finger in the packet and then pulled it out empty. He patted his stomach and pulled a face. "I don't wanna be one of those old people spewing over the sides of their chair like bread dough."

Hana nodded and gave a wistful smile. "Good on you. I admire your willpower."

Will bent to retrieve a crumb from Mac's cardigan and popped it into the baby's mouth. He sighed as the child pushed it back out again and gave him a look of disgust. "Whose problems, Hana?"

"This thing with she-who-I-can't-mention, the small boy who's taken up residence with us, my brother who's done an amazing about-face and is now staying in New Zealand on the advice of strangers he met here." She drew her hand across her eyes. "Want me to go on?"

"Ryan's great here. You shouldn't worry about him." Will patted her knee and slapped her fingers as they worried at a loose thread in a seam on the cotton gloves. "Tama's happy in the fire service. What else is there?" His eyes strayed to her tiny son and back again. It was a momentary tell and Hana huffed out a sigh.

"He can't hear. I suppose you guessed too and didn't think to say anything either."

"I was working up to it," Will confessed. "It's a hard thing to say to someone but I would've."

"Logan knew. I've carried it for months thinking he'd freak out and he was doing the same." Hana sighed. "Why is my life a permanent mess?"

"Because you look outside your own wee bubble and spread your care to others, that's why. Look at me and my boy. Because of you, we've got a home and jobs instead of worrying about surviving and waiting for the bailiffs. You're burdened for others, Hana and there's only a problem with that when it weighs youse down so."

Hana nodded. "Alfred's been growing weed on the roof of the hotel. It's a nightmare and now Logan knows."

"Why's it a nightmare?" Will asked. "Isn't it Alfie's problem?"

"Yeah. But knowing about it made me complicit. It's Logan's hotel and a police raid would be disastrous. Leslie keeps asking to look after the children but I'm nervous when she takes them to the flat. I find myself checking she won't leave them with Alfred while she nips out. I don't want to offend them but can't trust them either; these children are my responsibility. Alfred promised he'd stopped driving and then he drove my brother around the mountain on a tiki-tour to goodness knows where. It's been a dreadful strain and telling Logan felt like a relief. Now they're mad as hornets at me. I don't know what Logan's said, but it won't be good."

"Jack smoked weed." The bristles moved under Will's hand as he stroked his gnarled face. She closed her eyes against the recurring image of Jacob Darcy Du Rose holding a pistol in her newborn's face. "It makes yer paranoid. Mebbe that was his problem." Will's brows knitted at the agony on Hana's face and he touched her hand. "What else, kōtiro? What hurts?"

"I can't get his face out of my head." Hana felt her chest hitch and clung to the fringes of sanity like a skydiver sans parachute. "It won't go away. Logan remodeled the ensuite bathroom after I shot the wall out but I can't use it. I can't sleep in our bedroom because of the smell of blood and fear, but I know it's in my head. I think I'm going crazy."

"Crazy?" Wiri's mouth dropped into a fearful 'o' and the biscuit crumbled in his fingers. "You're not allowed to go crazy." His grey eyes filled with tears.

Hana gulped at the realisation he'd listened to every word like a dry sponge soaking in knowledge and assessing threat. Her hands shook as she rubbed a finger beneath her lower lip. "It's just an expression, Wiri," she said. "It means nothing."

"My real mum's crazy." Tears welled in the child's eyes and Hana recognised an older man's words. She heard the intonation and felt the secondhand misery of Asher's spite repeated from the childish, rosebud lips.

"No, she isn't." She dismissed the fact with more surety than it deserved. "She's in hospital and doesn't feel well. But she isn't crazy, sweetheart. Mummy will be back home before you know it."

"But I live with Phoe now." Wiri's eyes locked on Hana's in challenge and she quailed under the fierceness of his gaze. "So it doesn't matter anymore."

"Get on with yer cookie," Will told him, jerking his head at Phoenix whose lips strayed towards the ragged end of Wiri's biscuit. He rustled the packet and held out another. "One more each."

Distracted, the children stuffed remnants into their mouths and took another, busying themselves in juvenile pleasures. Mac waggled his fingers and grunted, receiving another half which occupied him instantly. Will turned his chair towards Hana. "That's one problem less, anyway."

"What do you mean?" Her brow crinkled in confusion.

"Kid's all yours, girly. The decision's made."

Hana sighed and watched the small boy feed her daughter his cookie and felt the weight of one small problem fall away. Will spoke the truth; Wiri would travel to Hamilton as her son and she would allow him past the last barrier into her close-knit family. "I'll ask Nev for his birth certificate so I can register him in a school."

"Best get him to sign a release form too."

"A what?"

"Certificate of guardianship," Will said. He reached out and touched Hana's trembling fingers. "I'm proud of you, kōtiro. The creator broke the mold after he crafted you; 'cause there sure as hell ain't no more like ya on this earth."

20

One More Problem

"I'm hungry, Ma. Please can you feed me?" Wiri skipped along next to Hana as she poked her head through doors looking for Mark.

"Feed me too?" Phoenix begged, grizzling at the imagined threat of being forgotten.

"You just ate biscuits in the museum. You can't be hungry." Hana withdrew from the dining room doorway as a waitress emerged carrying used crockery.

"Nonie Leslie will feed us," Wiri asserted, craning his neck to see into the industrial kitchen opposite. "She still likes me and Phoe. Just not you."

"Not you." Phoenix shook her head with exaggerated sadness and patted Hana's thigh. "It be all right. I feed you."

Hana exhaled in a snuff as Mac rubbed his eyes and whimpered in his car seat, a muted, nonsensical sound which indicated extreme tiredness and dissatisfaction with his sitting position. "Fine! Go in the family dining room." Hana pushed the heavy door open and the children piled through. They dived for the oak dining table, dragging up the ancient chairs and clambering astride them. Phoenix's face barely reached high enough to see over the vast expanse of scarred wood. Hana released Mac from his restrictive straps and hoisted him onto her hip. Digging in a drawer she retrieved a feeder cup and approached the archway into the kitchen with care, eager to avoid a collision with the busy waitresses.

"I'll just grab milk," she told the large man at the sink, his arms buried to the elbows in sudsy water.

"Yes, missus Du Rose," he replied, turning an innocent face in her direction. A long tongue pushed from between his lips in concentration and the characteristic almond shaped eyes betrayed the Downs syndrome which gifted him an extra chromosome. "Nearly done with breakfast."

"Thanks, babe." Hana gave him a beautiful smile and filled the feeder cup with full fat milk. Mac watched her action with intensity and swung his legs in excitement as his mother pushed the cup into the microwave.

Hana searched the chiller cabinet for left overs and slung together sandwiches one handed. The bacon strips refused to lie flat and the slabs of cheese stuck up like ramps until she rammed the second slice of bread over the top. The microwave dinged and Hana retrieved the cup, swapping it for the plate of sandwiches which she slapped a plastic cover over. "Let's get you sitting down," she told her son, keeping the cup at arm's length even though he lurched for it and made sucking noises with his lips. Mac slid into the high chair and waved his arms like a windmill as Hana fixed the straps to keep him there. He lurched for the cup as she drew it nearer and she shook her head, getting eye contact with him and touching her fingers to her lips. "Thank you," she said and pulled her fingers away.

Mac ignored her, pitching back and forth in the chair and making it grind against the floorboards. Hana sat the cup away from him, aware of the other children's interest as she took his tiny hand and used the fingers to touch his lips. "Thank you," she repeated and saw a flash of recognition in the green eyes. His lips moved and his wrist relaxed, allowing Hana to perform the designated words of sign language. He huffed and puffed as she let go, snatching the cup with eagerness and snorting milk in tiny droplets as he rooted for the tip with his lips.

"Please watch Macky for me, guys?" Hana asked. "And I'll fetch your morning tea."

"Yes, Ma." Wiri slid from his chair and stood next to the baby, ready to bang him on the back if he choked. Hana gave the boy a smile of gratitude and contemplated life without Wiri's sensible head in it. She realised as she retrieved the sandwiches from the microwave and grabbed two small plates, the thought made her miserable. It wasn't her intention to steal another woman's child; it just happened that way.

The children tucked into warm milk and bacon and melted cheese sandwiches with enthusiasm while Hana watched her baby boy suck the dregs from the cup. His eyelids drooped from the soporific effect of the warm milk and his head wobbled on his neck. He jerked awake as the cup bounced against the table top and then drifted away. Hana released him from his bonds, wiped his creamy mouth and cradled him into her body. She snuggled him tight and reached for her phone, texting her errant brother.

'I'm at the main house in the family dining room. Are you coming to say goodbye?'

The lack of reply spoke louder than any message. Five minutes out of a disastrous relationship with Hana's former friend and he'd entangled himself again. She sighed and watched the view beyond the leaded squares of blown glass as guests moved around in the front car park, arriving with excited anticipation and leaving with a sense of sadness.

"I'm still hungry." Wiri's voice spoke into the silence, shocking Hana back to reality. He wiped his mouth with the back of his hand and Phoenix looked hopeful, picking the last crumbs from her plate.

"You can't be." Hana patted Mac's back as he slept. "You've had cookies and sandwiches and warm milk. Wait for lunch now."

"Mmmnnn, lunch," Phoenix repeated and Hana sighed and wondered when the endless round of food provision would end. Even in his late twenties, her eldest son still treated her home like a free larder so perhaps the answer was *never*.

"Uncle Mark's holding hands with a man." Wiri watched through the sash window, his eyes narrowed in curiosity.

"No, he'll be shaking hands," Hana corrected him. She peered through the sash window but other tourists blocked her view of the car park as they dragged suitcases across the gravel. "That's what grown-ups do when they say hello or goodbye."

"Like this?" Wiri seized Phoenix's skinny wrist and pumped her tiny hand. She grumbled with annoyance.

"No! Gently, gently," Hana chided. "Get Uncle Logan to teach you later."

"Like this?" Wiri clasped Phoenix's sticky hand with more care and Hana nodded her approval.

"Much better. Logan's good at it; he'll show you." Her lips quirked at the memory of how Logan's hand always ended up on top in the handshake, a deliberate action of superiority.

Hana listened to the footsteps issuing down the long corridor and waited. Mark pushed his tufty fringe around the heavy door and grinned at the room's occupants. "Glad I caught you," he intoned, his voice deep and comforting. "Any tea going?"

"I haven't managed it yet," Hana said, rocking Mac in her arms. "Please can you make me some?"

Mark nodded and disappeared next door, returning with a full teapot and mugs stuffed on a tray. A milk jug teetered near the edge and Hana held her breath, relieved when it all made it onto the table. Balancing her son in one arm, she opened a drawer in the huge Welsh dresser and yanked out a packet of baby wipes, which she tossed onto the table. "Wipe your faces and then get out a puzzle. I want to talk to Uncle Mark for a minute before he goes home."

Wiri took charge of operations, scrubbing cheese grease from his cousin's face until red marks remained. He cleaned his own with the same wipe and Hana cringed. He used four more to attack the crumbs on the table and Hana's eyes narrowed, seeing something of Logan's obsessive compulsion in the steady, determined action. Phoenix hustled to the dresser and retrieved a complicated jigsaw, losing half the pieces on the rug in her enthusiasm. Undaunted, Wiri knelt and began turning them face up, looking for edges to begin the picture.

"Clever lad," Mark mused, pouring tea and watching the child's concentration.

Hana nodded with deliberate slowness. "I'm beginning to realise that. It didn't matter when he was only staying with us on an ad hoc basis, but if it's permanent, I should make more effort."

"Permanent?" Mark cocked his head. "Is his mother worse?"

"No. But she's no better either. Nev's got his hands full with Asher and the farm so we're keeping this little man for a while longer. Logan's working at the school for a term so we're shifting back next week. He'll come with us."

"To Hamilton?" The hope in Mark's eyes sent a flicker of pleasure through Hana's breast.

"Yeah. Back to the Waikato Presbyterian School for Boys. Where we started."

"Yuk, not to that tiny staff unit I hope. Surely you'd need a bigger one."

Hana shook her head. "Logan's secured The Gatehouse again. We stayed there before we went to Europe. It's huge and old, but better than one of the cramped units."

"I'll enjoy having you more local." Mark smiled and poured the tea into two mugs. "While I'm still here."

Hana's answering smile drooped. "I thought you planned to stay."

"In the country, but maybe not in Hamilton. There's a permanent job in surgical at Auckland General and I might apply. I haven't decided yet. I've got a few options. The lease on my new place is six months and I've found a lodger. I'm not tied to the city."

"You found a lodger already?" Hana asked, sipping her too-hot tea. "You only mentioned it the other night."

Mark nodded. "One of the surgeons starts at the Waikato Hospital next week. It might be nice having company." His face flushed pink and Hana glared at him.

"Is this the person who's taking your mind off Anka? Why move so fast, Mark? Be careful."

Mark swallowed and changed the subject. "The emergency department in Auckland is run by a consultant called Michael Du Rose. That's a strange coincidence, don't you think? Any relation?"

Hana choked on her tea and her face paled. "Just stay away from him."

"Who is he?" Mark's eyes narrowed in curiosity. "Family, obviously."

"He's Logan's half-brother," Hana replied, glancing at the children as Wiri set Phoenix to work turning pieces the right way up in the box lid. She lowered her voice. "He's Ryan and Tama's father. He's got as much honour as a snake and you'd do well to stay away from him."

"Damn good doctor though," Mark concluded. "Well respected. The registrars spoke highly of him."

"They must be female then," Hana snapped but Mark's mind seemed elsewhere. His eyes glazed over and Hana heard alarm bells in her head. "Did you spend the night with this mysterious woman and her stethoscope last night, or is it the thought of Michael Du Rose that's getting you all hot around the collar?"

Mark's expression became coy. "Yes, I did, Hana. The relationship isn't what I expected but I think it might work for

me this time. If it doesn't, there's always this job in Auckland."
He screwed his face up. "I've never met Michael, have I?"

"No. Be careful, Mark?" Hana sighed and Mark raised
his eyebrows. "You just got burned by Anka; it could be a
rebound."

"I can assure you it's not."

"I hope not." Hana hefted her snoring son over her shoulder
and tipped him into the car seat where he lolled to one side. She
straightened him out and clasped the seat belt shut. "If you ever
come across Michael, you'd do well to never mention me. You
don't want favours from him, Mark, because he always expects
something in return." She stood up and fixed a steady gaze on
her brother. "Michael Du Rose thinks the world owes him. Just
don't ever expect us to pay your debts to him."

"I won't." Mark avoided her eyes, knowing he'd already
bandied his association to the Du Roses around the group of
doctors. Hana saw it in his face and her heart clenched in misery.
She watched him for a moment before delivering her verdict.

"You're already offside with Logan over Anka. Don't
compound it by using your link to him to influence Michael for
a job; it really won't end well."

Mark slugged his tea and stood with a hasty and
unconvincing nod. "I'm not likely to meet him, Hana. I only
mentioned it because of the association. Best be off now if I'm
to beat the Hamilton traffic. I'll grab my gear from your place
and leave the key under the mat. Thanks for letting me stay; it's
given me a chance to clear my head."

Hana let him hold her, feeling the strength in his long arms.
As children he'd been jealous of her and it fostered cruelty and
violence. He'd used his hands to hurt her and then years later,
to heal. She sighed, feeling the tension in him and praying he'd
change his mind about a new relationship. Instinct told her he
sought challenge and excitement and neither of those things led
to good outcomes in love. She waved him goodbye and watched
him crunch through the gravel to his car, the hand-blown glass

panes distorting his body. "Why?" she asked herself under her breath. "Why do you want to self-destruct so badly?"

Her head swivelled round at speed, her lips parting in surprise as the small boy joining the edges of a puzzle spoke wisdom into the room. "Because he's bored," Wiri said, his tone older than his years. "That's what men do."

21

Confusing Encounters

Hana wandered around the house in a daze, her son's pink cheeks radiating an unhealthy glow against the cream cardigan as he tossed his head from the pain of the new teeth cutting through his tender gums. He'd cried himself sick and Logan arrived home to find Hana coping with a sobbing baby and two children squabbling over a single Lego piece from a bucket full of identical clones. "I'm driving into town to get my hair cut," he said. "I'll take these two with me to give you some peace." Logan inclined his dark head towards the arguing pair on the hearthrug and Hana heaved a sigh of relief.

"That would be awesome."

"I'll be about an hour." Logan glanced at Wiri's tousled head. "I might get his cut too."

"Okay." Hana looked around the lounge which had formed her prison cell for the past six hours, wrinkling her nose in distaste. Mac pressed his nose and mouth into her shoulder, hurting the site of her pacemaker and she hissed.

"Hey, boy. Do you want your girly hair cut?" Logan asked and Wiri nodded, pushing his fringe out of his eyes at the same time as standing.

"Have my girly hairs cut?" Phoenix lifted the thin ponytail Hana had wrestled onto the top of her head in between soothing Mac and ordering Wiri to put pants on.

Hana opened her mouth to refuse but Logan winked and nodded. "Yeah, I'm sure the barber will cut one or two of yours."

Phoenix squealed her delight and dashed into the garage to retrieve her red gumboots.

"Doormat!" Hana called as she heard the crash of the shoe cupboard door. "Don't put them on indoors."

Logan pulled her towards him and wrapped his arms around her and the grizzling baby. "Why don't I drop you at the hotel with the pram? You could push him around the rose gardens and he might fall asleep. If he settles you can grab a cup of tea and I'll text when I'm heading home?"

Hana nodded with exhaustion. "Sounds good." She shook her head, her eyes downcast. "I'm too old for this. I'm making a mess of it."

Logan kissed her temple and loosed his hold on her shoulders to stroke Mac's cheek, pulling a sad face at the tearful green eyes. "You're doing good, babe. I know it's hard. It didn't last long with Phoe and it won't last long with this wee man either."

"If you say so." Hana yawned and gathered supplies into a bag which would fit under the pram and let Logan fill the ute with children and paraphernalia. She shoved a woollen hat over her unwashed hair and wrapped a scarf around her neck. Mac whimpered all the way to the bottom of the mountain and didn't stop until Logan stuffed him into the pram and swaddled him up in a blanket.

"What did you do?" Hana watched her son licking his lips, a confused look on his face.

"An old Du Rose remedy." Logan smirked and tapped the pocket of his jacket.

"Seriously, what did you do?" Hana felt caught between admiration and concern. Logan pulled a tub from his pocket and handed it over, grinning as Hana opened the lid and peered at the contents. "What's that?" She sniffed it, scenting something peppery. The stuff inside looked jellified with a greenish hue.

"Kawakawa." Logan's brow knitted and he searched Hana's face for scorn. "It's been made into a paste for Mac's gums."

"By who?" Hana sniffed again and twisted the lid back on.

"The kaumatua's wife." Logan jutted his chin out. "It's an old Māori cure, te rongoa Māori."

Hana narrowed her eyes and readied herself for an argument. "You can't just shove something in a baby's mouth. I don't even know what's in it."

"I told you. Kawakawa. And it's working." Logan jerked his head at the pram where Mac stared at the inside of the hood, moving his lips around in an exaggerated movement.

Hana opened her mouth to speak but Logan shook his head and climbed back into the ute, insulted by her lack of faith. He didn't give her the opportunity to debate the issue, slamming his foot on the gas and leaving the car park in a hail of gravel. Hana shoved the tub of goo into the bag next to the pram and closed the zip. She fitted it in the tray beneath Mac and pulled her coat tighter around her body. Mac wrinkled his nose and stuck his tongue right out, pulling a comical face. Hana bit her lip and forced herself not to worry about poisoning and emergency hospital dashes, followed by awkward questions from social welfare officers. "Look on the bright side, Hana," she told herself with a sigh. "He's stopped crying."

The hotel steps thronged with visitors checking in for a conference and Hana moved away from the hotel, pushing the pram through the thick pea gravel and hearing it crunch under the wheels. Miriam's rose garden showed her its winter face, the standards and bushes pruned ready for the coming spring. The blunted branches resembled stunted fingers pointing skywards and the air tingled with expectancy. Will's son served as the gardener and clumps of cut grass clung to the hem of Hana's jeans and scattered across the tops of her leather boots. The pram bounced along on the uneven surface, the wheels disappearing under a desiccated green covering and Mac turned his face to the side and closed his eyes, lulled by the movement. "Typical!" Hana hissed. "I criticise your father and you prove him right." She shook her head and continued pushing as her son settled into the rocking rhythm and slept.

The stable yard looked deserted, the loose boxes empty and a wheel barrow leaning on its end against the wall. Hana pushed the pram across the rippled concrete and stopped in front of the box Sacha occupied when she wasn't out in the paddocks. She stroked her gloved fingers across the bolt and closed her eyes, imagining the white mare stretching her head over the door and nuzzling her face.

"I don't bloody care!" The shout made Hana jump and she recognised Lincoln's raised voice. She darted a frenzied look at her sleeping son.

"I don't know what to say to him!" she squeaked. "He killed a woman!" In a moment of irrational panic, she cranked the bolt back on Sacha's loose box and pushed the pram inside, pulling the door behind her. It groaned on the new hinges Logan fixed in place. A glance at Mac found him still sleeping and Hana pressed herself and the pram against the far corner of the stall, trying to avoid tipping the water bucket near her feet. She watched grains and a blade of hay bobbing on the gently moving surface.

"Don't you speak to me like that!" Linc's voice cracked the silence and Hana pressed herself against the wall, her heart thudding in her chest.

"He's a murderer!" she repeated, mouthing the words as her legs shook beneath her. "He killed a woman."

Linc stopped outside the loose box and his voice echoed off the brickwork, surrounding Hana in tenor sounds. "They released me and aren't looking for anyone else; they said so."

Hearing no other voice, Hana realised Linc's conversation partner was on the telephone. She held her breath as his boots grated loose stones against the concrete. "I don't care what you think."

Hana breathed out through her lips in silent wisps of air, aware of her raised heart rate and the threat of the pacemaker beneath her collar bone. "Don't go off," she pleaded. "Don't go off."

"I'm grateful for everything you did," Linc said, his voice lowered. "I appreciated your help with the lawyer's fees but I paid the price for what I did. I'm doing this and I don't care who gets hurt."

Hana's brain worked through Lincoln's words, hearing them as an echoed repeat in her head. He sounded like a guilty man up to further trouble. Her eyes widened in horror as Mac opened his mouth and furrowed his brow, nudging the pram with her thigh to jog him back to sleep and hoping the action made no discernable sound. Lincoln's conversation included someone who paid his legal fees and her mind made the automatic leap to Logan. Her husband paid for his friend's lawyer. She struggled to remember who imparted that fact. Was it Logan himself, Leslie or Will? Hana breathed through pursed lips, trying to stop her exhale hissing and alerting Linc to her presence. But her heart pounded and fear pulsed through her body. Mac moved his head from one side to the other and whimpered in pain, rubbing a tiny fist across his mouth. Hana stretched her fingers beneath the pram and dragged the kawakawa gel from the pocket of the bag, snagging her finger on the zip. She pushed a blob of it into Mac's mouth and watched his brow furrow as his tongue worked in his sleep. She patted her sticky fingers against his chest through the blanket, offering maternal comfort in the hope it would be enough.

"Don't tell me what to do." Lincoln's boots shuffled on the concrete as he began walking away from the stall. "This is my life and I intend to take charge of it from now on. Don't get in the way!"

Hana exhaled as Linc's voice grew distant and she heard the office door slam behind him. Waiting a moment to be sure he'd gone, she peeked over the half door and unlatched the bolt, sliding it with painful slowness. The door creaked on its hinges and Hana caught the scent of Sacha's perfumed skin as she retrieved the pram from the corner and shoved it through the opening. Not stopping to close it behind her, she walked at speed, heading through the gate towards the hotel without looking back. Her breath came in frightened heaves and she loosed the scarf from around her neck and whipped the woolly hat off. "Oh no," she hissed, pressing her fingers to her lips. "What's he up to? Is he planning to hurt someone else?"

Half turning on the spot, Hana hesitated, wanting to go back and demand an explanation from the stable manager. A spirit of indignation on behalf of his next victim sent her back to the stables and across the yard, stopping outside the stable manager's door. Light glowed through the leaded glass and she paused before raising her hand to knock. In the heartbeat before her knuckles connected the glass she heard the sound of a heavy bottle clunking into place on the table and the chink of glass. Lincoln roared as though he'd poured fire into his belly and Hana halted her foolish plan.

She retreated, not keen to face a murderer but desperate not to have to deal with a drunk. She walked back towards the hotel, drawing her phone from her pocket. 'No secrets,' Logan said only days before.

"Okay, Logan, no secrets," she said, dialling his number.

22

Suspicion

Hana sent four voicemails and a text to Logan as she sat on the front steps of the hotel, pleading illness and begging him to return. He answered none of them and her fingers froze inside her gloves while she waited, the afternoon temperatures plummeting as the mountain obscured the sun. Guests arrived and left, bumping their suitcases down the front stairs and nodding to Hana. Mac slept and for that, she felt gratitude.

The ute slewed to a stop in front of the steps, spitting gravel at Hana and the pram. Logan leapt from the cab and Phoenix banged on the window nearest her to get Hana's attention. "Sorry, sorry," he said, wrapping her in his arms, bare despite the winter temperatures. His hair looked neatly cropped around his ears, the fringe left long and flipping forwards. "Phone battery went dead and I didn't realise. The kids played a game while I got my hair cut and I didn't notice until we got back to the car. I plugged it in and saw heaps of messages from you. What's wrong?"

"I want to go back up to the house." Hana shivered, supporting her sentiment and Logan rubbed his fingers along her spine.

"Something's wrong. Talk to me." His perceptive grey eyes sought out weakness like a missile, heaving the crack wide and peering in. "Hana!" His tone hardened and she pushed herself out of his embrace.

"I can't talk here."

A group of loud tourists emerged, their excited chatter conducted in French rapped out like gunfire. They waved a map of the site without understanding and Logan stepped forward. "The stables are that way." He pointed towards the north side of the house and smiled, his understanding rewarded by smiles and waves as he repeated the instructions in fluent French.

"Show off," Hana grumbled.

Phoenix blew kisses through the car window and pointed to her shortened ponytail. Hana stared in horror and Logan gave a low chuckle. "The barber snipped off two hairs and turned the wee bunch into a man-bun. She thinks he cut heaps off and showed everyone in the cafe."

"Cafe?" Hana frowned, her face betraying hurt that while she sat freezing on the hotel steps, her family enjoyed treats in a warm cafe.

"Yeah. Sorry. I was trying to give you some time to yourself." Logan ran a hand through his fringe, pushing it backwards so he could look at Hana's disgruntled expression. "It went a bit wrong though, sorry." Strong hands pushed Hana towards the ute and she clambered in, greeted by the children's enthusiasm and eagerness to show her their new hairstyles.

"Mine's just like Papa's," Wiri announced, unclipping his seatbelt and twirling for Hana to admire his head.

Phoenix became apoplectic, pointing at his disconnected state and hitting him until the boy clambered back into his booster chair and clicked the seatbelt closed. "Naughty!" she shouted at him, her eyes filling with tears of horror. "That very very bad!"

"Your hair's beautiful, but she's right, Wiri," Hana confirmed. "Don't undo it without asking, please."

"Okay, Mama." He sounded chastened but his eyes remained bright as he checked himself out in the reflection from the window.

Logan dismantled the pram and removed the car seat from the pram frame, inserting it into the ute and bringing a draught with him. When he closed the door, Mac's eyes opened and Phoenix leaned sideways and patted his hand. "Goin' home, Macky!" she shouted and Hana's eyes widened.

"Don't yell at him, Phoe!"

"He hearin' me, den," she said, nodding like a bobble-head toy. She reached across and touched the tiny mittened hand and smiled, her face embracing the movement with wholehearted enthusiasm. Mac watched for a moment and then returned her grin, closing his eyes and turning his face away, even though his expression remained smug. Phoenix kept hold of his hand and watched him with maternal affection.

Logan reached across for Hana's hand, his fingers straying above the glove to her wrist. "You're freezing, babe. I'm sorry."

"Can I play wiv the worm on your phone, Pa?" Wiri called, leaning forward and straining against his seat belt.

"No!" Logan turned his head as he cranked up the heat in the interior. "It must've beeped to warn you the battery was running out. You know you're meant to tell me."

"I fought it had loads left." Wiri's voice assumed a whine and Hana heaved an audible sigh.

"I need to talk to you when we get back." Her eyes strayed to the side of his face as the ute turned towards home, pushing up the steep mountain road with a growling engine. Logan's brow knitted and concern etched into his expression.

"That sounds bad. Am I in trouble?" He gave her a puppy-dog sideways look and Hana smirked, watching him squirm. A powerful, authoritative alpha male, few things rocked Logan's world except a threat to his whānau or Hana's displeasure.

"No." She shook her head. "But someone is and I'm afraid it'll backfire on you."

"Great." Logan floored the gas and forced the ute up the hill, a sense of urgency settling on his shoulders.

Darkness closed around them and Hana rustled up a quick meal of pasta and mince while Logan showered the children and got them ready for bed. Mac appeared in his highchair licking his lips and Hana caught the scent of kawakawa as she put his beaker of warm milk on the tray in front of him. "I'll just get the others," Logan said, shooting her a concerned glance as he left the room.

They conducted the meal in subdued silence, Logan worried and the children tired. Mac's face drooped over his bowl as Hana pushed food between his lips. Bedtime seemed faster than usual with Logan acting as the sheep dog, driving the little people into bed and ignoring their complaints and manufactured ailments. "I'll get cross, Wiri," he warned the boy as he dug his heels in, demanding drinks, stories, long conversations and a manhunt for his favourite teddy. "You didn't even bring that here!" Logan said, his voice sounding stressed. "Just get into bed."

"Stop!" Hana told the child, leaning over him and pressing her lips to his forehead. "You're playing up now and it's not fair. We're tired too so get to sleep."

Logan smoothed the gel onto Mac's gums as Hana kissed her daughter's head in the room next door. "Sleep tight, baby," she said with a smile, stroking the soft curls back from her forehead and listening to the gentle suck of her thumb between her lips. "I love your new haircut."

"Fanks, Mama." Phoenix smiled from around her thumb but didn't remove it. Hana dimmed the hall light to a muted glow and made her way back to the kitchen. She found Logan snagging the top from a bottle of beer and he indicated a glass of red wine on the table for her.

"Let's go in the lounge," Hana said, shivering against the sinking temperature. "Light a fire and we'll talk."

Logan made an art form out of fire making in the burner, laying kindling with precision beneath heavy logs cut from the bush and dried in the shed. He prodded newspaper between the gaps and struck a match. Hana watched as it flared, curling her toes beneath her and sipping the wine. Logan fiddled with the fire, checking the draw from the flu and then propping the heavy glass door open to monitor the flames. "What's up?" he asked, glancing once before shifting the handle to increase the air flow beneath the fire and closing the glass door.

"I went for a walk and ended up at the stables." Hana took a sip of her wine. "I heard Linc coming and he sounded angry so I freaked out and hid in Sacha's stall."

Logan snorted a laugh, but the smile faded from his lips at Hana's look of disapproval. "He's unpredictable, served prison time for murder and nobody knew where I'd walked to."

"Manslaughter." Logan corrected her. "Not murder. Accidental death caused by something he did."

"Whatever!" Hana felt her patience stretch and become frayed. "I heard him on the phone. Whoever he spoke to sounded involved with the court case. Lincoln thanked them for paying his legal costs. The thing is, he's up to something. He said it's his life and he'll do what he wants. What could that mean?"

"I don't know!" Logan shrugged with irritation. "Maybe he's gonna live on ice cream for a month. The guy can do what he wants."

"That's what he said." Hana narrowed her eyes. "The other person on the call tried to talk him out of it though, so it's something serious. I need to work out who he spoke to and then maybe I'll know what he's planning. Who else besides you helped him?"

"What if I said nobody?" Logan's eyes narrowed, glinting like crystals behind long, dark eyelashes.

"Then I'd call you a liar," Hana retorted. "Your phone battery died, which means Lincoln didn't speak to you and I don't think you had anything to do with his crime. There must be someone else."

Logan chewed on the inside of his cheek and laid back, long legs stretched out in front of him. He put his arms behind his head and gave her a lazy smile. "We've come a long way, Mrs Du Rose," he drawled. "You didn't even suspect me."

Hana swallowed more wine and held back her retort, seeing the truth in his statement. She daren't admit she'd marched their son across the stable yard to confront Lincoln and then bottled out. Logan crossed his legs at the ankles and Hana watched his brain move into gear. "A few of us helped him. He behaved like a dick but he didn't kill her so we all pitched in and funded his legal fees. We grew up together in the township and that's what whānau does, I guess. Linc worked for Jack after school. His wife got a partnership at a doctors' surgery in South Auckland and he commuted here in about half an hour in good traffic. Sometimes he stayed in the bunkhouse if it got too late to go home. I came back from England around the time the police arrested him and Lincoln didn't get bail. The evidence according to my sister was circumstantial, based on his affair with the dead woman and the presence of his DNA at her house. He promised us he didn't do it and we believed him."

"He cheated on his wife?" Hana's lip curled back in disdain and Logan gave a slow nod.

"Yeah. Stupid idiot."

"Where did the woman live?" Hana asked. "Nobody's mentioned it until recently."

"In the township." Logan sat up and examined a healing cut on his index finger. "I don't know why Lincoln got involved."

"But the point of my eavesdropping was that Lincoln's up to something and the other person on the phone tried to stop him doing it."

"Doing what?" Logan frowned.

"I don't know!" Hana bit. "That's why I'm asking you. Is it possible he did kill her and you're all wrong about his innocence?"

Logan shook his head and then halted the movement, doubt creeping into his eyes. "What exactly did he say?"

Hana stared at the ceiling to get her facts straight and then repeated Lincoln's sentence. "He said, 'I appreciated your help with the lawyer's fees but I paid the price for what I did. I'm doing this and I don't care who gets hurt.' What could that mean? Who might get hurt?"

"Dunno." Logan chewed his lower lip. "I'll ask him tomorrow."

"No!" Hana squeaked, slopping wine over her hand and licking it off. "Then you'll have to tell him I hid in the stable listening to a private conversation."

"Well, you did." Logan's smirk curved his face and the scar under his right eye crinkled. A dimple appeared to the left of his mouth from another old injury and Hana squirmed in her seat.

"Please don't?" she begged. "I'll do anything." The words were airborne before she realised her mistake and she flapped her hand trying to take it back.

"Anything?" Logan crawled across the hearth rug on all fours and settled himself in front of Hana. He lifted the wine glass from her fingers and his lazy smile oozed sex appeal. "I like the sound of anything. What's it worth?"

Hana giggled as he dug his fingers into her waist and tickled the sensitive flesh. She caved forwards and his lips nibbled at her neck, drawing a groan from deep in her throat. "The kids might come in," she whispered, glancing towards the door as Logan undid the buttons of her blouse and slipped it off her shoulders.

"Let's go to bed then," he murmured from beneath her hair.

Hana sighed and glanced at the flickering flames behind the glass doors of the stove. "Seems a shame to waste a good fire."

23

No conclusions

The chill air gnawed at Hana's skin and forced a groan from her lips as she settled her face on Logan's chest. "You've got all the warmth," she grumbled, pushing her hand across his stomach to where the fire glowed in the darkness.

"We can swap," Logan offered. "I'm melting."

Hana clambered across him, taking the blanket with her and exposing him to the cool draught. "See, it's horrid," she muttered, plonking herself down nearest the fire.

"Yeah, thanks for sharing that," Logan sighed. "I believed you when you said it was cold on that side; you didn't need to prove it by nicking the blanket."

Hana replaced the hairy woollen throw diagonally across them both. It covered her but left Logan's long legs and slender feet exposed. "You should've left your socks on," she commented, rewarded with a disgusted snort.

"Yeah, because wearing only socks is sexy." Logan cuddled her close into his chest and rested his chin on her head.

"Who else gave Lincoln financial backing?" Hana asked and Logan snuffled.

"I hoped you'd leave that well alone but I guess not."

"Who?" Hana persisted.

Logan sighed. "I gave some, Alfred did, Michael, Toby, quite a few of the stockmen. Even Jack donated. Lincoln's mum sold her car and threw that in and heaps of the township helped. Some could only give ten bucks but they believed he didn't kill her so they pitched in with what little they had."

"Who didn't donate?" Hana looked for a different approach.

"I don't know if anyone on the other side of the mountain got involved." Logan scratched his stubble and Hana listened to the sound of his fingernails on the rugged flesh. "Even if they believed Lincoln innocent, Rueben might've stopped them chipping in because he always chose contrary to everyone else."

"Well, whoever Lincoln spoke to on the phone gave him money for his defence. They don't want him to do something. What could it be?"

Logan shrugged. "Not sure. Pania died about seven years ago and Linc served five years of a seven-year sentence. He turned up at the hotel after they released him early. It made sense to give him a chance; he ran the stables under Jack before so it seemed a good solution."

"Who goes back to where it all happened and settles there?" Hana mused.

"Lots of people." Logan turned on his side and snuggled her into his chest, tickling her nose with the downy hairs. "Liza said the evidence against him was circumstantial; wrong place, wrong time. The prosecutor put a convincing enough case together to prove him guilty."

"Lincoln's poor wife." Hana sighed. "Isn't it tragic enough to find out your husband's been having an affair with another woman, only to discover he's accused of killing her as well?"

Logan shifted on the hearth rug. "Doesn't it sound familiar?" His voice lowered to a rumble. "You thought I'd moved Ryan's mother in last year and then the boys found her dead behind Nev's place."

Hana shivered. "Yeah. Maybe that's why it's affected me so much. Shades of familiarity."

Logan pressed a kiss on the top of her head. "I didn't cheat or kill Sylvia. Lincoln did cheat but maintains he's innocent of Pania's death."

"Why manslaughter?" Hana felt the heat burning the base of her spine and wrinkled her nose in discomfort, wishing she'd stayed on the other side of Logan.

He groaned. "You're not letting this go, are you?"

Hana snuffled into his chest. "Nope."

"The original charge was murder, but half way through the trial Linc's defence collapsed and the judge directed the jury to find him guilty of manslaughter."

Hana pushed herself up onto one elbow. "How can a defence just collapse?"

"Dunno." Logan sighed. "Ring Liza and ask her."

Hana snorted. "No thanks. I don't want to know badly enough to risk getting my head ripped off by your sister."

"It started as murder and ended up as a lesser charge of manslaughter as far as I recall. I still don't think he did it. I do remember that at the last minute, Linc refused to take the stand in his own defence. It disappointed everyone and that's why there's animosity to him now; people backed him and felt cheated. It put doubt in their minds and left a nasty taste."

"What happened to his mother? She sold her car to help pay for his defence so where is she now? Why doesn't Lincoln live with her instead of at the motel?"

Logan closed one eye and stared at the ceiling. "I think she died."

"How?"

"Can't remember, Hana. I'd got problems of my own by the time the trial happened."

"Did you go to it?"

"No. I worked during the week on the north shore and drove home at weekends to stick the farm back together. I spent that few years riding around with a dark cloud over my head."

Hana pursed her lips and tried not to focus on his relationship with Caroline during that period of his life, but jealousy flashed in her green eyes and she directed it elsewhere. "What's his wife to you?" She pressed to the core of a different sort of pain, remembering Fiona's open animosity towards Logan.

"Second or third cousin." Logan shifted and Hana heard the smile in his voice. "Why? You jealous? I think I had my first French kiss with her. Ouch!" Logan pushed his hands between his legs as Hana lifted her knee with force.

"I didn't want that much detail!" No humour laced her tone, only aggression and pique.

"Good job I didn't then," Logan groaned. "Can't you take a joke?"

"No." Hana's lips lifted in an evil smirk. "Only I get to French kiss you, do you hear?"

"Fine!" Logan snapped. "Then get here because you need the practice." He rolled her onto her back and pinned her in place with his thigh, tickling her ribs until she collapsed beneath him like a jelly, weak from giggling.

24

Pulling Uphill

The move to Hamilton wasn't without its stresses as Hana readied three small children and three adults for the shift south. Phoenix and Mac went without fuss but Wiri and Caleb proved more difficult.

"What about school?"

"I've found you one along the road and I'll organise a uniform when we get there."

"But I like my school."

"You said you didn't!" Hana swallowed her irritation and fixed a smile on her lips.

"But I like it better than a new one." Wiri's bottom lip stuck out and his grey eyes widened with anxiety.

"Logan, help me," Hana hissed, appealing to her husband's wisdom as the small boy dug his heels in, removing everything from the suitcase that belonged to him and piling it on the floor.

Logan stopped tapping on the laptop and turned his body to face the suitcase and distressed child. Hana walked behind him to snag Mac's toy rabbit off the back of the sofa and saw a bank account statement sprawled across the screen in a complicated spreadsheet. "Sorry," she said with a sigh. "You're busy."

Logan smiled with his eyes and laid the laptop on the sofa cushion next to him. He beckoned to Wiri with a crooked finger. "Come sit on my knee," he said, his voice soft. The child slouched over, resistance in his feet but he snuggled into Logan's torso without fuss. "You have two choices," Logan said, lowering his voice. "We're going to Hamilton for a whole term. I thought you'd want to come with us but if you don't, that's fine too."

"But what will I do then? I can't open the front door without a chair. How will I get in and out?"

"You can't stay here alone, mate." Logan pushed a lock of Wiri's dark hair away from his forehead. "You'll go back home and live with your father and Asher."

"I don't want to." Wiri raised his voice and the tears came, spurting from his eyes like an overflow. "I want it to be like it is now. You have to stay here with me. Here!" He slammed his hand into the back of the sofa and Logan dodged.

"We can't. Me, Hana, Phoe and Mac are moving to Hamilton. You decide which you want to do and we'll be cool with that."

"I can't choose, I just can't!" Wiri's panic seemed pitiful and Hana turned away so he wouldn't see her sadness.

"Would you like to talk to your dad about it?" Logan asked, his voice level and soothing. Hana gritted her teeth, angry that Nev hadn't yet bothered to see his son, signing the papers with cool efficiency and callous disregard for a small boy's fate. She left the room and busied herself packing baby clothes for the trip, rolling the little items and fitting them into a suitcase. Logan's voice rumbled through the wall, a one-way conversation as he spoke to his half-brother on the phone. His tone rose an octave and Hana cringed.

"Mummy?" Her daughter stood in the doorway, balancing on one leg with her other foot swinging. Her grey eyes channelled anxiety and tears pricked at the corners. "Wiri's crying. He told me to go away."

Hana sighed and her brow furrowed. "He's got some things on his mind; he'll be okay. Papa's dealing with it."

"Sad fings, Mama? He's crying hard like he fell down on the floor." Phoenix punctuated her sentence by jabbing an index finger at the tiled surface beneath her feet. Hana held her arms out and the little girl skipped over, burying her face in her mother's thigh.

"Your daddy will make it better, baby," she whispered, hoisting the child onto her hip. Phoenix cuddled in close and laid her head on Hana's shoulder.

"I no like Wiri crying."

"Me neither." Hana kissed her forehead and swaddled her under her cardigan like a mother hen gathering her chicks for the night. "Your dad will sort it."

"Sort it?" Phoenix bobbed her head up and sought Hana's green eyes, searching for certainty. "Papa big an brave, aye?"

Hana smiled. "Yeah, baby. Papa's big and brave. And real smart. He'll sort it out."

"And mart." Phoenix snuggled down and then uttered childish logic. "I get Wiri biscuit. And I get Macky biscuit and Phoe biscuit."

Hana rolled her eyes and bit her bottom lip to stop the smile spreading across her face. "No, baby. Food isn't the answer to all your troubles. Let's find Wiri and see if cuddles will cheer him up."

Phoenix wiggled her nose and released a sigh of defeat, swinging her legs as Hana walked along the corridor. They found Wiri in the room he'd appropriated, his face pushed into his favourite pillow on the double bed. Hana sat on the end and Phoenix pitched out of her arms, crawling across the mattress to her cousin. The little girl fitted her tiny body into his back and reached her skinny arms around his shoulders, her delicate frame shuddering with his sniffs. "All better now, Wiri?" she asked, her tone pleading as her fingers twirled a lock of his dark hair.

"Uncle Logan's talking to your father," Hana said, her tone soothing.

Wiri gave a disgusting sniff and wiped his eyes with the back of his hand. "No. He's shouting at him. I heard him say he didn't have time to come up and see me." Wiri turned his head to face Hana, grey eyes red rimmed and watery. "I want Pa to biff him good."

Hana swallowed. "Logan's not going to hit Nev. It's not how family deals with things." Wiri raised an eyebrow with far more adult understanding than a five-year-old should ever accrue and his skepticism acted as a knife in Hana's gut. She winced and corrected herself. "It's not what family should do, Wiremu. There are better ways."

"Uncle Kane would biff him so hard he'd make his teeth rattle."

Phoenix giggled around the thumb she'd pushed into her mouth and repeated half the sentence. "Teef rattle."

"Yeah, well Logan's not Uncle Kane." Hana kept the silent prayer of thanks to herself. The thought of Caroline's incestuous pregnancy to Kane sent a dart of fear up her spine.

"I don't like Uncle Kane," Wiri muttered under his breath. "He's scary and he locked me in a cupboard once for touching his stuff."

Hana's eyes widened in horror but she managed to mask it as Logan's feet pattered along the corridor. She heard him peering into rooms. "We're in here," she called. "Macky's having a nap."

"And Wiri's havin' tears, Pa." Phoenix sat up and looked at her father with childish hope. "Can you fix him? He don't wanna be in a cupboard though, fanks."

Logan's features jerked in surprise and he ran his fingers along the back of Hana's neck, infusing her with comfort and solidarity. "Your father's asked me to drive you down to his place." Logan corrected himself. "Your place. He'd like to talk to you."

Wiri took a last sniff of the pillow fabric and Hana felt his isolation. Tama's scent must be long gone but the child wouldn't let her banish the imaginary remnants in the washing machine. He sat up and Phoenix rolled away like a rugby pro. "Na, fanks. I'm not going." He used the hem of his sweatshirt to dry his eyes and nose. "I'll come wiv you guys."

Logan's perplexed expression made Hana suppress an inappropriate laugh. "But your dad's waiting for us." His eyes spoke of the angry battle he'd endured to achieve the small concession in the face of Nev's disinterest. "We need to speak to him." Logan ground his teeth in irritation, having gained victory over Nev only to lose ground to a child. "He wants to see you."

"Na, he doesn't. I heard what he said. He don't have time for me so I don't have time for him."

Logan floundered, looking to Hana for help. "He didn't say he wouldn't make time. What he actually said was…"

"He said he didn't want to drive all the way up here just to pat me on the head and wave me off. He said it was a waste of his time." The child's repetition of his father's words left a searing trail in the air molecules which took Hana's breath away. Logan closed his eyes and they were stormy with the texture of a wind torn lake when he opened them again. He shook off the awful legacy of his own unwanted status but the effort left him ragged.

"Who wants to help me dig up veggies?" Hana took charge, breaking the silence with practicality. "I'll make homemade chips for tea with the special crinkler and you guys can help."

"Crinkle chips!" Wonderment passed across Phoenix's face and she clapped her hands over her mouth. "I do, I do!" She stood up on the bed and raised her hand in the air as she'd seen Wiri do in class on a family visit. "My wants crinkle chips, pees."

"Right then. Wellies on and away we go." Hana pointed at the bedroom door and Phoenix slithered off the bed, giggling.

"Them's not wellies. Them's is gumboots, silly Mama."

Hana stood and slipped past her husband's static body, dragging her fingers around his waist and down across his neat butt. His hand was a fist and she tugged the bunched digits straight until they relaxed. "She's wrecking the joint," he muttered, cocking his head to listen to his daughter yanking boots from the cupboard in the garage.

"It's fine." Hana leaned in and kissed his upper arm through his shirt, feeling the muscle flex beneath her lips. "Go help your nephew and I'll occupy Phoe." She left the room with a quick glance at Wiri. The boy sat upright on the bed, bottom lip pushed out and his arms folded around his body as though encasing himself in a strait jacket of protection. Her heart ached for his misery but age and wisdom told her she wasn't the best person to deal with his fury.

Phoenix bounced around in the garage while Hana stuffed her feet into her own boots and collected the pitchfork from the shed. The greenhouse was a new addition to the property, snuggled against the boundary fence and given necessary protection from the furious storms which encased the mountain during winter. Logan used a pile driver to punch vertical logs into the ground, determined the wind shouldn't get its wily tendrils around the structure and throw it to the far reaches. Only two sides and the roof housed safety glass, aluminum forming the windward walls. Somehow the greenhouse survived, set into a dip in the green plateau and sheltered by native punga and silver ferns waving overhead. Hana held her daughter's hand as Phoenix exercised her new found skill; skipping. "Last of the potatoes," she mused, her inner vision consumed by the sight of Wiri's sad face. "Do you think they'll be big ones?"

"No." Phoenix shook her head, doubt filling her mind. Then her brain reasoned there would be no crinkly chips. "Yes." She changed her answer and increased her speed.

They harvested the last of the veggies, packing the potatoes into a wooden crate and dumping the foliage in the compost bin. Phoenix grunted as she tried to lift the box, finding it impossible as the tendons stuck out in her neck and she breathed through her mouth like a weight lifter. Hana laughed. "Leave it, Phoe. We'll get Dad to lift it with his big muscles."

"Dad lift it." She looked relieved, smacking her hands together to loosen the dirt as she stood. They went back to the house the long way, stopping to watch the falcons soaring on the up draught overhead. Phoenix clutched the metal rungs of the fence and pushed her face through. "Birdies," she said, pointing with excitement as one flew close. The sheerness of the cliff seemed terrifying up close, more frightening with the protection of the fence than it ever seemed without. Hana glanced down into the bush canopy sloping below and imagined Bobby's last letter to her moldering in the damp soil below. She sighed.

"You sad, Mama?" her perceptive daughter asked, touching Hana's jeans with her dirty fingers. "I do crinkles for you. Special ones."

"You're a beautiful person, Phoenix Du Rose." Hana smoothed the dark curls back from the tiny forehead, thwarted by the wind which whipped them up again. "You're like your sister."

"Sister," Phoenix repeated. "Baby sister."

Hana winced. "Nope. No more babies my dear. I meant Isobel, your big sister. We don't see enough of her, do we? We're surrounded by men in the Du Rose world. Men everywhere."

"Men eweewhere." Phoenix nodded her head as though she understood, safe in her cocooned world of family; regardless of their sex. She turned and held her arms upwards. "I wide on your head, Mama."

"No." Hana took one of the hands, feeling the coolness of the slender fingers. "That's a Daddy thing. I'm for cuddles and nice playing. He's for rough housing and messing about. Besides, you sit on his shoulders, not his head."

"I ngā pokowhiwhi." Phoenix tapped her shoulder with her free hand and Hana nodded and smiled without replying. Her daughter's fluency in Te Reo isolated her; she'd tried hard to learn but the complicated structure of the language messed with her head and emerged on her tongue as awkwardness and embarrassment, especially in front of Logan.

Indoors the boys had settled before the fire, a game of cards between them. "Snap!" Wiri shouted and Logan jumped and let him collect the pile on the hearth rug.

"No!" Phoenix began. Her keen eyes spotted the queen of hearts mistaken for diamonds and Hana put her hand over the child's mouth and distracted her from budding mayhem.

"Come on, Miss Crinkly. Let's get chipping."

"Chipping! Chipping!" Phoenix bounced to the kitchen in her socks, eager to find the wavy cutter which produced crinkly shaped chips. Hana heard the long drawer being yanked out and smiled to herself at her daughter's natural enthusiasm for life.

With the crinkler found, Logan was commandeered to fetch the crate of vegetables and he took Wiri with him. The child moved like a shadow, aligning and bonding himself to Logan's masculinity like a safe anchor in a troubled port. The darkness of a bitter spirit shrouded him, smothering the lightness that was Wiremu Du Rose and Hana feared for him.

Caleb proved the other fly in the ointment and made his reluctance to leave the hotel clear. "Maybe Mr Du Rose will give me a job when my leg's better. Then I can pay you back for the free food and lodging." The teenager twisted the bottom of his jacket in writhing fingers.

"You need to get your cast checked at the Waikato Hospital." Hana gritted her teeth ready for the ensuing battle. "With Logan gone there'll be nobody free to drive you all the way there and back again. It's easier if you're in Hamilton so I can do it."

"You don't want me hanging around," Caleb protested. "What will I do when the cast's off?"

Hana sighed. "Why don't we work that out when it happens?"

"If you leave me here, I'll find a way to pay for my stay." The crutch slipped from his fingers and crashed to the floor and Caleb reached for it and missed. The chair creaked and he winced with pain as he stretched too far, nearly pitching himself onto the carpet. Exasperated, Hana left the motel room and slid the door closed behind her. She almost missed the sound of the boy calling her name, fear in his voice. "Hana! I'm sorry, I'm sorry."

She leaned against the weatherboard wall and put both hands up to her temples, massaging away her anxiety. Mac's needs dictated her desire to move back to town, but it felt as though the weight of the world pulled backwards like a noose around her throat. Vibrations came through the floor as Caleb retrieved his crutch and moved towards the door. Metal clattered against glass as he fought the ranch slider and poked his head through the gap. "I'm being an ungrateful dick." His eyes narrowed with relief at Hana's presence and he stepped across the threshold, his face pinched into an expression of tearfulness. "You've been awesome and I'm throwing it back in your face."

"Yeah, you are." Exhaustion and frustration made her bitchy. "Do what you like, Caleb. I'm taking my baby to the city and you're welcome to come; there's room for you. If not, stay here until you're healed and ask one of the stockmen to drive you to Auckland or Hamilton. Get Marla on reception to watch for the appointment coming through and change it to wherever you want. There's no charge for staying here; it's on me." She pushed off from the wall and strode along the deck without looking back, tired of trying to shepherd a resistant flock. Hearing Caleb call her name she kept walking, releasing herself from responsibility and absolving herself of the flicker of guilt.

25

Memories

"**Y**ou all right?" Logan took his left hand from the steering wheel and reached across, stroking Hana's fingers under his.

She nodded. "I think so. It feels strange coming back after so long away."

"Eighteen months."

"What?"

"We left eighteen months ago."

Hana looked out of the window as the Waikato spiralled by, its legendary greenness lush against the browner tones of further north. "The Godzone," she murmured, watching the off ramp for Huntly looming ahead.

Logan stroked her thumb and smiled. "Do you know where that phrase came from?"

Hana shook her head, accepting his encyclopedic knowledge as a distraction ploy. "No."

"It's from a poem." He took his hand back to use the indicator, overtaking a tractor on the dual carriageway.

"Thomas Bracken wrote it in the late 1800s. He called it *God's Own Country* and it's been abbreviated to *Godzone*."

Hana nodded and felt her chest tighten. She used to be a city girl, hankering after five-star comfort and resenting the rural isolation of Mātakitaki and the insular nature of the Du Roses. She shivered, wondering when the switch happened in her mind and one represented freedom while the city enfolded around her like barbed wire.

"He wrote *God Defend New Zealand*," Logan said, glancing sideways and wincing as her attention wandered.

"The national anthem?" Hana asked, her voice listless. "I love that. Such beautiful words. Do you think he does?"

"Who? What?" Logan put his hand back over hers.

"God." Hana turned to face him, her teeth gnawing on the inside of her bottom lip. "Do you think he defends New Zealand?"

"Yes." Logan's confidence halted her and she pushed it no further, aligning to the peace in his spirit and drawing comfort from the assurance, even if he'd lied just to soothe her.

They drove through the suburbs in silence as the three children slept in the back seat, Wiri's hand resting on the side of Phoenix's car seat so his fluttering fingers could seek out hers if he needed to. Hana glanced backwards at the boy's pink cheeks, seeing the torture which assailed him even in slumber. Her own children slept in comfort, understanding nothing of their cousin's agony; witnessing his outpourings of grief and temper as concerned but baffled observers. "Wiri cried all the way to the highway," she said, keeping her voice low. Logan's face set in a hard line and she watched his jaw working beneath the beard growth.

"I saw."

"What do I say to him?" she asked, floundering. "I don't know how to make it better."

"You can't." Logan swallowed and made the turns to steer the ute towards Fairview Downs. "Whatever you did for Bodie when your first husband died; just do that."

Hana snorted with disdain. "No. I made dreadful mistakes. I wrapped him in cotton wool because I couldn't get to him emotionally and I created a monster. I won't do that again."

"Then do the opposite!" Logan's patience sounded frayed, Wiri's difficulties overlaid with memories of his own childhood. "I don't bloody know, Hana. Just do whatever you think. I'm not a freakin' psychologist, am I?"

Hana turned away stung and withdrew her hand from beneath his. Logan shook his head and fixed his face into an impenetrable mask. She fought the urge to retort, knowing from experience it wouldn't give her any satisfaction, but Neville Du Rose wasn't dead and nor was Anahera. One was pig-headed and the other incapacitated. Hana sighed, hoping her fumbled attempts at helping the damaged boy would be enough.

"He just needs you to love him." Logan's words sounded stilted and angry. "Just bloody love him, Hana. Please."

She opened her mouth and wisdom made her close it again. Instead she watched the boxy houses whizz past the window. The rural school had lost its street appeal and Hana gaped as Logan made the final turn through the magnificent wrought iron gates. In the past year someone with planning permission had buried it beneath a housing estate, surrounding it in a brick siege. Ugly boundary fences ringed the soccer fields like sentries, protecting the new builds from marauding teenage boys. The absence of green and openness caused her to take a sharp intake of breath. Logan wrinkled his nose; his only comment on the progressive march of the human desire to conquer and occupy every square centimetre of earth and air.

The Gatehouse stood where it had for almost two centuries but a panelled fence protected its blank windows from the street. Hana turned in her seat to assess the damage as Logan launched the ute up onto the small driveway. "I bet it's dark at the back of the house with that fence now."

"Yup." Logan tipped himself from the driver's seat and left her sitting there as he skipped up the front steps and onto the villa's wrap around deck. The front door opened at his touch and she heaved a sigh of relief. He disappeared for a moment and Hana watched him walk back outside, his cowboy hat and riding jeans incongruous against the formal backdrop of the private school. Her lips quirked at the memory of him in a suit, expensive Italian fabric hugging his neat bum and the shirt sleeves containing his veined biceps. He'd make the switch from chopping wood to teaching boys without breaking his stride but the cowboy boots would remain; a silent rebellion against the propriety of academia.

"Do we unload the car or the kids?" Logan pulled open the passenger door and leaned his forearm on the sill above Hana's head. She smelled the familiar scent of New Zealand bush and summer.

"Neither," she replied. "Just get back in and let's go home."

Logan smirked and the scar beneath his right eye wrinkled. "Whatever. Sorry about before. I'm just angry at Nev."

"I know." Hana's fingers sought his face, tracing the line of his jaw and stumbling against the coarse hair breaking through the skin. "Don't be so hard on him. He's lost everything these last few years; his father died, his brother left, he lost Rueben's half of the mountain, his eldest son cost you both a fortune with his stupidity and now his wife's been sectioned. It's not unreasonable to enjoy a well-deserved meltdown." Hana watched her husband's face cloud over and narrowed her eyes. "I know it sucks, Loge. Wiri's caught in the crossfire but it'll work out."

"Like it did for me?" Logan's tone held bitterness and sarcasm. "Don't think so, somehow."

"We can't change the past." Hana's eyes strayed to the wooden pillars on the porch and the detailed filigree on every surface of the old house. "Let's just keep moving forwards, hey?"

"I love you, Mrs Du Rose." Logan caressed her name on his lips; anchor and lifeline. He tugged her from the ute and crushed her into him, keeping her balanced on the slender footboard while his nose pushed into her neck and his fingers roved under her shirt to touch the clasp on her bra.

"Not in front of the children." Hana whispered and nibbled his ear lobe.

"They're not looking." His voice sounded muffled by her sweatshirt and she shivered at the touch of his warm fingers on her skin.

"Ah-hem." The delicate throat clearing made Hana jump and Logan banged his head on the top of the door. He leapt back with a hiss and put his fingers up to look for blood, fearing an episode with his hemophilia. Hana held her breath and watched as he brought clean fingers down to inspect.

"Sorry to disturb you when you're moving in." The female voice drew Hana's attention and her gaze met that of a smart woman in her forties with *get-me-the-manager* styled blonde hair, cut into her nape.

"Hi." Hana's eyes darted to Logan and back, seeing a lack of recognition. The woman took a step forward.

"I'm Ava." At the couple's obvious confusion, she elaborated. "I'm the principal here at Waikato Boys'. You must be the Du Roses."

Logan recovered with incredible speed, dropping into a businesslike manner with frightening ease. He took the proffered hand and nodded, his face a blank mask. Hana straightened her shirt and looked away, fighting the urge to giggle like a cornered teen. The woman appeared clipped and professional unlike Hana; caught necking with her husband on school premises. She turned away, her eyes watering and reached into the ute to get her purse, her mirth compounded by a line of dribble running its course from Wiri's mouth onto his jacket.

Sunlight and optical illusion made it look as though the drips travelled up as well as down it like a zip line. Smothering a snort, Hana retrieved her purse and emerged backwards into a conversation about changed bell times and lessons lasting only fifty minutes. "It works well," Ava explained. "It adds an extra period to the school day for enhanced learning and I've introduced a Semester A and B timetable to align our boys with university processes."

Hana plastered a fake smile onto her face and offered her hand. "Hana Du Rose," she said. "Nice to meet you."

The woman smiled, a genuine expression of pleasure and Hana relaxed. "Angus Blair spoke highly of you both. It's wonderful to have you back." Ava addressed Logan, turning her perceptive blue eyes on him. "He'd earmarked you for deputy principal, I understand."

"Did he?" Logan sounded non-committal but only Hana knew the warning signs. She didn't understand what had occurred to ruin a lifetime's friendship, but Logan's eyes showed suspicion at his former mentor's name.

"That role's still vacant." Ava's features took on a beaked appearance as she hooked her prey and attempted to reel it in. Hana observed her efforts of persuasion with amusement; Ava hadn't experienced Du Rose stubbornness before. It would be a different form of education for her. Hana watched with cool disinterest as Logan sidestepped the blatant offer and indicated the ute with a jerk of his head.

"I'll settle my family and check in with you," he said, his mind already elsewhere.

Ava knotted her brow and then conceded. "No rush. Monday's teacher-only day so you can catch up with your colleagues and fit in where required. I'll see you at the staff meeting; we start at fifteen minutes past eight."

Logan gave an upward tilt of his head in acknowledgement and with a smile at Hana, Ava turned and whirled away on high heels.

Hana wanted to ask about Logan's broken relationship with Angus, but the more rational part of her didn't want to know. It happened during a traumatic time in her life and she figured it was best left behind.

"How do we do this?" Logan's question snapped Hana back to the present moment and she shrugged.

"No idea. Three grumpy kids, only the food I brought from home and no idea if there're even beds for them. It's our usual brand of chaos so I guess we'll work through it."

Logan's face broke into a smile. "That's what I love about you; your resourcefulness."

An hour later, the children sat around the kitchen table eating sandwiches. After the initial eye-rubbing and displays of pique they warmed to their new situation, helped along by the presence of food. Phoenix picked crusts from around her sandwich and left them to the side of her plate. "Nice kai, Mama," she mused and Hana smiled in her direction.

"Thanks, baby."

"Where Papa?"

Hana handed a stick of cheese to Mac and listened to the sound of Logan's footsteps moving overhead on the first floor. "He's putting up the travel cot for Macky." She winced at a crash and amended her sentence. "He's fighting the travel cot for Macky."

"He fightin'?" Phoenix formed her rosebud lips into a little 'o' of exaggerated surprise and nudged Wiri. "Not again!"

"What? Your dad doesn't fight," Hana said, keeping her voice level and maintaining the careful illusion of perfection for her children's benefit. The old Logan fought, but he hadn't needed to for a while.

"He fighted Uncle Kane." Wiri added his comment whilst eating the crusts Phoenix piled onto his plate like her own personal dustbin. "You fighted Uncle Kane." He raised an eyebrow and shot her the classic Du Rose look of disdain. Hana writhed with dismay at the child's enhanced memory.

"That was years ago." She dismissed it as insignificant although it paved the way for her acceptance and mana within the Du Rose family. She'd hit Logan's hemophiliac half-brother and he'd bled. "Fighting's wrong," she conceded with a wince of guilt. "It's never okay."

"Fightin's wong!" Phoenix stressed and piled more crusts onto Wiri's plate.

Logan appeared in the doorway, his dark hair mussed and his right index finger in his mouth. Hana cringed. "You cut yourself?"

"It's fine. I used my spray." He smiled over his hand, hiding the blood running into his mouth. "I'll run it under the tap."

"Fightin's naughty!" Phoenix yelled. She balled her fists and tensed her body as though enduring some kind of muscular episode. Hana jumped, Logan knitted his brow but Wiri laughed. Phoenix looked pleased with herself and performed again for her cousin's benefit.

"Don't encourage her," Hana chided the older boy and handed another stick of cheese to her silent son. His lips moved with anticipation, already sucking before the yellow wedge arrived in his fingers. Hana patted her mouth and Mac's eyes watched, his left hand mimicking the action. Tiny fingers flicked the thank you sign, pushing away from his mouth as his green eyes danced with pleasure at Hana's ready smile. She stroked his cheek and the silent communication felt like a milestone passed. Hana turned, finding her husband's grey eyes watching her.

"It'll be okay," he whispered and Hana nodded.

"Run your hand under the cold tap."

"I used my spray."

Ignoring his protests, Hana dropped into her role of family nurse, dragging sticking plasters from her purse and patching up the ragged wound. She prayed the bleeding would stop to allow Logan's body to behave as God intended. The city seemed to crowd in on her, cluttering her mind and pushing away anything except her role as wife and mother.

Hana Du Rose drowned out her fears by moving her mind through the details of bath time in the huge upstairs room, making a passable dinner and settling the children in the big classroom next door to their bedroom. The old house creaked and groaned with every movement and the temperature dropped, requiring the ancient, gravity fed central heating which added to the cacophony of unfamiliar sound. The baby monitor rumbled with strange vibrations on the kitchen table and Hana nursed a mug of tea and listened to Wiri telling Phoenix a whispered story about a rabbit with super powers, calling from his bed to hers. Mac snuffled and settled with ease, tired from the journey and an overload of sensory challenges in an unfamiliar environment.

"Hey." Logan turned aside from the old dishwasher which emitted a resigned hiss as it gave in and began to fill. He leaned his bum against the counter and folded his arms, observing Hana from across the wide room. "What're you thinking?"

Hana shrugged and cradled the mug, turning it round and round on the scarred table. "I'm thinking it was a mistake to come back here."

"Oh." His handsome jaw dropped and Logan tried and failed to hide his dismay. "Memories?" he asked and she nodded.

"Yeah. This city's not been kind to me and I can't cope with any more tragedy."

"It's not all been bad." Logan covered the distance between them in a few long strides. He pulled her to a standing position and settled himself in her chair, hauling her down onto his knee. "You met me here."

Hana's lips curved into a smile and she met his serious gaze with a coy look. "Not true. I met you on a Circle Line tube train in London, or have you forgotten?"

"I'd never forget that. But Hamilton held you until I returned and that makes it a great place for me." He ran a gentle finger down the side of her face and Hana felt the tingle of attraction. Logan's thighs felt solid and safe beneath her and she glanced at the strong biceps which once carried her upstairs and would again. She reached for his top button and saw his pupils dilate with immediacy, obscuring the stunning grey irises with instant darkness. A flicker passed between them as the button slid through its slot and Logan's lips parted as hope burgeoned.

Hana leaned down and tasted him, his mouth smooth and dry beneath hers. Powerful fingers settled either side of her waist and she revelled in the secure feeling his grip gave her. It would all be fine; Mac, everything. Logan Du Rose made it right just by being there with her, his kisses so soft but capable of furious passion. "I love you," she whispered, their lips touching as she murmured the treasured words. His body told her he knew, chest hard against her breasts and his hands pushing through the back of her hair and cupping her neck.

Logan stood in a fluid movement, the muscles bunching and flexing as he commanded his body to lift Hana, not permitting a millimetre of separation between them. He carried her up the stairs and past the room where three dependent children tugged on the umbilical cord of parenthood.

Closing the door with his foot he laid Hana on the bed and undressed her, stopping to admire every part of her body. His work-worn hands caressed the silvery traces on her skin where her womb stretched to carry his babies and grateful lips kissed and nibbled their curving trails. A patient man he took his time, relenting when the icy room temperature drove them beneath the sheets Hana brought from home. He enveloped them in a tent which smelled of the mountain and Hana responded to his touch with a frenzy of frustration only satiated when he bound her to him and rocked their bodies in familiar pleasure.

"It will be okay," he promised again as they hid in the warmth of their joint body heat. Hana moved her head on his chest and nodded, listening to the sound of her hair moving across Logan's soft skin. The fingers of her left hand sought the whakapapa tattoo on his right shoulder, tracing the memorised genealogy, reading it like braille and seeking reassurance from the tangata whenua honoured there.

"Mac's deaf. We both know it. Tests won't change that." Her voice sounded loud and aggressive in the darkness but Logan responded by pulling her closer and wrapping the sheets tighter around them.

"I don't care. He's my son."

"I think I caused it." Hana let the statement do its worst, waiting for Logan to react and surprised when he didn't. She lifted her head. "Say something."

"What's to say? You didn't."

Hana raised herself up onto her elbows and chewed her lip, seeking Logan's gaze in the darkness and failing. "I discharged a loaded shotgun right next to him only minutes after he was born. It might've burst his eardrums." She heard Logan's head move on the pillow and his fingers clasped around her shoulders, forcing her down onto his chest. He resettled until she lay on top of him, their bodies molding together in a familiar posture. Her toes wiggled against the hair on his shins and she nestled in, seeking comfort and absolution for her terrible crime. Logan's arms wrapped around her back and his fingers locked.

"You protected our son, Hana. I've never told you how grateful I am and I should've. It took courage to sit in that bathroom in the state you were in and face whatever came through that door with a loaded twelve bore. I admire you wahine and even if Mac's deafness is the result of that, nothing will change how I feel about you and him. You and my tamariki are the only thing that matters to me. Don't forget that. There's nothing else I value more. We'll deal with what happens next just like we always have but please, Hana, give yourself a break."

She cried then, silent tears rolling across Logan's shoulder and tumbling onto the mattress with a faint plop in the darkness. He smoothed his large palms across her soft back but refused to let her dwell on her guilt, banishing it with easy kisses and mind blowing sex which drove all other thoughts away. Hana's sleep when it finally came was laced with exhaustion and she stayed close to Logan throughout the night, seeking his warmth and surety like oxygen.

It would all be fine. He'd promised.

26

Drama and Blessing

"**I**'ve left him!"

Hana stood at the front door with a blue plastic baby spoon in her fingers. Her lips moved, but no sound emerged. Leslie gave her a hearty shove and weaved past her into the house. Her buttocks wobbled in the too tight dress as she bent to prod off her shoes with a practiced finger. "Nasty old man. I've come to live with youse."

Logan emerged from the kitchen with a grizzling Mac on his hip. "Hana, this kid's hungry. What's going on?" He gaped at the sight of his stepmother hauling ass towards him with her arms outstretched. "Hi." He sent a nervous glance Hana's way as Mac tipped forward into his grandmother's arms and pushed his face into her shoulder. He tensed and pressed sore gums into her ample flesh and Leslie dropped into the role with ease, patting his back and ruffling his ginger hair.

"Is my bub teething?" she demanded, entering the kitchen. Hana heard the squeals of delight from Phoenix and Wiri as they spotted her. Loud chatter commenced and Hana swallowed and looked at Logan with apology in her eyes.

Logan ran a hand over his face and rolled his eyes. "Great!" he bit. "We haven't been here twenty-four hours yet and already they're hunting us down like possums."

Hana chewed her lip and stifled a laugh. "Drama queen," she chided him, leaning against the front door to close it.

"Hey!" The shout sounded muffled through the heavy wood and Hana spotted a shape moving behind the stained glass beyond. She jumped in surprise and Logan stiffened and shielded her, his defensive stance offering protection. He snatched the door open and Caleb stood on the tufty mat, balancing on his crutches. His eyes widened in alarm at Logan's balled fists and the determined look in his eyes. "You said I could come!" he insisted. His voice rose. "You invited me!"

Logan exhaled in a hiss and stood back with exaggerated aplomb like a doorman. "Course we did. Everyone's welcome. All it needs now is..."

"Hi. There's no room on the drive so we've parked near the school. Hope that's all right." Hana's eldest son waited with impatience for Caleb to clack his way across the threshold and then he reached for her, drawing her into strong, brown hands. "Is there a party?"

"Kind of." Hana accepted his embrace and greeted her daughter-in-law who carried their daughter. Hope buried her face in Amy's shoulder, needing time to warm up to Hana after time away. Jas shoved his way between everyone's legs and looked up at his grandmother, his mouth opening to issue immediate demands.

"I want Phoe to line up outside. We're doing a parade and she's my colour sergeant." He leaned back so Hana could see the tee-shirt; designed to resemble an army uniform complete with green tie and epaulettes.

"She's having breakfast," Hana said, bending for a kiss and feeling disappointed as the child strode along the hallway.

"Everyone outside!" he bawled entering the kitchen and Bodie jogged after him to deal with the ensuing chaos.

As the crowd moved away from the door, Logan slipped outside and stood on the deck in his socks. Hana followed him and laid a hand on his shoulder with a light touch. "You're not leaving?" Her face betrayed anxiety and he drew her into his side with a strong arm around her waist.

"I feel like it."

"Me too. Can I come?" Hana listened to the hike in volume coming from the villa and felt her heart sink. "What just happened?"

"We got invaded," her husband replied, shielding his eyes to stare at the school buildings scattered throughout the distance.

"Will you stay?" Hana turned and pushed her face into Logan's chest, wanting the same security he offered the night before. "I know you're avoiding Bodie but please stay this time."

Logan shrugged. "It's best if I'm not around him."

"Why?" Hana heard the whine in her voice.

Logan planted a kiss on the top of her head. "Because smacking the snot out of a cop isn't on my list of things to do today."

"Stay with me." The begging edge in her voice forced Logan to relent.

"Fine. I'll try," he sighed. "I'll be the bigger man."

Hana snorted. "You are the bigger man, idiot."

Logan bent his neck and sought her lips, dragging her hips in to meet his body. Determined hands cradled her back and desire sparked between them as he made the kiss last long enough to leave Hana gasping.

"You're always kissin'!" Wiri's admonishment made Hana smile, her lips against Logan's. He sounded sulky, the presence of Jaspal like salt in his raw wounds.

"We're allowed to," Hana retorted. "You'll kiss lots when you get married."

"No, I won't!" Wiri squished his face into an ugly blob of mismatched features and stuck his tongue out. "Scustin!"

"What's up, mate?" Logan pushed his hand into the back pocket of Hana's jeans and she felt his fingers against her bum, warm and teasing.

"That kid's bossing me. I don't like it. And Caleb needs to pee but he can't get up the stairs on his sticks. Macky's crying and Nonie's pissing me off already."

"Wiri!" Hana gave him the benefit of her shocked expression. "No swearing."

"Sorry." He didn't look sorry, eyeing the lush green grass of the soccer pitch in the distance. "Can I play on that?"

"Not by yourself." Hana released herself from Logan's grasp but kept hold of his hand to stop him bolting from the whānau overload. She yanked his fingers to make him follow her indoors and then closed the door behind them. She turned the key and put it in her pocket, glaring at her tall husband.

"There're other doors," he muttered, his grey eyes glinting with mischief.

"Use them at your peril," Hana hissed and he wiped the smile from his lips.

"I'm whipped, Wiri," he sighed, ruffling the boy's dark hair. "Whipped by my kō. What's the world coming to?"

"You love it, Pa," the child chortled, catching Logan's hand and skipping through to the kitchen.

Hana watched their progress, tasting the Du Rose testosterone in the air and scenting trouble already.

Leslie fed Mac at the table, pushing porridge between his pink lips and burbling baby talk into his face. He grinned and accepted the food from her, slapping the table top with his hands and balancing on her knee. Logan busied himself boiling the kettle for drinks and ignoring the visitors, casting a pall of grey cloud over the proceedings. Hana watched the hard set of his shoulders and saw the back of his neck stiffen as Bodie made his first demand of the visit. "It's great that you're here; Jas starts back at school tomorrow and Amy's rostered on the same shift as me. Hope can go to her childminder as usual but we need you to pick Jas up and then get Hope. I'll give you directions."

Hana opened her mouth to speak but Logan turned wielding an ancient looking blue teapot and answered for her. "She can't. Wiri starts his new school so she'll be there."

Leslie parted her lips to volunteer her services but one look at Logan's raised eyebrow silenced her.

"Can I get Nonie's car keys, Ma?" Wiri's small voice came from the doorway and Hana looked at the distress on his face. She heard Jas bossing Phoenix around in the room next door, his voice raised as he delivered a series of barked orders. "Caleb's got stuff in her car. Then can I go back to bed? I'm tired."

Hana crooked a finger and invited the child onto her lap, pushing the chair back to accommodate him. She kissed the back of his head and wrapped her arms around him. "We'll go for a walk later," she promised. "We'll take a ball."

"Will Papa play footy with me? Can I go in goal?" He turned to look at Logan, comforted by whatever he saw there. Slipping off Hana's knee he snatched Leslie's keys off the counter. He strolled through the doorway, turning left away from Jas and his personal army. "I'll just help Caleb, Ma. He's got bags."

Hana winced and met the accusation in her son's eyes. "Why's he calling you, Ma?"

Logan dumped the teapot on the table and clattered in a cupboard rounding up mugs. "Help yourselves." He darted a quick smile at Amy and then made towards the door. "I'll check on Caleb."

"Why is he calling you, Ma?" Bodie demanded. "He's not your kid. Doesn't he belong to that other loser up at the hotel?"

Leslie hissed through her teeth at the insult and lifted a dozing Mac over her shoulder. "I'll change this wee pirinihi." She exited and Hana cringed, her body tensing in the faint hope that Bodie didn't understand the Māori word for prince. He'd barely accepted Phoenix and Mac without hearing his baby brother elevated over his delicate ego.

"So," Bodie launched, "you can't get your grandson because you're picking someone else's kid up instead." Statement not question. Hana felt her heart quail at the instant attack. "You hardly ever see your proper family anymore; you're so consumed by the bloody Du Roses and their problems. What're you doing, Mum? Is this what you want?"

"Stop!" Hana's shout took him by surprise and Amy turned to look through the window, bouncing her daughter on her hip. "Do you not have any other topic of conversation? I'd love to see more of you. I'm desperate to see my grandchildren but you do this every time; pick a fight over the same thing." She stood and shoved her chair under the table with a loud scrape, not sure how to proceed with the air hanging around her like a choking mist. "If you'd given me some warning, I'd have done my best to accommodate you just like I've done the millions of other times I've helped you out."

"Told you," Amy muttered under her breath.

"So, you won't do it then!" Bodie stood and let his chair skitter across the tiles. "Thanks for nothing and welcome back! I don't suppose I'll see much of you with all the other demands on your precious time." He stalked from the kitchen, his dark skin contrasting with the whiteness of the paintwork. Hana felt her heart snap as he shouted to his son. "Jas. Come on; we're leaving. Now!"

"Sorry," Amy said, touching Hana's arm as she moved past with Hope, who'd just warmed up enough to begin a smiling game with her grandmother.

"I don't want to!" Jas yelled and Hana heard his little feet pounding along the corridor. He burst through the doorway and launched himself at Hana, clutching her legs. "Hanny, tell them I'm staying here! I've got stuff to do."

Hana stroked his hair and held onto her nerve as Bodie appeared in the doorway, his face channelling hatred and rejection from a wounded ego. "The front door's locked!" He held his hand out for the key Hana retrieved from her jeans pocket and placed into his brown palm, her heart quailing in her chest. Bodie grabbed Jas by the arm and hauled him away, glaring at his mother with venom in his eyes. "You've changed!" he snapped. "You've forgotten what really matters!"

The front door slammed and they left, the blood tie aching against the growing feud. Hana put her face in her hands and felt the wetness on her palms as she struggled to process the fifteen-minute disaster. Caleb's crutches clicked into the kitchen but he hovered in the doorway before clanking away along the corridor. Hana heard him scrape his way to the classroom next door where Logan had lit a fire and put the TV on for the children.

Her husband gave her time before he scooped her up in his arms, enfolding her in his strength and trying to sap some of the pain. Hana dried her tears on his white tee shirt, seeing the mascara blotches arc out in strange lines. "You knew he'd start making demands, didn't you?"

She felt Logan shrug against her. "I guessed. Every time you do what he wants it makes him feel like he's gained ground; got an edge."

"It shouldn't be a damn competition!" Hana wailed. "Why can't he just be pleased to see me?"

"Because of me, Hana." Logan kissed her temple. "He won't stop until he gets what he wants; me and my whānau out of your life."

Hana shook her head. "He won't win."

Logan lifted her chin with his finger and his grey eyes looked stormy like grit, sadness in his face. "One day, Hana. One day he will."

Her eyes widened in determination and she shook her head. "I've given him everything, Loge. Too much. I raised him the same as Izzie and yet they're so different. He wants it all. I gave Amy my car, I sold them Culver's Cottage, I've run around after them both and bent over backwards to be their instant babysitter. I've shown him unconditional love even though I disliked his choices. What else can I do?" She shook her head again. "I've had enough."

"Do nothing today." Logan threaded his fingers through hers. "He's family; be careful not to make decisions you'll regret."

"I know," Hana whispered. Her husband's wisdom came from bitter experience; his own and those of others whose choices had shaped and distorted his world beyond what it could have been in an alternate universe. "What do you suggest?"

Logan stroked her hair and Hana looked up at his angular jaw and the long, majestic nose of his forebears, waiting for his royal pronouncement. In an older tribal structure Logan Du Rose would rule as chief, commanding respect and authority with his God given right as rangatira. The tribes clung to their heritage against the tide of pakeha law but Logan's mana still sang of his birthright and nobility. "Let him cool off and then ring him," Logan said, his voice low and confidential. "Write down how you feel about everything and then meet him somewhere neutral. Ask him to read your words and contribute. Find a resolution and walk through it."

Hana smiled and sniffed away her tears. "A hui? Like in the old days."

Logan shook his head. "Not just the old days, kōtiro. It's how we still sort things out. We just can't sit on the marae for weeks until it's sorted anymore." He sighed. "I'd love to go back to the old days." His grey eyes fixed on her face and he brushed a stray curl from near her mouth, following it with a smoldering kiss. Hana's lips trembled against his as he attempted to drown out the awful sense of loss and the knowledge that something valuable had cracked. Nothing but the strongest glue could repair its fractures.

"Will you come with me to meet him?" Hana asked, her green eyes troubled. She searched Logan's face for help and salvation, quailing at the sad shake of his head.

"No," he replied. "It's best if I don't."

27

Teasing Out the Details

"So, why did you leave Alfie?" Hana pushed another log onto the fire and watched Leslie rock Mac to sleep over her shoulder.

"I can't tell youse." The old woman pouted and Hana stared at her with curiosity; fear lit her features ahead of sadness.

"What did he do?"

"Never you mind." Leslie pursed her lips and Hana felt a shiver of anxiety run through her damaged heart, accompanied by an awful foreboding.

"Now you're worrying me." She knelt up and eyeballed Leslie. "Tell me what's happened."

"It's best you don't know." Leslie patted the baby's back and eyed the door before lowering her voice. "But I've removed the problem so there won't be any more of it."

"Removed the problem?" Hana shook her head, hearing herself parroting Leslie's words. "What problem? Stop talking in riddles."

"Your phone just went off. I think you've got a text." Logan covered the space between them on long legs and put the device into Hana's hand. He ran his fingers through his hair. "Pete rang me. He wants me to pop over to his staff unit and look at some gadget he's made." Logan rolled his eyes. "It's probably broken and he wants help to fix it."

"That didn't take him long," Hana mused. "We've been here less than twenty-four hours and already it's like we never left." Her own words condemned her at the memory of Bodie's meltdown earlier.

"Wiri and Phoe are in bed asleep. I've set up a single bed in the room to the left of the front door and there's another bed in the attic room still." Logan directed his last comment towards Leslie and she avoided his eyes.

"Thanks, Logan." She rested her cheek against Mac's and turned to face the fire.

"I can't get the fire going." Hana's fingers reached for another log and Logan shook his head in irritation.

"You've put the paper on top of the kindling and added the logs too soon. It's closed off the oxygen and there's nothing for the flames to grab hold of once they've used up the paper." He fished a ball of charred newspaper from the edges and wrinkled his nose. "And you used wet paper!"

"I didn't know." Hana sulked in the face of his superiority and jumped as Leslie stood and turned towards the door.

"This tamaiti tāne is tired. I'll put him in his cot and take a shower if you don't mind?"

Hana nodded. "There's another bathroom downstairs if you'd rather have your own. It's past the laundry and turn left."

Leslie shuffled from the room without answering and Hana watched her retreating back. "Something's going on," she whispered and Logan glanced sideways at her. She leaned closer and watched his deft fingers place more paper in the fireplace at the bottom of the pile and stoke the ailing flame back to life. "She won't tell me what happened up at the hotel or why she's here. But she did say she 'removed the problem.' What could that be?"

"No idea." Logan didn't sound much like he cared. He unfolded two large sheets and stretched them across the chimney, holding them in place either side with his hands. Orange flames flared behind a photo of Fairfield Bridge and the fire roared as the newspaper drew the air harder through the flames. "Who knows how their marriage works?"

Hana laid her cheek against Logan's bulging bicep. "Stay home with me," she murmured and saw the corners of his lips quirk upwards.

"Why, babe? What's the matter?"

"Dunno." Hana sighed. "Bedroom's cold and I don't want to go up there by myself."

Logan gave a low sound like a chuckle. "I'll just nip to Pete's and come straight home. I won't be long." He kissed the top of her head. "Then I'll warm you up. Promise."

"Hi there." Caleb's crutches clattered into the room and Hana watched Logan turn away from him with a look of distaste. Her heart sank.

"Hi. You settled in?" She fixed a smile on her face and summoned up a spirit of welcome, knowing from the set of Caleb's shoulders; she'd failed. Logan stood up and stretched his long body, lifting his arms above his head and yawning. Hana admired his physique but a glance at Caleb's face showed her he saw something different. The air crackled with testosterone as the powerful alpha male issued a silent, physical threat and the teenager quailed. Hana raised an eyebrow at her husband and watched the smirk begin on his angular face.

"See you in a while," he said, leaning down to stroke her cheek with gentle fingers. The look he gave Caleb as he passed him was fierce enough to draw colour from the boy's face.

Hana listened to Logan putting his cowboy boots on and the sound of the front door shutting with a click. "I'll just leave the front door unlocked for you," she said to Caleb. "We're safe enough on the school grounds and besides, they only gave us one key. Everyone on site with a master key can get in so it's just as well we brought nothing valuable."

"I won't be going far, will I?" He slumped into a stuffed armchair with a sigh and clattered his crutches to the floorboards. "I'm stuck here now."

Hana narrowed her brows and shrugged. "Why did you come, then? I thought you were adamant about staying at the hotel."

"That old woman made me." Caleb pouted and Hana heard the alarm bells in her brain.

"Why?" She narrowed her eyes. "I know something happened after we left but Leslie won't tell me what."

Caleb swallowed. "She had a massive argument with the old bloke. I missed you and the kids. After you left nobody came to see me and it got lonely."

"Ah, sweet." Hana mellowed, suspicion laid to rest in the face of the teenager's admission. "So you hitched a ride with Leslie?"

"Yeah." He looked pleased with himself. "You said there'd be room." He cocked his head to one side and levelled blue eyes in her direction. "Who was the Indian dude? Is he your son?"

Hana nodded. "Yep, that's Bodie, my eldest son. His sister's called Isobel and she's awesome. I need to make the trip down to see her again soon, but Invercargill's ages away with three little children on a plane."

"Invercargill? That's like, the other end of the planet."

"No, just the other end of the country," Hana mused. "I'll talk to Logan; maybe he'll come with me to help with the little ones."

"He hates me." Caleb picked at a fleck on his jeans, wincing at how the action moved his plaster cast. "He doesn't want me here."

"Logan hasn't said that." Hana stood up and brushed dust from her trousers. She heard Leslie moving overhead and wondered how she could get the wily old lady to spill her secrets.

"He doesn't need to. Asher said he makes it real clear when he wants rid of you."

"Asher!" Hana fixed a steely gaze on Caleb's face. "How do you know Asher?"

He licked his lips, focusing his attention on the rolled up leg of his jeans and neatening the uppermost edge against his cast. "I met him at the hotel."

"Asher's not allowed near the hotel." Hana put her hands on her hips and stared Caleb down. "He's allowed to live with Nev but not set foot on the rest of the property. I'm guessing you didn't go for a stroll to the other side of the mountain, so how did you meet him?"

Caleb groaned. "It's no big deal, Hana! His dad sent him around with some gear for the old bloke who lives upstairs. Please don't tell Logan?"

"For Alfred?" She felt her heart rate hike and instinctively touched the outline of the pacemaker. "He knows Asher's not allowed there. Logan needs to know."

"No!" Caleb jumped up and balanced on one leg, reaching out for Hana. "Please, don't do that! I wasn't meant to tell you. If your husband charges in there and chucks him out of his home, he'll blame me." He hopped towards Hana, his cast trailing behind him. The effort pained him and as he passed the sofa he sank down into its folds with relief.

Hana swallowed and her fingers fluttered in front of her. Keen to busy them, she seized a decorative mug from the mantelpiece. "It's not like you'll ever see him again," she said, her tone tight and wooden. "Once your cast is off, you'll move on. You won't go back to Mātakitaki."

Caleb's eyes widened in surprise. "Yeah, I will! I need to go back to where my dad lived last. That's there, at the hotel."

"Your dad lived at the hotel?" Hana's lips parted in shock. "You've never mentioned it."

"He did though. I followed him there. People know him. I have to find him."

"Who's your dad?" The words emerged as a husky whisper but as she watched Caleb writhe in discomfort, the similarities were startling and she wondered why she'd never seen it before. The teenager's reply drove her hands to her face in horror and Hana sank to her knees in front of the fire.

28

The Worst of Shocks

"What did you say?" The colour drained from her porcelain skin as Hana struggled with Caleb's words. The mug slipped from her shaking hand and bounced on the floorboards, sprinkling shards around her from tiny chips in the surface. Hana stared at the mess and ran a trembling hand over her face, the horror in her green eyes mirroring the devastation on the floor.

"Hana?" Caleb grappled with the sofa arm to haul himself upright, reaching sideways for the crutch nearest the armchair and bending double to retrieve it. He grunted. "Why are you being like this?" He resembled a pantomime pirate as he bounced towards her on one leg with the crutch sticking out sideways.

"No! Don't touch me!" Hana raised a hand towards him, warding him off and backing away as he reached her.

"What did he do?" Caleb's face filled with panic. "Did my dad hurt you? What happened?"

"Not him! You!" Hana shouted, her eyes wide with manic fear. "You ruined my life!"

Caleb's crutch scraped across the floorboards as he dragged his body towards her. Confusion reigned in his blue eyes. "No. No, I didn't. I'd never hurt you."

Hana continued to back away from the young man on her knees, causing him to swivel on his crutch and risk tipping over sideways. "Which one were you?" she spat. "Did you attack me or were you the one who broke my windscreen?"

Caleb's face paled. "Neither. I did none of those things. I don't know what you're talking about."

"Your family made my life hell!" Hana gasped, backing up so her spine rested against the sofa. "Nothing was ever the same again. They came after me for a year and I didn't know what they wanted. Now you turn up here pretending to be lost. How could you do that? You've taken our hospitality and kindness, when all the time you were lying!" She waved her hand at the damaging photograph in Caleb's hand, her lips curling back in an ugly sneer.

"I'm just me!" Caleb's face held all the emotion of a kicked puppy. "None of this makes sense. I wouldn't hurt you; I'm happy with you."

"Oh, I bet you are!" Hana snapped. Hot tears dusted her cheeks and bounced off her clothes. "You must have a real laugh at me, foolish, gullible woman!" She sniffed and wiped her nose on the back of her hand and her voice hitched. "Why am I always so stupid?"

"You're not, please listen? You're kind and beautiful and I appreciate everything you've done for me. Don't judge me, please, not when you've been so open-hearted until now."

Hana put her hands over her eyes and swallowed. She wanted the young man to leave and narrowly stopped herself yelling at him to get out. A voice in her head told her not to be cruel. Caleb hovered in front of her, resting his weight on the good leg, his face a mask of pain and confusion. "Can I explain?" he begged. The faded picture of a much younger Flick holding hands with a slender blonde woman seemed to mock Hana's foolishness. It dangled from Caleb's fingers like his greatest treasure.

"I don't know if I want to hear it." Hana squeezed the bridge of her nose. "I thought you didn't know who the Du Roses were and believed you were genuinely lost. Was it all lies?"

"No!" Caleb risked hobbling forward, his expression fearful. "None of it was lies. Please, hear me out and then I'll leave if you want me to."

Hana nodded, the still small voice in her ear telling her to give the kid a break. Caleb shuffled backwards and hefted himself into his armchair. He sighed. "I told you the truth; my dad died and Mum's new bloke killed him. We sat through court for weeks during the trial after we'd given evidence and the jury found him guilty. We walked out of court and stood on the steps and my mum turned to me and said, *'Can we try to get things back to normal?'* She said it like it was no big deal to watch her partner convicted for her husband's murder and I stared at her for ages wondering if she was serious."

Caleb gulped and ran a hand over his face. "I asked her who my real dad was and she shook her head. *'Just a man I loved once,'* she said. *'But he left before I could tell him about you. He's gone, Caleb. Come home and let's make this work, just the two of us.'* I looked at her and realised I never knew her. She didn't care when her boyfriend knocked the shit out of me and she didn't care that my dad was dead because of him. I asked her for his name and she said, *'Robert, Robert Dressler, but you'll never find him.'* I said goodbye and walked away. She didn't come after me and I've spent months looking for my dad, Hana."

Hana squeezed the bridge of her nose between her finger and thumb. "You said you lived with a girl in Auckland. Was that the truth?"

"Yeah." Caleb nodded. "I met the girl I told you about and lived with her folks, working at a dairy in town for an Indian family. Dressler's not a common name, so it was easy to track down an uncle in Henderson, who put me on to a step family in the north, although they had a different name." Caleb smiled with pride. "New Zealand's not that big and I'm quite good at following leads and keeping notes. The dairy owner let me make local calls from the landline during my breaks."

His face clouded. "I made so many phone calls, word got back to my half-brother; I'm guessing he's the one you met. The day after he got out of prison, he tracked me down in the dairy and turned up with some nasty mates. He told me to stay away from his family and robbed the till while his buddy held a knife to my throat. They terrified the owner's wife and told her if she didn't get rid of me, they'd come back. The Indians family were good people, Hana. They were nice to me so I gave a statement to the cops and then quit. I got home early to find my girlfriend in bed with another guy and couldn't stay."

Caleb glanced at a misshapen index finger on his right hand. "I think I broke his nose; hope so anyway." He shrugged. "I hitch hiked south to Rangiriri where I asked around about my dad and described him to a few locals. They clammed up and went quiet. I figured they knew him but didn't want to tell me, so I hung around to see if he turned up."

He wiped his hand frantically over his face, masking the sadness in his eyes. "I didn't know who the Du Roses were until I met a guy fencing a paddock at the bottom of the mountain. He said Logan Du Rose would kill me and hide the body if he found me on his land. I pretended to leave, back tracked and booked myself into the camp site for a few weeks. I bought a knackered tent from a couple going home to Holland and that lasted a while, but then it ripped in that big storm two months ago and I've lived rough in the bush ever since."

"What did you hope to achieve doing that?" Hana asked, curiosity budding in her chest. "How could you find your father from a shack in the middle of nowhere?"

"I didn't stay there all the time." Caleb looked pleased with himself, puffing up his chest and seeking Hana's approval. "I stored my gear there and moved around. It seemed easy to pretend to be a back packer and watch Logan's men. I learned their names and listened to what they talked about. One afternoon I hid from some stockmen and heard them talking about Flick as they rode by on horses. It's the name my half-brother used in the dairy so I got excited. I knew my father lived there."

Hana sighed. "He's not on the mountain, Caleb."

"Yeah, he is," the teenager argued. "That's his nickname. I heard them say it but they moved away too fast." He glanced down at the cast on his leg. "I broke my leg the next day as I packed up. I figured if I went down to the hotel I might find work in the kitchens or something. The pig ran past and I thought I'd kill it and save the meat in case I needed to go back to the hut."

"Was David one of the stockmen you heard talking?" Hana asked, the afternoon's events falling into place like a jigsaw puzzle.

Caleb's eyes widened. "Yeah, the one with curly blonde hair. He knows where my dad is."

Hana slumped with her head in her hands, the huge sigh escaping her lips. "He doesn't. I promise you, David's the last person to know where Bobby is."

"Bobby? His family up north called him that." Hope burgeoned in the teen's eyes and Hana bit her lip.

"I'm the only one who used that name," Hana said, her jaw working. "We became allies at a time when life with the Du Roses wasn't easy. I miss him." She pursed her lips.

Caleb's eyes looked red with the effort of not crying, the last of his fragile ego holding on by a thread. "He's dead, isn't he? I came all this way and he's dead. I've got nobody." His chin sank to his chest as the teenager jumped to wrong conclusions. "Did Logan kill him? I bet he could."

"No!" Hana regretted the irritation in her voice. "My husband killed no one." *Not as far as I know.* "And Bobby's not dead. He left and he can't come back."

"He's still alive?" Caleb gulped. "Where is he? Can I see him? At least tell me what happened to him, preferably before you throw me out?"

Hana edged towards the sofa and sank into its folds. She wrung her hands together. "Bobby's not dead, but I can't tell you where he is because I don't know. Logan took him to the mountain for his own safety and he worked for us for a couple of years. He became a great stockman and Logan trusted him. He oversaw our house build and became a friend to both of us. The day Mac came, Logan's grandfather tried to kill us but your father stopped him. The last time I saw Bobby, he handed me a gun and went outside to find him. When they found Jack's body I thought your father killed him and panicked. I persuaded Logan to give him a new identity and get him away from the mountain. Bobby left the same day."

Hana studied the young man's face through the silence. Caleb's eyes opened wide, pitching between disbelief and something she couldn't read. He inhaled and swallowed. "But he's not dead?"

"No, he's not dead!" Hana's stress emerged as irritation. "He's fine. He wrote to me and returned something of mine. I had heard nothing about him until recently, but that's not surprising."

"What did you hear?" Caleb leaned forward.

"Just that he'd got a new girlfriend." Hana chewed the inside of her lip. "But I heard it third hand so I can't promise it's true."

"Did my dad kill the man who hurt you and your baby?" The strain put an involuntary croak into Caleb's voice. "Is my real dad a murderer?"

Hana shook her head, careful with her words. Bobby offered to kill Logan enough times and she couldn't be certain he hadn't killed before he reformed into a trustworthy employee. "A horse kicked Jack to death," she said. "Bobby didn't kill him. But he'd been in trouble with the police before. That's why he stayed on the mountain so long; to avoid arrest. He witnessed Jack threatening to kill me but couldn't give a statement and risk being jailed, so Logan moved him."

"To another town?" Caleb's intense gaze burned holes in Hana's soul as she shook her head.

"To another country. Sorry."

The teenager let out a huge sigh. "I found something of his at the hut." His voice sounded pitiful. "It's a knife with a wooden handle. The blade shoots out when you flick the catch. A flick knife. My half-brother said it's how he got his nickname."

"I recognised it when I cut your trousers." Hana swallowed. "How could you know it belonged to him?"

Caleb shrugged. "Just a feeling. It's what I'd choose too, simple but deadly."

"I thought your brother threatened you and robbed the shop." Hana's eyes narrowed. "You make it sound like you sat down and talked."

Caleb's blue eyes flashed with confusion and he shook his head. "He did rob the dairy. Don't you believe me?"

Hana swallowed and dismissed her misgivings. "Yes, I believe you. Bobby perhaps left the knife by accident. He stayed at the hut when he guarded the house." The memory still tasted fresh in her mind. "Jack Du Rose watched me for months from the bush. If Bobby didn't come when he did, I'd be dead." She gulped. "I owe him my life and my son's."

Caleb's smile looked watery. "I never had my dad pegged as some kinda hero."

"Well, he was that day." Hana sounded defensive. She avoided thinking of the blonde stockman's shameless adoration. In those last months of her pregnancy, Bobby proved Hana's staunchest protector. She thought of his vibrant blue eyes and the way he looked at her and allowed the sensation to flood back into her heart. "I miss him," she breathed.

"Did you love him?" Caleb's voice wavered. "Did you..."

"No!" Hana shouted the word. "It wasn't like that!" *It wasn't for me, but it was for him.* She stood and stalked to the window and her eyes raked the dark soccer pitches beyond the glass. "Why does your generation make everything dirty?"

"Sorry." Caleb hung his head. "Tell me how I can contact him?"

Hana shook her head and avoided his flashing blue eyes, her arms folded tightly across her chest. "I can't, sorry. Only Logan knows; he won't tell me and I can't ask."

She heard a sniff behind her and turned, catching the teenager wiping his eyes on the corner of his sleeve. The fabric did little to stem the gentle flow of salty tears traversing his pale cheeks and his body jerked with the effort of not drawing attention to himself. Hana closed her eyes and shook her head, willing herself not to be moved but she wasn't hard wired to ignore suffering.

Caleb's head sank onto Hana's shoulder as she dropped to her knees next to him. His body heaved with misery and he cried with quiet dignity as she folded him into her. She struggled not to cry with him, feeling the raw edges of his grief at having come so far and achieved nothing. Hana stroked his soft hair and patted his back, feeling her shirt grow more sodden with every passing minute.

Her words returned to bite her. She told Robert Dressler's son the truth; missing Bobby's true friendship with a tangible ache as his absence condemned her to the testosterone laden Du Roses. Hana gulped and patted Caleb's back, whispering soothing words devoid of any practical cure. "It's okay, baby," she whispered. "I know it hurts."

"Do you?" he sobbed and felt Hana nod against the back of his head.

"Yeah, Caleb, I do. I know how it feels to be fatherless and so does Logan."

"Please talk to him for me?" he begged. The teenager sat up, his face soaked and the skin tight and flushed. "Please, Hana?"

She smiled and shook her head. "I can't, Caleb. But you can. It's between you and my husband; I have to stay out of it. Sorry."

Hana's features appeared wooden and fixed in place. Bobby told her he loved her and she wouldn't let it damage her marriage again.

"How do you know the Du Roses didn't bury him?" Caleb asked, punctuating his sentence with a disgusting sniff.

"I told you; your father wrote me a letter. It arrived in the mail after he left." Hana disconnected and stood, wanting the conversation over. "Logan heard recently that he got a new girlfriend. He'll be back soon; you can ask him then." She stared through the window, her expression distant.

Caleb raised his hand as Hana turned to leave the room. "Can I read the letter? Please?"

She swallowed and avoided his eyes. "No. I destroyed it." Her brow narrowed and she fixed a determined look on her face. Hana felt the suspicion in Caleb's glare as he watched her. "I'm tired. I need to go to bed."

Hana mobilised herself and headed to bed after checking on her sleeping children. Something felt wrong and she couldn't put her finger on it. Sickness flooded her senses and she checked on Mac four times more before she could settle. "I'm sorry," she whispered into the silent room. "I'm sorry if your deafness is my fault." Her chest hitched as thoughts of Flick strayed inevitably to the last time she saw him, helping her load the gun and telling her to fire at the next face which appeared in the doorway. She lay in the cold bed and craved her husband, needing Caleb out of her house with a desperation which frightened her.

29

The Truth Hurts

"What did Pete want?" Hana dropped her book onto the bed and sat up, fluffing pillows behind her for support.

"I wasn't long." Logan stripped his tee shirt over his head and shivered in the cold. "Just an hour."

"I know; I need a cuddle." Hana pouted and watched Logan unzip his jeans and drop them to his ankles. Muscular legs stepped out of them and his thighs tensed as he bent to retrieve them and folded the fabric with precision, laying them over the bedroom chair in the corner.

"It's freezing!" he exclaimed. "Bloody hell!" He disappeared beside the bed and Hana leaned over to see where he'd gone. She watched his head bob up and down as he performed twenty press-ups on bunched biceps before slipping beneath the covers. "That's warmed me up." He sighed. "Come here, baby. I've a promise to keep."

Hana snuggled into his armpit and sniffed his distinctive scent; mountain air and sunshine. "What did Pete want?"

Logan snorted. "Henrietta bought this trampoline to exercise on and he saw a thing on the TV which literally wobbles the fat out of you. It's a load of crap but he thought it might work. Instead of buying a real device, he nicked some crocodile clips from the physics laboratory and wired it to the metal on the trampoline."

"You're kidding!" Hana gasped in horror. "He'll kill her."

"Yeah, that's what I told him. I've confiscated the crocodile clips."

"Far out!" Hana buried her face in Logan's side and imagined an electrified Henrietta bouncing her buxom self on a wired trampoline. "Doesn't he want to stay married to her anymore?" She heard the smile in Logan's voice.

"Nah, he's just a cheapskate. He wanted me to help him wedge the clips onto the frame because they wouldn't open wide enough."

"That guy's scary," Hana sighed. "He wore the same clothes for nine years and only washed them in the holidays. I don't think he ever cleaned his jacket."

"He did when I moved into the flat; I dragged it from his wriggling body every Friday night!" Logan turned on his side and wrapped his arms around her, pulling her close. The hair on his chest tickled her nose and she relaxed, shrouded in safety.

"Logan, I need to talk to you." Her voice sounded plaintive in the darkness and she heard her husband sigh. He covered her lips with his and smothered them in softness as he strengthened the kiss. Tender fingers slipped beneath the waistband of her pyjamas and tugged. Hana moaned and then remembered her dilemma. "Logan," she began and he silenced her with another long kiss. He spoke against her mouth, reluctant to break their connection.

"I rushed home to keep my promise," he whispered. "I'll listen to you later but right now, kōtiro, I just wanna show you how much I love you." He nipped at the soft skin beneath Hana's jaw and she exhaled in a rush. Easing the ugly flannelette pants over her rounded buttocks, Logan groaned with pleasure at the action of her wandering hands and his breath felt warm on her cool cheeks.

"I love you, Logan." Hana allowed him to pull her on top of him, her pants legs trailing across the bed and tangling their ankles together like a noose. His boxer shorts felt rough against the tender skin of her stomach and she wiggled against them.

Logan bit his lower lip and his long lashes swished closed. "You have no idea," he whispered. His hand moved behind Hana's head and forced her lips over his while the other hand made light work of her pyjama shirt. The temperature between them hiked and Hana forgot the biting air which seeped around the joints of the old window frames as she lost herself in Logan's warm attentions. She placed her palm over his mouth as his enthusiasm produced more than a decent level of noise. "Stop!" she hissed. "Leslie and Caleb will hear us from opposite ends of the house."

He laughed at her when she cried out with pleasure, nibbling the soft skin of her neck. Logan honoured his promise, leaving Hana breathless and forced to kick off the covers. When his fingers brushed along the curve of her breast, she giggled and pushed his hand away. "No, you've paid in full," she protested, dodging the questing hand. "You've worn me out."

"Lightweight!" Logan scoffed. "Call yerself a Du Rose; you've no stamina, wahine."

"You're probably right." Hana rolled onto her side facing his outline in the darkness and reached out to touch his firm chest. "I still need to talk to you."

"No, not talking; more kissing," he grumbled and Hana swallowed and steeled herself for the awkward conversation.

"We promised no more secrets and I need to tell you something."

Logan exhaled into the darkness and turned to face her, snagging the sheet in his fingers and hauling it over both of them. "Okay. Hit me with it," he breathed and Hana felt his body tense on the mattress.

Hana's words emerged as stilted and afraid; making her admission in the confessional of the borrowed marriage bed. "I think I know what's rattled Leslie," she said, inhaling and holding the breath as Logan made no sound. "Nev used Asher to run errands to Alfred, despite you saying he wasn't allowed on the property."

"Did he damage anything?" Logan asked and Hana flushed in the darkness; a child telling tales out of school.

"I don't think so."

She heard Logan's hair swish against the pillow. "I'll let it go this time. It's not worth the cost of their marriage. I'll make sure Leslie knows that, although it seems a bit extreme doesn't it?"

"That's not all." Hana swallowed. "I found out tonight who Caleb's father is."

"What?" Logan faced her and she sensed his confusion. "What's that got to do with anything?"

"It's why he's here." Hana pushed herself to a sitting position and hugged her knees. "He heard his dad worked for you and tracked him to the hotel. He stayed in the camp ground until his money ran out and then slept rough in the hut."

"Worked for me?" Logan repeated the words, his brain running through possibilities. "Is he a Du Rose?"

"No." Hana gulped and released the damaging words. "He's Flick's son."

"What?" Logan sat up using his stomach muscles and turned to face her. Leaning across he gripped her wrist. "Promise me you didn't know!"

"I didn't." Hana fixed the fingers of her other hand over Logan's, attempting to loosen his grasp. "Bobby doesn't know about him; it's okay, he's not one of the two sons from Hamilton. Caleb only found out a few months ago and he's been looking for him ever since."

"Bloody hell!" Logan dropped Hana's wrist as though she might contaminate him and spun from the bed naked.

"Where are you going?" She slipped into the freezing cold air and blocked the doorway, arms outstretched either side of her.

"I'm throwing him out!" Logan snarled through gritted teeth. "I should've known. There were a couple of times when I saw something in his face and felt like I knew him. I don't want Flick's kid here, Hana, not near you or my children." He punched his balled fist into his other palm.

"He's done nothing wrong," she protested, hugging her cold body. "Apart from looking for his father."

Logan stood in front of her, tall and imposing. His might dwarfed her and Hana felt a shiver of fear. "We promised no more secrets," she grumbled. "I've told you the truth and this is how you react; like I'm the bad guy?" Her hands gave into gravity and slapped her thighs in defeat. "Great! Thanks Logan. You've really restored my faith in honesty and confession. It's been such an amazing experience." She stepped out of his way and slunk back to the bed, still warm from their passion. "Go for it, Logan. Throw him out. Wake the children and scare them with the inevitable shouting and the sight of someone they respect throwing an injured man onto the street." Hana covered herself with the sheet. "You never know; your new boss might promote you for your kindness to humanity." She lay down and turned her back on her seething husband. "You might want to cover up before you go startling everyone."

Hana jumped as the bed moved behind her and Logan's body slipped beneath the covers. He shifted her hair aside and kissed a line down the back of her neck. She jabbed her elbow to the rear and met his ready hand. "Too slow," he hissed and ran his hand from waist to breast. Reaching forwards in slow, deliberate movements he cupped the soft globe in his fingers and let out a shuddering sigh. "I'm sorry."

Hana held her breath. Du Rose men didn't apologise and hearing Logan say the words stilled her troubled heart. He kissed the rise of her shoulder. "You're right. Thanks for being honest and I'll decide what to do in the morning." His beard grazed the space beneath her left ear. "When I've got clothes on."

Smirking, Hana rolled onto her back and put her arm around Logan, pushing her fingers through his dark hair. "Can you say it again please?" she murmured.

"What?" Logan's hand roved across her stomach and his fingers closed around her waist. "I'll kick his ass when I've got clothes on."

Hana snorted. "Not that bit. I wanna hear you say sorry again."

Logan's head jerked backwards and she dug her fingers harder into his hair. "No way," he groaned. "That was a one-time only offer."

"I like hearing you apologise," Hana whispered. "It makes you sexier; an alpha who knows how to bend to his woman's will."

"Whatever!" Logan covered her body with his and pinned her in place, reasserting his dominance and wanting her to massage his wounded ego. "What if I don't mean it?"

30

Self-saboteurs

"Why would Asher disobey you?" Hana yawned and stretched, feeling Logan shift next to her. "He's lucky you allowed him to live with Nev."

"That kid pressed the self-destruct button years ago. Now it's all about waiting for detonation."

"Why though?" Hana turned onto her stomach and shivered in the early morning chill of the old house. She peered at the floor looking for her pyjamas in the gloom. Spotting them over by the window she gave up trying to cover her dignity and pushed her body closer to Logan's.

"Oosh, wahine!" he complained. "Not the feet; they're blocks of ice."

Hana grinned and ran her cool soles up the inside of his warm thigh until Logan clasped them in his big hands and massaged her freezing toes. She purred with pleasure. "Why, then?" she persisted. "What made him press the self-destruct button?"

"No idea," Logan mused. "Maybe it's the cost of living in Reuben's house. Kane didn't provide the greatest role model and Nev's weak. Look at Tama; he'd started along the wrong path as well, but you brought him round."

"Not me. Us." Hana pressed her cold nose against Logan's ribs and he shivered and grumbled his dislike. "You nurtured Tama long before I appeared on the scene."

"Yeah, but what you gave him was different, probably something only a woman possesses. I couldn't match that."

"Asher had that. Anahera's a good mother."

Logan shifted and put an arm out of the covers, testing the chill and knowing he needed to brace himself to face it. He sighed. "But some kids just self-sabotage. Haven't you noticed that?"

Hana nodded against his chest. "Bodie did that heaps. I'd haul him back onto the straight and narrow and things would improve, but the second I let my guard down and trusted him, he'd blow it. There'd be some dumb mate who suggested he did something for a dare and he'd do it without thinking about where it might lead. Then I'd find myself sitting in Angus' office yet again. Bodie would cry, apologise, promise he'd try harder and then back we'd be a few months later sitting in the same seats. It felt endless and exhausting."

"Same with Tama," Logan sighed. "Helping a self-saboteur is like holding the tide back with your hands. You know you're gonna end up slammed face first into the shale, but you stand there anyway and hope you're wrong. Heaps of times I told him I was done and walked away. He'd cry, I'd relent and believe his promises. Then I'd get an email from his primary school as soon as I got back to the UK and wait up until midnight to talk to his teacher. He seemed to get worse after I came home to New Zealand and I hoped Angus could sort him out. Neither Kane nor Michael intended to."

"Did you ever visit this school while I worked here?" Hana's lips caressed Logan's pectoral as she spoke, poking out her tongue to gauge his reaction.

"Yeah. Just day trips to sit in Angus' office and get lectured about responsibility and what goes into creating a respectable young man. I never saw you." Logan sighed. "Five years earlier and I could've saved myself a whole heap of time and trouble." His fingers roved down her thigh and Hana felt him hold his breath, seeking her out in a familiar telepathic link to assess her interest.

"Ma!" Their bedroom door swung open and hit the side of the oak wardrobe with a crash. Hana heard the suitcase edge across the floorboards. Logan jumped, but she'd half expected an interruption and clamped a hand over the cuss word which escaped his lips.

"What?"

"Mac's made a massive stink in the bedroom." Wiri stood in the light from the hallway, his small body a dark silhouette. "Phoe's gonna puke."

Hana groaned. "I'm coming now. Just go to the bathroom and hop in the shower for school."

"You're nudey dudey." Wiri sniggered and Logan turned his head to eyeball the child.

"No, I'm not."

"Yes you are," Wiri giggled. "I can see youse nono stickin' out the bed. It's a big, fat nono too."

"Bathroom!" Hana growled, lifting her head so she could see over Logan's chest. "I won't ask again!"

The child turned away, shoulders slouched in mock irritation and Logan shouted to him. "Shut the door, man!"

Wiri returned, reached up to grab the handle and dragged the door closed behind him, slamming it so hard the house shook. Hana's brow knitted. "You don't think he's pressed a self-destruct button, do you? I don't think I've got the energy."

"Na." Logan sat up and stretched, his gold St Christopher resting against his collar bone as he moved. Hana watched as it swung down to its proper place and nestled between the dark, downy hairs. He leaned across and kissed her forehead. "And at least we can give that one back."

Hana snorted. "You reckon?"

Logan stood and reached for his shorts and Hana lay back and watched his graceful movements. He caught her eye and tried to see behind him, spinning like a dog chasing its tail. "I don't have a fat ass, do I?"

Hana laughed out loud. "No." She pulled the sheet over her face. "But you've got a stronger stomach."

Logan grumbled as he pulled a tee shirt over his head and left the room. Hana heard him shouting along the hallway. "Where's the bugle bum then?"

The voices of the older children chimed in with shouts of, "He's there!"

Hana showered with Mac sitting in a corner of the cubicle, with the jets turned away from his face. He chewed on his fist and grinned up at her. "Good morning," Hana cooed. She squatted in front of him and used the sign to match her words. She brought the back of her right hand towards her left for 'good' and then reversed them and lowered her left hand to her inside forearm. "Good morning," she repeated and Mac's lips moved in a silent response. "Good morning," Hana said again, remembering to smile and her son cocked his head and watched with intense green eyes, soaking in every small movement. "My mummy taught me sign language," Hana told him. "It's how we spoke together." She closed her eyes and imagined Judith McIntyre's slender fingers moving like graceful swans as she communicated. When Hana opened them again to dispel the ready tears, Mac's emerald irises met her gaze with steady understanding.

Hana heard the sound of the water change as the nozzle jerked on its flexible hose and stopped pounding the glass cubicle. Instead it aimed itself at the back of her head and doused her with cooling liquid. Her eyes widened and she gasped, leaping up to slam on the handle and stop the cold water. She whirled around outraged and Mac laughed, a pleasant sound like tinkling bells. Hana smiled with delight. He loved it when she played the fool and Phoenix possessed a knack for making him giggle until he threw up. "You liked that! You're a Du Rose male; you thrive on other people's discomfort!" Hana slapped her naked thighs with her hands and pulled a face at the baby. His lips opened wide to reveal four pearly teeth and his eyes became happy slits ringed with dark eyelashes.

Hana rubbed shower gel into her hands and soaped him up where he sat, tickling him and enjoying the return of the happy infant. "All better now?" She smiled into his face and he flashed the teeth again, the gums still red and sore but no longer distressing him. Hana set the nozzle to a slow drizzle and cupped her hands, spreading the liquid over the soap to clean her son. "Let's not tell Daddy his te rongoa Māori stuff worked, hey? He'll look smug and we don't want that." She tapped the end of her nose with her finger and Mac turned his face and gave a pitiful wail, his gaze fixed on the plump breasts in his eye line. Hana shook her head. "Bedtime and emergencies," she said, forming the words he couldn't hear. "I'm reclaiming them!"

Mac kicked and grizzled as Hana wrapped him in a towel and pinned him against her. Her hair hung limply down her back like cold rope and she shivered in the cool air outside the bathroom. Eating sounds came from the kitchen downstairs and Hana skittered along the corridor to the bedroom, opting to cling onto the mummified child harder than her own towel. In the bedroom she thrust a nappy onto the baby before he peed and gave in, settling him with a conciliatory breast feed to satiate him before she got dressed.

A knock on the door heralded Leslie, looking like she had slept little. "Logan's feedin' the other tamariki. I've made some toast fingers for this tamaiti tāne if you want me to take him."

Mac spotted Leslie, craning his neck and straining to sit up using his stomach muscles. His arms and legs flailed with excitement at her presence and his lips blew out grunts of exertion. Leslie held her arms out and he squealed a high pitched noise. "Will I give him a beaker of milk?" she asked, lifting the child over her shoulder. Mac gave a hearty burp and she patted his back and eyed Hana as the other woman struggled into her jeans while still damp. "Too late, I see. Ah well, the Du Rose men do like their titi." She turned away and Hana gasped, her cheeks flushing red.

"Leslie! Don't be vulgar!"

"Nothing vulgar about nipples, kōtiro. We've all got them."

Hana put her hands over her ears. "It's too early for this conversation."

Leslie grinned. "And you're too English."

"Probably. Please tell Logan I'll be down before he leaves." Hana sighed with relief as the door clicked closed behind Leslie. The woman called a spade 'a spade' and Hana shuddered, preferring to call it a 'digging thing' whilst working up to the truth. Sometimes the testosterone haze which hung over the Du Rose males made Hana uncomfortable and their easy Māori ways and openness of speech left little to the imagination. Tama could be baldly explicit, often finding Hana's fingers clamped over his mouth. Alfred was the worst, hiding little of his relationship with his seventy-year-old wife. Only Logan behaved with any degree of privacy, making his alpha image even stronger for those desperate to test his prowess.

"What're you thinking?" Logan's hand on her shoulder sent the blush from Hana's chest to her fine boned neck and she twisted the sweater in her fingers.

"You." Her eyes narrowed and she turned, pressing her breasts against Logan's crisp white shirt. She ran a tentative finger up the line of buttons and he groaned. He wrapped his arms around her and his thumb traced the line of her lacy bra.

"You pick your moments, wahine," he complained, resting his soft lips against hers.

Hana let her hands roam over the expensive fabric of his grey trousers, feeling the neat backside beneath its folds. Cursory exploration further revealed a straining at the seams near the front and she sighed with satisfaction. "Leslie mentioned Du Rose men and nipples and then there you were," Hana whispered. "Like an apparition of pure..."

Logan's lips closed over hers, severing her sentence. "Pure school teacher," he reminded her with a raised eyebrow. Clearing his throat with a wince, he adjusted his trousers. "Pure respectability."

"If you say so." Hana stroked her breasts through the material and taunted her husband with deliberate intent. A thought occurred to her and she stopped and jabbed an index finger in his direction. "Stay away from those horny women in the social sciences department. They were definitely headed your way before you asked me out. I wouldn't put it past them not to care about the wedding ring on your finger." Hana narrowed her green eyes to slits. "Don't go near their staff room or you'll come out divorced."

Logan put his head back and laughed. "Okay, Mrs Du Rose. Whatever you say. Is there anyone else's character you'd like to malign before I go to work?"

She shook her head, pretty face screwed into a scowl. "I can't think of any right now."

Logan shoved a dark tie around his neck and knotted it with deft fingers. "Good. Then have a great day. I wished Wiri and Phoe good luck at their new school and kindy. Leslie said she'd ride shotgun in case of trouble." Logan flung his jacket over his muscular shoulders, shrouding the multi-millionaire farmer in expensive Italian cloth and looking even less like the average high school teacher. "I'd best meet my new boss and pretend to look interested in the staff briefing."

"You met her the other day." Hana shrugged the sweater over her bra and pulled it down to her hips.

"Yeah, today I get to meet the new head of department."

Hana pushed her feet into socks. "Won't it be weird; going back as a teacher when you used to be a head of faculty?"

"Not really." Logan lifted her chin for one last kiss. "I'm not staying. As long as my classes run like I want them to I don't care about school politics. I'll get the hours to satisfy the teacher registration rules and go home. Easy."

"What about Caleb? Do you still want him out?" Hana tensed as Logan's brow furrowed and he thought for a moment in silence.

His steady gaze made her quail and a flicker of enjoyment crossed his face. Then he shrugged. "He's your guest so that makes him your problem, Hana. If you want him out, I'll back you. Otherwise, you deal with him." He gave a wink as he left the room and Hana sat on the bed feeling colder, less safe and as though he'd taken some precious life force with him and left her in the shade.

31

Different

"I'll drive." Leslie held out her hand for the ute keys and settled herself in the driver's seat while Hana secured Mac's car seat. "You tell me where to go."

Hana sank into the passenger side and closed the door, already exhausted from dealing with the other two. She waved a tired hand at Caleb who stood on the front porch resting on his crutches. "Have a good day," he called to the children in the back seat and Phoe waved with enthusiasm. Wiri stuck his tongue out and Hana reached behind her and tapped his leg.

"I saw that! Don't be so rude."

"We don't like that big boy," Wiri replied, dropping his bottom lip.

"I like that big boy." Phoenix leaned forward in her car seat and stretched around Mac so she could look at her cousin. "I like that big boy."

"But I don't," he repeated. "He's a bad boy."

"What makes you say that?" Hana turned in her seat to face the angry, grey eyes. Wiri scowled and opened his mouth.

"He won't find his stuff again. Serves him right for making me carry it in from Nonie's car."

"Which way do you want me to turn?" Leslie's voice screeched like nails on a blackboard, panicked by the excessive Hamilton traffic.

"Right," Hana said, staring at her mother-in-law. "No need to yell at me. I was happy to drive!"

"I don't like that boy," Wiri began again and Leslie snapped at him.

"Hush, Wiremu Du Rose! Tō waha!"

"Don't tell him to shut up!" Hana sat up in her seat. "What's with you today?"

"Aua atu rā."

Hana looked around at Wiri and raised her shoulders in question. He pouted. "She said never mind." His brow furrowed. "I don't feel like going to a new school anymore. I want to go for cuppa teas instead."

"After school," Hana said, reaching her hand out to him. "Be a good boy at school today and we'll go for coffee afterwards and you can tell us all about it."

Wiri leaned forward and grasped her fingers. Mac grumbled in his throat and caught hold of her sleeve, hauling Hana's arm towards him and opening his mouth. Phoenix gave a fake, pitiful cry. "Cuddle me too," she protested.

"He wants to eat your hand," Wiri said, watching Mac reeling in Hana's sleeve. "He's got a bogey on his cheek. It's brown."

"It's toast." Leslie squinted in the rear view mirror at the baby in the centre of the back seat. "I missed it with the wipe."

"Turn left up here." Hana peered through the windscreen. "The school's next door to the kindy. Whoever thought that up is a genius."

"Developers. Gotta love 'em," Leslie snarled, pushing the ute through the other school traffic and grimacing as the neat family vehicles bowed to the might of the hefty farm truck's nudge bars and the mud clogged in its wheels.

"I'll drive home," Hana remarked as Leslie snatched a parking space in the car park, as another mother indicated possession with the orange blinker at the front of her tiny car. Leslie grumbled and plopped from the driver's seat with a curse.

"It's bloody freezin' down 'ere. Hamilton sucks!"

"Hamilton sucks!" Wiri repeated and Hana put her hand over his open mouth.

"Don't say things like that to the people who like it here," she whispered in his ear. "You want to make friends today otherwise it'll be a very long term."

"I just won't go then." Wiri stuck his chin in the air and Hana's heart quailed.

"You chose to come with us," she said, bending down on her haunches to look the child in the eyes. "You could've stayed at your old school back in Rangiriri. Now you've chosen and you can either go home and back to that school, or you can stay here and treat it like an adventure. But you're not misbehaving here with the intention of going home whenever you feel like it. Do you understand?"

Wiri nodded. "I'll be good."

"I'll be good too." Phoenix held Leslie's hand and hopped about on the pavement. "Wiri be good, yeah?" Reaching out she grabbed his fingers in a firm grip and hopped again, her thin arms spread like a washing line. "You stayin' wiv Phoe Phoe, yeah?" She asked the question and nodded to herself, judge and jury. "Not go home by self?"

Wiri gave a reluctant smile and put his arm around the toddler with latent possessiveness. "I'm bein' wiv you," he said, his grey eyes sincere. His other hand plucked at his sweatshirt which sported a cartoon character. "But I look stupid in my mufti clothes."

"Then let's get some uniform for you." Hana smiled and held out her hand, investing her energy into the suffering boy and leaving Leslie to trail behind carrying Mac. Phoenix maintained her death grip on Wiri's other hand. He stopped just inside the front doors, halting like a stubborn horse with anxiety in his face.

"What if you buy me uniform and I don't like it? What if everybody hates me and wants to kill me? What if they all do tarukino all day and I don't wanna?"

"Do what?" Hana stopped and peered at the child's anxious face.

"Cannabis. He's just rambling!" Leslie spat, pushing Wiri on with her stomach. Mac made a swipe for a handful of black curls and she pulled him upright in the nick of time. "Stop it, tāne. He kutukutu ahi."

"What's nonsense?" A male voice boomed and a tall Polynesian man approached them. He shared Logan's height but not his muscular build and he'd scraped straight, dark hair back into a ponytail behind his collar. Kind brown eyes stared down at the reluctant Wiri. "Is this my new student? I'm Mr Rōpata." He pronounced his words with Māori vowel sounds.

After a moment of hesitation, Wiri let out a sigh. "You're brown," he said. "Fank goodness for that."

Hana swallowed in a moment of horror until the tall man let out a deep laugh. "Māori blood and bones, man. Nice to meet you." He stuck out a large paw and Wiri's tiny fingers disappeared inside.

"I need a uniform," Wiri said, tugging at his sweater. "I've got my old school shorts on but I need clothes like them." He pointed at a group of children moving past, his grey eyes missing nothing when they put their small heads together and whispered about him behind their hands.

"And that's why I'm standing here waiting for you." Mr Rōpata winked at Hana and took Wiri's hand, leading them towards the reception. In seconds Wiri wore the correct maroon sweatshirt and grey uniform shorts. Hana clutched the relevant sports kit in her hands. Wiri looked ready to embark on his new adventure and Hana felt grateful to the man who'd made such an effort to immerse the frightened child into this new chapter.

The receptionist's sing song voice chirped out the amount for Hana to pay for uniform and school fees and she jumped and dragged her credit card from the front pocket of her jeans. She handed it across the counter and then crouched down to look into Wiri's face. "You good now, baby?" she asked. He nodded and Hana pressed a kiss to his forehead. "Have a great day and we'll go for afternoon tea when I pick you up. How's that? You can tell us how it went."

Wiri nodded and let go of his teacher's hand to wrap his arms around her neck. "Promise you'll come for me yourself?" he whispered and Hana nodded.

"Promise."

Wiri let go and she stood, feeling emotional. The lack of blood tie seemed to make no difference and Logan's comment about sending him back rang hollow in her brain. It couldn't happen; she'd invested too much love in the boy already. Mr Rōpata caught Wiri's hand and gave her a smile. "Thank you for your phone call last week, Mrs Du Rose. It's helpful to understand the background issues."

Hana swallowed and glanced down at the back of Wiri's dark curls, feeling like a betrayer. She'd stumbled through her account of the five-year-old's tortured situation, explaining the reasons why Logan's half-nephew lived as their son and called them Ma and Pa. She knew the teacher had heard worse but cringed against the unusualness of their circumstances. Glancing at her green eyed son, she imagined giving him up, the thought causing her chest to clench in agony. "Thank you," she said. Lifting the backpack from her arm she handed it over. "Wiri's snack and lunch is in there. I'll name his sports kit and he can have it tomorrow."

Mr Rōpata nodded and accepted the bag in his spare paw. "We don't do sport on Mondays so that will be fine. Is it Wiri or Wiremu? Which do you prefer?"

Wiri shrugged. "People I love call me Wiri. You can call me Wiri but everyone else can call me Wiremu Neville Lincoln Du Rose."

Mr Rōpata threw his head back and laughed. "They might struggle with that my little tangata whakahangareka."

Phoenix heard the Māori words and pouted, tugging on Leslie's skirt. "I don't like clowns!" she insisted, staring at Wiri's teacher in alarm. "I don't like clowns!"

Hana spun and picked her up, struggling to hide her surprise. She hadn't looked at the birth certificate in the file on the counter, just adding it to the pile of documents required to register Wiri at the school. The list of names left her reeling and Leslie reached across to accept the pale Manila folder from the receptionist's fingers. Mac lurched for it and Leslie held it at arm's length. "Bye Wiri." Hana waved to the little boy and he kissed his palm and blew it, involving a whole lot of spit. Then he wiped his palm on his new shorts with a look of distaste and walked through the door with his teacher.

"He spit in my eye!" Phoenix complained and wiped her face on Hana's shoulder.

"One down, one to go," Leslie commented, turning and heading for the main door.

Hana watched the disconsolate slump of Leslie's shoulders and wondered what ailed the elderly woman. Her patience seemed more frayed than usual and her temper boiled close to the surface. "Just shoot me," Hana whispered under her breath and Phoenix let out an exaggerated hiss.

"No! Naughty!" she complained and Hana realised her mistake. Too late. "Papa won't shoot you." Phoenix tipped so she could look beyond Hana's red curls and peer into her face. "Poppa Alfie won't shoot you." Her diatribe continued through the front door and onto the pavement, changing as she thought of people who'd rather like to shoot her mother. "Toby might shoot you. No. Yes. No. Will can do it." Her grey eyes grew round like saucers at the thought of the stroppy museum curator. "I ask him?"

"No thanks love, I'm good."

Phoenix smiled and pointed at the sign for her new playschool. "Kindy?"

"Yep." Hana kept her tone matter-of-fact. "Lovely kindy."

"I don't wanna go kindy." Phoenix looked anxious and a low keening sound came from her throat. "I go home wiv Macky."

"It's until afternoon tea time, just like your other kindy, Phoe," Hana persisted. "Then I'll come find you and look at the toys you've played with. I think Mac would love to see them."

"See them." Phoenix repeated the words around her thumb sucking, a whine in her voice. "Toys."

"Ooh, look at the climbing frame, moko!" Leslie turned with a smile on her face and pointed through the railings at the wooden fort in the middle of a playing area. Children swarmed all over it and Phoenix popped the thumb from her mouth.

"I don't like them kids," she said, forming a snap judgement of the crowd of undersized people.

"Oh." Hana made her voice sound disappointed. "I quite like that little girl in the red dress. She has pretty hair and a kind face." The small girl pivoted on one leg at the top of a slide, her dark curls blowing in the breeze. As she made the decision to drop to her bottom and slither down, another child pushed past her, almost toppling her off. A teacher rushed over and intercepted him at the bottom, wagging her finger and pointing back up to the little girl.

"Dat naughty!" Outrage filled Phoenix Du Rose's face and Hana saw the imprint of her husband's sense of injustice blazing in the grey eyes. "Not do that!" She peered into Hana's face and formed her words with exaggerated movements and wiggled her legs to be put down on the ground.

"The teacher's sorting it." Hana caught hold of the indignant child's hand as she surged ahead along the path and through the front doors.

Phoenix fidgeted while the staff introduced themselves and then she kissed Hana with a quick and cursory peck on the cheek. Leslie got a kiss on her stomach and Mac received one to his woolly booted foot. Then the Du Rose child was gone, stomping through the outside doors and making a beeline for the climbing frame.

"Geez, she's like her pa," Leslie chortled, her breasts wrestling in their undersized bra. "Got a bee up her ass."

"Er, excuse me." Hana grabbed the attention of the nearest teacher and pointed at her daughter's retreating back. "Phoenix saw another child push a little girl on the climbing frame. She's gone to sort it out."

"Ohkay." The teacher dragged the word out and shot after Phoenix, attempting to divert her attention to something else. With a daughter as stubborn as Logan, Hana didn't fancy the woman's chances with any tactic other than the head on version.

"I should probably stay a while." Hana rose on tip toes and her posture screamed separation anxiety.

"Well, I think you should run." Leslie hoisted Mac up onto her hip, his legs almost doing the splits in the effort required to clip on. "Before the trouble starts."

"What?" Hana whirled around, her mouth open.

"Get!" Leslie seized her slender wrist in her beefy fingers and hauled her towards the doorway. "She's Logan Du Rose's daughter and her whakapapa included Phoenix Te Wehi and Rongomai Te Wehi, the warrior. She'll be fine."

Hana groaned and squinted her eyes, watching through the open doorway as the teacher squatted down in front of Phoenix. The delicate child in the red dress seemed drawn to Hana's daughter, her lips moving as if in slow motion.

"She's an elective mute."

"Sorry?" Hana jumped at the voice in her ear and moved away. A slight woman dangled a small boy from her hip, older than Mac but skinnier and blonde. "Josie. She's never spoken, not as long as my daughter Hayley's been coming here. I saw you arrive; is that your little girl?" She jerked her head towards Phoenix, who let go of the teacher's hand and stood next to Josie. The older girl dwarfed her but accepted her presence, looking down on the top of Phoe's head with interest.

"Yes. That's Phoenix and I'm Hana."

"Nice to meet you, Hana. Hayley's on the tricycle outside; it's the only reason she comes. She goes to school next term and then it'll be this one's turn. I'm Elisha by the way." She bounced the grizzling child on her hip.

"Oh dear, what's the matter?" Hana down-turned her lips in a sad face and looked at the child.

"Teething," his mother said. "Big back ones, I think."

"We just had that with Mac," Hana replied, wincing. "My husband got this amazing gel stuff and it worked overnight."

"What's the name of it?" The blonde woman looked interested, her brow furrowing as though to remember every detail Hana spoke.

"I can't remember. It's homemade. It's got a Māori name and I'm sure he said it was made from kawakawa leaves. I felt skeptical at first. It's in the car; would you like me to get it? He looks in pain."

"No thanks." The woman's face shut down and Hana felt the animosity rise. "I'll get something from the pharmacy."

Hana nodded, the moment turned awkward and uncomfortable. She fought to retrieve the former camaraderie. "I didn't believe either at first, but it worked."

"Let's get you home little man." Elisha gave Hana a sweet smile and turned away. "See you again," she called over her shoulder and kept walking, her grizzling son dribbling on her patterned blouse. In the distance Hana saw Leslie putting Mac into the ute, rubbing noses with him and making him giggle.

"Hey, don't worry." A dark skinned teacher touched her hand. "Pakeha don't understand our ways. I'm glad you do though, kōtiro." She winked at Hana and passed, trailing a little boy who ticked his head upwards at regular intervals. Hana smiled at him and waved, rewarded by soulful brown eyes and the hint of a smile.

"Youse took yer time," Leslie chided her as Hana clambered into the passenger seat. "This rūruhi needs a coffee."

"You're not an old woman," Hana grumbled. She watched Elisha fitting her son into the tiny car Leslie beat to the parking spot and her heart sank. She turned to her mother-in-law with misery in her face. "I don't know how that happened."

"What, me getting old? I didn't notice it either. Don't stress." Leslie patted her knee. "I'm fine with it."

"No, one minute I'm walking into a new place and the next minute, someone dislikes me."

"Who?" Leslie peered around the car park, spotting numerous women and one lonely man slotting smaller children back into vehicles.

"Oh, just someone who didn't appreciate my offer of that teething gel Logan got for Mac. It didn't help that you'd already waged war over a parking space."

Leslie humphed and clacked her false teeth as she pushed her lips up in a disgruntled fish face. "Don't worry what others think of you, Hana. Worry about what you think of yourself."

Hana nodded and fastened her seatbelt which shifted the file on her knee. She opened it and fingered the documents inside. "Did you know Wiri had Lincoln as one of his middle names?"

"No." Leslie pulled out of the car park ahead of Elisha, forcing the other woman to jam on the brakes. "It's a common name. What's the problem?"

"So, you don't think it's anything to do with Lincoln, as in stable manager, Lincoln?"

"No idea. Ask your husband." Leslie turned left without indicating and Hana held on to the door handle and closed her eyes. "Where's a cafe then?"

"Back there." Hana jabbed with her finger without opening her eyes. "You've passed three."

Leslie stamped on the brakes and Hana screamed. "Please, just let me drive!" She opened her eyes and looked at her surroundings. "Pull over in this layby and bloody indicate first!"

"You're so damn picky!" Leslie growled. "Drive, don't drive. Make yer mind up!"

Hana ground her teeth to suppress the biting comments which rose into her mouth and almost escaped. She swapped seats with Leslie, annoyed when the old woman slid over to sit on her knee before she'd managed to hop out onto the foot rail. A fine drizzle prickled her skin and she peeked in the side window and met her son's curious green eyes. Settling in the driver's seat and altering the settings so she could see over the steering wheel, Hana made time to turn and smile at her baby boy. He responded with a shy grin and kicked his legs, looking away and then peeking back at her. "Right," she said, grinding the gears by accident, "Time for coffee."

She hid Wiri's documents in the glove box while Leslie seized Mac and ran for the cafe door. The old kuia barged other customers out of the way in her single minded quest for caffeine. By the time Hana stood on the welcome mat shaking raindrops off her jacket, Leslie stormed towards a table like a heat seeking missile. "I've ordered," she called to Hana and the occupants of the cafe turned to stare.

"Thanks." Sinking into a hard backed chair, Hana ran her hands through her damp, frizzled hair. Mac giggled and she did it again to amuse him. "I forgot how wet Hamilton can be after the mountain."

"Aye," Leslie replied. "From drought to drench. Like my sex life." She cackled and Hana darted nervous glances at the nearest table.

"Don't you mean that the other way around?" she dared to ask and Leslie sighed, bending to strip the heavy jacket from Mac's shoulders so he could bend his torso. "You did just abandon your husband."

Leslie snorted like a bull and Hana jerked backwards and changed the subject at speed. "Tell me why Wiri has Lincoln's name in his. Was there some doubt about his parentage?" Her brow knitted thinking of the small boy; a carbon copy of a Du Rose, his likeness to Nev and Logan undeniable.

"Na. He's pure Du Rose. No way some blondie fathered him." Leslie echoed her thoughts and Hana nodded.

"I shouldn't cast aspersions," she sighed. "Especially not after what Jack tried to do. Mac and I nearly died because of his suspicions."

"Yeah, but you birthed a karaka babby!" Leslie cackled and Hana's expression faded into irritation.

"Stop calling my son orange!" she hissed and the old woman's eyes lit with mischief.

"Will if I want to; he doesn't mind. He can't hear me."

"I mind!" Hana gritted her teeth and then relaxed her facial expression as the barista brought over their coffee. "Anyway, we don't know that and you shouldn't listen at doors."

"One latte, one affogato and a fluffy," the barista said, leaning the tray on a corner of the table to unload.

"Thank you." Hana watched the movement of his strong hands, the olive skin and slight build reminding her of Bodie and making her heart sting. No more than nineteen, the young man chucked Mac under the chin and winked at him as he turned and left them to their drinks. Hana dragged her phone from her pocket and peered at the empty screen. Still no response to her text message to him.

"Here you go, moko," Leslie said to Mac, shifting him round on her knee. She seized the teaspoon and gathered a blob of the frothed milk onto it, inserting it between his eager lips and laughing at the confused face he pulled as the bubbles crushed against his tongue. "It's miraka kore kirīmi. Won't hurt you."

"Why did you order trim milk?" Hana asked and Leslie shrugged.

"Just did. Why do you want to know about Lincoln?"

Hana sighed and reached for her latte, watching as the ice cream in Leslie's affogato slid lower in the glass, hot coffee turning it into a light brown syrup. "I overheard a phone conversation between Lincoln and someone else. I don't believe he's as innocent as he claims; somebody else was involved."

Leslie shook her head. "What's done is done, kōtiro. Let it go. He's been in prison a long time for an innocent man or one covering for another."

Hana stopped with her mug resting against her lips. "I never mentioned him covering for anyone else. What made you say that?"

Leslie's cheeks adopted an uncomfortable flush and she licked her lips, reaching for her affogato while Mac pushed bubbles in and out of his pink mouth. "Please, Hana. Just leave it."

"Then tell me the truth!" Hana snapped. "A man I loved and respected held a gun to my baby's head not so long ago. Forgive me for not being comfortable around a man who served time in prison for murder."

"Manslaughter," Leslie corrected, a moustache of coffee stained ice cream across her top lip. Hana opened her mouth to point it out and then closed it again in revenge as the barista grinned across from the counter. "It's over now. You need to leave well alone." She spooned a knob of ice cream into Mac's open mouth and he jerked in shock and pulled a face.

Hana squeezed the bridge of her nose between thumb and forefinger and sized up her mounting issues in order of importance. "Please don't give him coffee." She sighed. "Bodie hasn't called and you've abandoned your marriage and won't tell me what's wrong. Caleb's keeping a secret and I don't know what to do about it because Logan won't help me. Now there's a murderer waiting for me at the hotel. Oh and apparently someone's seen Asher hanging around the hotel when he's not allowed."

Leslie laughed. "Linc's not waiting for ya, honey. Looks more to me like he's avoiding you. Your son's pig-headed and will need you before you need him. Don't worry about me and Alfie and I don't wanna talk about either of those bloody teenagers right now."

"So, Caleb did something at the hotel? With Asher? That's why you brought him here." Hana spread her hands wide in placation. "Just give me a clue, please?"

"Nev and Linc were best friends growing up." Leslie's eyes narrowed as she chose to throw Hana a lifeline which didn't involve something closer to home. "Michael and Logan knocked around with them too, although they weren't meant to. It couldn't be helped in a small township like ours and boys will be boys. When Logan reached nine, his mother found the four of them drinking behind the cow shed and took all her boys out of school. She home-schooled Barry, Michael and Logan after that. She didn't want Logan around Reuben's boys in case they gave away the secret of his parentage and she may have involved him, because Nev stopped visiting. Lincoln didn't though. He stayed friends with all of them although it wasn't always easy walking the line between the two sides of the family."

Leslie reached for her drink again, Mac's head lolling against her shoulder as he grew sleepy. "Jack liked Linc and employed him when the boy left school, wanting to train him to take over the stock and horse side of the business. Miriam stopped worrying about keeping the boys apart as they grew up because Logan went to boarding school on the north shore in term time and then university and away to England. She didn't have a problem with Linc anyway, only Nev. Linc married Logan's second cousin, Fiona Du Rose, but they were too young. She always wanted to be a doctor and started at the university in Auckland. She came home at weekends and they seemed to cope all right. Linc lived in the bunk house with the stockmen and it worked for a while. They hit a rocky patch and he went to live in Auckland with her, driving back to the stables six days a week. He did that for years. Nobody knows why he started an affair but these things happen. Next thing, the mistress is dead and Linc's on a murder charge."

"I guessed he and Fiona weren't still together." Hana remembered the strain which accompanied their chance meeting. "Who came back to the township first? Lincoln or Fiona?"

"No idea." Leslie looked bored with the conversation. "Doesn't matter. She divorced him even before his case went to trial. Reckon a marriage is over the minute one of them cheats."

Hana nodded and watched the rain pound against the huge shop front. Her mind strayed to Bodie's father, who'd cheated on her and left her to find out after his death. "It sure is," she said with a deep sigh, the pain long since dulled by her marriage to Logan. But the humiliation of having not been quite good enough for someone remained to undermine her confidence and render her suspicious and untrusting. "What's worse? Finding out your husband's had an affair or that he's in police custody for killing his mistress?"

"It saved Fiona a job," Leslie cackled. Hana's eyes opened wide in horror.

"What?"

Leslie shook her head, looking amused. "Slow down, girly. The cops questioned her, but she'd spent six weeks as a locum in Christchurch. Nobody suspected Fiona. I can't imagine how awful she felt." Leslie lowered her voice as an elderly couple took possession of the table behind Hana. "Linc didn't mean to kill her; they argued and he pushed her backwards. That's what the police said."

"Isn't that what happened?" Hana leaned forward.

"It's not what he says happened. Linc always maintained he left her alive. The cops set up one of those drink driving road blocks on the mountain road and stopped him on his way back to the farm. He realised he didn't have his licence with him and went back to Pania's for his wallet. When he got there, he found her lying on the floor bleeding and called an ambulance. Linc admitted to the affair straight away and they found his DNA in the bedroom. The prosecutor made a case for her wanting to end the affair and him getting angry and pushing her. They started with murder and bargained down to manslaughter. The whole township chipped in towards his defense and Liza acted as his barrister. But he gave in overnight. Alfie thinks he received Fiona's divorce papers and just gave up. And then his poor mother died during the trial from an overdose of antidepressants and Linc wanted it over."

"Maybe." Hana finished her drink and viewed her beautiful, sleeping son across the table. "I meant to go to the supermarket after this but Mac's gone to sleep. There's no fresh food in the house. We've eaten everything I brought with us."

"I'll do it," Leslie offered, her face brightening. "I'll drop you back at the house and go to the supermarket; I'd love a chance to see what these Hamiltonians have on offer. Reckon they think they're better than the rest of New Zealand, so I can look for myself."

"Thanks." Hana reached into her purse for Logan's credit card. She slid it across the table into Leslie's waiting fingers. "It's the same pin number as last time. Please don't drive like a maniac and ding the ute; I can't bear any more tension in the house."

"I won't." Leslie bundled the small boy to her copious breasts, almost smothering him as she stood. Hana paid cash at the till and followed her mother-in-law outside to the ute and helped buckle the snoozing baby in. The rain eased for long enough to get home and with her ill humour abated, Leslie drove with as much restraint as a hoon in a drivers' education class.

"It's just a supermarket," Hana warned her as she stood on the front porch and watched Leslie crank the ute into reverse. "I think you're overestimating the level of excitement on offer."

32

Backbone

Leslie waved and screeched through the school gate, armed with Logan's ute and his vulnerable credit card. Hana pushed the front door open and took her sleeping son upstairs, laying him in the travel cot and turning on the baby monitor. Then she went on the hunt for Caleb, figuring he must be on the ground floor somewhere. "I didn't hear you come in," he stammered, a guilty look on his face. He removed the boot of his cast from the low coffee table in front of him and muted the TV.

"I dropped the children at school and kindy. Leslie's gone to the supermarket." Hana sank into a wing-backed chair next to the sofa. "Are you hungry?"

Caleb nodded. "The fridge is empty, but I found bread and a few biscuits."

"Yeah, sorry about that." Hana eyed him with curiosity. "What happened at the hotel?"

The atmosphere crackled with tension as the teenager licked his lips and searched for a ready lie. Hana scented deceit before it passed across his lips. "Just lonely after you left." He widened his eyes to puppy-dog proportions and turned on the charm as easily as flicking a switch. Robert Dressler's huge personality filled the room as Caleb exercised the genetic code with precision.

Bile rose into Hana's throat as she realised she'd been played, accommodating a stranger into the Du Rose clan without regard for her own children. The gap in her life left by Tama ached like a wound and she'd filled it with Caleb; but something in his blue eyes drove a warning into her heart like an arrow. Her expression hardened. "Tell me the truth or leave now." No smile accompanied the command to soften the delivery and Caleb's mouth opened in an unattractive gape.

"I just did! Nobody came to see me after you left and it got boring."

"So where does Asher fit into all this?" Hana's green eyes lacked empathy and she watched the boy baulk at this new, combative side of her nature.

"We hung out a bit is all. He knew my dad and told me some stuff."

Hana snorted with disdain. "Yeah, I bet he did. Most of it would be make believe too. Bobby didn't waste his energy on Asher Du Rose and you'd do well to copy him. That kid's on the road to nowhere and he won't stop until he runs into a mirror and sees his own reflection. He's lucky he's not in prison."

Caleb shrugged, keen to end the conversation. "I thought he seemed fine."

"Well, he isn't." Hana drove her point home and rose from her seat. Caleb's body language reminded her of Bodie during his rebellious years and the memory induced a deep bone tiredness which made it hard to move one foot in front of the other. "I'll get some wood and light a fire," she said with a sigh. "This house is freezing."

"It's better than the streets," Caleb muttered, determined to invoke guilt seeing as he'd failed at sympathy. Hana chose to ignore the veiled threat within Caleb's words and busied herself with finding kindling and logs in the shed to start a hearty blaze.

Leslie returned after two hours with enough food to feed the school population. Hana helped her unload the ute and put everything away before her son demanded attention via the baby monitor. "I'll get him!" Leslie demanded as Hana moved towards the kitchen door. The old woman shifted her bulk around Caleb, who balanced on one leg in the doorway. Hana watched as a silent communication of dislike passed between them and she hefted the tin of peas in her hand and narrowed her eyes at the boy. "You need to tell me what you did," she said, giving him another opportunity to come clean. "I'll find out, anyway."

"She doesn't like me," Caleb offered. "Thinks I'm a free-loader. She said my sort trail trouble like the smoke from a fart and she didn't want to bring me here."

"Well, that's obvious," Hana snorted. "She doesn't want to be in the same room. The journey here must have been entertaining!"

Caleb wrinkled his nose. "Yeah."

Hana moved into the living room, hearing Caleb's crutches scrape across the floor behind her. She seized the poker and pushed it into the flames, watching as it stirred up the oxygen, causing the light display to turn a brighter shade of orange. "I wish Logan could see this fire," she mused. "I always mess it up when he's watching."

"Have you talked to him about me?" Caleb shifted in his seat and chewed his bottom lip.

"I told him you're Bobby's son, yes." Hana avoided his eyes and stirred the kindling again, sending up sparks and ash.

"Did you ask him where my dad is?" Hope filtered through his words and Hana suppressed her natural sense of compassion.

"No."

"Why?" Caleb's tone became urgent and demanding and Hana felt a familiar flicker of fear. Bodie's antics caused the same clenching in her gut when he dumped his problems on her shoulders and panic assailed her rational thought.

She stood up straight, poker in hand and squared her shoulders. Her gaze on Caleb made him quail. "Because I told you to ask him yourself. I won't act as your go-between to soften up my husband. If you want to know something; ask him."

"He doesn't like me." The sulky teenager returned, anger replaced by self-pity. He sank into an armchair. "You said you'd help me." Caleb's bottom lip turned down and his eyes narrowed, peering out at her from beneath hooded lids.

The poker clattered against the tiled hearth, dislodging a log which hissed and sprayed orange sparks into the chimney. "I have helped you!" Hana raised her voice and put her hands on her hips. "How dare you!"

"You know I'm looking for my dad!" Caleb persisted, pushing himself back into a standing position and reaching for his crutches. He held his injured leg off the floor and wobbled as he bent forward. "It's the only reason I'm here."

"Nice!" Hana spat, shaking her head in disbelief. "The only reason you're here is to heal. After that, I can't help you." She whirled from the room, clattering into Leslie outside the door.

"Hana!" Caleb yelled behind her and the old woman's eyes widened.

"You've made a big mistake taking him in, kōtiro," she hissed. "Youse need to get Logan to throw him out."

"Just leave it!" Hana snapped, holding out her arms for Mac. In response to her barely concealed anger he turned his face away, burying his nose in Leslie's neck. Hana dropped her hands, pain in her eyes.

"Let's make morning tea." Leslie's head bobbled on her shoulders; food and sex her all time answers to life's problems. "You hungry, moko?" She planted a kiss on Mac's ear and set her battleship body on a course for the kitchen and the full to bursting fridge.

Hana leaned back against the wall and sighed, watching Leslie's buttocks fight with each other beneath her skirt as she schlepped away. Caleb's face appeared around the doorframe, his eyes dark and foreboding. Hana raised her index finger. "Pressure me again and we're done," she said, her voice dripping acid. "I will not go against my husband, not for you or anybody else." She pushed away from the wall and navigated the crutch he'd placed at an awkward angle, a flicker in her breast sensing he'd done it on purpose to trip her. "There's food in the kitchen," she shot over her shoulder, avoiding his eyes but sensing his gaze on her back.

33

Instinct

The heaviness on her chest made breathing a challenge and Hana roused herself from sleep with difficulty. Mac's head filled the space between her neck and shoulder and her right arm ached from his dead weight. She groaned and opened her eyes, confronted by the sight of Leslie asleep in the chair opposite, the heat from the fire acting as valium in their blood. The old woman's jaw hung open and her top set of false teeth readied themselves to eject as her tongue swelled back and forth like the tide. Chunky thighs parted and her floral skirt rode up to expose a pair of old-fashioned, greying bloomers. As Hana squeezed her eyes tighter shut against the vision, Leslie snorted like a kune-kune piglet.

Mac stirred as Hana laid him on the sofa, piling cushions against his legs to keep him from rolling. She stretched her arms above her head and yawned. Pictures flashed across the TV screen but no sound emanated from the speakers. Hana cast around the room searching for Caleb and not finding him. A memory lingered in her mind of a clattering noise breaking into her sleep and she shook her head and tried to recall the exact sound. Crutches. Caleb's crutches.

Every floorboard protested against her stealthy footsteps and Hana winced at the orchestra which betrayed her attempt to creep across the room. Shuffling and then a click issued from the hallway and she followed the sound, curiosity driving her forward. Metal scraped across tile and the voice came from in front of the main door. "Bloody hell."

Hana poked her head around the door frame and spied Caleb lying just beyond the abrasive front door mat. He prodded at the crutch nearest his right foot, succeeding only in driving it further away. "What happened?" Hana moved into the hallway and increased her pace, arriving next to him in seconds. "Did you fall?"

"Something like that. Thought I'd walk up and down to get some exercise but it didn't work out. This bloody floor's slippery." Caleb accepted Hana's outstretched hand and hauled himself to a sitting position. He turned his body away from the stairs and tried to kneel up on one knee, cursing as his broken leg stuck out behind him. "How do I do this?" he demanded. "How can I get up again?"

Hana stood behind him and hauled upwards, her hands fixed beneath his armpits. Caleb used his good leg to flex until he stood upright, towering over Hana. She ran an anxious hand across her eyes and glanced up at the back of his blonde head. Something about the incident felt wrong, but she banished it as fanciful and busied herself retrieving his crutches. "Where do you want to be?" Her fingers shook as she handed them over, instinct flashing a warning she didn't understand.

"Just in the kitchen. That owd bitch won't wanna wake up and see me staring at her." He fixed his hands around the crutches and set off at a steady shuffle. Hana followed behind, glancing backwards at the spot in front of the door. The tiles stared back, offering no sheen of slipperiness to back up Caleb's story.

"I've never slipped on that floor," Hana said, keeping her tone even and without challenge. Her glance strayed to the single trainer on Caleb's good foot and her confusion deepened.

"It's this moon boot thing." Caleb twisted towards her, his face open and conveying honesty through the bright blue eyes. "I'm still not used to it. I fell a couple of times at the motel." He gnawed at his bottom lip. "It's hard to get back up when you're by yourself. It's one of the reasons I wanted to be here."

Hana nodded and allowed her face to relax into a smile. He needed her. He just said so. Her eyes strayed to the dark coloured plastic bag just inside his bedroom door. "What's that?" she asked pointing and Caleb's eyes widened.

"Those second hand clothes you got for me. I brought them here; I didn't have a proper bag so the old man gave me a bin liner."

Hana nodded and pushed it further into the room, moving it out of the way of the door. A tee shirt fell out onto the floorboards and she picked it up and placed it on top of the bag. "Go into the kitchen and I'll find you something to eat. Leslie bought enough to feed an army." She followed him along the hallway, sensing the unease coming off him in waves.

"There was another bag," Caleb began. "I can't find it."

"That dumb ass friend of Logan's is here." Leslie stood in the lounge doorway and inspected her bottom plate of false teeth. She brushed off fluff as Hana looked away. "I can't help it." Her wrinkled face puckered into something a bloodhound might be proud of. "I fell asleep and they popped out onto the rug."

"Rinse them under the tap." Hana pushed her into the kitchen and leaning across her ran cold water into the sink. "What friend?"

"The weird one with the fat wife." Leslie dumped her teeth into the sink and watched them jig beneath the flow of water. Her speech sounded muffled and peculiar.

"I'll let him in before he bangs on the door and wakes Mac. Can you grab that salad out of the fridge for Caleb?" Hana headed for door. The apocalypse couldn't wake her sleeping son but the excuse to escape the floating teeth seemed too good to be true.

"Heeeeeeyyyy! Have you missed me?" Peter North slammed his car door and the sickening sound of grating metal set Hana's teeth on edge. The temporary paralysis as her body tensed made her too late to avoid the inevitable bear hug. Dandruff showered around them like snowflakes and Hana inhaled the scent of chip fat and Tweed; essence of deep-fried-old-lady and sweat.

"Sure have," Hana lied, extracting herself from the spindly arms and taking a step back. "Congratulations on your wedding. Is Henrietta well?"

"Bouncing!" Pete exclaimed and Hana stifled a snort at the thought of Pete's overlarge wife on her electrified trampoline. "She's away at the moment for work. Have you got any left-overs?" He rubbed his stomach like a child and Hana nodded and jerked her head towards the kitchen.

"Hana, can you put this rubbish out? I don't know where the outside bin is." Leslie waddled forward with a dustbin liner and pushed it into Hana's hand.

"I've shown you twice now!" Hana sounded exasperated and Leslie gave a sheepish grin and dodged Pete's outstretched arms.

"Don't touch me, loser!" she snapped and picked up speed on her return journey to the kitchen.

"I'll just put this rubbish bag in the outside bin. Don't wind her up; she has the use of kitchen knives," Hana warned Pete. She carried the bag outside on the porch and stood for a moment inhaling the cold, fresh air. "I swear nobody else in this place possesses legs."

"Cheers." Pete took the steps into the house two at a time, tripping over the top one and splatting into the door post. Hana rolled her eyes and wondered whether to get the ambulance on speed dial. Seconds later, Leslie's angry shout made her drop the lid of the wheelie bin with a crash and follow the sound of yelling.

"I'm not bloody Miriam!" Leslie yelled, her face puce and her lips drawn into a tight line. "You call me that every damn time and yet youse know I'm Alfie's second wife! I swear you do it on purpose to annoy me."

Pete seated himself at the table in expectation of food as though the raging woman would calm and feed him within the next few seconds.

"Just give him some lunch," Hana sighed. "If you fill his mouth I find the talking stops for a little while."

With a humph, Leslie pushed her face into the fridge and yanked out the remains of a sandwich Mac hadn't finished earlier. Hana heard her baby gurgling from the living room and retrieved him from his nest on the sofa. His nappy smelled like a sewage works and she diverted to the bathroom, hoping nobody died in the meantime.

"How's my mokopuna?" Leslie cooed as Hana delivered him, cleansed and joyful to the high chair at the table. The little boy's quick eyes spotted the food from his vantage point and his enthusiasm hiked, wrists twirling and tiny fingers grabbing at air. "Youse love your cheese, don't you moko?" Leslie winked at the baby, slicing the sandwich into chunky fingers.

Pete tapped the table in an annoying staccato beat and Leslie landed him a back hander as she crossed behind him to place the sandwich in front of Mac. Hana fixed a bib around the baby's neck and he looked up at her and squeezed his eyes shut tight in acknowledgement.

"Cheese or ham?" Leslie snapped and hit Pete again on the way to the fridge.

"Both," he replied, anticipation making his face pink. The old lady shook her head in irritation and slapped two pieces of bread on the bread board.

"Is it nice to see me?" Pete looked up at Hana like a child seeking approval. Her face softened and she nodded.

"It always is, love." Hana sat next to her son and smiled across at her former colleague, jerking her head towards the other diner at the table. "This is Caleb. He's staying with us for a while." She avoided catching Caleb's eye. "What's new with you, Pete?"

Pete's brow knitted and he leaned forward and lowered his voice. "Henrietta can't get pregnant. We've tried everything." He looked hopefully towards Hana and his eyes drifted over Mac's fluttering fingers as they pushed breadcrumbs into his teeny mouth. "I thought you might give me some tips."

Hana opened her mouth as colour leached from her cheeks, wishing he'd asked her anything else but that. A snort from Leslie broke the awkward silence and Hana stared in horror at the woman's heaving shoulders as Leslie buttered bread with her back to the room. She closed her eyes as the old kuia whipped round. "Try teckin' yer pants off!" she cackled and Hana cringed.

"I do!" Pete took her seriously and rose to his feet. His elasticated shorts dropped around his ankles to reveal spindly white legs and Hana clapped her hand over Mac's eyes and closed her own.

"Pete!" she squealed. Mac battled her fingers as his world went dark and his sandwich disappeared.

Caleb swore and placed a hand over the salad he'd pushed between two slices of bread, as though the airborne essence of Peter North might contaminate it.

"I need you to look, please," Pete pleaded and Hana opened her eyes at Leslie's sharp intake of breath. The sports teacher stood with his hands on his hips, a tuft of belly hair rising above the waistband of his undies. "Henrietta says they're too tight but they're my favourites. She got me Batman ones which are bigger but I love Superman best. What do you think?"

Hana groaned and forced herself to look. Every part of Peter North spewed from the child sized underwear like a tube of toothpaste squeezed by a moron. There were bulges where there shouldn't be and nothing in the expected places. He flattened his lips in a rueful smile at Hana's look of confusion and pointed to the large, yellow 'S' on his crotch. "I'm a bit cold," he announced. "It will come back out."

"Youse wahine's right!" Leslie grinned. "Them's your problem. The little tadpoles can't do their stuff if they're in prison."

"But these're my favourite!" Pete groaned, clasping his groin with both hands although only one would've been sufficient.

"Pants or babies?" Leslie demanded and Pete's flaccid features dissolved.

"Babies," he mumbled.

"They must do a bigger size," Hana said. "They look like they'd fit Wiri."

Leslie snorted. "Wiri would fill 'em better too."

"These were the only pair," Pete grumbled. "I've been wearing them for two weeks because I don't want Henri to steal them." He jabbed at an unpleasant looking rash at the junction between his thighs and his nether regions. "Do you think that's jock rot?"

"Oh, for frick's sake!" Caleb closed his eyes in disgust and turned away. Hana swallowed down the acid which threatened to make an entrance and communicated her distress to Leslie. Pete hopped around some more and Mac giggled at the floor show. Leslie reached into a drawer behind her and seized a pair of kitchen scissors. Hana opened her mouth to stop her but the old woman possessed fast reflexes for her age. Pete wailed in horror as the cool metal touched his bare buttocks and with a snipping sound, Leslie cut the elastic. Galvanised, Pete hopped around the kitchen table with his shorts around his ankles, clutching his groin and screaming. Leslie followed, chuckling and skipping behind him, administering random snips and making the slit wider. "Off, off, off!" she cried, getting into the spirit and enjoying herself. Carried away like a bride-to-be at a strip joint, she hurled the scissors into the sink and lurched at Pete's rear, wrenching the damage apart with her bare hands. A tearing sound filled the room and with a high pitched scream,

Pete's doughy body released the undies and Leslie raised them high above her head in victory.

"Oh, no!" Hana covered her eyes with her hand and looked away in disgust.

Pete's voice came out of the silence with a frisson of hurt in his tone. "Henri says I'm magnificent," he complained. "Don't be scared, Hana."

Hana made baulking noises in her throat like she might vomit and Leslie sniggered. "Youse just a little tiddler, man. I've been round Du Roses all me life and…"

"Stop!" Hana removed her hand and glared at Leslie. It gave her a full frontal view of Pete's nudity. "Pull your shorts up!" she snapped and Pete bent from the waist, his head disappearing towards the floor.

"What the hell?" Caleb's voice held a mixture of terror and disgust as Pete's full moon greeted him at close range. "Don't you show me your ass!" He took a swipe at Pete's bare bum with his crutch and missed, getting it stuck in Pete's shorts as he hiked them up. The shorts popped up with a hearty yank, taking the knobbly end of the crutch with them and Pete produced an admirable soprano. "Eugh! Eugh!" Caleb dropped the crutch at speed and hobbled backwards from his seat, clinging to the door frame with white knuckles. "I'm not touching that now!"

With a sigh of resignation Hana soothed the angst from the room with a healthy dose of English-sensible. "Why don't we eat?" she suggested. Caleb hobbled to the table and eyed Pete's sandwich on the bread board with eager anticipation, although he refused to sit next to him. "I didn't get ham and cheese," he stated, giving Hana the stink eye.

With a dirty chuckle, Leslie dropped the pants in the dustbin, washed her hands and returned to her sandwich making.

"It keeps popping out of my shorts now," Pete said, his tone sulky. He pushed his face under the lip of the table and performed some rearranging, bobbing up and down and making Mac laugh at the impromptu peek-a-boo.

"I'll walk along and get the children," Hana announced as the small crowd ate. Her soul sought escape from the presence of the confusing males. "Please can you watch Macky for me?"

"Course I can." Leslie spoke with her mouth full, spitting crumbs across the airwaves. "Ain't you teckin the ute?"

Hana shook her head. "Nah. Fresh air will do me good." She kissed Mac's forehead and waved at the rest of the room, seeking her jacket in the closet by the front door. When she turned towards the door whilst fitting her arms into the sleeves, she met Pete's face at very close range and screamed. "Bloody hell, Pete! Are you trying to give me another heart attack?"

"I'm coming with you," he said, yanking on the leg of his shorts.

Hana groaned, but he ignored her audible protest and followed her out onto the street, walking like a man with hemorrhoids. "You're making everyone stare!" Hana hissed as a group of pushchair touting women passed them on the pavement. Two of them looked back with confusion in their faces.

"My thing keeps popping under my shorts leg," Pete announced, grabbing flesh and material in one hand and walking a little easier.

"Just go back to the house," Hana begged. "I can't walk along with you while you interfere with yourself."

Pete's jaw gaped. "I'm not!" he snapped.

"Then walk normally!"

"I can't; it's rubbing!"

Hana exhaled and a sob of misery went with the whoosh of air. Pete's knobby knees strode along next to her like hairy white lighthouses in her peripheral vision. "Please behave!"

Phoenix seemed pleased to see Hana and performed a cute wrist wave for her mother's companion. "Hello un-cool Pete," she said, hiding behind Hana's legs and acting silly.

"Time to get Wiri," Hana urged. "Did you have a nice time with your new friend?"

"Yes, Mama." Phoenix skipped along holding her hand as they escaped into the street.

School opened up a whole new set of challenges. Phoenix brushed her hair out of her eyes. "Need a wee," she announced.

"Can you wait until we get home? It's not far." Hana's brow knitted in consternation.

"Nope. Need it now."

Wiri emerged from the classroom sporting a painting made up of black and brown splats. "Hey Ma. I've done a painting of the last muster." He jabbed a finger at the wet paint. "That's when Toby fell off in the mud."

"He'll love it." Hana cast around for a toilet sign. "Where's the bathroom?"

"Over there." Wiri pointed with an outstretched finger and Hana instructed him to stay with Pete in the playground. "My teacher wants to see you about my tatts."

"Okay. In a minute." Thinking she'd heard wrong, Hana pushed her daughter up the steps and into the toilet block, suffering Phoenix's squeals of delight at the neat row of porcelain sinks along one wall. "Hurry." Hana pulled the door closed as the child wrestled with her clothing and she leaned against it to wait. "Don't lock it!" she added as an afterthought.

"I likes these loverley toilets!" Phoenix announced with appreciation. "I comin' a school 'ere, aye?"

"Don't know, sweetie," Hana said, glancing over the top of the door. "Hurry up."

Phoenix flushed twice and washed her hands three times, fascinated by the blower which dried her fingers with warm air. Hana chased her out of the bathroom and down the steps to find a small woman pointing at Pete's shorts. "That's illegal!" she said, jabbing her finger in the direction of Pete's crotch. "It's flashing."

"It's accidental," Hana said, stepping between them. "And a very long story."

The woman rounded on her. "I want to know why my daughter apparently spent all playtime drawing tattoos on your son's chest in black marker pen. I'll never get it out of her school skirt and the blouse is ruined."

Hana gaped. "Pardon?"

"Look. I've got tatts like Pa now." Wiri pulled up his shirt and pullover to reveal a mess of black lines coating his torso. "It's my whakapapa."

Speechless, Hana stared at the myriad lines and patterns, some coloured in and others filled with odd shapes and speckled patches. The chest part circled his tiny nipples like a wonky bra. "It's...it's..."

"Magnificent." The male teacher appeared behind the woman and Hana heaved a sigh of gratitude. "But I've told both children that we don't do ta moko in our school; not during the day anyway." He chortled a good natured laugh and the small woman bristled.

"It's not funny!" She raised her voice and the handsome male met her look of disdain with calm assurance.

"No, it isn't. It's technically assault seeing as your daughter was the ringleader. Had Mr Du Rose not been fully accepting of their actions; I would have referred the matter to the principal."

"What?" The woman's face coloured bright red and she took a step back. "My Samantha's not a bully!"

The teacher smiled a slow expression of mirth and the woman jogged back to her gaggle of supporters. A group of small girls milled around the adults' legs.

"Need a wee again." Phoenix crossed her legs and Hana groaned.

"I'll talk to Wiri," she promised the teacher, abandoning the males to accompany her daughter back to the toilets. As Phoenix made straight for the hand dryer, Hana rebuked her. "You're just messing around! I don't have time for this."

Thwarted, the child plonked herself on the toilet and made a pretense of squeezing another small one out.

"Let's just go home." Hana emerged onto the top step with her daughter's hand gripped inside hers. Wiri's teacher had moved across the playground to speak to another group and Hana stared at the sight of Pete and Wiri surrounded by small girls. Wiri looked fed up.

"These reckon they're all coming back for a play date." Pete shrugged and Hana shook her head from side to side with determination.

"No way!" she hissed. "I only left you for a second!"

"I don't want them," Wiri announced. He jabbed a finger at Pete. "He said they could come."

The band of females oohed and aahed at Wiri's words, attracted by the powerful Du Rose X factor. It didn't seem to matter that his tone sounded insulting and he paid them no regard. "I'm Liesel," a pretty, blonde girl announced. "Will we be having cake?"

"Hello weasel," Phoenix said and gave a cute wave, mishearing. Wiri laughed and the girls crowded closer.

Hana leaned into Pete's face. "Put every single one of these children back where you found them," she growled. "I don't have time for this."

Pete's bottom lip curled downwards and he stomped around the school yard, making excuses and handing children back to reluctant mothers. Hana shook her head and glanced at Wiri. "What kind of mother lets her child go with a stranger?"

"Dunno." Wiri smiled at Phoenix and curled his fingers around her small hand. "Especially one wiv his willy hanging out his shorts."

34

Missing Stuff

"You promised us afternoon tea." Wiri's face crumpled in dismay. "You promised."

Hana chewed her bottom lip. "Will a trip to the dairy do?"

Wiri and Phoenix bent their heads together with conspiratorial ease and then nodded with smiles. "Pie and a fizzy drink?" Wiri asked, a natural negotiator.

"Okay." Hana's sigh signified defeat and they walked to the end of the road and turned left into a side street with a dairy.

"Do I get one too?" Pete asked, clutching his crotch one handed and hopping from foot to foot.

"Fine! But you wait out here with the children."

Hana emerged with hot pies, bottles of fizzy drink and three ice creams bundled together in her other hand.

"Ice creams first!" Pete declared and the children giggled at his rebellion. They sat on the low wall outside the dairy and watched as school children swarmed into the shop like ants. Pete snarfed his cornetto and laid into the pie and drink.

"Uncle Pete," Wiri said, his lips white rimmed with ice cream. He pointed a delicate finger at Pete's shorts. "It's popped out again."

Pete swore and Phoenix bugged her eyes in horror. With both hands around his hot pie, Pete looked hopefully at Hana. She pulled a disgusted face. "No way, dude! Ask me again and I'll tell Logan."

"I technically didn't ask," Pete replied, swallowing pastry at an astounding speed.

"You can tell him that as he chucks your dead body in the river," Hana replied, her tone dull.

"What's the matter with you today?" Pete's blue eyes radiated surprising perception as he glanced sideways at Hana. "Is it something to do with that kid?"

Hana groaned and nodded. "Yes. And no."

"Which is it?" Pete sprayed pastry over the pavement and Hana watched the flakes dance around in the breeze.

"Yes, Caleb is part of the problem and no, he's not all of it."

"So which bit is he?" Pete stopped chewing to glare at a boy from one of his classes and the child moved away, glancing at Pete's shorts leg with something like horror in his eyes. "The big bit or the little?"

"He's just some of it." Hana sighed. "His father used to work for us and Caleb broke his leg on our property. I took him in because I felt sorry for him and I suspect it wasn't my finest hour. Logan said he would be trouble and I don't want to admit he was right."

"Logan's always right." Pete grinned and adjusted his shorts. "Don't tell him I said so."

Hana shook her head. "I won't. I left Caleb up at the hotel with free board and lodging but he turned up here. Now he's making me nervous."

"Do you think he's got a crush on you?" Pete smirked. "Tell Logan. He'll sort that one out real quick."

"No." Hana narrowed her eyes and shook her head. "He didn't come to be nearer to me. It's something else. He's mixed up with Logan's nephew, Asher."

"What's my bruvver done now?" Wiri's expression accused Hana of betrayal as he fixed grey Du Rose eyes on her face. "What did Asher do?"

"Oops," Pete hissed under his breath and Hana exhaled in a rush of regret.

"Nothing, baby. Just a misunderstanding. Don't worry about it. Are you ready for your pie?" She fumbled in the carrier bag and fished out a steak and cheese, hoping to distract Wiri from an interrogation.

"My 'ave pie?" Phoenix turned guileless eyes on her mother and Hana's heart melted. "Peez, Mama," she added.

Hana handed out the food and drink and rolled her eyes at Pete. She jumped as her phone rang. "Hey, gorgeous." Logan's voice sent tingles down her spine and Hana closed her eyes, wishing she could conjure him up before her and bury her face in the safety of his muscular chest.

"Hey," she replied. "What's up?"

"Is Pete with you?"

Hana glanced sideways and grimaced. "Yes, but he's covered in pie so I'm not handing my phone over. Shall I put you on speaker phone?"

Logan laughed. "No babe. I don't want the kids to hear swear words like that. Tell him he's missing a staff meeting and is in big trouble. His balls are on the line."

Hana wrinkled her pretty nose and glanced down at Pete's shorts. "Not just his balls," she whispered.

"What?" Logan's jealous tone made her heart sink and she struggled to cover her error.

"Nothing. Nothing to worry about. We're just at the dairy and he's having a pie with Phoe and Wiri." She leaned across and placed the phone between the munching children. "Say hello to Daddy."

"I got pie, Pa!" Wiri called, mumbling over the goo in his mouth.

"Pie, pie!" Phoe's eyes rounded like tennis balls and Wiri laughed at her inability to say more than one word.

Hana put the phone against her ear and felt a wave of tiredness overtake her at the need to constantly prove herself worthy. "I'll send him back," she said, her voice terse.

"Hana?" Logan's voice raised as he shaped her name into a question. "What's wrong?"

"Nothing," she said with a sigh. "Nothing. We're just having afternoon tea as a treat and then we're walking home."

Logan's tone softened. "I trust you, Hana."

"Really?" She didn't mean it to sound so scathing.

"Yeah. Really. I know he's got his dick out; Leslie told me." His smirk leaked through his words, rounding them out and making them sound less dangerous. "Tell him he'd better find a pocket to stuff it into; our new headmistress is not amused by his absence. I'd better go. She's glaring at me through the glass doors."

The phone clicked and the absence of Logan's voice in her ear left a void. Hana sighed and turned to Pete. "Mrs Whatsit is taking the staff meeting and your absence is noted. Logan said you need to get back there as soon as you can."

To her surprise, Pete shrugged and slugged a mouthful of drink. "Whatever," he said and burped.

The children giggled and Hana turned to face him. "He wasn't kidding, Pete. She's there right now."

"Yeah, yeah." He turned a benevolent smile in her direction. "They just wanna stand at the common room window and watch me run across the soccer fields with my thing flapping out from under my shorts. I'm not stupid, Hana. I know that old woman told him she snipped my dags off."

Hana frowned. "No, he sounded pretty serious." Her eyes narrowed with concern. "You should head back."

Pete stood up and brushed crumbs from his shorts and hairy legs. "I'll walk back to yours and take the car."

Hana shrugged and helped the children off the wall. "It's your funeral," she muttered under her breath.

They set off walking and reached the edge of the soccer fields just as Pete's phone vibrated in his pocket. "Oh, that's what that funny feeling was in my shorts." He sounded surprised, fishing it out and putting it on speaker phone. He winked at Hana as though they shared in some secret joke. The caller's voice broke into the stillness of the green field and the expression on Pete's face made Hana snort and turn away. "Mr North! Is there some pressing reason why you've chosen to absent yourself from a prearranged staff meeting?"

"Er, what?" Pete peered at the phone in his hand as though it threatened to burn his fingers.

Recognising the voice of the new principal, Hana shooed Phoenix and Wiri away from the ensuing disaster and made a game out of following the white lines on the soccer pitch. She chased the children until they giggled. "What's un-cool Pete doing?" Phoenix asked, stopping so that her cousin ran into the back of her. Wiri swerved to the left and glanced at the teacher in the too-short-shorts, who argued and gesticulated at the black phone in his hand.

"Gettin' hisself into trouble," the child answered and Hana sighed, forced to agree with the juvenile wisdom.

"Logan! This isn't bloody funny!" Pete yelled into the phone and Hana held her breath. Wiri and Phoe burst into spontaneous laughter as Pete stamped around the edge of the soccer pitch, his shorts riding up and flesh making a reappearance. With a gasp, Hana covered both children's eyes and they wriggled to free themselves. "Whatever!" Pete screeched. "You just wanna see my man-bits wobbling and I'm not gonna give you the satisfaction! Besides, it hurts when it slaps against my thigh!" He pressed the button to disconnect, fumbling in his irritation and failing. Hana caught the horror in the principal's voice as she stammered in disgust.

"I beg your pardon? Mr North, get back here right now or you're fired!"

Pete adjusted his shorts and sauntered across to Hana, peering at his phone in annoyance. He shook it in Hana's face. "Do ya know what he did? That nasty old woman told him about my Superman pants and he got one of the food tech teachers to ring and pretend there's a staff meeting." His bottom lip drooped with petulance. "He thinks he's so bloody funny!"

Hana swallowed and gnawed on her bottom lip. She opened her mouth to speak but Wiri got there first. "There is a staff meeting. Pa told Ma he'd be late tonight because of it." The child poked a forefinger up his nose as the words tumbled from his mouth, wreaking havoc. "Yeah. That new lady boss is a bit mean. Pa said she's got rocks up her ass."

"Wiremu Du Rose!" Hana covered Phoenix's ears and glared at the little boy. He shrugged and ate the bogey from his fingertip.

"Well, he did say that. I heard him."

Phoenix swallowed and shook Hana's hands away. "Mama. Won't that hurt if you have stones up yer bum?"

Hana fixed a wooden smile on her face and turned to her daughter. "It would hurt. And that's why he didn't mean it."

"Oh no!" Pete hopped from foot to foot, his shorts flapping in the breeze. "Oh no!"

"Mama!" Phoenix patted Hana's thigh in panic. "Un-cool Pete's gonna poop stones! Quick, get the potty!" Anxiety made her grey eyes widen in fear and a sob escaped her rosebud lips.

"You'd better run across the paddock," Wiri said, his face creasing into a grin. "She's gonna skin yer alive."

"Hana! You have to help me!" Pete squealed, his colour ashen. "Say you're sick and I'm helping you. Say anything. Here, ring her back." He shoved his phone into her stomach and Hana recoiled.

"No! I'm not lying for you, Pete. Logan rang me because he knew you wouldn't believe him. We tried to tell you." Hana pushed the phone away and pointed towards the school building in the distance. "Wiri's right. You should run."

"Hurt me!" Pete dropped to his knees. "Break a bone and then call the ambulance. Give me a good excuse. You have to help me."

"I'm not breaking your bones!" Hana stepped back in horror, mortified to feel Pete's knotty fingers gripping her jeans. "Get off me."

"I'll hurt ya." Wiri put his rucksack down on the grass and stepped forward. "I'll kick youse in the head. Let go of my ma or I'll smash you good."

Phoenix gave a sharp intake of breath and Hana came to her senses. "This is ridiculous! Wiri, pick up your bag; we're going back to the house. Pete! Get up. Start taking responsibility for your actions!"

"No! No! You don't understand!" Pete lurched for her legs and Hana stepped back, clattering Phoenix in her haste. Rage charged through her blood and her temper snapped.

"That's enough!" She scooped up her daughter and breathed apologies into the side of the downy head, turning on her heel and hurrying towards the house in the distance. "Come on, Wiri!" she urged, glancing over her shoulder.

"Can't I just give him a little slap?" Wiri protested as Pete hobbled along on his knobby knees, wailing like a sick cow.

"No!" Hana felt her heart rate increase and her breath came in short rasps as anger took hold. "Come here right now!" She balanced Phoenix on her left hip and snatched up Wiri's wrist with her free hand. The short walk to the house seemed to take an age with the sound of Pete wailing behind her as he thrashed around in the grass. When the noise stopped abruptly, Hana turned and saw him running towards the school building, holding onto the bottom of his shorts with both hands. Wiri let out a snort of laughter which stuck in his throat as Hana glared at him.

"Nonie's gone out," Phoenix announced as they crossed the driveway. Hana fumbled in her pocket for the door key.

"How do you know?" She set the child down on the porch.

"Pa's ute's gone." Wiri put his hands on his hips and raised an eyebrow. "Om. That's naughty."

"Yes, it is." Hana fitted the key into the aged lock, hissing with annoyance as it wouldn't turn.

"It's unlocked." Wiri stepped up and pushed the front door open. Hana's blood ran cold at the sight of the unwelcome visitor standing in the hallway.

35

Unwelcome

"Hey, bro!" The grey-eyed man turned as Wiri ran into his legs, hoisting him up into his muscular arms with ease. "Have you missed me?"

"Yes!" Wiri buried his face into his brother's neck and Hana fought to keep the grimace from her face. "I thought you didn't love me anymore." The child's voice sounded muffled against Asher's sweater and his tiny knuckles showed white as he gripped around his neck.

"Egg!" Asher exclaimed. "You moved away from me, remember. I'm still where I always was."

"Where's the whānau?" Wiri asked, referring to his birth mother and father. "Did they come for me?"

Hana bit her lip and turned her face away from the child's agony. She excused herself and carried Phoenix through to the kitchen. Caleb shifted out of her way on his crutches, something like guilt in his eyes. Hana gave him a filthy look and passed him, setting Phoenix on a kitchen chair. "Where's Macky?" the little girl asked, pointing to the crumb littered high chair.

"With Nonie, hopefully," Hana said, reaching for the kettle and filling it with cold water. "Would you like some afternoon tea?"

"No, Mama! I had pie, member?" Phoenix covered her mouth with a tiny hand and giggled at her mother's error.

"Oh, yeah." Hana forced a smile onto her face. Her phone buzzed in her pocket and she pulled it out and removed the screen lock. She winced at Logan's unrepeatable text message, a litany of swear words punctuated by perfect grammar and punctuation. "I think Uncle Pete made it to the meeting," she muttered and Phoenix nodded with fake understanding.

"I tired," she said, yawning and rubbing her eyes. "Wanna go sleepies."

Hana moved to soothe her daughter. "But you won't sleep tonight," she crooned, stroking the dark curls.

"I will. Wanna go bed." Phoenix's face creased and she squeezed her eyes closed. "Promise. I just tired."

"Okay. Let's lie on my bed," Hana suggested. "We'll cuddle for a while and I'll wake you up for Dad coming home."

Phoenix nodded and allowed Hana to pick her up. Her body felt like a dead weight as the busy day at kindy caught her up and stripped her of all remaining energy. Hana went out into the hallway and caught the tail end of a conversation. Asher balanced Wiri on his hip and stared at Caleb, his expression worried. "Where is it?" he asked and Caleb closed his mouth as Hana passed carrying her daughter.

"Excuse me," she said with forced politeness, working her way between the teenagers. Asher watched her struggle, making no attempt to move and Hana gritted her teeth and resisted the urge to hurt him. Her skin prickled at his nearness, his sabotage of her home and business still uppermost in her mind.

"I'm hungry, Hana." Wiri's words cut deep and she steadied her breathing, his abandonment of her as a mother figure jarring and painful.

"You just had a pie," she said, keeping her voice quiet. Without looking back, she crested the stairs and carried her daughter along the landing, closing the bedroom door with her foot. The upstairs of the old house felt like a silent graveyard and Hana shivered and laid Phoenix on the bed, pulling a woollen shawl around them both. The little girl snuggled into Hana and wrapped her tiny arms around her mother's waist, providing comfort without meaning to.

Hana didn't intend to fall asleep. The threat of Asher Du Rose in her home should have been enough of an impetus to remain alert. She woke with a start as darkness pushed into the bedroom, extracting herself from Phoenix's arms. The scream escaped her lungs before she properly woke and Leslie jumped backwards, clutching Mac. "Nice!" Leslie snapped. "I'm not so ugly, am I?"

"Sorry, sorry!" Hana sat up and Phoenix uncurled from her ball, stretching and smiling at her grandmother. "You scared me. Why did you push your face into mine?"

"Macky gave you a kiss," Leslie grumbled. "I thought I'd give you one too, but my bottom teeth kinda popped out at the last minute. We were looking for them."

Hana turned sideways and saw Leslie's bottom plate sitting on Logan's pillow. She shrieked and moved away. Mac flapped his arms and giggled. Phoenix leaned over her mother and made a grab for them, almost succeeding as Hana batted her hands away.

"Is this a private orgy, or can anyone join?" Logan sounded tired and summoned up a wink for Phoenix as she reached out to him.

"Cuddles Papa." She sat up and stretched her arms, squeezing her eyes closed in enjoyment as he reached down to hoist her up and onto his hip. Logan's face creased into a look of disgust as Leslie grappled around on his pillowcase for her teeth. She shoved them back into her mouth and stood up with a smile.

Mac giggled and reached out to put his finger in her mouth. Hana shook her head and watched Logan grow pale.

"Grab Mac." His eyes widened and Hana opened her arms to her son, who plunged forward into her chest.

"He's fine," she whispered under her breath, turning and setting her feet on the floor. Leslie spun on her heel, yanking her underwear out of her bottom.

"Do you have to?" Logan bit, his expression threatening. "You chuck your choppers on my pillow and then dance around with your fingers up your..."

"Logan!" Hana's voice held a warning and Phoenix pushed her thumb between her lips. "Not in front of the children."

"I'll make dinner." Leslie shimmied from the room with her fingers seeking the source of the discomfort. Logan shoved the door closed behind her with the heel of his cowboy boot.

"Look at my pillow!" he groaned, pointing to the wet patch in the centre where his head usually rested. "Why's she here, anyway?"

"What's wrong, Logan?" Hana stood, cuddling Mac into her shoulder. He rubbed his nose against her neck and settled with his face tucked into her hair.

"I don't want that kid here." Logan stood in front of the window and stared into the darkening sky. Phoenix sucked her thumb and twirled a lock of her father's dark hair. "I've got a bad feeling about him."

Hana swallowed. "Sorry," she conceded. "I jumped in with both feet and I made a mistake. I agree with you, but don't know how to fix it. I can't throw him out on the street with a broken leg, but I don't want him here either."

Logan turned to face her, his brow knitted in surprise. The scar beneath his right eye seemed to pulse in line with his heartbeat. "Did you just defer to me, Mrs Du Rose?" A smirk lit his mouth, tugging it upwards on one side. His teeth grazed his lower lip and he looked away.

"I know you're laughing at me." Hana pouted, tossing her red hair in defiance. Mac giggled as the fiery tresses stroked his face. "I can't put my finger on it but he's up to something."

Logan nodded, his expression tired. "With Asher. I saw the loser drive away as I walked across the soccer pitch." He turned to face her, eyes narrowed in suspicion. "Why did you park the truck, so it blocked the road? The principal bawled me out on the phone. She left before the faculty meetings started and complained because she needed to mount the curb to drive through the gate."

"I didn't," Hana began, the realisation crossing her face as her sentence ended. "Leslie used it. I walked to get the children from school and when I got back, she'd taken Macky out somewhere."

Logan sighed. "I wish you'd done it. Leslie won't listen to a word I say." He laid his daughter on the bed and tickled her tummy, resorting to baby-talk for his next statement. "Now all we need to do is get rid of our unwanted house guests and life can go back to normal."

36

Problem Children

"Wiri, no!" Hana caught sight of the small boy hovering in the doorway, his tiny fingers clasping the frame. He moved fast and her heart sank as she shoved the baby towards her husband. "Logan didn't mean you, Wiri!" She ran after him, intercepting his skinny body at the top of the stairs and scooping him up.

"Get off me!" he shouted, flailing with his arms and catching Hana on the collarbone in a direct hit. The pacemaker beneath took the force, bruising the tender skin above it and dragging an agonised groan from between Hana's lips. An old fear overtook her and she bent double, feeling the blood rush to her head as she waited for it to administer the electric shock she'd spent the last two years expecting.

"Sorry! Sorry!" Wiri screamed and stepped backwards the moment his feet touched the floor. "I didn't mean it. It was an accident." His voice caught and he almost tumbled down the split-level staircase, stopping himself with scrabbling fingers on the bannister rail. His eyes widened to the size of gold coins as Logan's powerful frame loomed in his vision.

"What the hell happened?" Logan seized Hana's shoulders and held her still. His presence offered comfort and she felt her raging pulse slow. Her chest eased and her fingers fluttered against the painful flesh beneath her collar bone. In her peripheral vision she watched Wiri's socks disappear down the stairs, his little legs pumping beneath him. Caleb's crutches scraped on the tiles in the downstairs hallway and Leslie grumbled and complained as she hauled herself from the kitchen.

"Phoe, keep Macky in the bedroom please baby." Logan dropped to his haunches as Hana slid down the wall. "What can I do?" he whispered. "Do you need an ambulance?"

"No." Hana gasped out the word. She laid her head back against the plaster and closed her eyes, hissing out shallow breaths through pursed lips. "He lashed out and caught me here." Her fingers fluttered against the metal shape under the porcelain skin and Logan unbuttoned her blouse to look at the damage. Then he snorted like a bull.

"Bloody hell, Hana. It's made a blue line around two sides of it. I'll fricken kill him."

"He's upset." The words escaped with a sob. "He thinks you want rid of him too." She lowered her voice. "He heard what you said."

Logan winced. "Sorry. But he's hurt you, Hana." He shook his head. "Can you stand?"

"Just leave me here for a minute." Hana rolled her neck, willing the sickness away from her soul. "I'll be fine." Her complexion looked pinched and grey. "The pacemaker didn't go off. Do you think mine's a broken one?"

Logan stood and shook his head. "You've got this idea that it'll throw you across a room, Hana. I've told you heaps of times; your heart rate gets too low and that's when it shocks you. There are parameters it operates within, but it goes off when your heart rate drops, not spikes." He opened his mouth to speak and then closed it again.

"What's going on?" Leslie demanded from the middle of the staircase, peering around the corner with concern etched into her features. "What happened?"

A squeal from Phoenix drew their attention towards the bedroom, Leslie craning her neck around the newel post. "Mama, look! Mac's coming a see youse!"

Hana's eyes widened as her son rocked on all fours, determination creating hard lines in his baby face. Backwards and forwards he swayed, his bottom touching his heels and then lurching again. His weight shifted and a hand edged forward, then another. Left knee, right knee and then he got it, the rhythmic movements of a crawl. "Mama!" Phoenix bounced next to the baby, her excitement feverish and at the same time afraid. "He's walkin' Mama! He's rescue youse."

Logan watched his son with pride and gave Mac a thumbs up. Leslie clutched her ample bosoms and beamed at Hana. "See, kōtiro, my mokopuna's good in every other way."

Hana swallowed at the backhanded compliment, recognising in Leslie's rumpled face the doubt created by a legacy of wives' tales. She bit back the urge to scream at her that deaf didn't mean disabled in everything, the pressure of Logan's hand on her shoulder providing fortification. "She guessed," he whispered. "But she means well."

Mac plummeted onto his face, rocking on his rounded tummy and wailing with rage at the abrupt end to his victory. Phoenix squatted next to him and patted his wriggling back, murmuring encouragements which his useless eardrums wasted. Her voice soothed and cajoled and Logan strode across to retrieve Mac from the floorboards, touching Phoenix's hair in approval. He whispered something to her in Māori and her face opened into a beam of pride. Leslie nodded.

"Yeah, she's a good big sister," she translated with affection and Hana felt the doors of their shared language bang closed in her face for the millionth time in her marriage. She shut her eyes against her own inability to learn their beautiful dialect, with its lilting inflections and taste of bubbling rivers and mountain air. Hauling herself to a standing position using the bannister rail and Leslie's outstretched arm, Hana placed her fingers over the tender spot on her chest and remembered Wiri.

"Find Wiri for me," she asked Leslie. "We need to talk about this whole mess."

Leslie nodded and backed away, turning on the stairs to obey. "Mind your own business," she said to Caleb who waited at the bottom. "It's family stuff, nothing to do with youse." Her voice sounded sharp and Hana cringed. She wanted to rebuke the old lady for her cruelty but something about the young man jarred at her nerves.

Logan held Phoenix's hand and carried a struggling Mac. He kissed Hana's forehead. "You okay?" he asked, his voice soft.

Hana nodded. "Yeah. It just hurt at the time and I still panic that the wires might pull out and then where will I be? I don't even know if the bloody thing works!"

"It works!" Logan sounded exasperated. "They check it every time you go to the hospital, Hana. They've told you how to check it on your phone if you're scared. You still don't trust it?"

"It's never gone off by itself!" she snapped, rubbing at the sore spot. Delicate fingers wound their way through the hem of her sweater and she looked down to see Phoenix staring up at her, anxiety in her eyes.

Logan heaved in a breath and set his jaw. "Hana, it does go off, okay. Just trust me."

"What?" She turned to him, brow knitted in confusion. "You don't know that."

"Yes I do." He gritted his teeth and wrestled with the words forming on his tongue. "It goes off a few times every night. I didn't want to tell you because I knew you'd freak out, but it works, babe. It works just fine."

Hana's fingers caressed the aching bruise on her chest. Logan focussed on it as the blue line grew and Hana put her hand over it to force him to look at her. "What do you mean?" She shaped her words with care and her green eyes blazed in a heady mixture of anger and fear. "How do you know?"

Logan's shoulders slumped. "The muscle in your chest twitches. I've felt it." He swallowed. "It terrified me the first time it happened. I started taking your pulse at night and it drops real low sometimes. The pacemaker kicks in when it gets too bad." He shifted on his cowboy boots and Hana heard the floorboards creak beneath him. "I asked the cardiac specialist about it on your second appointment and he took a closer look at you. He said it's unusual to get muscle movement but not unknown. Once or twice a night is okay but if it's in quick succession, I need to get you to the hospital." Logan focussed at a spot on the ceiling. "I know it works, Hana. I thank God every time it does its job because I can't lose you." He closed his eyes against emotion he couldn't deal with and his jaw worked beneath the dark shadow of beard on his skin.

Hana lowered her head, the anger expelled from her soul as she watched her strong husband struggle. She felt torn. "I should be cross you didn't tell me," she said. "But I feel an idiot for worrying about it." Her eyes narrowed in confusion. "When did you speak to my specialist? I sat there with you the whole time."

Logan shook his head. "You went for a blood test and I didn't go with you. Now he just sends you to pee in a jar or any excuse he can think of so he can ask me how you're really doing."

"So, I don't need to keep peeing in a jar?" Hana's jaw hung open in indignation.

"No idea." Logan shrugged. "Maybe. Maybe not." He shifted Mac on his hip and winked at Phoenix.

The commotion at the bottom of the stairs made everyone except Mac jump. Leslie's voice rose from a shout into a screech. "Where is he?" she hollered.

"Where's who?" Logan leaned over the bannister as horror crept into his expression. He swore, knowing the answer before the old woman spoke.

"I don't know!" Caleb shouted back and they heard the sound of metal banging on bone. Logan took the stairs two at a time still carrying his son. The baby clung to his neck and grinned at the unexpected rollercoaster ride. Hana hoisted Phoenix onto her hip and followed, rounding the dogleg and gasping at the scene before her.

Logan stood with Mac on his hip and his other arm raised, gripping the crutch against Leslie's tugging. Caleb was boxed into a corner by the front door, balancing on one leg with his arms protecting his head. "She's broken my wrist!" he shrieked. "It's nothing to do with me!" Logan's biceps bulged beneath the sleeves of his shirt and his vice-like grasp on the crutch turned his knuckles white.

"Wiri's gone!" Leslie wailed. She let go of the weapon and sank to her knees. "Asher stole him!"

"What?" Hana hurried forward, her heart thudding in her chest. "No!" Panic drained her colour and widened her eyes as the awful sense of loss seeped through her body. "Please, don't say that. He wouldn't. Tell her, Logan. Asher knows he can't take him."

An explosion of misery erupted from Phoenix as she cast around looking for her small companion. She sobbed and wriggled, begging for release from Hana's grasp. Her mother set her on the floor and took a step back, her hands covering her mouth and her shoulders heaving.

Logan strode towards Caleb and dragged him from the corner one handed, forcing the teenager to hop on his good leg. "Where is he?" he demanded, his voice cold and threatening. Mac covered Logan's mouth with his hand, absorbing the tension in his father's body and deciding he didn't like it. "Get up!" Logan snapped at Leslie. "Take the kids."

"No!" Hana wailed, pulling Phoenix against her leg. "Give Macky to me. I'll keep them safe." Wiri's absence caused a void to open up in her soul, threatening her other babies. Her rational mind told her to strap them to her body. "Call the cops, Logan," she begged.

"Asher left hours ago," Caleb interjected, his voice wavering. "The kid ran down the stairs and through the door. I couldn't move fast enough to stop him."

"Asher took him!" Leslie screeched. "Why else did he drive all the way down here?" Her wizened face paled, her eyes bugging, so the whites glowed around the dark irises. "You rotten boy! How could you?" She lurched for the crutch, surprising Logan into letting go. The old woman jabbed the rubber end into Caleb's stomach with surprising agility and force. "If you brought trouble here after these good people showed you nothing but kindness, I'll kill you!" She swiped again with the crutch and Mac let out a wail, not liking the game anymore.

"Hana take Mac!" Logan thrust the child towards her, strengthening his grip on the metal. "Leslie, stop!" He yanked the crutch away from her and rounded on the teenager. "Did Asher come to take Wiri?"

Caleb swallowed and Hana spared him a moment of pity. Logan's brand of interrogation knew no bounds and she imagined the expression on his face as he leaned in closer to the frightened boy. She noted the square set of his shoulders and the tendons showing in the back of his neck. She knew his grey eyes must be flashing danger signals and she gave the teenager a way out. "Tell him, Caleb. He'll get it out of you, anyway. I'm calling the cops, so if you're not honest with us they'll make you tell the truth."

"No, not the cops!" Caleb squirmed, pushing his backside as far into the corner as it fitted. "You can't call the cops." His cheeks pinked and he slid down the wall until his good leg formed an arch beneath him. "Please don't."

"I don't have time for this!" Leslie screamed and waddled into the kitchen to retrieve her mobile phone. "I'm calling them. My moko's out there alone in the dark. This boy doesn't know what truth is."

Logan's fingers closed around Caleb's throat as he lost patience and bodily lifted him to a one-legged standing position. Hana heard the teenager gag and put her fingers over Phoenix's eyes. "Logan, don't!" she said, authority in her tone.

"Asher didn't come for him. He wanted me. He left hours ago after Hana went upstairs. I couldn't give him what he wanted, so he hit me in the guts and drove away." Caleb reached under his shirt and displayed his ribcage. A black smudge started under the bottom rib on his skinny frame and curved towards his midsection. "The kid ran out the door crying. I wasn't quick enough to stop him."

Logan let go and Caleb sank to the tiled floor, his body shaking. "He can't have gone too far," Logan said, snatching the ute keys from the sideboard. He didn't look at Caleb again but stepped over him, slamming the front door on his way out.

"Cops is coming," Leslie announced, emerging from the kitchen with the phone in her hand. "They'll be here in five minutes."

"No! No! No!" Caleb screeched. He writhed on the tiles in an effort to get up and seized hold of his crutches. "You bloody stupid old woman! Why did you do that? I asked you not to!"

Hana's heart quailed and the women exchanged a look. "What have you done, Caleb?" Hana asked, her voice terse. "I asked you that question once before and you assured me you weren't in trouble."

"I wasn't," he gasped. "But I am now and so are you."

37

Unwanted

"You didn't bring it here?" Leslie's shout made Hana jump and her dozing son jerked on her shoulder.

"Bring what?" Hana pressed her daughter closer to her leg as she sensed disaster looming. "Bring what here?"

"The weed!" Leslie snorted. She advanced on Caleb. "What did you do with it?" The teenager cowered back into the corner and Phoenix let out a wail.

"Hana!" Logan's sharp admonishment from the open front door drew her attention back to her distressed daughter and she nodded at him and grabbed Phoenix's hand. "Take the kids into the kitchen. Wiri's not out here; I've checked. I'll wait for the cops and then drive around."

Hana nodded and edged backwards to the kitchen, her gaze never leaving his face. She watched as a vein pulsed in his forehead; part of his early warning system.

"It's fine, baby, it's fine." Hana nursed both children on her lap at the kitchen table, able to hear only raised voices from the hallway.

"Papa's mad," Phoenix whimpered. "Wiri's gone."

Hana shook her head and kissed the little girl's downy curls. "Dad will find Wiri. He's worried, not mad."

"Papa's mad," Phoenix repeated and Hana winced. The pulsing vein told its own tale. She tapped her foot on the tiles, desperate to hear the outcome of what sounded like a heated discussion. Police sirens broke the sound of steady traffic along Maui Street and her whole body tensed.

"Peese can I have biscuit?" Phoenix asked, rubbing the back of her hand across her eyes. Hana opened her mouth to say no but her mind ran ahead of it, welcoming the distraction.

"That's a great idea, sweetie," she answered, smiling at her daughter. "Sit up at the table and I'll get some." Planting her daughter on a chair, Hana lurched for the pantry and retrieved a packet of chocolate-covered biscuits. Mac's head shot up in interest and she plonked the pack in front of the little girl. "Take one and give one to Macky." The baby went into his high chair with ease, slipping beneath the restraints like a knife through butter. His delicate wrists twisted and turned with excitement as his fingers flexed and he made sucking noises with his lips. Phoenix shoved a biscuit across the table and Hana put it into her son's hand. "I'm just here, Phoe," she told her child, slipping through the kitchen doorway and waiting, one eye on her babies and the other keeping tabs on the adults in the hallway. "Logan," she hissed, "I think the cops are here."

"Ooh, my bro' Bodie," Phoenix muttered and Hana's heart missed a beat. She hoped and prayed her son didn't get out of the police car whose blue and red lights clambered onto the driveway and reflected through the glass in the front door.

Logan nodded and swore, shoving Caleb aside to intercept the officers on the porch. "Get inside. I'll deal with you later," she heard him growl and the skinny teenager hopped sideways out of reach. Leslie gave him a rotten glare and headed towards Hana, shoving her through the doorway.

"Just listen," she whispered. "One of the reasons I left Alfie was because he paid that stupid boy, Asher to clear the drugs off the roof. I begged him not to because the kid can't keep his mouth shut, but Alfie said he couldn't do it himself. Asher cleared it away, hosed it down and disinfected the lot but I saw him through the kitchen window." Leslie's fingers writhed on her skirt hem and she hauled it up past the point of decency. During Hana's moment of extreme distraction, Phoenix took another biscuit and grinned at her brother.

"Saw him do what?" Hana's urgent tone brought Leslie to her senses.

"Put the bin bags of marijuana into the back of his car," she whispered, her voice high and squeaky. "I followed him to Caleb's place and watched him unload it there. I told Alfie, but he said it wasn't his problem no more. Said his own son called him a junkie for trying to fix his arthritis, so he didn't care if the kid sold it to all the hotel guests. I got scared. Logan and me don't like each other, but he's done right by me over the years. I didn't want to see his business hurt. I fought with Alfie and he told me to leave, so I did. There was something else, but that's staying between me and him. It's private. But that Caleb hung around with Asher from the minute he arrived and I knew they'd be up to no good. Alfie stormed off and I packed my car. I made Lincoln load that kid's bag in so I could drop him off somewhere along the way. We don't need his kind making trouble on the mountain."

"So you brought him here instead?" Hana heard Logan's cowboy boots moving around on the porch outside and a flashlight drifted past the kitchen window. "How did he get it here?"

"What? The marijuana? No idea." Leslie's stage whisper filled Hana's brain with panic and she clapped a hand over her mother-in-law's mouth.

"Stop saying that word," she begged. "The cops are outside!"

"I know." Leslie patted Hana's upper arm with an expression of sympathy. "I called them, remember kōtiro?"

Hana gritted her teeth, watching her mother-in-law view her with forced compassion, like someone who'd walked into a room full of laughing people having missed two thirds of the joke. "I know you called them." She forced the words out. "Wiri's missing."

"No, isn't." Phoenix giggled and swung her feet, reaching for another biscuit. Mac beamed and licked the chocolate off his and Hana halted, her mouth half open. Her son coughed on an abundance of coloured sprinkles and she stared in confusion.

"How did Mac get that one? He's not allowed the ones with bits on."

Phoenix giggled again. "Wiri done it."

Leslie shook her head. "Moko's talkin' rubbish."

"Phoe!" Hana's voice turned her daughter's head. "How did Mac get another biscuit? Did you give it to him?"

The front door opened and Logan's voice drifted down the hallway. "Hana? Can I borrow your phone so I can grab a recent photo of Wiri? I'll email it to these officers so they can circulate it."

Hana stuck her head through the kitchen door and nodded, noting the strain on her husband's face. The back of Caleb's head showed through the bannister railings where he'd slumped onto the bottom step. "Come out, Wiri."

Leslie looked at her like she'd crossed the line into crazy, but Hana persisted. "Come out, Wiri, or I'll get cross." A snuffle sounded from somewhere in the pantry and Hana narrowed her eyes. "I mean it!" she said, trying and failing to keep her voice level. "I'll count to three and I want you standing right in front of me. One."

"You called the cops on me," Wiri wailed from beneath the bottom shelf and Hana saw the outline of a bare foot in the gloom.

"Told youse," Phoenix chirped and reached for another biscuit. Hana ignored Leslie's open mouth and leaned forward, sliding the packet out of her daughter's reach.

"Two," she said.

"I'll go call them off," Leslie muttered, stamping out to the hallway. Hana heard low voices at the front door.

"Do I need to use three?"

"No." Wiri's voice sounded muffled. "Are you gonna let the cops rest me?"

"Arrest you? No." Hana sighed.

Wiremu Du Rose slipped from his hiding place and emerged, dusty but unharmed. His feet made no sound on the floorboards as he handed over a jam flavoured biscuit to Mac. The baby boy screwed up his face and head butted the gift, shattering it onto the high chair tray. Phoenix giggled again and her tiny brother set about putting the broken pieces into the slot in his face. Wiri watched, refusing to get eye contact with Hana.

"I ran away because you don't want me no more." His voice sounded heavy with sadness and rejection. "It's 'cause I called you Hana instead of Ma when Asher came. I hurted your feelings so you don't want me." He swallowed back tears, the weight of the world pressing down on his slender shoulders. "And I was naughty and moved the nasty boy's gear."

"Do you want a cuddle," Hana asked and watched as the dark curls bobbed up and down. "Come here then." She held out her arms and Wiri marched across, his little body stiff with anticipation of more rejection. Hana collapsed onto the seat next to Phoenix and pulled him into her lap. "I felt surprised when you called me Hana, but I understand why. You've got a mummy and Asher probably wouldn't like it. You overheard what Logan said but not all of it; just the ending. He didn't mean you. You're family." Hana stroked the dusty fringe back from Wiri's face. "Nothing will change that."

Logan's tread sounded heavy as he led the concerned police officers along the hallway, Leslie following close behind. Hana recognised neither of them and relief flooded her soul. They insisted on speaking to Wiri alone to ascertain his reasons for disappearing, without adult coercion. Logan rolled his eyes at

Hana and leaned his backside against the counter, reaching for a pre-licked biscuit and then changing his mind.

"Logan," Hana began and he shook his head at her, placing a slender index finger over his lips.

"Not yet," he whispered.

The police officers returned Wiri to Hana's knee and accepted the apology for wasting their time. "Not at all," the youngest of the two said with a smile. "We're never sorry about happy endings."

The older one jerked his head towards Logan and he followed them down the hallway. Hana waited until the front door closed and her husband's imposing figure returned to the kitchen, running a hand through his dark hair. "Bloody hell!" he exclaimed.

"I said I'm sorry hundreds and thousands of times," Wiri grumbled, his face creasing into a pout.

"I like hundreds and fousands," Phoenix declared. "My 'ave some of dem too?"

"No!" Hana heaved out a sigh. "Wiri, Caleb saw you go out the front door, so how did you end up hiding in the pantry?"

Wiri wrinkled his nose. "Easy. Go out the front and come in the back."

"Right." Hana rolled her eyes at Leslie. "I think Nonie would love to bathe you all so Daddy and I can make dinner." She shot a look of pleading at her mother-in-law and for once, Leslie didn't argue.

"I feel sick," Phoenix announced. "I don't want dinner."

"I feel sad. I don't want dinner." Wiri slid off Hana's knee and waited by Leslie as she hoisted the baby from the biscuit rubble. Phoenix followed, leaving a streaky brown chocolate mess on the table.

"What did the policeman ask you?" Hana asked and Logan raised an eyebrow.

"What do you think, Hana?"

Wiri sighed and his slender shoulders slumped. "He asked me if youse been bashin' me or if I did hidin' for a game." The boy got eye contact with Hana and his chin wobbled. "I telled 'im that my real ma and pa don't want me no more because I'm a bad boy." He reached out tentative fingers and latched onto Leslie's skirt.

Hana opened her mouth to refute his version of the truth and Logan shook his head. Leslie left the room with the sad crowd trailing behind her. "You're wasting your breath," Logan said, his voice soft. "The kid won't hear what you're saying. It can't compete with the crap in his head."

Hana put her hands over her face and heaved out a sigh as the group made its way up the staircase. "What a night," she groaned.

Caleb's crutches scraped their way along the hallway, click, click, click. Logan snorted and shook his head, fringe bouncing against his dark eyelashes. "Did you think it was over?" he asked, amusement lighting his grey eyes. "Sorry to disappoint you, but the trouble's only just started."

38

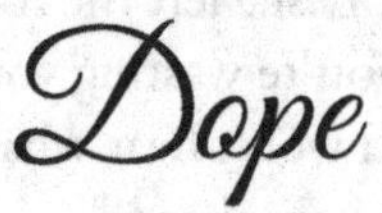

"Hey! Get in here!" Logan's voice held command as he summoned Caleb. Hana sank deeper into Phoenix's vacated chair to wait while the crutches clicked closer. She flicked at a stray crumb and pursed her lips as it pinged out of control and hit the draining board.

Caleb limped into the kitchen and headed for the furthest corner away from Logan. "It's not my fault," he started, not waiting for Logan to close the door behind him.

"Shut up." Logan leaned against the counter and bent one leg, resting the sole of his cowboy boot on the cupboard door. Hana stiffened at the warning tension in her husband's body. "You brought weed to my house." Statement not question. Logan's voice dripped menace and Hana gnawed on her lower lip, anger and fear mixing into a heady combination.

"Why?" she snapped, standing and gripping the edge of the table. "Didn't we give you enough help or support?"

Caleb shook his head and his stance epitomised sulky teenager. "It's not that. You wouldn't tell me where my dad is.

It's why I'm here." He worked his jaw and Hana shook her head, finding it impossible to feel compassion for him.

"So, you put my family in this position to force my hand?" Temper flared in her green eyes and she let go of the table, moving past its wooden corner to get closer to Caleb. Logan stopped her with a hand on her upper arm.

"Tell me the whole story," he demanded and Caleb eyed the chair nearest the high chair. He clicked across to it and slumped down.

"You left me," he said, his tone accusing. "You left and now you won't tell me where my father is."

"I offered you to come with us!" Hana shouted. "You said no!"

"Hana, Hana." Logan slipped an arm around her waist and pulled her into his side. With a tender hand which belied the tension in his stance, he stroked her cheek and forced her to look up at him. "Let me do this, sweetheart. He'll tell me what I want to know."

"Or what?" Caleb snorted, hatred in his eyes. "Asher told me all about you, big man! What will you do?"

"Break your other leg." Logan said it without inflection, his tone level and easy, but his grey eyes flashed danger and his smile offered no sense of play.

Caleb swallowed and his eyes bugged. "You wouldn't." He jerked his head towards Hana. "She won't let you."

Logan's smile widened and Hana held her breath. "Asher doesn't know jack about me, but if you wanna try me, keep going little boy. Talk about my wife in that tone again and I'll break it just for fun."

Caleb's nerve disappeared with the dawning realisation that Logan meant what he said. Hana watched him eye the tall Māori, searching for weakness and finding none. A glance upwards showed her a man who never backed down from a fight and didn't know how it felt to lose one. His vehemence terrified her and mana poured from him in waves of power. Her mind cast back to the photo of Logan on a madman's wall, aged sixteen and clutching a soccer ball for a team photo. Perhaps he possessed it even then; a faulty off-switch which removed boundaries and levelled fear. His body against hers resembled a coiled spring, waiting for Caleb to provide an excuse to release the tension in the muscular shoulders and ramrod straight back. But the hand around Hana's waist remained gentle, the fingers caressing the gap between her sweatshirt and jeans.

"Okay, okay." Caleb caved in the face of a man with enough stubbornness to beat him hands down in the war of silence. "I'll tell you everything."

"Damn straight," Logan replied, his voice sounding unconcerned but his body saying otherwise. "Because you know an awful lot about me for a kid who allegedly hung around a camp site for a couple of months."

Caleb dodged the inference. "The old man in the hotel had this crop of weed," he began, shifting around on the hard seat. "He asked Asher to help him get rid of it for a bit of extra cash. Asher started clearing it before you left but he told me about it and asked if I'd store some of it for him." Caleb swallowed. "I didn't realise it would be so much; bags of the stuff. Ash got rid of heaps to a guy in the township, but he kept some back just for us." He paused and shot a look of resentment at Hana. "I wanted you to tell me about my dad but you don't even talk about him."

Hana's head shot up with indignation in her eyes. "How was I supposed to know you're his son? I'm not telepathic."

Logan's eyes narrowed. "So that's why my dead beat nephew turned up at my house. Why did he send the stuff here with you?"

Caleb's shoulders dropped. "He promised to find out where Flick went if I did this for him. Said he's got friends with a house on the outskirts of Hamilton and they might have a room for me. We were gonna smoke it with them, to soften them up for me moving in. They knew Flick from before, or that's what Asher said."

Hana closed her eyes and exhaled through her nose. Caleb shifted from dangerous to gullible in the space of two sentences. Logan's fingers moved over her skin in a slow, calming rhythm. "And?"

Indignation flooded Caleb's face. "He's a liar! I brought it here and hid it under the stairs. He said we'd go today and meet his mates. I upset that old lady to make her go out, but Asher didn't turn up when he promised and the bag disappeared. Now he won't tell me where my dad's gone or take me to see the house!" Caleb's voice raised to a shout and Hana jumped. "He lied to me!"

"There's no house and no mates and he doesn't know jack about your dad." Logan's voice maintained its even keel, creating a bubble of safety around Hana. She leaned against him, grateful for the warmth beneath his arm.

Caleb hobbled to his feet and leaned on the table. "There is. One of them knows my dad real well. I need the weed to get the information." The teenager's jaw worked from side to side as he ground his teeth, hurt blazing in his eyes. "And the room sounded perfect."

"You idiot!" Logan's nose wrinkled with disgust. "You're not Flick's son; he's got more street smart in his left eyebrow than you'll ever have. Is that the other part of your con?"

"No!" Caleb's eyes filled with tears and unless his acting ability outweighed his skills in character judgement, he told the truth. "My mum told me Robert Dressler is my dad." The first tear fell and he brushed it away with a rough hand. Hana felt the ice in her heart thawing but as she shifted on her feet, Logan's hand around her waist tensed, locking her against him.

"We just had the cops here, idiot. Where's the hash?"

"I don't know!" Caleb's voice rose to an irritating wail. "It's gone! Asher went mad. He said these guys at the house paid good money. He punched me in the gut and stormed off."

"They already paid?" Logan's head shook from side to side. "I doubt that. What else did they want?"

"Nothing. Just the weed. Asher thinks I double crossed him and hid it at the hotel." Caleb's voice lowered and shame crept in. "He's going back there to look."

"Geez." Logan released Hana and ran both hands over his face, stopping to rub at his eyes. Cold seeped back into her bones without the warmth of his arm and she realised how much she relied on his protection. A life without him became unthinkable.

"What will you do?" Hana heard the wavering of her own voice and hated the fear there.

"I need to think." Logan pressed a kiss to her forehead and stepped away, already reaching in his trouser pocket for his phone. Turning at the door he jabbed a finger at Caleb. "You crossed the line, kid." The door clicked shut behind him.

"Where did you hide the stuff?" Hana watched as Caleb sank back into his chair. She heard the children running around overhead as Leslie tried to round them up to put into pyjamas. Glancing at the ceiling she wanted to be up there with them, not left in a room with a snivelling traitor.

"Under the stairs." Caleb gave a huge sniff and Hana reached across and threw him a roll of kitchen paper. He snagged a couple of sheets and blew out a disgusting stream of snot.

"Where? Show me."

The hallway felt cold after the kitchen and Hana shivered as she walked towards the front door, Caleb tapping out his beat behind and reminding her of his crippled status. "Where?" she repeated and he pointed a crutch towards a panel beneath the newel post.

"Kick it at the bottom and it pops out." Caleb jerked his head forward. "All these old villas have a space there. I thought everyone knew that."

Hana pressed a tentative toe against the triangular panel and nothing happened. She stared at Caleb with accusation in her eyes. "No, kick it!" He mimicked the movement, almost overbalancing. Hana nudged the panel with more force and felt it move a fraction. A harder push popped it out at the top and she bent to wrest it free. Kneeling, she peered inside, seeing a cavernous space the full width of the staircase and the height of the bottom two steps. A sweet but musty scent filled her nostrils. Hana sighed and sat back on her haunches. "Did Leslie know what you brought? She must have seen you put it into her car."

Caleb shook his head. "She came to me real angry and said she watched Asher unload some of the bags into my motel room the day before and guessed what they were. I think she asked her husband to sort me out, but he didn't care. Asher had already sold all the bags except one and I'd hidden that. The old lady searched the whole room but couldn't find it. She lost her temper and said I disgusted her and needed to leave. When she brought her car around I sneaked the bag into the boot while she spoke to the stable guy in the end room. She kept jabbing her finger at me so I knew she couldn't keep a secret."

"Why did Leslie bring you here? It's the last place she'd take someone she wanted rid of; near her grandchildren."

Caleb lowered his eyes in shame. "She wanted to drop me off once we got to the city." He swallowed. "I told her to let me out at the nearest police station and I'd tell them about the hotel growing drugs and selling them to kids at the camp site. She went mental." He cringed at the memory. "She nearly crashed the car."

"So she brought you here?"

Caleb nodded. "But not willingly. I'm sorry, Hana. I just wanted my dad."

Hana put her hands over her eyes. "I don't know where he is, Caleb! I've told you that a million times."

"But your husband does!"

Hana sighed and removed her hands, hopelessness flooding her senses. "And I told you to ask him. I can't get involved."

"He won't tell me." Caleb's hands balled into fists on the table.

"He actually said that?" Hana cocked her head and the teenager's cheeks flushed pink.

"No. He said he doesn't know anymore. He paid for the flight, dropped him at the airport, gave him an address and hasn't heard from him since."

"Then that's the truth!" Hana slapped her thighs in frustration as she brought her hands down to her sides. "Logan never lies!"

"I know he killed him." Caleb's eyes welled. "He's a nasty bugger and if my dad crossed him, he'd think nothing of putting him in a hole and burying him."

Hana swallowed, Caleb's thoughts mirroring her own earlier fears. But she shook her head. "Bobby wrote me a letter and posted it from the airport. Logan wouldn't bother taking him to a public place like the airport and then killing him; he's not stupid."

"No, he's just lethal." Caleb swallowed, perhaps considering how lethal Logan might be under any more pressure.

"You'd better hope not." Hana bit back her sarcasm, resentment bubbling in her throat. "Because you brought drugs into a home with small children and now they're missing. What if Wiri found them? Has that even crossed your selfish little mind? And if Asher bashes up the hotel, you'd best get praying because Logan will hurt you for sure." She replaced the panel and stood. "At least I know why you were grovelling on the hall floor earlier. Is that when you discovered the bag gone?"

Caleb nodded and Hana shook her head. "Your father would be disgusted at you, Caleb. He did dumb things in his life; but drugs weren't one of them."

"It wasn't my fault!" Caleb began and Hana raised her hand in a universal stop sign. She shook her head and moved towards the stairs.

"You say that a lot, Caleb. When someone says it's not their fault as often as you do, it's time for them to examine their own character. They might find they're the common denominator!"

39

Safe and Secure

"How do you feel now?" Hana cradled Wiri in his fluffy towel while Leslie chased a naked Phoenix around the bathroom and Mac sat on the floor giggling.

"Okay." Wiri shifted on her knee and rested his head against her collarbone. Hana winced and shifted her bum on the toilet lid. "Sorry I hurt the thing in your chest. And sorry I called you Hana when I really wanted to call you Ma."

Hana shook her head. "It's okay to be confused, Wiri. I would be in your shoes."

"I fink I lost my shoes at school." He sighed and yawned.

"No, you didn't. I carried them." Hana stood and kept the child swaddled in her arms. "Can you cope with madam here, Leslie? I'll go down and stoke the fire so they can get warm before bed. I think we'll have to put hot water bottles in with them tonight."

Leslie nodded and caught an escaping Phoenix before stuffing her wriggling legs into pyjama bottoms. "You go. I'll bring this pair after you."

Hana clattered down the stairs and turned towards the classroom they used as a lounge. Wiri's pyjamas dangled from her hand as she laid him on the sofa. "Hana," he said, sitting up and dragging the bottoms over his bare feet. "Why can't I see my real ma? Where'd she go?"

"Hospital, sweetheart." Hana grabbed the poker and prodded at a dying ember in the bottom of the fireplace. "Remember, Logan and I talked to you about it."

"But why can't I see her? Doesn't she love me anymore?"

"Wiri, she adores you!" Hana stopped mid-prod and faced the boy, feeling his agony radiate across the room. "This isn't something she chose." With a sigh, Hana threw a log into the flames and lifted it so the orange tendrils got a chance to reach for their next feast. They slid up the sides of the wood, crackling with excitement and joined by different jets of red and blue sparks. The flames licked at the log until the sides grew charred and cracked. Wiri's small body slipped in next to Hana's behind the fire guard, his slender frame close to her side.

"When can I see her?" he persisted, his grey eyes stormy with loss.

"I'll ring the hospital soon," Hana said, pursing her lips. "We'll do whatever they say to allow Mummy to get better again. Okay?" Her arm felt heavy as it slipped around the skinny frame. "Wiri, you know the story of how my father sent me away when I was a teenager, don't you?" The child nodded. "It hurt, sweetheart. It really hurt. I've wasted twenty-six years of my life thinking badly of him and then when I believed he died, I couldn't even put it right. Do you think I'd be mean enough to keep you away from Anahera if she could see you?" Hana cuddled him into her ribs. "As soon as the hospital lets us in, I'll take you there, I promise."

Wiri nodded and graced her with a beautiful smile. "Thank you." He skewed his lips sideways and frowned in concentration. "Until then, can I still call you Ma? And then when my real ma sees me, I'll call you Aunty Hana?"

Hana smiled and kissed the top of his head. "I think that's a great plan; you're such a clever boy."

Logan walked into the room with a downy Mac on his hip, the small boy's red curls standing up on his head like candy floss. Phoenix trailed behind with a grumpy face and Leslie waddled through the door last. "I'll make us some dinner," the old woman said, puffing and shoving an arm under each of her copious breasts for support. "Them mokos fair worn me out today."

"Then sit down." Hana raised herself up on her knees and nudged Wiri out from behind the fire guard. "I'll do it."

Leslie shook her head. "I need to phone my Alfie. I think better when I'm cooking." She left the room and closed the door behind her.

"Where's Caleb?" Hana asked, looking towards the empty sofa where he usually sat.

"I'm here." The voice sounded sad and came from the bench in the bay window, over which the curtains were drawn against the cold night air. Hana glanced at Wiri and then over to the window seat, regretting the lack of privacy in their conversation. Wiri pursed his lips in annoyance and then calmed at Logan's hand ruffling his hair.

"Wanna watch a movie?" Logan asked the children and their mood lightened during the process of choosing and arguing over which one they collectively wanted. Mac crawled around behind them, lifting cases and throwing them; laughing as they skittered across the floor boards.

Hana latched the fire guard and waited until the children settled in front of the TV before following Logan to the window seat. "What's happening?" she asked, sitting next to Caleb.

Logan leaned against the side window and shoved his hands into his pockets. "Linc drove up and locked the main gates. There're no guests expected late and the conference party won't leave the hotel tonight." He narrowed his eyes at Caleb. "Unless you're messing with me, kid."

Caleb shook his head with the kind of vehemence teenagers muster up from somewhere and use to good effect. "No, I promise. That's what he said."

"What if they get in another way?" Hana chewed her lower lip. "They might go through the bush or the camp site. Then what?"

"On foot?" Logan shook his head. "There's a barrier arm at the holiday park and robust security on the whole site. Linc's alerted the stockmen and they'll keep watch. We can lock that place like a safe, Hana, honestly. Trust me."

Hana swallowed. The two significant words set off alarm bells in her brain and she tried to focus on Logan's sense of confidence and lack of concern. Insecurity niggled at the back of her head even so. "I'll check on Leslie," she said, feeling the testosterone arc between the two males. Whatever Logan needed to say to Caleb didn't involve her.

40

Here Today, Gone Tomorrow

"Want some help?" Hana closed the kitchen door behind her and washed her hands under the hot tap. Leslie gave a disgusting sniff and nodded.

"That stupid old man caused all this." She waved a meat cleaver in front of her face and Hana winced.

"With the marijuana? Yeah, I guess so. But you and I both knew he did it so we're as much to blame."

"I'm not!" Leslie's voice rose to a screech and Hana patted her upper arm and glanced back towards the door.

"Shh! For goodness' sake, Leslie! Please don't wind Logan up any more than he already is."

"He'll blame me." Leslie triangulated a ham sandwich with one swipe. "He always blames me."

"Does not." Hana snatched the cleaver away and cut the crusts from the next victim. "I wish I knew why Alfred asked Asher to help him; of all the people who weren't a great idea, he's one of them. He couldn't know that Asher would sell the stuff. No, this is on that ratbag teenager. Logan can sort him out; I don't want him anywhere near my family."

"Talking of ratbags, did Bodie text you back?" Leslie used her sleeve to dry her eyes.

Hana hissed out a sigh of annoyance. "Thanks so much for that. Let's poke my sores instead of yours, shall we?"

"Well, did he?"

"No!" The word seared Hana's heart with as much force as the cleaver dismembered the next sandwich.

"He's got everything he wants from you, that boy. He bought your lovely house for a pittance and now he's realised Logan won't let you act as his private babysitting service, you won't hear from him again."

Hana swallowed and let her redheaded temper get the better of her. "Bloody hell, Leslie. Just because you're hurting, there's no need to take it out on me!" She slapped the knife onto the bread board, watching as the blade stuck in the wood and balanced there. Shaking her head, she left the room, slamming the door behind her.

Logan appeared as she seized the rounded end of the newel post and swung onto the bottom step. "Give me your phone!" she demanded. "Mine's in the kitchen and I don't want to go back for it."

Her husband eyed her with wary curiosity and Hana watched his thought process churning through the options. The redheaded temper didn't frighten him and she started up the stairs, assuming he wouldn't give in.

"What did she say to you?" His level tone fanned the flames of injustice in her and Hana pouted.

"She said Bodie won't call me ever again because there's nothing left to take."

Logan wrinkled his nose and cocked his head. "I don't think that's fair, Hana. There's other stuff going on. You can have my phone babe, but I don't recommend you ring him right now, not while you're feeling upset. Ignore Leslie; she knows nothing."

Hana nodded and flexed her fingers on the bannister. Her green eyes filled with glittering tears and she lowered her head. "Can I have a hug?"

"Course you can. Let me just check the kids." Logan ducked his head around the door and smiled at what he saw. He withdrew and pulled the door closed behind him. "Mac's sitting on Wiri's knee sucking his thumb and Phoe's asleep on the rug." Strong, scarred hands opened to Hana and she clambered down the steps and met Logan half way across the hall, burying her face in his warm chest. His arms pressed her into him and she inhaled his gorgeous scent of mountain air and sweet, green grass laced with the heat of a summer sun. Hana pushed her fingers beneath his shirt and Logan snuffed at her cold hands and shivered as she ran them up his spine. Kisses began at her temple and moved down to her cheek. "I love you, Hana Du Rose," he whispered in her ear and a warmth began in the pit of her stomach.

"Do you?" Her voice held a tease and Logan lifted his head and put his hands either side of her face.

"What do you think?" Soft lips brushed hers and Hana sighed and leaned into him, enjoying the intimacy of his touch. Her lips parted to allow the gentle brush of Logan's tongue and her fingertips roved beneath the waistband of his trousers as though by themselves.

"Dinner's ready." Leslie banged through the kitchen door bearing a tray and the couple sprang apart like guilty teenagers. Hana stifled a laugh but Logan's eyes darkened to thunderous shades. His expression snapped closed to hide his frustration and Hana reached up and stroked his cheek, her fingers lingering over the rugged scar beneath his right eye.

"Stop wahine," he groaned, his voice a hoarse whisper. "It's driving me crazy having a house full of people. I need some time with you by myself." Gentle fingers strayed to the back of Hana's neck, caressing the delicate skin beneath her red curls.

"A little help here!" Leslie's voice sounded acerbic and she balanced the tray on her knee and battled the door. "I'm not your bloody housekeeper anymore."

Logan's eyes flashed and Hana pushed her hands up his shirt further, so her fingers rested on strong, muscular pectorals. She gave a small shake of her head and stood on tiptoe to kiss her husband. "I'll help her," she whispered. A smirk lit her green eyes. "Now who needs to cool off?"

Logan's jawline worked beneath his skin and he exhaled, bringing himself back under control. "You'll keep," he said, his voice low and sultry. His teeth grazed her bottom lip and Hana felt the hunger for him grow in her chest, craving more of his nearness. She left to help Leslie with the tea tray, feeling far more rattled than her husband.

The little family seemed subdued as they huddled in front of the warm fire devouring sandwiches. Even the children hung together like a flock of wary birds. Hana sighed with relief as she kissed the last child goodnight and closed her bedroom door against the chill in the hallway. Logan met her by the bay window, pulling the curtains closed in front of her. "It's freezing!" he exclaimed, removing his pullover and mussing his dark hair. Hana sat on the bed and watched as he unbuttoned his shirt.

"It's only eight o'clock," she said in surprise, focussing on the tight muscles either side of his spine. "What are you doing?"

Logan groaned. "It feels much later." He ran a hand through his hair. "What a bloody day!" The pullover and shirt went onto a chair near the window and Logan stood with his back to her, hands pushed into his trouser pockets. "Whose stupid idea was this?"

"Caleb? Mine." Hana rose and slipped her sweater over her head, hauling a thermal vest after it. Her jeans seemed to stick to her flesh in the bone chilling cold and she walked across the room to Logan in her socks and underwear. "It's my fault. I'm sorry." Her tiny hands barely touched as she splayed her fingers across Logan's broad back. His warmth radiated through to her soul and offered relief from the dark cloud hanging over her head. Silky soft flesh slipped beneath her touch and she added her lips, sensing Logan's interest as though through a telepathic knowing. Little darts of desire sparked in the pit of her stomach and she longed to tumble in the big, cold bed with him. "I'm sorry," she said again, her voice a hushed whisper.

Logan turned under her hands and Hana felt the roughness of his scars brush beneath her questing touch. She traced the longest of them with an index finger, moving from beneath his armpit to the waistband of his trousers and knowing he couldn't feel it. "I didn't mean that." His grey eyes narrowed, the pupils black and round in their quest to obscure the smoky irises. "Coming back here to Hamilton seemed a great idea, but it's not." Logan's lips twitched and he wrapped coarse fingers around Hana's wrists, pulling her arms up and around his neck. "Now I'm here, I just want to go home."

Hana's fingers played with a stray curl at the back of Logan's head and she stood on tiptoes to reach, pressing her breasts against his stomach. "You don't like school?" She struggled to keep the surprise from her voice. "But you love teaching."

"Yeah, I do," he conceded. "But I'm getting too old to play management games with principals and boards of trustees. I wanna make a difference to a child's learning, not tick boxes and lay paper trails." His lip curled back in distaste.

"It's just a blip." Hana let her bottom lip trail close to Logan's nipple. "You'll feel different after a few weeks."

Logan's eyes closed and he nodded, running his hands along Hana's arms to her shoulders. He dug his fingers into the soft hair at her nape and sighed as the coils caressed the backs of his fingers. "Hana," he began, "there's something I need to say."

"Shh." Her finger against his lips sealed the words into his mouth, expecting further admissions of disappointment in his career choice. "It's okay," she whispered. "I know." She reached up and nibbled the supple skin near his sternum and heard the moan of satisfaction escape Logan's lips. Her fingers wrenched at the top button of his trousers and fumbled the zipper, snagging her flesh and drawing blood in her haste. Hana sucked at the wound, her lips full and enticing, eyelashes fluttering as Logan dealt with his own fasteners and laid the trousers over the arm of the chair. He turned back to her, urgency in his eyes. "No!" Hana protested, flashing him a heart stopping smile. "No talking." Taking his hand, she led him to the bed and slipped out of her underwear, pushing herself beneath the cool sheets and giggling as he followed.

They pulled the sheets over their heads and barricaded themselves against the chill. Logan's kisses busied Hana's lips and her thirsty soul soaked up his affection. Rough hands stroked her leg from thigh to ankle and he pulled back, a smile in his voice. "You've still got your socks on, Mrs Du Rose."

"It's cold!" she complained and pulled his mouth over hers. "Warm me up."

Hana flushed with embarrassment at the noise they made, broadcasting their activities for the household. "Shh!" she told Logan once, pausing for a moment to listen for voices or creaking floorboards. The silent house wrapped around her and she relented, falling under her husband's spell with the same degree of wonder as she did the first time. He touched her and she lost herself.

The silence of the house seemed oppressive when she emerged from the sheets to breathe, hair on end and her cheeks flaming. Logan exhaled and threw himself back on the pillow. Hana's hair tickled the soft skin over his ribs and he lifted the red tresses in his right hand and twirled the curls in his fingers. She sighed, pressing her lips to his pectoral and feeling it flex against her kisses. "What're you thinking about?" she asked.

"Nothing much." Logan turned on his side and wrapped his arms around Hana's slight frame. Her hand strayed to his taut stomach and then lower. Logan groaned. "I'm getting thoughts in my head now. I don't think you wanna know what they are."

Hana sniggered. "Are they X-rated?" She sighed and snuggled deeper, absorbing his warmth against her chest and shuddering against the cold at her back.

"They are now, but they weren't." Logan moved his head, making his hair swish against the pillow. He sighed. "The school's different without Angus. This new woman rules with a rod of iron but the staff don't respect her. It'll end in tears."

"Whose?" Hana pressed her nose against Logan's right nipple and darted out her tongue. He moved away with a jerk and grunted.

"Mine. Behave."

"Why yours? You only just got here." Hana adjusted her head so her cheek rested on Logan's shoulder. "I thought she'd be more likely to go after Pete because of his indecent hundred metre dash."

Logan snorted. "Yeah. Idiot. She watched him through the window. It looked like she threw up in her mouth."

Hana shivered. "So why you, babe? Do you think she's singling you out already?"

"Yeah, I do actually. She wants a deputy and Angus led her to believe I might be interested. I blew her out ten minutes after arriving and she's been spiteful ever since." He exhaled through pursed lips like a smoker. "I just wanna renew my teaching registration and get the hell out of here."

"Why don't you like Angus anymore?" Hana chewed her lip in the darkness, knowing Logan wouldn't answer. He sighed.

"He did something I don't approve of and it's not up for discussion."

Hana pouted and dug her fingers into his ribs as punishment, enjoying his deep groan of discomfort. "I'll ring the hotel tomorrow," she mused, reality forcing its way back into her peace. "Macky's appointment at the hospital can't be very far away. It's why I agreed to come back to Hamilton."

Logan pulled her closer. "And I thought it was to support me." He kissed the top of her head.

Hana tilted her head back. "Did you read all your grandmother's diaries?" She waited a beat for him to answer, feeling his chest tighten against hers.

"Why?"

Hana sighed. "Because the one you gave me is boring. It's got cattle prices and things I'm not interested in."

Logan snorted and she gritted her teeth, suspecting a set up between her husband and Will. "Well, is that so?" he said, amusement in his voice. "Fancy the kuia having nothing to say. Are you sure she doesn't mention a dead body in there somewhere? There must be some family mystery left for you to solve, babe. Geez, you're slipping."

"Not funny!" Hana prodded him again and smiled at the resulting groan. "You did it on purpose to put me off reading them. As soon as I get home, I'll make Will tell me where they're hidden and I'll read the bloody lot!"

"Yeah, whatever. Shut up and cuddle me."

Hana wriggled but gave up when Logan pinned her to his chest. His forearms felt rock hard to her touch and she couldn't break free. She protested enough to make a point and then allowed herself to be held, loving their closeness after the busyness of the move. "Logan?" Her question broke into the silence and her husband jumped, his momentary relaxation disturbed.

"Mmmn?" His voice sounded lazy and the word slurred next to her ear.

"Did you move Caleb's drugs from under the stairs?"

41

An Old Tragedy

Logan pushed himself up the bed, running a hand over his face. Hana heard the stubble scrape against his palm and pitied her chin, the skin burnt from her husband's enthusiastic kisses. "Is that where he hid it?"

Hana tensed in anticipation of anger, but Logan sounded amused. "I thought it seemed quite clever," she said and felt Logan shrug.

"Not really. Everyone knows that turn-of-the-century villas have a hiding place at the bottom of the stairs."

"I didn't." Hana frowned and her husband sniffed.

"You weren't raised here."

She smarted under the distinction; the remark forming a boundary she couldn't cross. The reminder she didn't belong acted as a knife in her soul and she sat up in bed, the sheet tumbling from her breasts. "I can't sleep," she stated. "I think I'll get up for a while."

Hana heard Logan swallow, but he offered no alternative and she pulled pyjamas over her nakedness. "Hana." His voice sounded soft in the eerie light from the moon which intruded through a crack in the curtains. "Believe nothing Caleb says, babe. He's full of crap. Toby went up to see Alfred and he reckons the marijuana got incinerated. He admits he gave Asher cash to pull it down from the roof garden and to power wash the greenhouse and roof space. But he says he shipped the bags up to the incinerator himself and stood there while it burned." He paused but stopped Hana interrupting by raising his hand. "I know what you're gonna say. Alfred's lying or Asher nicked only some of it, but these people are family and that kid isn't. He's trouble, Hana. You know it, I know it and as soon as he's healed, he'll be on his way. Make sure he knows that and don't let him fill your head with anymore roke."

Hana winced at the Māori word for excrement and pulled a dressing gown over her pyjamas. The metal cornering of the diary glinted in the moonlight, balancing on the dresser where she'd left it and Hana snatched it up, angry with Logan and his grandmother for their abandonment of her. She left the room without answering, the bloom of their intimacy still warm in her veins. "Bloody men!" she grumbled, descending the stairs and avoiding the creakiest ones.

Light showed under the door of Caleb's room and she passed by with care, not wanting to draw his attention and hear yet more excuses for his recent behaviour. In the lounge she found Leslie, kneeling in front of a struggling fire. "You finished yer bouncing around?" the old woman asked, not looking up. Hana felt her cheeks blaze and pursed her lips.

"Tell me exactly what happened after we left the hotel," she demanded. "I want to know why you fought with Alfred and how you came to bring Caleb here."

Leslie leaned back on her haunches and fed a hefty log to the hungry flames, nodding with satisfaction as the fire revived under her ministrations. "I thought you might," she grumbled. "I'll make tea first." She stood, using the arm of the sofa to creak her old bones into a standing position and Hana plonked herself on the deepest of the armchairs and waited.

"Was it over the weed?" Hana asked, following her to the kitchen when she didn't return. Leslie stood by the sink watching steam pump from the kettle without focussing.

"In part," she answered, pulling herself together and reaching for the teapot. "He started with a wee tub of seedlings after Miriam died and he'd go onto the roof and tend them. Next it's a herb garden and then the greenhouse and he's up there all the time; watching the world go by and smoking his baccy as he called it. I felt relieved when he agreed to clear it away without a fuss, but I saw that boy take the bags. When I searched his place I didn't find it. Alfie wouldn't help me and we argued but it would've been okay but for the other thing." She gave a heavy sigh and went after the tea bags with a spoon as though imagining Alfred's head being squashed beneath the metal.

"Alfred told Logan he incinerated the weed." Hana's brow furrowed in confusion.

"They did some of it that way." She winced. "It made such a stink they stopped." Leslie sighed and a tear sprang onto her cheek before she could wipe it away. "He misses his wife. We married too quick and this is my punishment. Atua wants to see me hurting."

Hana shook her head. "No, you're wrong. God doesn't enjoy people's pain; you can't blame him."

"It is." Leslie nodded so hard she banged the mugs together. "It's my punishment for all the other times."

"All the other times?" Hana cocked her head in confusion and then winced at Leslie's raised eyebrow. "Oh. Other times. Like, you and Alfred had other times?"

Leslie nodded. "Yes. Two people in unhappy marriages, growing up together and working side by side. It's bound to happen. Both as trapped as the other, him more so because of the land the old woman left him. He loved the bones of Miriam and she never deserved it. Every time she went back to Rueben he sought me out, right up until the last time."

"The last time?" Hana fingered the diary in her hands, Leslie's revelation obliterating any secrets held within the crinkled pages. "What happened the last time?"

Leslie sniffed and wiped her nose with the back of her hand. "I got pregnant."

The diary fell from Hana's fingers with a clatter, depositing shards of aged paper onto the kitchen floor. "You got pregnant? Does Logan know?"

"No!" Leslie's eyes widened, the whites glaring like the stare of a maniac. She turned to face Hana, her face filled with latent threat. "And you won't tell him."

Hana groaned and put her hands over her face. "Then you shouldn't tell me this stuff! I'm not keeping secrets from him; we promised each other."

Leslie swallowed and ignored her. "She looked like your Phoenix, dark ringlets and grey eyes. I loved her so much." She sighed and Hana waited for more, frustrated with Leslie's faraway look. The old woman's eyes filled with misery and her chin wobbled. "The day she died I knew I'd never be happy again. And I haven't been."

Hana swallowed. "I'm so sorry, Leslie. I didn't know."

The sad old woman wiped her eyes and nose on the hem of her dress and sighed. "You can't go back in life, kōtiro. She would've turned thirty-five last Sunday and I decided we'd been together long enough, me and Alfie. I told him the truth and he threw himself into a temper like I've never seen before. Figure he broke every plate and cup in the apartment and screamed at me to get out." Her heavy lidded eyes sought Hana's, the heart reflected in them broken. "He said what kind of woman gets a papa to carry his own pēpi to the urupā in her coffin without telling him she's his kin?" Her chest heaved and she struggled with her next breath. "Why did I marry him, Hana? Why did I think I could make it right?"

42

Verdict

Hana watched as a female staff member teetered on too high heels, straightening her back and attempting to look Logan in the eye. She fingered the material of her tight skirt and shifted her legs into what she thought might appear as a sultry stance, throwing out her left hip in his direction. Hana's steady walk towards the school building slowed and Phoenix bounced next to her, singing a little song under her breath. She looked up as Hana stopped and followed the direction of her mother's gaze. "Papa's talking to lady," she announced and Hana winced at the reminder, jealousy flaring in her breast like a nasty flush.

"I can see," she said, her voice low and controlled. She studied Logan's body language, hands shoved in his pockets and his stance casual. As the woman moved towards him, his cowboy boots took calculating steps away, matching her for pace and distance so she didn't notice. When she laughed and reached out as though to place a hand on his arm, Logan ended the conversation with a shake of his head and turned away. Relief flooded through Hana. It didn't matter how many times the poor man proved himself, she tarred him with the filthy brush belonging to her first husband.

"Logan," she called, forcing herself to speak and seeing the woman jump in surprise in her peripheral vision.

"Papa, Papa, Papa," Phoenix sang and he turned back to them, a ready smile spreading across his whole face.

"How're my girls?" he asked, scooping up his daughter and putting an arm around Hana's shoulders. He bent his head and kissed her temple, whispering in her ear. "Thanks for rescuing me, babe. That chick can't take no for an answer."

Hana pushed her hand into Logan's back pocket, displaying possession like an angry lioness. The woman allowed a vengeful look to cross her attractive features before realising who and where she was. Hana felt jealous eyes boring into her back and wished she'd dressed ready for competition, her sense of victory short lived. "Who is she?"

"Head of English." Logan fixed his eyes forward and resisted looking back at her. He lowered his voice. "She's already bedded a physics teacher; can't imagine what she'd want with me."

"I can!" Hana grumbled. "But she's not getting it."

The teacher watched for a moment and then flounced away, her face fixed back into a mask of indifference. Her heels clicked up a set of concrete stairs and into the bowels of the school.

Logan snuffed out a laugh and clasped Hana closer. "Nope, for sure. I'm happy with my life as it is, thanks."

"Why did you text me?" Hana asked, matching her step to his. Phoenix snuggled into Logan's neck and popped her thumb into her mouth.

"Receptionist at the hotel rang me earlier. A letter arrived for you last week and got put into the wrong pigeon hole. I asked her to open it and scan to email. When I tried to forward it to you, something stuffed up and I got a mailbox error. I need you to read it." Logan pulled his phone from his pocket and pressed in the passcode to unlock the screen. His eyes softened at the look of fear on Hana's face. "It's nothing bad.

Macky's appointment came and it's short notice, that's all." Gentle fingers reached out to stroke her cheek and he jerked his head back towards where they met. "You saw me trying to get cover so I could come with you. I don't think it's a good idea to accept favours from her; she's a little too familiar."

Hana heaved out a sigh and accepted the phone, turning her attention to the tiny screen. "If that's the cost of covering a couple of hours; don't ask for a week off."

Logan shook his head and tickled Phoenix under the chin, ignoring the barb in Hana's voice. "She didn't ask me outright," he said.

"I don't think she needed to. Her pheromones smelled strong enough to reach me." Hana gaped at the screen and then swore. "It's today, Logan. Don't they realise we have lives too?"

Logan shrugged. "I've got a health insurance policy which takes a chunk of money off me every month for this stuff. Why didn't you use it?"

Hana chewed her lip in embarrassment. "You didn't know I took Mac to see the doctor. I needed to be sure something was wrong before I involved you. It seemed unfair to rake over old wounds without being certain."

Logan tutted and leaned to kiss her brow. "Idiot! We're in this together, remember?"

Phoenix slipped an arm around Hana's neck and dragged her closer into the embrace, sighing with contentment. Logan's free hand traced a pattern at the bottom of Hana's back. "We'll be fine," Hana said. "It's just tests and questions and I can do that by myself. I'll see if Leslie will take Phoe and Wiri to kindy and school and free me up to go to the hospital with Macky." She bowed her head and peered at the phone again. "I've got two hours to pull it all together and get there."

"I got kindy?" Phoenix asked, lifting her head and popping out the thumb. "Phoe-Phoe like kindy."

"Yes sweetheart," Hana said, stroking the dark curls from her daughter's face. "Two big days and one half one."

"No." Phoenix shook her head from side to side hard enough to rattle her brain. "No. All the days."

"You're too young, pirinihehe. Maybe next year." Logan's eyes crinkled at the corners and Phoenix pouted and leaned in close, trying to open his eyes wide with her fingers.

"I princess?" she asked, her lips pursed as she translated the Māori word.

"Truly," her father replied and winked at Hana.

"Do I need a copy of that letter?" Hana asked, worrying at her lower lip. "I might need to show it at the clinic?"

"It didn't say so." Logan placed his daughter on the ground and her feet wiggled in mid-air before touch down. "Mead building, reception E. The appointment time is ten o'clock but they want you there earlier to fill in paperwork. You should change the address to The Gatehouse for now."

"Okay." Hana took her daughter's hand and steeled herself to face the extent of her son's disability. "Wish me luck."

"Hana." Logan's voice sounded soothing and he snaked his fingers behind her neck, leaning his forehead against hers. Their vast height difference caused him to form an arch above their daughter. "My life is brilliant; better than I ever imagined it could be. We have two beautiful kids and I love you. We don't need luck." His lips brushed against hers and she closed her eyes and sighed.

"I know." She forced a smile onto her lips and set off for the house, waiting a moment on the pavement while Phoenix waved over her shoulder. Logan watched for a while before moving away with heavy footsteps, caught in the impossible gulf between work and family.

"I'm not a kid," Phoenix announced as Hana led her home. "I'm a lamb."

"Okay, but it's still a baby," Hana argued. "What difference does it make?"

"Mrs Alison at kindy says little lambs. Kids is naughty. They eat things and bounce around. Lambs is for sweet babies what Jesus loves."

"That's interesting," Hana acknowledged, pondering the matter. "Fair point. You can be a lamb if you like."

"Can Wiri be lamby too? And Macky?"

"Yep. For sure." Hana opened the unlocked front door and stepped across the threshold. "Let's see if Nonie minds taking you to kindy."

"Yeah, I can do that." Leslie met her at the door playing hunt-the-school-shoe with Wiremu. "What did you do with it?" she demanded, turning her attention back to him as he cocked a leg over the bannister rail. "Stop messing around and find your shoes."

"I fink I lost them," he grunted, sliding a little way before clattering his backside against the newel post. "Oof!" he complained. When he opened his mouth to describe the part he'd hurt, Hana cut him off.

"Get ready. Nonie's taking you to school this morning. Phoe, grab your backpack, it's got morning snack and lunch in it."

"Yippee!" Phoenix bounced to the kitchen and seized the bag from the table, fiddling with the straps.

"It's for later!" Hana protested. "Don't open it now; you just ate breakfast." She turned her attention to Leslie. "Please can you walk or take your car? I need the ute for an appointment."

"Where?" Leslie cocked her head on one side and Hana gritted her teeth. "It doesn't matter. Your car might be easier. Take the ute."

Her mother-in-law looked thrilled and Hana cringed, doubting Logan would appreciate another fender bender at his expense. "I'll drive real slow with the kids in the car," Leslie promised and Hana nodded, ignoring the deadline contained in the assurance. After she dropped them off might be another matter.

"Not kids!" Phoenix shouted from the kitchen. "Lickle lambs."

"Where's Macky?" Hana asked, seeing his empty high chair through the doorway.

"Here!" Phoenix piped up and pointed. "He got bare bum."

"Aye? What?" Hana groaned and skirted Leslie and Wiri, arriving in the kitchen to see her tiny son crawling under the dining table, his bare butt a skinny pink beacon. A wet nappy trailed from his fingers and he flicked it out sideways with the effort of hauling it along next to him. "Fantastic!" Hana complained, scooping him up and holding him at arm's length. "Just brilliant."

"You deal with him and I'll sort these two out." Leslie waved Hana up the stairs.

"Kiss, Mama! Kiss!" Phoenix tottered after her with a wrapped sandwich in her hands.

"Put that back, Phoe!" Hana bent to kiss her and then puckered her lips to receive a wet slobber from Wiri, who grinned as she wiped her face on her sleeve. "That's gross!"

"No, it's good. It puts the girls off," he snickered, sticking out his pink tongue.

"Please help Nonie with Phoe?" Hana begged, still holding her son outstretched in front of her. Wiri nodded and confiscated the sandwich, reverting to adult mode and putting Phoe's lunch back in the backpack. Leslie continued the shoe hunt alone.

When peace engulfed the old house with the click of the front door, Hana heaved a sigh and withdrew her splashing son from the bathroom sink. His lips formed silent sounds and his brow furrowed at his removal from the water. Hana pulled his face towards hers with a finger on his cheek and pursed her lips. "Come on, dude. This is the day we find out what you need."

Her son screwed up his mouth into a gummy grin, green eyes focussed on her face to read her expression. Hana forced herself into fake happiness and cajoled and jollied him through the process of dressing and getting into the car. She groaned in dismay when she surveyed the car seat in the back of Leslie's vehicle. "Damn!" she complained. "She took the portable one." With no way of fixing the seat to her pram, Hana resigned herself to carrying her son around the kilometres of hospital corridors on her hip instead, knowing he'd eat most of her hair on the way to the appointment. She settled herself in the driver's seat and plaited her auburn locks to one side in anticipation, muttering to herself. "I'll have jelly-arms after carrying you, baby." She turned to face him and he grinned and kicked his legs in response.

The drive to the hospital proved without incident but reaching level fourteen in the multi-storey car park, Hana's cheeks flamed with heat as fear touched her heart. "There must be a space soon," she panicked. "I'm running out of floors!" She glanced in her rear view mirror and saw her son snoozing in the car seat. "You're no help," she grumbled, missing Wiremu's quick eyes and jabbing finger pointing out spaces from a distance. A car reversed out up ahead and Hana waited, trying not to worry about the traffic bunched behind her. She nosed Leslie's car into the gap between an SUV and a ute, grateful she'd ended up with the smaller vehicle by default.

"Right, little man." She peeled the sleeping baby from the car seat and lifted him over her shoulder, smiling at Mac's enormous sigh of contentment. He wound his baby fingers into the loose curls which escaped the plait and held on, turning his warm breath onto her neck and squeezing his eyes shut.

Hana carried the baby and her giant bag full of supplies over great lengths of corridor. A blue line painted onto the floor steered her to the Mead building and she searched for the relevant reception desk. A man around Logan's age looked up as she approached the desk and he smiled. "How can I help you?" he asked, in a sultry Irish accent.

"Our surname's Du Rose. My son has an appointment for this morning at ten." Hana held her breath while the man searched a screen in front of him, his brow furrowed in concentration. "The letter went to my other address," she began. "I didn't get the opportunity to confirm the appointment."

The man glanced around the busy waiting room and shook his blonde head. "No matter. Come on through."

Hana looked around her at the groups of parents with children of varying ages, chewing her lip and looking doubtful. The man smiled, a lovely smile in a face filled with kindness. "It's fine." He held his arm outstretched to indicate an opening at the side of the reception desk and Hana took a tentative step forward. Like a gentleman, he stood back to allow her through first and she almost collided with a portly woman approaching the gap at speed.

"Ooh, sorry," the woman said, taking a step back and smiling at Mac's sleeping face. "Thanks so much, doctor," she gushed to the man, waving a stack of papers in her hand. "Everything all right?"

"Yep." He jerked his head backwards to the waiting room. "I've collected my next patient but don't know what to do with the others. They're all for Nathan. Can you sort them out?"

"Yes, yes. Admin will get someone else to bring up the notes for this afternoon's clinic. They're not sure what's gone wrong. Oh!" The woman reached into the stack of papers and dragged out a stapled set. "Here's the referral for this young man," she said, handing it over. With a blur of paisley skirt and wiggling hips she moved away, resuming her position at the front desk.

With a deep breath which came from her diaphragm, Hana followed the long legged walk of the doctor, scuttling behind as he made a left turn and stopped at an open door. He nodded and paused to tuck his shirt back into his trousers, reminding her of Logan's constant battle to keep his long torso in check. Something about him seemed familiar and Hana paused before accepting his invitation. "Do I know you?" she asked.

He peered at her. "Perhaps." His easy smile displayed nice front teeth and Hana nodded, allowing the feeling of déjà vu to slip away from her. She stepped through the doorway, her heart heavy with dread and the weight of her son's head numbing her collar bone. Gritting her teeth, Hana willed herself not to cry but knowing despite her best endeavours; she would.

Sweating in a visitor's chair near the window, Hana cradled her son in her arms and watched his peaceful, sleeping face as the doctor read her referral letter from Fiona Haines. When he laid the paperwork on his untidy desk and moved to sit next to her, she felt her terror hike. "Your GP says your son's paternal great grandfather and maternal grandmother both suffered from profound deafness," he said in his gentle Irish lilt. He reached out a bony finger and slipped it into Mac's hand, smiling at the sleeping grip reflex. "He's a sweet wee man. Let's start at the beginning."

The doctor kept hold of Mac's hand, sitting back in his seat with one leg crossed over the other and the laces undone on his black shoes. Hana took a gargantuan swallow and began her story, fixing her gaze on the man's psychedelic socks and listening to her robotic voice.

Ten minutes later her chest heaved and the doctor handed over a box of tissues, waiting while she took one. "There's no evidence to suggest that a shotgun blast would make your son deaf," he said, raising an eyebrow at Hana's shaking head. "So stop blaming yourself. Prolonged sounds such as aircraft engines or machinery can cause difficulty, but it sounds like you protected him best you could under the circumstances. Did Logan cry out in shock at the blast?"

"What?"

"Your son, Mrs Du Rose. Logan. Did he cry out when the gun went off?"

Hana swallowed. "Sorry. We call him Mac and no, he didn't."

"But he cries normally at other times, when he's hungry or needs his nappy changed?"

She nodded. "Yes, he grizzles like his sister did and I can differentiate between the cries he makes. But he doesn't hear other noises."

The doctor cocked his head. "I would suggest your son's lack of reaction to a gunshot nearby as a newborn means he already had the issue at birth. So, take yourself off the list as a contributor. The genetic history is something else and we may never determine how significant that is. What we need to do is run tests on Mac and see what we discover. Science is a different game from your mother's day and Mac's hearing may be salvageable. Do you sign with him?"

Hana nodded. "Yes. He understands me and tries to emulate my hand signals."

"Good." The doctor looked pleased. "Then you're ahead of many mothers already. You have a universal method of communication which facilitates interaction. What about other family members; how do they deal with it?"

"Various ways." Hana swallowed a sense of hopelessness. "My daughter pulls Mac's face towards her when she's speaking to him. I haven't said anything; she just seems to know to do that. Our older boy waits until Mac's looking at him."

The doctor nodded and reached backwards over the table for the papers. "You've three children?"

Hana sighed. "Three children live with us but only two are ours. But I have a son and daughter from a previous marriage."

"No hearing difficulties with any of the others?"

She shook her head and hiccupped from crying, embarrassment flushing her cheeks with a pink glow. "No, they're all fine."

"Do you have a supportive family?" The doctor's brown eyes drifted over Hana's face as he waited for an answer. She thought about her fractured relationship with Bodie, the physical distance between her and Izzie and the mess of Du Rose egos. She wanted to ask him to define the term *supportive*.

"My husband's great." She blew out through pursed lips. "When he speaks, I've noticed Mac puts his hand on his father's chest or throat. I think he likes the vibrations."

The doctor nodded with a smile. "Awesome." He jerked his head towards the comatose baby. "It's time I met the wee chap myself. How about it?"

Mac behaved with his usual inimitable charm, taking a few moments to wake up, rubbing his eyes and nose against Hana's shoulder and straightening his legs. He became interested in the doctor once the stranger caught his attention with bright, colourful toys and a shape with moving parts which swivelled around a central pillar. He followed the Irishman and his array of gadgets with his eyes, but when the doctor hid behind Hana, Mac contorted his body to see and when he couldn't, grew bored. The baby bent himself double to play with his socks and didn't respond to the squeaky toys behind Hana's right ear or the rustling of metallic paper which the doctor rubbed right behind Mac's head. Yet when he tapped the baby on the right shoulder and offered a plastic rabbit, Mac squirmed around with a look of curiosity and reached for it, grabbing it by the ears and poking it straight into his mouth.

Hana's pulse rate picked up as the doctor strolled to his desk and wrote quick notes about his findings. "Observations indicate significant problems." He wrote and spoke out loud, confirming what Hana knew in her heart as the medic spewed long Latin terms into the air and onto the page in his slanted scrawl. When he looked up and caught her gaze, she felt her stomach drop into her toes and despite valiant efforts, failed to contain the sob which rocked her whole body. Macky flopped backwards onto Hana's stomach, driving the air from her lungs in a whoosh. He stared up at her through huge green eyes and grinned around the rabbit in his mouth, shiny wet lips and a look of innocence so pure, it hurt Hana's soul. He patted the toy against his tongue as the Irishman delivered his verdict and Mac's tiny existence filled an A4 sheet of paper in a medical file.

43

Strange Coincidences

Hana reached for her phone, fingers shaking as she took a seat at a table in the downstairs cafe. The barista worked behind the coffee machine, creating Hana's order of espresso with artistic flourish. Mac lolled in her arms, his eyes half closed in an attempt to reclaim his ruined nap and unaware of the doctor's verdict or the hitching of his mother's chest. Hana made the call, knowing he wouldn't answer but the reassuring sound of his voicemail comforted her. "Logan? Please call me back," she begged, feeling her resolve crumble in the face of overwhelming odds. "I know you're teaching but please call me."

Cradling her son brought calm into her tumult and Hana closed her eyes and kissed the red, downy head below her chin. When her phone rang, she jumped. "Logan?"

"Hey, babe. I've nipped out of class. How'd it go?"

"Awful." She felt her chest tighten. "Just like we knew."

"But what did the doctor say? I'm sorry, Hana. I should be there. Do you want me to come?"

Hana gave herself a mental and physical shake. "No. Stop beating yourself up. It was too short notice. The doctor made an appointment for another kind of test. Macky sits on my knee with headphones on and then there's another one a few weeks after that where he needs to stay asleep with electrodes on his forehead. I need you to come to those. I don't want to do it on my own."

"Oh Hana." Logan's voice reached out to her across the city, their shared sadness linking them in a gossamer thread of pain. "I'll be there even if I jack this job to do it. Nothing's more important than you guys. If Cruella hadn't already seen me, I could've faked sick."

Hana snorted. "You're never sick."

"Are you kidding me?" Logan's voice lightened. "I went for so many Factor 8 infusions my first year here, I'm amazed Angus kept me on the payroll."

"That's different." Hana smiled at the barista and took her coffee with a muted thank you. "Hemophilia isn't sickness. It's a medical condition."

"So is deafness, babe. I love my son and nothing will change that. It's not about imperfection or disability. I'll learn the signing thing I've seen you do and we'll make sure Mac achieves everything he needs to. I'm still leaving him and Phoe the mountain when I die, so he'll just have to work a bit harder than her at communicating. We both know he's quick and intelligent. It's not like the lights are on but nobody's home. He's in there raring to go."

"I know." Hana sipped her coffee and looked around at the busy hospital. A man caught her eye, tall, mousy haired and familiar. She missed Logan's next sentence. "What? Sorry."

"I said I've got a free period last so I'll come home early. It'll be okay, Hana, you know that, don't you?"

"I do. I love you." She raked the milling bodies for the man's figure, not seeing him and convinced she'd mistaken someone else for him.

"Love you more." Logan's sultry voice pushed through Hana's misery and she smiled.

"Probably."

He laughed and ended the call, leaving her happier than before he rang. Her heart pricked with gratitude with his ability to make her feel safe. Nothing seemed impossible around Logan Du Rose.

Glancing at her watch, Hana realised she had time for one last errand. Kissing Mac's cheek as he flopped over her shoulder, she sipped coffee and followed the orange line through a maze of corridors until she reached the mental health unit. Dumping the empty cup in a bin outside, she walked through the sliding doors and approached a reception area. A harried looking woman greeted her with a forced smile. "Hi." Hana tried not to listen to the mumbled rantings of a scruffy looking man who paced back and forth next to the reception window. "Is it possible to see Anahera Du Rose?"

The woman sighed and smiled, forcing herself to ignore the man who turned on his heel and walked into a plant pot. "Are you a family member?"

Hana nodded. "Sister-in-law."

The woman's eyes strayed to the man as he picked himself up and began pacing again. "Yes, that's fine. She's not in the secure unit anymore." She consulted her computer screen. "If she's in with the counsellor, you can either wait in the visitors' lounge or come back here."

Hana glanced sideways as the unhinged man lectured the rubber plant about something in gibberish. "Yeah," she replied, not committing to waiting anywhere. Despite the pleasant surroundings and efforts made at making the environment feel like home, an air of unpredictability shrouded the building in a spirit of fear.

"Room 5," the receptionist said. Losing patience, she stood and pointed at the pent-up man. "Kenneth! Sit down or wait for Dad outside. He said he wouldn't be long."

Like the flick of a switch, the man sank his bottom into a nearby chair, resorting to foot tapping instead. The receptionist relaxed and went back to her computer screen; order restored.

Hana gripped her son harder to her body and proceeded along a carpeted hallway, her gaze flicking from one laminated number to the next. Someone smiled and waved from Room 4 and she halted in confusion as a snowy haired old man beckoned to her and pointed to Mac. He sat on the edge of a bed and beamed without a tooth in his head. Advancing with caution, she entered the doorway and stood ready to run if the man lurched towards her. "It's okay," he said with a smile. "I'm completely sane."

Hana's cheeks pinked with embarrassment at her uncharitable thoughts and she allowed herself a smile. "Then you're more than I am," she joked.

The man grinned, olive skin crinkling around his eyes. "He's a little whitey, isn't he?"

Hana laughed and nodded. "Yes. Like me. My husband's Māori and when he first saw Mac, he kept calling him orange."

"Karaka." The man chortled a deep, low sound like tumbling rocks. "Funny." He flapped his hand towards the doorway. "You don't have to stay, kōtiro. Thank you for stopping by and letting me see your boy. He's waiwaiā." He translated for her benefit. "Beautiful. He'll bring you much joy."

Hana nodded and inhaled. Of course he would. She turned to leave, but the man spoke, forcing her to face him again. "You looked so sad. I wanted to encourage you."

Her body stilled, eyes filling with salt water. "Thank you," she whispered. "I am."

Kindness radiated from the wise brown eyes. The stranger sat on the edge of a hospital bed in a mental health unit; driven there by forces unknown. Yet he'd noticed a woman with the weight of the world on her shoulders as she hurried through unfamiliar territory on a reluctant mission. "Don't be," he said, crinkling his eyes. "Things are never as bad as they seem." His final smile dismissed her and he bent to pull up his socks, humming a Māori tune in a gentle, lyrical tone. The familiar sound filled her soul with thoughts of Logan, his strong, scarred fingers strumming the strings of his battered guitar as he sang of an abandoned world of folk lore and ritual. It comforted her and she left the man, more confident footsteps steering her across the corridor to a room opposite. Hana stared at the crinkled number five clinging to the doorframe and took a deep breath. Her phone nestled in her pocket, photos of Wiri meant to encourage Anahera to let her son visit and Hana reached out a hand and felt the rectangular shape through the fabric of her trousers. Wiremu needed his own mother; not someone else's.

Raising her hand to tap on the open door, Hana stepped beneath the doorframe and froze. The couple sat on the bed with their backs to her, a strong male arm wrapped around Anahera's emaciated frame. Her long dark curls tumbled down over his forearm and their heads touched. His voice sounded low and cajoling, Anahera nodding like a toy as they whispered shared secrets. Hana tried to withdraw backwards, not wanting to disturb them. Mac grunted in his sleep and she froze as the man swivelled his head and looked her in the eye.

"Sorry," Hana gushed. She backed into the corridor, tangling with a medicine trolley in her haste. Pressing her hand against Mac's slender back she hurried towards the main doors without looking back.

The nurse pushing the trolley called out to her. "Sorry, that must've hurt." Ignoring him, Hana limped through reception and outside into the fresh city air, disbelief making her chest hot. The walk back to her car seemed endless with Mac flopping like a dead weight over her left shoulder. The change bag filled with nappies and a flask of warm milk dangled from the crook of her right elbow and dragged her down, making her count each footstep. She validated her parking ticket and parted with cash by the lift. But the sight of Leslie's car nestled between a pillar and a ute caused Hana to hurry and she reached it breathless and exhausted as though she'd run a race to the finish.

Mac continued to sleep as she loaded him into the car seat and stowed the bag in the foot well. Once in the driver's seat, Hana examined her ruined right heel, mopping up the blood from a deep graze with a stray tissue. Her knee, thigh and hip felt bruised and she sat for a moment and caught her breath. Licking a piece of tissue and gluing it to the cut, Hana tried not to worry about what Leslie might have used the tissue for. The back of her sock looked blood soaked and the heel of her shoe scored and spoiled. "Should've worn my boots," she muttered into the rear view mirror. The dashboard clock told her it was lunchtime and Hana dragged out her phone, fingers hovering over the keypad. She knew Logan would be in the gym, snatching a forty-minute workout between classes. She sent the text anyway, hoping he read it before his next teaching session and wondering what he'd say.

'Went to see Anahera. I think she's having an affair with Lincoln Haines.'

44

Expect the Unexpected

Mac snoozed in his cot after lunch as Hana chopped potatoes for dinner, wondering where Leslie disappeared off to with Logan's ute. She watched through the side windows as a posse of young men practiced at the cricket nets, swinging wooden bats through the air at nothing and occasionally, each other. The empty house relaxed around her with a creak of settling boards and the odd groan as the old building reshaped itself. She'd searched for Caleb on her return but found him missing, his bag of second-hand clothes still on the floor of his bedroom.

A knock on the door sent her to dry her hands and Hana flung it open, expecting to see a young man on crutches or an old woman wielding shopping bags. "Go away." She kept her tone level and swung the door closed, failing as Asher pushed his way through the gap.

"No." He strode into the hall and looked around him, ducking his head into the lounge and clicking his tongue with annoyance when he found it empty. "Where is he?"

Hana left the front door wide open and ignored Asher, striding into the kitchen and hoping he got the message. She heard his feet scuffing on the floorboards as he searched each room for Caleb, the drugs or both. "Fine!" he shouted, his tone arrogant. "I'll look upstairs." Heavy footsteps slammed against the stair treads as he moved to the upper level. Fear bridled in Hana's heart at the thought of her sleeping baby and her eyes darted towards the monitor sitting next to the pile of naked potatoes. She didn't wait to see if Asher would dare accost her infant, flying up the stairs and running to the bedroom where she barred the way with her body, arms outstretched across the frame. Asher clumped down from the attic level, his lips curled back in a spiteful grin. The handsome Du Rose features lost their devastating effect against the twistedness of his heart.

"You're not touching my son!" Hana's green eyes flashed with a mother's fury as she watched him pass her. He laughed, a cruel, hollow sound and moved to her marital bedroom where she heard him flinging things around. The sound of shattering glass identified Logan's aftershave as the most recent casualty but she stood her ground; protecting her son.

Asher wreaked destruction on the upstairs level as he went, tossing off sheets and knocking things over. He paused in front of Hana, his chest almost touching hers. "Did you hide it in here?" he demanded, his tone sing-song as though he thought it a game.

"The only thing in there is my son." She said it through gritted teeth and Asher snorted.

"Yeah, that's right. He is your son. Not Logan's though, hey?"

Hana's eyes narrowed and her redheaded temper flared. "You know nothing about genetics, do you, Asher? But then I guess you didn't stay in school so what can I expect? Mac is Logan's son and when we're gone, he'll inherit everything you ever wanted, money, land, fortune; all of it."

"That whenua is mine!" Something in Asher's eyes snapped and Hana regretted going so far. She held her nerve and did what it took to protect Mac. She shook her head, willing courage from her stomach into her chest.

"Never. Logan paid for that land with hard cash and blood. You don't get to take it back. No matter what you do, Asher, it'll never be yours. Get over it." She kicked him hard in the shin, her foolishness evident in his reaction. She made the confrontation physical and he responded in kind. Slender hands forced their way around her throat and Asher's grey eyes turned to gun metal, hazing over as Hana fought for breath. She kicked out again but Asher dodged the blow, ramming her head against the doorframe as punishment.

"Not so damn mouthy now, are we, Hana? You just don't know when to shut up." His thumbs pressed against her larynx and Hana saw lights flash in her vision as he cut off her airway. Her brain screamed for oxygen, begging her to fight. She scrabbled at his hands, digging in her nails and re-enacting a primeval desire to survive. She gouged his skin and he hissed in pain. Asher's rational mind whispered sense over the anger and she saw the moment come and go in his stormy Du Rose eyes.

"Stop!" The commanding voice resonated around the hallway, seeming to bounce off each of the walls in turn. Asher's vice ended and Hana sank to the floor with a strangled breath, clawing at her painful throat.

"Uncle Linc." Asher backed away from Hana, his gaze darting between her and the imposing man standing at the head of the stairs. "It's not how it looked. I wouldn't really do it."

Lincoln took a step forward and Asher reversed until his spine touched the doorframe to Hana's bedroom. "You okay, Hana?" Linc asked.

She tried to nod, the action painful. Rage blossomed in her heart and she clambered upright, resuming guard duty for her defenseless son. Asher's face darkened. "Don't ask her if she's okay!" he exploded. "It's all her fault. Everything went wrong the minute she turned up."

Lincoln looked at Hana and then back to Asher. The rage inside her increased. "He's lying! The Du Roses were screwed long before I married Logan. Don't you dare hold me responsible for your family's stupidity!" She rubbed at her throat with her left hand, the other braced against the doorframe.

"It's true, Uncle Linc. She turned up and then Poppa Reuben died, Dad lost the farm, Kane and Caroline left and then Tama went to live with her." He spat the final word, jabbing the air with his index finger to list his grievances. "Then Mum got sick and left and Logan made Dad throw me off the property. I've got nothing and it's all down to her. She's taken everything, even my baby brother!"

Hana shook her head at the blatant truth twisting. "You're such a liar," she hissed, knowing she diced with death.

"Enough." Lincoln sounded calm; a man who'd witnessed more prison fights than prison dinners. "Asher get out."

"No!" Hana ventured from Mac's doorframe, pulling the door closed behind her and holding onto the handle. With the other hand she grappled in her pocket and pulled out her phone. "I'm calling the cops. He just tried to kill me. I'll call my son." She fumbled with the keypad, alarmed when Lincoln snatched it from her fingers.

"No, you won't. That's not how we deal with things." Lincoln held the phone above his head and Asher's face lit up in victory.

"No, that's not how we deal with things," he parroted, taunting Hana with an upturned mouth and spiteful sneer.

Tears of anger gave her green eyes a metallic sheen as she delivered her ace. She'd heard that sentence too many times before to feel intimidated at its utterance anymore. "Maybe not." She lifted her chin and glared at them both. "I'll let my husband think of a more permanent solution." She forced her shoulders into a shrug and watched Lincoln's left eyebrow raise in surprise. "Get out of my house!" she shouted. "Both of you!"

She didn't give them time to respond. Slipping inside the baby's bedroom she closed the door behind her with a satisfying click. The wood felt solid beneath her palm and she waited for a moment, her body aching from the excess adrenaline coursing through her veins. "Why do they always try to strangle me?" she whispered to the silent room, stroking the painful skin beneath her throat. "Can't they think of something else?"

The irony of the question brought a bubble of mirth to the surface at the ludicrousness of her thoughts. She sighed. "Thank goodness they haven't." Hana stumbled across to her baby's cot, peeking over the sides into his open green eyes. He beamed at her and kicked his legs, one tiny foot bare and the sock waving in his hand. He squeaked with pleasure at her presence and Hana wrinkled her nose at the gift in his nappy. "I'm so grateful you heard none of that," she breathed, his innocence like a balm to her soul.

Hana dealt with her son's bum and carried him downstairs, grateful for the closed front door at the bottom of the stairs. Unable to find the key, she shot the bolt across and hurled the dirty nappy onto the fire in the lounge. "Shall we get a nice drink?" she asked Mac, kissing his button nose and carting him through to the kitchen to heat up a bottle.

"I made tea." Lincoln's voice brought Hana to a skidding halt in the doorway, anger crossing her face like a hot flame.

"I don't care. I asked you to leave."

Lincoln shrugged. "I heard ya." He reached for his mug and took a sip of the dark brown liquid. Hana snatched a bottle from the fridge and Mac's legs wiggled against her painful hip. His fingers opened and closed in anticipation as though reminded of why he'd woken. He grizzled and pushed his face against her shoulder while the bottle rotated in the microwave, filling with heat and zaps of radiation. Hana pulled it out after thirty seconds and he grabbed it with clumsy fingers and helped the teat into his eager mouth.

Hana glanced at the clock. "Logan will be home in a minute. Then you'll leave."

Lincoln put his elbows on the table. "Why? Because I stayed to make sure you were okay or because I didn't call the cops?"

"Both. And give my phone back!" Hana sat down opposite, near enough to the door to escape if needed.

"It's behind you." Lincoln watched her through narrowed eyes as she turned her head and spotted it next to the kettle. "You're a surprise, Hana Du Rose. I expected a timid little flower who did what Logan said and popped out babies to order." He cocked his handsome face to one side and Hana noticed a scar along his jawline where the stubble didn't grow. "You're like the old kuia reincarnated."

Hana blinked with deliberate slowness to illustrate her annoyance and refused to meet his eye. "Just leave; I don't want you here."

"I need to see Logan."

"Then wait outside!"

"I'm fine here, but thanks."

"Then I'll go." Hana scraped her chair back and Lincoln shook his head, standing opposite and dwarfing her.

"No, sit there. I'll get a cold pack for your throat. Do you have frozen peas?"

Hana shrugged, not sure what Leslie packed away in the fridge and cupboards. "I don't know. There's another freezer in the laundry at the end of the hall."

Lincoln nodded and left the room, returning with a packet of frozen stir fry mix. Hana gave him a disparaging look and he laughed. "Have it for dinner with the potatoes." He jerked his head towards the browning vegetables on the draining board and Hana groaned.

"I forgot about those."

Lincoln left her holding the baby as Mac fed himself back to sleep. To Hana's surprise, Linc rolled up his sleeves, washed his hands and finished peeling the potatoes, putting them into a water filled saucepan. "You'll expect a dinner invitation next," she said with sarcasm as Mac pushed the empty bottle out of his mouth with his lips.

"Was that it?"

"What?"

"The invitation." Lincoln smirked as he dried his hands on a cloth and sat opposite Hana. "It would give me a chance to get to know you."

"I don't want you to know me!" Hana snapped, lifting Mac over her shoulder and feeling embarrassed by the burp which popped from his lips.

"So why does it matter what I think of you then?" Lincoln watched her exasperation with amusement, qualifying his question. "You seemed keen to make me believe Asher was a liar, rather than you being a trouble maker."

"I really don't care what you think." Hana pulled the packet of floppy vegetables away from her throat and flung them onto the table. "If you want to blame me, then do it. Logan knows I caused none of it and it's his opinion that matters; nobody else's."

"Good answer. But I don't believe Asher, for what it's worth. Reuben caused his own catastrophes in life and from what I remember of the man, he took ownership of every one of them." Lincoln's brow furrowed. "Kane and Caroline were a surprise though. Let's hope they don't breed."

Hana looked up from her son's sleeping face. "I think they're trying to."

Lincoln pulled an expression which showed open distaste. "Isn't it illegal?"

"You know about them?" Hana's eyes widened. "About them being related."

"Half brother and sister? Yeah, I worked it out. I thought everyone knew."

"Nobody mentioned it. They mustn't know otherwise they wouldn't be together."

Lincoln shook his head. "Don't bank on it, Hana. Some families are stranger than fiction."

Hana rolled her eyes. "This one is for sure." She sighed. "I wanted to see Anahera to ask her if Wiri could visit. He's struggling and I don't know how to fix it."

"So why didn't you?" Lincoln fixed a steady gaze on Hana's face. "Why run away?"

"You're having an affair!" Hana's voice raised in irritation. "Nev's my brother-in-law. You can't think I'd chat to you both and show photos of Wiri and then come home and say nothing." She glared across the table. "I can't stand cheats!"

Lincoln raised an eyebrow and nodded, the action slow. "Is that the problem between us, Hana? You hate me because you think I'm a cheat."

Hana patted her son's back and thought about the question without answering. She reasoned through her feelings about Lincoln Haines, picking through the remnants of their very first meeting and cringing. "It's part of it," she admitted. "But our first meeting involved you threatening to shoot Sacha."

"Followed by you threatening to shoot me in the balls." Lincoln grinned. "Doesn't that make us even?"

Hana closed her eyes and absorbed the peace coming from Mac's steady breathing and the beat of his tiny, regular heart against her collar bone. "I don't know anymore."

"I'm not having an affair with Anahera." Lincoln pushed his mug away. "I went to get answers."

"Why?" Hana screwed her face up in disbelief. "What could she possibly know?"

"She gave someone an alibi which led to my arrest. I wanted her to validate it to my face."

Hana shook her head and Mac shifted against her chest. "I don't buy this; you put your arm around her. That's more than asking questions." She ran a hand across her throat and winced.

"I didn't know she'd get so distressed." Lincoln jerked his head towards Hana's throat. "Put the cold pack on it."

"It's defrosted. I don't know if I want to eat it."

"Nobody will know." Lincoln smirked. "Unless you tell them."

Hana's brow knitted and she stood, hoisting Mac higher over her shoulder. "Well, that's it right there." Her smile looked sad as she turned away from him. "That's the difference between you and me."

45

Threats and Promises

Hana didn't expect Lincoln Haines to still be sitting in her kitchen when she returned. Her neck felt better after a period of sponging it in the bathroom with a cold flannel. Mac snoozed in his cot upstairs and Hana rolled her eyes with annoyance as she turned up the monitor on the kitchen counter and faced the stable manager. "Why are you still here?" She put the potatoes onto the stove to boil and waited for his answer, tipping a block of mince into a frying pan.

"I don't wanna be like this with you." Lincoln's brow narrowed in a flickering movement as he rubbed a hand across his chin bristles. Hana watched his reflection in the kitchen window and shook her head.

"It doesn't matter; we don't have to see each other and I can be civil."

"It does matter!" Lincoln stood, his jaw flexing. "I'm not a liar, Hana. Please believe that."

Hana pointed the wooden spoon at him. "You had an affair and cheated on your wife, killed a woman and went to prison. I caught you with your arm around my sister-in-law, you wouldn't call the cops on Asher and now you want me to feed my family something I wouldn't eat."

"I threw it in the bin; the stir-fry." Lincoln's gaze bored into her face, his need for her approval unsettling. "And I didn't have an affair or kill a woman." He licked his lips and stood, thrusting knuckled fists deep into his jeans pockets.

Hana paused with the spoon in the air, dripping juice into the mince. "You didn't cheat?"

Lincoln twisted his face, causing a dimple in one cheek. The large man looked cowed. "I cheated but not in an affair."

"What other kind of cheating is there?" Hana waved the spoon in exasperation. "You bumped uglies with someone who wasn't your wife!"

Lincoln snorted. "Bumped uglies. That's gross even for me."

Hana shook her head and stabbed at the meat. "I don't care, Lincoln. Please go away."

"The woman I slept with took payment, Hana. I didn't have an affair with her."

"No." She shook her head. "Logan keeps all that stuff away from the township. You're lying again."

"Logan wasn't here when it started." Lincoln pushed his backside against the counter and chewed his lip. "While he stayed away in England, the township went to hell in a handcart. Reuben focussed on chasing out the drug dealers selling to his boys, but he didn't have the motivation to deal with anything else. Alfred spent his time ruining the hotel business and fighting Jack over the running of the beef herd and stables."

Hana winced at the mention of Jack and gave an involuntary shiver. "Please don't talk about him."

"Okay."

Hana sighed and went back to stabbing the mince as it turned from red to brown. The potatoes bubbled on the stove. "If this woman sold sex for a living, the police would know that another of her clients might have killed her. Why were you convicted?"

Lincoln sat down in a chair and rested his arms on the table; the slump in his shoulders showing defeat. "Pania had a private arrangement between a few of the local men. After she died, the cops found evidence I'd been with her and managed to make a case around an illicit affair. Serves me right." He raised his mug in salute. "Is a five year stint in prison serving a manslaughter conviction enough punishment for you?"

"I don't know. It's none of my business. Why would you spend so long locked up for something you didn't do? What if the client wasn't local that one time and killed her?"

"It couldn't be a stranger. We had an arrangement and there were only four of us in it. Two died while I was in prison and the other one had a cast iron alibi at the time Pania died." His eyes flickered closed, shutting Hana out of his innermost thoughts. "Nobody wants to talk about it now. I paid the price and in their eyes; it's done."

"You said Anahera alibied someone. Who?"

Lincoln shook his head. "It doesn't matter. He wasn't involved and she stood by her statement. I upset her and it wasn't fair. It was just a longshot."

"Were you the last person to see her alive?" Hana laid the spoon down and turned to give him her full attention.

"Apparently." Lincoln gave her a sad smile. "Biggest mistake of my life seeing her that day. I argued with Fiona about trying for a baby. She kept putting me off because of her career and refused to discuss it, so I drove away and went to someone who made me forget my problems. Instead it detonated my life from the inside out."

Hana shook her head. "That's so messed up on too many levels to count." She resumed her stirring. "My son's a police officer and often deals with murder enquiries; I'll ask him to look into it. There might be things they overlooked back then which could exonerate you now. Maybe if Fiona knew you were innocent, she might want to reconcile." Hana narrowed her eyes and glanced at him sideways. "I wouldn't but she might be more forgiving."

"Don't you dare!" The bile in his voice halted her musings and Hana's eyes widened in fear at Lincoln's tone. "You tell no one what I just said. Nobody. Do you understand me? They've had ten years to exonerate me and haven't. I'll do it myself. Pania was alive when I left, but I went back for my wallet and when I got there, she lay on the floor with the back of her head caved in."

"So you still say you're innocent." Hana pressed her back against the counter as Lincoln crossed the kitchen in three big strides. His rigid body seemed to suck the oxygen from the room as he towered over her.

"Why do you think the township funded my defense, woman? You think it was out of kindness?"

"I thought they wanted to help you get off the charges." Hana's face paled and Lincoln shook his head, his laugh spiteful.

"Get real! They needed me to stay quiet and take whatever came. I refused to go on the stand in my own defense, Hana! That was the deal. They decided my marriage was over and I may as well serve the time without ruffling the feathers of our precious township any further. They didn't want the cops scratching harder and finding out the truth. They sacrificed me, Hana. I lost a decade of my life for a quick shag that cost me twenty bucks."

"So the other members of your gentleman's club made you take the blame?" Hana's voice wavered with realisation. "And you think one of them killed this woman?"

"I don't think it; I know it!" Spit escaped from Lincoln's lips and Hana resisted the urge to wipe her cheek. He'd invaded her personal space to the point of discomfort.

"Is that why you're back?" she asked, her voice trembling as the second male of the day made her feel afraid in her own skin. "To get revenge."

"Sure am." Lincoln's handsome face curled into a sneer.

"Why are you telling me this?" Hana's eyes widened as the tall man brought himself back under control and ran a gentle finger down her cheek.

"Because you're gonna help me, Hana Du Rose."

"But I know nothing." Her mind wandered back a decade to the trauma of her first husband's death and everything that happened afterwards. She shook her head. "I lived in Hamilton ten years ago. I didn't know I'd met Logan before or that he'd been looking for me. I can't help you."

"Oh but you can, Hana and you're going to. In fact, I think you'll want to."

"No, I don't." Hana shook her head. "I don't even know who the other men were in your horrid little gang."

Lincoln smiled, the grimace of a desperate man. "There was a fifth person who remained anonymous. Only the two dead ones knew his identity and you're gonna find out who he was."

"How?" Angered, Hana shoved at Lincoln's chest to make him move backwards. "How can I find out?"

"Ask." His eyes glinted like granite in his tanned face, instilling terror into Hana with his next sentence. "Ask Logan why he paid such a big portion of my defense costs. Ask why he got Liza to pull strings and get herself assigned to my case. Ask him, Hana. I think we'd both like to know the answers."

"But I'll have to tell him the truth about why I want to know." Her voice wobbled with emotion, her chest tight and painful.

Lincoln shook his head. "You do that and I'll tell him I walked in on you and Asher."

"He won't believe you." Relief flooded through Hana at the ludicrous suggestion. "My son's older than Asher. He'll know you made it up."

Lincoln shrugged, not caring that he threatened to ruin her life in the exoneration of his own. "But it'll be there festering like a sore in your marriage, Hana. He'll never be quite sure that you're telling the truth again. If you're willing to take the risk; go for it. If not, do your job and I won't bust up your happy family." He turned and walked from the kitchen and she heard the front door slam behind him. He'd peeled potatoes for her and then stabbed her in the heart with the knife.

46

An Unusual Trade

"Spaghetti Bolognese, yum." Logan paused in the middle of washing his hands to lean across and kiss Hana's cheek. She tried to stop her shoulders tensing and failed. "What's wrong?"

"Nothing." Hana moved away, setting the mince and spaghetti on the table separately.

Wiri smacked his lips and grinned at Phoenix. "My pa calls it spaghetti bollock naked."

"Hey!" Logan stamped on the mutiny with a well-placed glare and his shout frightened the life out of the small boy. Wiri glowered at his empty plate and Phoenix patted his arm in sympathy. Then she poked her tongue out at Logan's back.

"Phoenix Du Rose, that's enough!" Hana chided her. "If you two can't behave, you can go straight to bed; I don't mind."

"You said you'd make shepherd's pie." Wiri shot her a glare of betrayal. "Like my ma makes for me. It's my favourite."

Hana nodded, guilt budding in her chest. "I know, baby. I'm sorry but I forgot to buy more potatoes."

"But I bought them." Leslie stopped dishing up the food and went to the pantry, peering into the basket they kept the vegetables in. "Where'd they go?"

All eyes fixed on Hana and she felt her temperature spike. Mac kicked his legs in his high chair and reached for the plastic bowl in her hand, making it clear he wasn't impressed with the delay. "They weren't nice," Hana lied. "I peeled them but they weren't good enough." She glared at Leslie. "Check the bin if you like. The bag is by the front door ready to go out although I'll be the one to walk it around the side of the house; as usual." Hana pushed a mouthful of mince and squished spaghetti between her son's lips and his pupils dilated with pleasure.

"I put bags in the bin. I can reach." Wiri's lips parted in a grin of evil proportions and he narrowed his eyes to slits and looked sideways at Phoenix. She smiled back at him like a getaway driver who thought they all just went for pizza and didn't hear gun shots.

"Is there any for me?" Caleb walked through the kitchen door balancing on his crutches. A clean cast encased his leg and he looked happier.

"Yep." Phoenix patted the chair next to hers and smiled at him. "Nonie, Caleb's got empty puku. He wants some of dis." She tapped her fork on the plate and laughed at the sound.

"I got a new cast." Caleb sat down and smiled at Phoenix. "Surgeon said I'm a quick healer. I've got a week in this one while he double checks the X-rays and then I go back to the fracture clinic. I might get a different moon boot so I can walk more."

"How did you get to the hospital?" Hana pushed food into her son at speed as he swallowed and opened his mouth for more, his slender fingers wiggling in midair.

"I took him there and gave him the money for a bus home." Leslie glared at Logan in challenge and Hana's husband ate his dinner and made no comment. "Quicker he heals, quicker he's gone," she mumbled under her breath. Hana cringed, but the men ignored her.

She felt relieved when the baby turned his face sideways, so the spoon wiped a smear of red Bolognese across his cheek. "Mac's done. Please excuse me and I'll sort him out for bed."

"Don't he want purini?" Leslie sounded indignant at Mac's denial of the sweet delights hiding in the back of the fridge.

"Mmmmnn! I do!" Wiri pushed his last mouthful in and slammed his cutlery onto the plate. He glanced back at Hana. "Fanks for that, Ma. I liked it better than shepherd's pie, anyway."

"You're welcome, Wiri. No thanks, Leslie. He's tired; I'll take him upstairs so he can get a head start before the others come to bed." She exited from the kitchen feeling Logan's grey gaze drilling holes in her spine.

Upstairs in the bathroom the little boy slapped the water beneath his palms, giggling at the sensations it created. "You'll be too big to sit in the sink soon, little man," Hana cooed, stroking his damp hair back from his forehead. "Then what will I do?"

"Take him in the shower like you did with Phoenix." Logan perched on the side of the bath and peered down at his cowboy boots, appearing engrossed in the view.

Hana glanced back at the door, a gap showing the hallway bathed in a glow from the lights downstairs. "I locked that."

Logan shrugged. "I unlocked it."

"Ugh!" Hana managed to hold onto Mac's shoulders as he gave the water an almighty slap and soaked her. He watched her reaction and laughed, attempting to repeat it and causing a tidal wave. Logan reached across and pulled the plug. Mac squealed as the water sucked at his skin and then looked confused as the last drips trailed between his toes. The expression in his green eyes asked what the hell just happened?

"What's going on, wahine?" Gentle hands moved Hana's long hair aside and he tutted as he saw the welt around her neck.

Hana rolled her eyes, knowing the futility of lying to her perceptive husband. "I can't tell you."

Logan raised an eyebrow and took the swaddled child who snuggled into the warm towel with a look of contentment. "Why? Did you say you wouldn't?"

She shook her head. "No, but there was a threat attached."

"Who put their hands on you, Hana? Was it that kid downstairs? If it was, I'll kill him."

"No, no." She raised a hand to placate him. "Not Caleb; he wasn't here." She squirmed, busying herself with mopping puddles off the floorboards with another towel. "But I've got a problem and don't know what to do."

"You could tell me." Logan kissed his son's downy amber head and watched Hana struggle. "We promised not to keep secrets from each other."

She sighed. "I know, Logan! I'm meant to ask you some questions otherwise he'll tell you that he walked in on me and Asher."

Logan snorted. "What? You killing him?"

"No." Hana widened her eyes and Logan pulled a face of disgust.

"And I'm what? Meant to believe it?"

"I guess so. He said he'd make it convincing."

Logan sat on the side of the bath and helped Mac get his thumb free, so he could push it between his rosebud lips. "So did he walk in on you and Asher?" His eyes blazed a path though her soul and she sat down on the floor opposite and leaned against the wall. "How long before the kids come up?"

"Ten minutes maybe." Logan jerked his head towards her throat. "You look like someone throttled you. Who was it?"

Hana held up both hands, palms facing him. "I need you to not go off the deep end," she pleaded. "I can't tell you if you'll race off and kill people."

Logan shook his head in exasperation. "Why do you always say that? I don't kill people, Hana."

"Maim them then!" she bit. "You can't."

"I'll ask you one more time, Hana. Who put their hands on you?"

She inhaled and her words emerged in a rush. "He did walk in on me and Asher, but the kid tried to strangle me. I opened the door thinking it was Leslie, but he came back looking for Caleb and the drugs. He searched the house and messed stuff up." She raised a finger. "I cleared up afterwards, but he broke your expensive aftershave. I'm sorry. The bedroom smells like a rugby changing room."

"Gee, thanks." Logan's eyes filled with irritation. "I thought you liked that scent. You bought it for me in Paris."

"I love it, but not all in one hit."

"Now I'm really pissed. I loved it too." Logan let Mac loll back in his arms and Hana watched as his muscles dug through his shirt. "I need to sort Asher out."

"That's not all." Hana chewed her lower lip.

"Are you okay?" Logan leaned forward and peered at her throat. "That looks sore. Did you ice it?" He spoke the words like a rational man but rage blossomed in his grey eyes. His irises turned to pewter.

Hana sighed. "Yes."

"So who's blackmailing you? Evidently someone walked in on Asher throttling you. And explain that weird text you sent me. Why do you think Linc's having an affair with Anahera?"

"I went to see her and found him with his arm around her. He followed me here and walked in on Asher strangling me. Asher wanted to check Mac's bedroom and I didn't want him near the baby. I got in the way. Lincoln chased Asher off but wouldn't let me call the cops."

"Strangling you?" Logan's jawline hardened and his pupils obscured his irises altogether. "I'll kill him. And Linc. Why didn't you call me?"

"Lincoln took my phone downstairs and then waited for me." Hana swallowed. "He's back to prove his innocence and he wants me to do it for him. He asked me to find out if you killed the woman because he says he didn't."

"Why would I kill her?" Logan's brow furrowed.

Hana inhaled. "There were four local men including Lincoln who went to the murdered woman for sex. He knows a fifth became involved, but only two of the men knew his identity. Those two died while Lincoln served his sentence. He thinks you might be the fifth man."

"Me?" To Hana's surprise Logan laughed. "I'm insulted. I've never paid for sex in my life."

Hana peered at the floor and her stillness alarmed him. "I hope not." When she looked up at him again, his expression of disbelief told her everything. She shook her head and sighed. "But you said if I died then you'd hire a hooker."

Logan's mouth opened in surprise. "I joked, Hana! You know that thing couples do where one of them laughs?"

Hana wrinkled her nose. "I can't always tell with you. Sometimes it sounds like a joke but you look serious." She sighed. "You're gorgeous. You'd never need to pay. But Lincoln's not ugly; not on the outside. What makes someone like him pay a prostitute?"

Logan inhaled and his chest looked strong and safe. Hana scooted across the bathroom floor on her bottom and pressed her hand against it, seeking the security she always found there. "Promise you didn't sleep with her?"

"I said I didn't."

"No, you said you didn't pay. It's different."

Logan rolled his eyes. "I didn't do either, Hana. Te tātea o te tāne is too precious to waste on casual sex. I told you that before. My seed is sacred." He stroked Hana's cheek. "And I didn't kill her either." He shook his head and the dark waves escaped onto his forehead, obscuring his eyes. "So she was te kairau? I didn't see that under my nose."

"I don't think you were in New Zealand full time when it started. Did you even know the dead woman?"

"I remember flying back and forth a fair bit during that time so I might have been here. I needed to stop Alfred wrecking everything, so I flew home every six weeks during the school holidays and then came back for good around the time the cops arrested Linc. Yeah, I knew her; we all did. Are you sure you've got this right? Anahera's sister was a prostitute?"

47

Creating Her Own Monster

"Anahera's sister died?" Hana's jaw gaped open. "Wiri's aunty?"

Logan nodded and pinched the bridge of his nose between thumb and forefinger. Mac's head lolled backwards and he sucked on his thumb with tiny noises. "Yeah. Pania was older than us. Michael got sweet on her for a while before we went to boarding school. We came home for the holidays and she'd gone loco; running around with the farm boys and pregnant at sixteen. My ma wouldn't let us near her; said she was out of bounds."

Hana snorted. "Yeah. I've seen out of bounds to your brother. Isn't that what turns it into a challenge?"

Logan grimaced. "Half-brother." He spat the words with venom, the correction aimed more at the unfairness of life than at Hana. "Yeah, he had a go. Of course he did. Every menstruating female within a ten kilometre radius was fair game to his ego; he wasn't fussy."

"Why ten kilometres?" Hana contemplated the riddle without success.

"He only owned this old bicycle." Logan's lips quirked into a sad smile. "He always said a round trip under twenty was worthwhile, but over and it better be fantastic."

"He's such an ass!" Hana commented, her brain already working. "Could he be the mysterious other man?"

"I don't know Hana." Logan patted his son's bottom through the towel. "Can we get a nappy on this kid before he does something I'll regret? I want you to leave this alone. I'll deal with Linc." His brow furrowed. "And bloody Asher."

Hana exhaled and leaned back against the bath. "That was easy. All the times I kept things from you because I expected you to kick off. I never realised how reasonable you could be." She rubbed her neck and frowned. Logan stroked his son's little toes as they peeked from the towel, his brow knitted in concentration. Hana watched his jaw work through the skin and her heart sank. "Well played, Logan. You almost fooled me."

"I'm good." He kept his tone light but the smile he offered Hana failed to reach his eyes. "Let's get these kids to bed shall we?"

"Don't do it, Logan. Please."

He snuffed out a laugh and stood, giving her a look she knew well. "What? I'm just gonna put a nappy on my boy." He left her sitting on the floor of the bathroom and she heard him chatting to the other children as they pounded upstairs. Phoenix burst through the doorway, already peeling herself out of her dress.

"Zip, Mama?" she asked, turning around so Hana could slide the fastener free. The happy girl stripped naked in seconds and bounced on the spot while Hana started the shower running.

"In you get." Hana lifted her over the side of the bath and smiled as her daughter stood under the deluge, her pretty face tilted upwards to meet the spray. "You're like your father," Hana whispered. "You face life head on."

"Head on?" Phoenix called, spitting out the water which strayed into her mouth. "I got head on." She patted her damp curls with a small hand and Hana smiled.

"Yeah, so you do. Come on missy. Hurry up and soap yourself so Wiri can come in."

"I don't need a shower; I'm clean." Wiri pushed through the doorway with his pyjama bottoms over his head. Phoenix pealed with laughter and covered herself with shower gel. She looked like a foamy snowman until she rinsed off and then she raised her arms to Hana.

"Look, Wiri. Wiri look at me." Phoenix pulled funny faces and wiggled her legs through the bottom of the towel Hana swaddled her in.

"Get in the shower, Wiri. I left it running. You stink." Hana jerked her head towards the stream of water.

"Stink!" Phoenix repeated and giggled. "Stink."

"That's man smell." Wiri whipped the pants off his head and his hair stuck up in a static haze. "I like it."

Hana pointed towards the shower curtain. Water pounded the bottom of the iron bath like a drum roll. "I don't. Get in there and have a proper wash, your feet are black."

"No peeping then." Wiri pouted. "No girls allowed. Only Nonie."

"Charming!" Leslie waddled through the door and glared at Wiri. "I'm a girl."

He rolled his eyes and hopped over the side of the bath. "Maybe once," he muttered. "But now you're just Nonie."

Phoenix buried her nose in the towel and yawned. "I got kindy morrow?" she asked and Hana shook her head.

"No, baby. You get to stay home with me and Mac and Nonie."

"Papa's at work?" Phoenix sounded disappointed, used to him popping home for meals, starting before dawn and finishing at tea time. She screwed her nose up in disgust at the new regime.

"You've got me." Hana ignored the twinge of sadness as the daddy's girl regarded her with the signature grey Du Rose eyes.

"Okay." She made it sound second best.

"How'd it go at the hospital?" Leslie slapped Wiri's bum as he waggled it at her through the shower curtain.

"You don't miss anything, do you?" Hana frowned as Leslie smirked. She relented, seeing the kind intention behind the old woman's nosiness. "Not good. Mac's deaf. Now they just need to find out how deaf and whether it can be fixed." Hana sighed.

"Logan put my mokopuna in his cot before he went out."

"Went out?" Hana froze. "Went out where?"

"Didn't say." Leslie leaned over the side of the bath and passed shower gel to the small boy dancing behind the curtain. "Youse meant to be washing tamaiti. Use the soap!"

"Don't call me 'boy'," Wiri replied in a sing-song voice. "I'm Wiremumu."

"Moo moo." Phoenix screwed up her eyes and rested her face on Hana's shoulder. "Moo moo."

Hana left the steamy bathroom and helped her daughter dress, buttoning her pyjama shirt and settling her into bed. The room felt cool so she switched on the heater in the corner, leaving it to fill the cavernous classroom with its warmth. "Nonie read it?" Phoenix waved the picture book in front of her face and Hana nodded.

"Okay. Kiss." She pressed her lips against the perfect cheek and ruffled her daughter's damp hair. "Love you, baby. I'll tell Nonie."

Wiri pouted when Hana asked Leslie to read and put up a protest. "She doesn't do the voices!"

"Her name is Nonie, not she. And aren't you lucky to have a choice of people to read to you?"

"Suppose so." Wiri stood on the bath mat wrapped in a towel and held his arms out to Hana. "I love you."

The smile lit her face from the inside. "I love you too, Wiri."

"Will I live with you forever?"

Her heart sank. "I don't have control over that, sweetheart. But whatever happens, I'll always be here for you."

"Does my real ma not love me?"

"She does, but she's ill. I tried to see her today to ask if you could visit but she was busy. I'll try again though."

Wiri smiled, his grey eyes trusting. "Fanks. I do want to see her."

"I know." Hana stroked his hair and stood up. "Hop into bed before Phoe falls asleep. Otherwise nobody will get a story." She kissed his soft cheek and went to check on her son.

Mac slept with his arms above his head, his breathing steady and tiny chest rising and falling to a rhythmic beat. "Beautiful boy," Hana whispered and stroked the warm forehead.

Downstairs, she hugged the diary written by Phoenix Du Rose and let her fingers run over the clasp which held it closed. The lounge felt warm and soporific with Caleb dozing on the sofa. He turned the television down as she entered. "Hey, Hana. I'm sorry about before. You've been kind and I took advantage. I shouldn't have brought drugs into your home or listened to Asher. As soon as I get this second cast off I'll be gone. Logan doesn't know where my dad is; I asked him. Said he put him on a flight to England and never heard from him again."

Hana sighed and sat down in a nearby armchair. She cradled the soft leather of the book in her fingers and nodded. "Logan wouldn't keep a man from knowing his father. A whole family kept him away from his."

"He's gone to sort out Asher." Caleb chewed his lower lip. "I told him where I think the house is. Will he get hurt?"

"Logan?" Hana shrugged. "Probably. The hemophilia makes him bruise and bleed, so yes, if there's physical contact, he'll get hurt."

"I meant Asher." Caleb nibbled on his fingernails, his body language stiff with anxiety. "I don't know where that bag went but Asher said he'd send the guys round to find it. He's already taken the money; he showed me over a hundred dollars. He promised them. They don't like missing out, not people like them." He stared at her sideways with a curious sly smile on his lips and Hana shifted in her chair with discomfort.

"Logan will be back soon." She opened the book and stroked her finger down the yellowed pages, seeking reassurance and wisdom from a woman she no longer liked. In sleeping with her own brother and producing Reuben Du Rose, the kuikui set in motion a disaster which took three decades before her heirs repeated it and seven more before it detonated.

"Good book? It looks old."

"It is." Hana ran her finger down the list of cattle prices and earnings, finding nothing to satisfy her soul. "And disappointing." She snapped it closed and huffed in annoyance as one of the pages bent. Opening the book again, she tugged at the page and found it thicker than expected, realising as she turned it over that she held a black-and-white photograph in her fingers. Three men smiled up at her and she peered closer to see their faces. Age spots dotted the surface and it held the pinkish hue peculiar to 1970s printing ink. One man held a shot gun slung across his shoulder and his hand rested on the shoulders of a light haired boy. The flared jeans they both wore looked incongruous against the tight fitting shirts and wide collars. The tall, imposing man in the centre rested his hand on the head of the dark boy in front of him. Hana's heart clenched as she recognised Reuben Du Rose and guessed the dark, gangly boy would be Neville. The third man carried a baby wrapped in a blanket, his face beaming in an open smile. Alfred Du Rose looked handsome once, slighter than his brother but no less defined. "Wow!" Hana breathed out the word and Caleb looked across at her. She held up the photo for him to see.

"That's neat; three old dudes and their kids."

Hana nodded and pointed at the baby. "It's Logan. This was taken before the family imploded. I don't know who the other man is though."

"It's on the back." Caleb jerked his head towards the photo. He leaned across. "Look. It's in pencil near the top corner. If you move your fingers, you'll see."

Hana turned the photograph over and peered at the slanted writing in the top right corner. "Can you read it?" She handed it over and Caleb took it with exaggerated care. He bent forwards and back to catch the light and read the faded words in a faltering sentence. "Alfie and Logan." He tipped the fragile paper and squinted. "Ru-something and Karl? No, Kane. That bit's too faded." Caleb handed the photo back. "That other one is Haines but I can't read the kid's name."

"Lincoln." Hana wrinkled her nose. "Lincoln Haines. Of course it is. The boys stayed friends after the family divided but I don't know what happened to Lincoln's father. He must've trodden a tightrope trying to please both sides; I'm not sure I'd bother."

"Me neither." Caleb turned the television back up and the conversation ended. Leslie joined them and Hana retreated into her thoughts. The kid leather of the diary felt soft under her fingers and she stroked it without thinking, pondering mysteries she couldn't seem to solve.

"Leslie?" she said and the old woman looked across at her, peeling herself away from the English soap opera which she and Caleb stared at goggle-eyed. "How close was Lincoln to Logan and Reuben's boys?"

Leslie shrugged. "Pretty close although Linc's more Liza's age I think. He kept very tight with Kane too until he married the doctor-woman. She didn't like Reuben's boys but he's always defended his friendship with Nev. They were real bad boys when they were younger. They roped Logan in and Miriam tried everything to keep them apart. I'm sure Linc was there when Kane split Logan open with a machete."

Hana winced and her brow furrowed in remembrance of the awful tale. She steered the conversation away from it, knowing Logan's version included his older brother Barry's complicity. It made her sick to think of it. "How many deaths have there been in the township during the last ten years? Can you remember?"

"Youse lookin' for a superbug, kōtiro?" Leslie snorted and Hana shook her head.

"How many?"

Leslie harrumphed as the credits rolled for her programme and she glared at Hana. "Now look what you made me do." She held up her hand and counted on her fingers. "Miriam, Reuben, him whose name makes you go loco." A pudgy hand yanked her glasses down her nose and she raised an eyebrow at Hana. "My hoa tāne, may Atua bless his lazy, gambling soul."

Caleb snorted. "Nice. I hope my wife doesn't talk about me like that."

Leslie leaned over the arm of her chair. "Little shits like youse don't get wives, tamaiti. Decent wahine look for men who can feed and clothe them, not wandering vagrants who bring drugs into other people's homes."

Caleb blanched and Hana didn't defend him. His apology failed to negate the current threat to her children or to her. She touched her neck and felt the soreness abating, her mind turning to the whereabouts of her husband.

He still hadn't returned by the time Leslie shuffled up the stairs to bed and Caleb left soon after on his crutches. Hana heard a peculiar rustling in the hallway and laid the book on the sofa, sticking her head through the doorway and feeling the cool night air in the hall. "What are you doing?"

Caleb bent over the dustbin bag by the front door, sifting through the rubbish in the dim light of a lamp. Hana remembered the lie about the potatoes Lincoln peeled and bit her lip. "Just checking something," he said, his voice hushed. "I thought the weed came back."

"The drugs? Why would it come back?"

"I dunno!" Caleb exclaimed and his eyes darted up the darkened stairs. "I wondered if the old lady played a trick on me."

"Wait!" Hana jabbed her finger at the black rubbish sack. "You put the drugs in a dustbin bag?"

"Yeah. They wouldn't fit in my diamante suitcase."

Hana narrowed her eyes. "Don't get smart with me. You're in enough trouble." She chewed her lip in thought but the fragment of memory eluded her as headlights spun onto the drive. "Logan!" She flung the door open before he even descended from the ute, her eyes grazing his body for injury.

48

Solved, Not Solved

Logan walked fine and his expression showed more peace than anger. "I filled the ute." He smiled at Hana and handed the keys over, frowning when she didn't take them. With a shrug he laid them on the hall table.

"Did you find the house and see the dealers?" Caleb moved backwards on his crutches, edging nearer to his doorway as though believing he could escape Logan if necessary. Hana gave a slight shake of her head, wanting to tell him how fast her husband moved and how she knew not to bother running anymore. Running, hiding, even locking herself into bathrooms. Pointless, all of it.

"Yeah, I saw them. The shoes hanging over the telephone lines gave them away. They're hard core dealers but they won't be coming here."

"Shoes over telephone lines? Is that why people put them there? I never knew why they laced them together and threw them up there." Hana's brow furrowed in concentration, missing Logan's grin and slight shake of his head.

"Was Asher there? They gave him a room but only if he got the weed." Caleb sweated with nervousness, a damp stain beginning beneath his arms.

Logan smirked and the scar beneath his right eye crinkled. "He's not there anymore," he replied. He jabbed a crooked index finger at Caleb. Hana saw the scar from an untreated childhood break for just a second as the white flesh glinted in the lamplight. "As soon as that cast comes off; you're gone, man. I don't know where Flick went because I told him not to come back. And you? You bring the kind of dumb ass trouble I ain't got time for, kid. That cast comes off and you're outa here."

Caleb nodded and backed into his room, closing the door behind him. Logan's eyes roved over Hana, sensing her tension. "It's sorted," he promised. "Fancy a drink?"

They settled in the kitchen with a bottle of merlot and Logan sipped and scratched the bristles on his jaw. "Why am I surrounded by stupid boys?" he demanded, pushing his fingernail into a dent on the wooden table.

"What happened?" Hana steeled herself for the truth, not wanting to hear it but knowing she'd prefer it to lies. "You've been gone for hours. I almost called Bodie."

Her husband raised his eyebrows in a look of disdain and Hana swallowed as he chose to ignore her lack of faith. "I went to the address Caleb gave me. It's an old state house in Horsham Downs. I told them Asher thought hibiscus leaves were dope and they wouldn't get high smoking it." He laughed. "I told them they'd smell pretty though." His expression changed with such subtlety, Hana almost missed it.

"What's wrong?"

"Nothing." His brow knitted and he worked to return his face to a blank slate. "Just something one of them said. He mentioned a name I didn't wanna hear."

"What name?" Hana pressed.

Logan shook his head. "It doesn't matter. It's not relevant to this."

"Was Asher there?"

Logan nodded. "Yeah. Kid took a swing at me and made himself look even dumber." He smirked. "I didn't expect it to be so easy. But I don't think he'll be staying with them much longer; the humiliation will send him packing."

"But where? He'll go back to Nev's place and we don't want him there."

Logan shook his head. "No he won't. I warned him. He's persona non grata on the mountain now. Banished. The guys won't let him back."

Hana heaved out a sigh and Logan reached for her hand. "No, Hana. We're not taking him on in the hope that he'll turn out good like Tama. Some people don't wanna be helped, babe. Learn when to quit."

"Don't throw your pearls before swine." She repeated the scripture; a remnant from her father's sermons and nodded. "I always hope there's something salvageable in everyone."

"There is." Logan sounded definite. "But they have to want it. Flick, Tama, Ryan; they all wanted a second chance and they got one. Asher's too twisted up to work out what he wants and Caleb wants his dad. End of. I can't give what I haven't got. And the more poking around he does up at our place, the more likelihood of someone in a cop uniform getting interested. How will that help a guy who's started a new life in England?"

"True. Bodie knew Flick was there but I doubt he'll protect us from his snooping colleagues now." Hana winced. "Not that he comes close enough to hear anything anymore."

"He will." Logan squeezed her fingers. "You bit him and he didn't like it. He and Amy seem to think I'm a wallet full of spare cash and you're a free babysitting service. It had to end sometime."

"Wallet?" Hana's eyes narrowed. "What do you mean?"

Logan realised his mistake too late and chewed his lower lip. "Oh, I lent him a grand to auction off Amy's house and never got it back. He hasn't looked me in the eye since he borrowed it. It's probably part of the problem."

"I'll pay you back." Hana licked her lips and looked embarrassed. "I'm sorry; I didn't know."

"What a good idea." Logan's sarcasm cut through her maternal shame. "Why don't you pay his mortgage while you're at it; you reduced your asking price on Culver's Cottage so he could afford it. Tell you what; he could give up work and send all the bills to you. Hell, they could both give up work and let you worry about the credit card statements. Geez, Hana!" Logan stood and dumped his mug in the dishwasher. Red wine dribbled through the rack before he closed the door. He turned to her and narrowed his eyes, not bothering to hide his irritation. "You're the problem but you don't see it. You've wiped his ass his whole life and the one time he didn't get what he wanted, he threw a hissy fit like a toddler. The punishment is that we don't get to see Jas anymore which hurts us and him, but doesn't touch Bodie. He's a dick, Hana and you enable him."

Hana inhaled, the words hard to hear. She went into defense mode, her heart pricking from Logan's criticism. "I do not! Isobel's not like that. I raised them the same."

His face softened and he shook his head. "Izzie's gorgeous. She's generous and loving. Marcus and Izzie feed their family on the smell of an oily rag; they've got nothing and yet they're proper happy. She's a breath of fresh air and nothing like your twit of a son."

"He knew about Vic's affair." Hana swallowed and stared at the table. "It isolated him before and after his dad died because he couldn't tell me."

"So what?" Logan folded his arms and leaned back against the counter. "He's not sixteen anymore, Hana. If he thinks his life was hard, he should've tried living Tama's. That's effed up for sure."

"But what about Jas? I'm desperate to see him."

Logan nodded. "Write to him, Hana and post the letters. Keep copies so that one day when he comes looking, you can prove how you felt." Logan's jaw flexed and pain crossed his eyes.

"Are you thinking of Reuben's letters to Will's brother?"

Logan nodded. "Yeah. He spent forty years talking about me to his friend and I grew up believing he was the outcast uncle. It helped and took the pain away just knowing he'd loved me. That's what you can do for Jas." Logan tilted his head sideways. "I don't think Bodie will stop Jas having them though. He's not spiteful; just a big baby."

Hana sighed. "I wonder if that's how Caleb feels."

"What? Like a big baby. Probably."

"No! Wanting Bobby to tell him he loves him."

Logan grinned. "Nice try, Hana. God loves a trier."

Hana pouted. "Sure he does."

Logan held out his hand to her. "Come on, Mrs Du Rose. Come to bed with me."

Hana rolled her eyes and feigned reluctance. "If I must."

"You do." Logan pushed her wine glass aside and took her hands, wrapping her arms around his waist and joining their fingers behind his back. Dark curls slipped into his eyes and he smiled. His lips pressed warmth against Hana's, soothing her battered soul from the outside in. Her soft tongue strayed into his mouth and Logan sighed. "Come on," he whispered. "Let me love you better and then we'll talk about Mac."

49

Cleaning Duty

Logan's alarm woke them at five in the morning and Hana groaned. She'd got up twice in the night to the baby and she pulled the covers over her head. "Why do you need to go to the gym so early?" she grumbled and Logan leaned sideways and kissed the back of her head.

"Because otherwise I go at night and that leaves you alone. I try to go at lunchtime but I've got a duty today."

"You're all heart." Hana pushed her face into the pillow and yawned. "You kept me up half the night and now you wake me at the crack of dawn."

Logan snorted. "It's not dawn yet." He dug his fingers into her ribs and she let out a muted squeal. "Anyway, we did as much talking as romping."

"Yeah, we did." Hana sat up, her nightdress on inside out and her amber curls coiffed into a messy wedge at the back of her head. "I might take a shower now before everyone wakes. It'll give me a head start. I need to put the bins out. The rubbish truck will be here in two hours."

"No, it won't." Logan pulled on gym shorts and slipped a sleeveless tee shirt over his head. Hana watched as it rippled down his chest muscles and she patted the bed next to her.

"Come back to bed and yes it will."

Logan dodged her grasping hands and laughed. "No, wahine. I need to stay fit so I can land running when we go back to the farm. I'm no good to anyone with spindly arms."

"You don't have those." Hana snorted. "And it's bin day today. When we stayed here last year, I always forgot."

"I did it yesterday." Logan bent to tie his trainers. "It's changed since then. And we can't leave it at the end of the drive anymore; we need to wheel it over to the school and put it with theirs."

"Did you do that yesterday then?" Hana's brow knitted in confusion.

"Yeah. And I wheeled the damn thing back again after work." He quirked an eyebrow. "So there Hana-who-sorts-all-the-rubbish and nobody-else-bothers. Play that on your violin."

"Oh, no!" Hana put a hand up to her mouth, her green eyes widening and glinting in the light from the bedside lamp. "Oh, no!"

"What?" Logan sat up and faced her.

"I put a bin bag by the front door last night."

"Yeah but I'll put it out this morning."

Hana shook her head in impatience. "It's not about that. I found Caleb going through it last night because he thought it might be the weed. Apparently he brought it to Hamilton in a dustbin liner."

"Stupid idiot." Logan stood and looked through the window at the blackness outside.

"I've thrown heaps of rubbish away this week; people keep leaving it by the front door."

Logan shook his head. "Why would he bring weed in a bin bag?" He lifted his hand and performed a corkscrew motion next to his temple. "Bad news, Hana. I don't think he'll make it to twenty. Kid'll fall off the flat earth and end up in space."

Hana's eyes narrowed at a faint memory. "Oh crap! I think Wiri did it. Remember when Bodie picked a fight with me and Wiri came in for Leslie's keys? Caleb got him to get something from her car. A couple of times Wiri's mentioned taking a bag away from Caleb because he doesn't like him. If he helped him inside with the dope, he'd know where to steal it from. What if he put it into the dustbin to spite him?"

Logan rolled his eyes. "Kid's got brains."

"Don't be dismissive!" Hana's face clouded. "I'll bet that's where it went. What if it's found at the landfill site and traced back here? Logan, what if the cops turn up?"

He shrugged. "Then they'll turn the school inside out looking for a marijuana plantation." He closed his eyes and shook his head. "Priceless."

"I need to ask Wiri if that's what happened."

"No, don't. Leave the kid alone, Hana. He's got enough worries and it serves Caleb right."

Hana huffed. "Then at least I should hose out the wheelie bin in case they send the drug dogs here again." She shivered at the memory of another time and a scary Alsatian eyeing up her pram.

Logan nodded, his face still wearing a smirk. "Bleach it out and use the hosepipe from around the side. I'll do it later if you can't manage it."

"I'm doing it now!" Hana leapt from the bed and ran around finding clothes.

"At five past five in the morning?" Logan checked his watch and raised an eyebrow. "Want me to set up flood lights so you can create more suspicion?"

"Shut up!" Hana slapped his bum as she passed him on the way to the stairs. "It's not funny."

"It's bloody hilarious," he laughed. "I wish I could hang around to see it."

She took an hour and Hana fell into the dustbin twice trying to wipe around the bottom. She appeared in the kitchen looking like a banshee and the children giggled at her hair. Leslie plopped toast onto Wiri's plate and put her hands on her hips. "Where've you been, kōtiro?"

"I fell in the dustbin." Hana peered at the stains on her sweatshirt. "It was difficult to get out, but I managed it easier the second time because there's a knack to it." She wiggled her fingers. "You have to do this thing with your legs and it falls over, but it hurts." She rubbed her stomach.

Logan managed to keep a straight face as he walked into the kitchen. Sweat darkened his tee shirt in a long stripe along his spine and his hair looked slick to his head. "Did you hose yourself down too?" he asked.

Wiri laughed, the action explosive enough to shower the table and everyone nearby with half-chewed toast. Hana pouted and glared at her husband. "I'll leave you to clear that up!" she snapped and exited, taking her last shred of dignity with her.

She left her dirty clothes on the floor and winced at the piece of onion skin clinging to the back of her track pants. Scooting to the bathroom in a towel, she wondered how to remove the traces of marijuana scent from the hiding place beneath the stairs. She pondered it as the hot water soothed her tired muscles and washed tomato sauce from the side of her face.

"Move over." Logan stepped over the side of the bath in all his glorious nakedness and Hana glared at him.

"Stop doing that!"

"What?" His eyes crinkled with mischief and he pulled her towards him.

"Unlocking doors; it's rude. Now wash my hair," Hana demanded, wriggling out of his grasp and turning her back on him. "I swear I mopped that thing out with the back of my head."

Logan snorted and massaged shampoo into her scalp. His strong fingers made her relax and she put her head back and closed her eyes. "I found a photo last night in the diary you lent me. You're in it."

"Oh, yeah?" Logan's hands strayed to her shoulders and then lower and he seemed more interested in his findings than hers.

"Your dad's there too. Alfred's holding you and Kane's standing in front of Reuben. Lincoln's there with what looks like his father. I can only see the word 'Haines' on the back. The names have rubbed out."

"Mmnnnn." Logan lifted her clean hair and kissed the back of her neck.

"You're not interested, are you?"

"Not one little bit right now."

Hana inhaled and exhaled a scream as ice cold water doused her from above. She almost flattened Logan in her attempt to get away from it. Her breath caught in her throat as she shivered on the bathmat, trying not to break her neck on the soaked floor. Logan laughed and stepped under the spray, soaping his broad chest and flexing his muscles to irritate her. "You're such a bloody townie," he jeered. "Have you never had a cold shower under a rusty hosepipe in a cow shed before?"

"No!" Hana snapped. She snuggled herself up in his towel as well as her own and glared at his shape through the flimsy curtain.

"Sorry!" Leslie's voice floated up the stairs. "I put the washing machine on and forgot it took the hot water. Stupid front loaders!"

Hana shook her head and warmed herself up enough to clean her teeth. Logan turned off the water and stepped onto the mat. "Please can I have my soaking wet towel back?" he asked, his lips quirking into a smile. Hana let him take it and spat toothpaste down the plughole.

"What about under the stairs? Won't there be residue?" She gnawed the side of her cheek with an expression of anxiety. "When it happened before, the dog tracked right to that spot underneath the dining table."

Logan sighed. "There won't be any dogs, Hana. The guys at the rubbish depot won't even notice it amongst all the other crap."

"What shall I tell Lincoln if he comes back?"

Logan's face lost its humour as though an unseen hand wiped the smile from his lips. There. Gone. "Tell him to see me."

"What will you do?" Worry turned Hana's pupils to black dots, accentuating the emerald of her eyes. She turned to watch her husband's spine grow rigid as he daubed the towel against his extremities.

"Just leave it." Logan ran the towel over his face and neck, patting his underarms and down over the rugged scar beneath his right armpit.

"I don't like it when you say that." Hana swallowed back dread. "It's dodgy."

"Dodgy?" Logan snorted.

"Yeah." Hana widened her green eyes in fear. "Dodgy. Once you said I should leave it and you ended up in police custody." She shivered out of the damp towel and reached above her head, scooping her hair into a knot. She jabbed a finger in his direction. "Then there was that other time when you got pushed into Hamilton Lake and almost drowned." Hana shook her head. "I'm not leaving it, Logan. Not this time. We're in this together or not at all."

Logan's pupils dilated and he stared at her, his face moving through a mix of emotions. Then he smiled. "I can't take you seriously while you're standing there naked with your arms above your head." He lurched for her and Hana squeaked as he pushed her back into the shower and turned the water on. He lifted her up against the wall of cold tiles and smothered her cries with his lips.

50

Missing

"Hana!" Leslie's voice squawked up the stairs like nails on a blackboard. "Hana!"

"What now?" She pulled her sweater over her head and buttoned up her jeans. "I'm getting dressed. Please, can you wait home with Macky while I run the others to school?"

"No. I'll take 'em. Your daughter wants a kiss."

Hana scampered down the stairs in her socks, almost breaking her neck on a slippery one at the bottom. "I'm here now."

"Kiss, Mama." Phoenix stood in the hallway with her coat and rucksack on while Wiri tied her laces with painstaking slowness. She puckered up her lips and closed her eyes in expectation and Hana bent and placed a gentle kiss on her mouth.

"You've got trainers for kindy," Hana said, her brow furrowing. "They're your best shoes."

"I'm not going kindy, member?" Phoenix replied. "I going take Wiri to school."

"Oh, yeah." Hana pulled her wet fringe away from her forehead and smothered her embarrassment. Logan's ministrations had a tendency to make her forget which day of the week it was. "I'll be fine; we'll all go."

"Nooooo!" Phoenix complained. "I wanna go wiv Nonie peese."

"Can't I come too?"

"Nope." She delivered her verdict and softened the blow with a beautiful smile. "Luff you Mama."

Hana sighed. "I love you too. So, you're not leaving me anybody?"

"Nope." Leslie chuckled and hoisted Mac higher onto the spare tyre around her stomach. "You got the morning to yerself. I'll bring 'em all back before Mac needs his nap."

"I'd rather be with you." Hana pouted and the assembled group viewed her with varying degrees of surprise.

"Oh. Well, have the morning to yerself." Leslie spun around before Hana could comment further and whisked the little family through the front door.

"Bye Ma," Wiri called over his shoulder and Phoenix gave a cute little wave. Then the door closed behind them.

"What's wrong?" Logan clattered down the stairs behind her and stopped at her crestfallen expression.

"I think I've just been ditched," Hana grumbled. "You kept me upstairs and now they've gone off without me."

A smile spread across Logan's lips and Hana shook her head, giggling as she backed towards the staircase. Her spine pressed against the wooden slats and she held her hands out in front of her. "Don't you dare. Logan, no!"

He bent and growled in her ear, catching her around the thighs and lifting her so her spine leaned against the bannister and her knees gripped around his waist. "I'm sure I can be a little late this morning," he crooned against her neck and Hana slapped his back and kicked her legs against his butt.

"No!" She lowered her voice to a whisper. "Caleb's not up yet. He might walk in on us."

"Bloody hell!" Logan groaned and rolled his eyes towards the ceiling. He let Hana slide down the rails and nuzzled her neck with his lips. "I'll be really quick," he promised and bit the soft skin beneath her ear lobe.

"Yeah, you will be because it ain't happening," Hana giggled. "Put me down and get to work."

"But Hana," Logan complained.

"No." She held firm and jerked her head towards Caleb's door. "His door's not shut."

"Maybe he's not here." Logan's eyebrow quirked upwards and a cute dimple revealed itself in his hopeful face. He set Hana's feet on the floor and slid away from her, nudging Caleb's door open so he could push his face into the room. "He's not here."

"Where is he then?" Hana's brow furrowed. "Kitchen?"

Logan checked the kitchen, lounge, downstairs laundry and the other two rooms. He returned with a smug look on his face. "He's not here, babe. No excuses."

Hana squeaked and bolted up the stairs, shrieking as Logan's feet pounded up after her. "You're so gonna get fired," she giggled as he pushed her onto the bed and climbed on top of her, his hands already roving beneath her sweater.

A lazy vibration began, pushing through Hana's leg from Logan. "Oh, baby!" she joked. "That's new."

Logan groaned in irritation and rolled over onto his side. "Damn phone!" he grumbled. "What?" His voice sounded snappy and without humour as he pressed the button and listened to the caller. Hana watched his brows knit in concentration and a look of dread pass over his eyes.

"What?" she mouthed, imagining awful scenarios with the children which made her blood run cold.

"Okay." Logan sighed. He swore a few times before shaking his head and ending the call. He stood and tucked his shirt back into his trousers. "It's not the kids. Anahera's missing."

"But she can't be. That place is like a museum; everything's locked up tight."

"Well, she is. Went out yesterday and didn't come back."

"What do you mean, she went out? She can't go out."

"Of course she can." Logan's expression seemed dismissive. "They're probably getting ready to send her home soon, so they must let her out on excursions just to make sure she can cope. Last I heard from Nev she was able to come and go during the day."

"Come and go?" Hana sounded disbelieving.

"It's not the middle ages." Logan fastened his belt and looped his neck tie back into a presentable knot. "It's a mental health facility, not prison."

"Did your mum spend time in one? Is that why you know so much?" Hana asked the question with sincerity but winced as Logan's expression darkened and he ignored her.

"Nev's driving to Hamilton. He's checking the places she usually goes and the hospital notified the cops. Expect a visit from your golden boy son."

Hana tutted and glared at him. "Where're you going? You don't know where she'll be."

"I'm going to work," Logan snorted. "It's not an emergency; she'll turn up."

"But what about me?" Hana leaned back on her elbows and tried to look sensuous. Her hair stuck up on one side and a streak of mascara graced her flushed cheek. Logan leaned down and kissed her pouting lips.

"You, my darling, need to think of a way to get rid of the old woman and the drop-kick before I get home."

"That's not fair." Hana sank back into the mattress. "Impossible in fact. Your grandmother said you were a dick."

"Kuia Phoenix?" Logan halted and dismay crossed his features. "No, she didn't. Did she?" He ran a nervous hand across his jaw and Hana smirked. "You bloody liar. I know what's in that diary, Mrs Du Rose; stock prices and land values for the early 1970s. Why do you think I gave you that one, huh?"

"I hate you." Hana pouted. "I looked forward to reading it and you've robbed me."

"Ah, poor baby." Logan leaned down and kissed her forehead. "Get rid of the interlopers, Hana. I'm kinda over it."

"You have no sense of charity!" Hana shouted at his retreating back.

"Marry a priest then!" he yelled back, his feet pounding down the stairs.

Hana sighed and flopped back on the bed, listening to the sound of the school bell tolling from across the field.

51

More Interlopers

"Logan." Hana blocked the front door with her body and placed her hand on her husband's chest, fingers splayed in warning. "Don't freak out."

Logan groaned and turned his back on her, running both hands through his hair and standing on the edge of the porch step. "What now? I'm tired, Hana. I want to eat, take a long shower and crawl into bed with a book."

"Ooh, what book?" Distracted, Hana tried to peer round his shoulder. "Will I like it?"

"No! What's going on, wahine?"

Hana winced. "Well, you know you told me to get rid of our extended family?"

Logan ground his teeth. "Yeah." He dragged the word out like a curse and shoved his thumbs in his back pockets. His sigh spoke volumes.

Hana took a step forward and stroked his broad chest, pushing her fingers into the crinkles of his shirt and choosing her words with care. "Nev's here. I said he could stay."

"What?" Logan closed his eyes and looked up at the darkening sky. "Why?"

"Don't be angry." Hana's green eyes widened and she put on her most cute face as she rested her chin against his chest and stared up at him. "He's anxious about Anahera. She's still missing."

Logan shrugged. "So, who's sorting the farm?"

"Toby." Hana pressed her cheek against him and snuggled in, looking for validation. "I did my best, Logan. Please give me a little credit."

"Why? Instead of getting rid of anyone; you've collected someone else."

"Not on purpose." Hana pouted. "And anyway, Caleb's gone. He took his bag of clothes and left. Must've gone during the night."

"Where's he gone?"

"You don't really care. You're trying to ascertain if he's coming back."

Logan snorted. "True. It's fine, babe. You did good." He put an arm around her shoulders and kissed the side of her face. "I'm starving."

Hana rubbed her palm along his tight stomach. "Good job one of the interlopers cooked dinner for you then, isn't it?"

"Okay, okay!" Logan buried his face in her hair and sniffed. "Geez, you're hot, wahine. I just want you all to myself."

"I know. Soon." Hana stepped across the threshold and allowed Logan to follow her. The family sat at the kitchen table and Nev rose as Logan walked in.

"Hey, thanks bro and to your missus." He jerked his dark head towards Hana. "You know why I'm here?"

"Yep." Logan sank into the chair next to his daughter and she patted his thigh and gave him puppy eyes.

"Luff you, Papa," she whispered.

Logan's smile spread across his face and he leaned in and kissed her upturned lips. Across the table, Wiri slid from his chair and plonked himself on Nev's knee. Hana shot worried looks in his direction, pleased for the contact with his father, but fearful of how to clear up the emotional fallout when he left again.

"Don't worry so," Leslie hissed, handing Hana a plate to pass to Logan.

She nodded in return and served the remaining plates with a fake smile. Half way through the meal Nev's phone rang and he jerked in surprise, tippling poor Wiri sideways. "Sorry, son," he muttered and went into the hallway to take the call.

"Who's that?" Wiri asked, his voice shrill.

"Somebody for your dad," Hana answered. "Sit on your own chair to eat, sweetheart. Let Daddy enjoy his food."

Wiri shifted onto his own vacant seat, his eyes never leaving the closed door. Hana felt her appetite leave, pretending not to notice as Phoenix's little hand popped over the side of her plate and stole the carrots one at a time. She gave her husband a watery smile above their daughter's head and he nodded in understanding, anticipating the revival of Wiri's abandonment nightmares and the bedwetting.

Leslie fed Mac in his high chair and he ate, humming to himself and clasping his hand around his throat to feel the vibrations. Hana smiled at her little boy and he beamed back, closing his eyes and putting his whole face into the action. "Beautiful boy," she mouthed to him and he mimicked her, opening and closing his mouth and tipping his head from one side to the other. He made no sound, but his enjoyment in Hana's attention induced a blossoming warmth in her chest.

"Still nothing." Nev shoved his phone into his jeans and sat at the table, his forehead creasing in irritation as Wiri crept back onto his knee and set to work on his father's peas. "I've looked everywhere."

"Have you checked under your bed?" Wiri asked. "I lose everything under there." He eyed Hana sideways, repeating the well-worn mantra of the last few months. "There's no monsters under there. God doesn't let them come near his children."

"Hmmmn." Neville wasn't listening and Hana glanced at Logan and receiving no silent glance of solidarity, stared at a knot on the surface of the table. "The charge nurse said someone visited and she's seemed subdued ever since."

"Hana visited." Wiri pointed her fork at her and all eyes turned in her direction.

"I didn't see her," Hana answered, her tone defensive. "She looked busy, so I left. Your mother didn't know I'd been."

When Mac sneezed and coated the side of her face with squashed peas and gravy, Hana excused herself for a shower, her heart heavy with foreboding and dread.

52

Night-time Antics

Logan dealt with the bedtime routine, accepting Nev's feckless assistance with Wiri. He sank onto the double bed as Hana finished drying her hair. "I don't know why he came here," he said, putting his arms behind his head. "It's obvious he doesn't wanna be here."

"He doesn't care about the fallout when he walks away either." Hana pushed the brush through her dusky curls. She turned to face Logan. "I'm worried about Lincoln turning up again." Her lips twisted as she chewed on the inside of her cheek. "He's scary."

"Don't worry about him." Logan wrinkled his nose. "He won't come back."

"He will." Hana fixed her hair into a clip and her nightdress flowed around her slender body as she moved, clambering onto the bed to kneel next to Logan. "He'll come when you're not here."

Logan shook his head. "He won't, Hana."

She narrowed her eyes. "Have you seen him?"

"Of course I've bloody seen him!" Logan's grey eyes flashed with anger. "I funded his defense and gave him a home and a job when he got back. He repays me by threatening my marriage with a crock of crap. Don't worry about him; he's gone."

"Gone where?"

Logan swore and rubbed his eyes. "Don't know and don't care, Hana." He groaned and ran his hands over his face. "It took me exactly twenty minutes to sort out that gang of idiots with Asher and I used the rest of the time to drive up to the hotel and rearrange Lincoln's attitude towards me. The boys made sure he left."

"Oh." Hana waited for details and got none. She lifted Logan's hands up to her face for inspection, seeing the blue bruising around his knuckles. "Aren't you scared you'll meet your match one day?" she asked, her voice soft and fearful. "Then what will I do?"

"Become a very rich widow." Logan smiled, his expression wistful. "Go kiss your kids. Watch they don't think you're a ghost in that granny nightie."

"Ha ha ha. I've been a widow once already, thanks. I don't want to do it again." Hana put as much sarcasm into her voice as she could muster.

In the children's bedroom, Nev looked like the most awkward storyteller she'd ever seen. He sat on the end of Wiri's bed like a sasquatch in a bean bag, all masculinity and no soft edges. Hana kissed a sleeping Mac and Phoenix, smiling at both her babies sucking their thumbs beneath the covers. She ushered a drooping Wiri into his bed and released Nev back into the wild.

Logan met her outside the bedroom door, running down the hallway pulling on his cowboy boots. "Trouble!" he said to Nev and ran back to the bedroom to collect his jacket and the ute keys. He ignored Hana and she floundered, not sure what to do. The brothers held an impromptu council of war at the bottom of the stairs and Hana panicked, running to the bedroom and pulling on track pants, trainers and a hoodie. Her flowing nightdress took some persuading to lie flat in her pants but she managed it, sneaking through the laundry door and running around the side of the house. Leslie watched her leave. The old matron peered through the kitchen window and shook her head in disbelief at the woman sneaking past. Hana put her finger up to her lips and Leslie shook her fist in return, making her feelings about the expedition clear.

Logan unlocked the ute from the porch, his face turned away as he spoke to Nev. Hana used their delay to hop into the open truck bed behind the rear seats. The air felt cold and she grappled around for something to hold onto. The men didn't even check the flat bed before climbing into the vehicle and Logan started the engine with a roar from the throttle.

Hana worked hard to keep low, not wanting to be seen through the rear view mirror. She felt grateful for the absence of sharp objects as she swung around on the slippery surface. They roared through Hamilton making myriad turns and she lay on her back staring at the stars and bracing her hands and feet against a toolbox and a wheel arch to keep herself from flying over the side. She moaned with relief as the ute slowed and made another turn, travelling with less urgency downhill. The reflection of the town lights lost their influence on the night sky overhead and bird calls and running water replaced the car noises and street sounds.

Hana peeked her face over the tailgate of the ute and absorbed her surroundings, recognising the car park at Hamilton Gardens. A lone dog walker clambered into his vehicle after pushing an enormous Labradoodle into the passenger seat. He squealed as the wet dog shook off the lake water from his late night swim and Hana suppressed a giggle.

The ute doors slammed and shook the vehicle as the brothers emerged. Logan pulled his jacket down over his bum and rubbed his palms together against the cold, holding the key fob over his shoulder to lock the vehicle. Hana slid towards the edge and waited for them to move away before attempting to clamber over the side and follow. The men walked with confident slowness, unfazed by the dark surroundings and long shadows. Hana slipped her feet over the side and hitched her bottom upwards, pushing herself over the tailgate with a decent shove of her palms against the ridged bed of the truck.

An almighty ripping sound rent the air and made both men turn around, their eyes widening in surprise at the sight of her dangling from the remains of her nightdress which caught around the metal clasp of the toolbox.

"Bloody hell!" Logan sighed. "I've seen it all now."

"A bit of help would be good." Hana sulked, swinging from the flannelette material.

"You look like a cow being airlifted out of a ditch," Nev laughed, the mirth disappearing from his face at the expression of rage on Hana's.

Logan separated her from the frayed edges of her nightie and waited while she tucked the remaining strands into her pants. "What the hell are you doing here?" he hissed at her. "This is no place for you, wahine."

"Don't be such a sexist!" she snapped. "If you'd tell me more about what's happening, I wouldn't have to sneak."

Logan fisted his hand in her hair and pulled her face into his chest. "You're doing my head in, wahine." She heard the laughter in his voice.

"What's going on?" she replied, ignoring his rebuke. "Why are we here?"

"Caleb called me." Logan's eyes narrowed. "Reckons he's in trouble and needs help. Asked me to meet him here."

"He can't have; he doesn't own a phone."

Logan raised a dark eyebrow. "Well, he does now."

"We're early. I'll get under the ute," Nev said and Hana pulled a face of disgust.

"What? Why?"

"Because he told my bro' to come alone," he replied as though he thought her stupid. "But I'm here if there's trouble."

"What about me?" She fluttered her lashes at her husband. "I'm not going under the car with him."

Logan grimaced. "I don't think they'll see you as a threat."

"They? I thought you said just Caleb."

"It won't be just Caleb, babe. There's more to this than you realise."

Hana pushed but Logan batted off her questions with one word answers which told her little. They waited for half an hour and the evening chilled into the minus figures, making Hana's teeth chatter in her mouth. Logan leaned back against the tail gate of the ute and sighed, the abandoned water tower looming ahead of him like an albatross. He settled his backside on the bumper and reached into his tight trouser pocket for chewing gum, feeling it soft and warm in his fingers. "Damn!"

Hana wrinkled her nose. "I hate that."

He nodded and shot her a smile which curved his lips into a slight arc, enough to send her scuttling to his side. "I thought I'd done with all this," he mused, his eyes narrowing to crinkle the scar beneath his right eye. "I'm too old, babe. I don't have the same desire to fight." Logan slipped an arm around her shoulder and gratitude filled her soul.

She nodded. "I know, Logan. But this is different; it's protecting what's ours. Phoenix and Macky; they're defenseless. And we did let Caleb become part of our family. I don't see that we have a choice."

Logan folded his arms and twisted his face into a frown. "No more strays, Hana. I can't do this again. I won't."

"Okay," she promised, surprised to discover she meant it.

Two battered vehicles pulled into the car park and halted opposite the ute. The headlights remained on, blinding the couple as figures slid from the passenger doors and formed a solid wall in front of them. "Nice to finally meet you, Logan Du Rose!" The male voice invoked a strong sense of déjà vu in Hana and she cocked her head to see past the light, failing as her eyes watered in protest. The owner of the voice moved before one of the headlights, remaining as a silhouette. "What? You have nothing to say to me?" The figure stepped forward, features discernible against the blackness.

Logan felt turned to stone next to Hana, every muscle ready to defend them both against attack. Her heart ached for the damage it might do to his vulnerable body and she balled her fists, ready to protect him with her own pathetic means. "Turn the lights off and we can talk like grown-ups." His tone sounded lazy as though the situation was common-place and normal. He lowered his head to stare at his cowboy boots but Hana saw his eyes raking the opposition for weakness from beneath long, dark eyelashes. "Get back in the ute," he hissed and she moved backwards enough to detach from him and then froze in position.

The car lights dimmed to only side lights, casting a yellow pall across the area. Hana counted eight bodies including the drivers of both cars. Thick set men, they looked ready for action. The sound of crutches scraping on the rough surface of the car park floor caught her attention and she spotted Caleb to the rear. A strong hand gripped him by the scruff of the neck and he hung there, limp and defeated. Eight and a half men.

One man stepped forward; dirty blonde hair and olive skin giving him bad-boy good looks. Hana gasped at the carbon copy of Robert Dressler standing between her and Caleb and Logan shot her a concerned glance. "I know you!" she spat, courage bridling in her chest. "You tried to steal my handbag!"

The man nodded, his smile cruel. "Full marks, miss. I used to see you all the time at that fancy school my ma put me in." He waved an arm behind him and another male stepped forward. "Remember my little bro'?"

Hana's lips parted at the sight of Flick's sons. Each possessed the same wary look he once displayed before kindness and safety mellowed him into someone affable and sweet. Hana's fists balled at her sides and rage blossomed, sending warning flares into her brain. "You made my life a living hell!" She took a step forward, dodging Logan's outstretched arm. "Your father would be so ashamed of you; he wanted you to be different, to take the better path. Look at you! You kidnap your own brother and call us up threatening to hurt him if we don't give you what you want. It's sick! You're sick!"

Logan let out a heavy sigh and relaxed against the bumper of the ute. Hana felt his irritation emanating towards her in waves but couldn't stop. She knew he'd given up the moment his legs crossed at the ankles and he let his weight rest against the car; readying himself for the ensuing floor show.

Flick's eldest son ground his teeth and glared at Hana. "You don't know my dad."

"Yeah, I do!" she snapped back. "He's our friend. He saved my life the day my son was born; he stopped a maniac shooting my baby in the head and put himself on the line. Bobby's a good man." She flapped her hand to encompass the gang of burly males, curling her lip back in disgust. "He'd look at you all pumped up with your fist-happy-mates and think you were pathetic. You've kidnapped your own half-brother over a dustbin bag full of shonky weed grown by a stupid old man with arthritis."

"Give us the dope and take the kid." Metal clanged to the ground as they shoved Caleb forward and he staggered, losing one crutch and balancing on the other with a complete lack of coordination.

"There is no dope." Logan stood, towering over the assembled crowd as his voice cut through Hana's anger. He sounded bored. "I already told the rest of your toxic little gang. A few wilting stems got collected onto the rubbish truck by accident; you're welcome to trawl the dump for it. You're getting nothing from me; keep the kid, he's your blood, not mine."

"Logan!" Hana looked shocked and he warned her with his eyes. She searched for Caleb in the darkness and saw his eyes glinting in the moonlight. He didn't look scared but his plight appealed to her rescuer mentality. "We're gonna have to fight our way out," she hissed to Logan and heard him suppress a snort.

"On your own, kid," he said and gave her a wink, his facial muscles fighting to suppress the amusement.

"I know you've got the drugs," Flick's son persisted. "Caleb here said he brought them to your place and you took them. You said they were crap just to get rid of Asher."

"That's right. You've still got the dope." Caleb pointed at Logan and Hana intercepted his gaze, her eyes narrowed. His betrayal stung.

"He knows we don't have it," she protested. "He lost it; it's nowhere in the house." She lifted her hand and pointed her index finger in Caleb's direction. "Now, he's on his own. I'm done."

"That's my girl." Logan smiled at her. He put his palms together in a loud clap and then made an action as though wiping them clean. "We're done here, guys. Don't call me again."

"But we know you've got more than that to trade with. We want cash and you've got lots of it." The surrounding males jeered in agreement and slapped Flick's son on the back. "Caleb said you're loaded. Millionaire or something."

Logan peered through the darkness at Caleb's ashen face. "Come near my home or family again kid and I'll hurt you worse than you could ever imagine."

Hana heard the scraping of shoes on grit as Nev crawled out from beneath the vehicle. He slipped into the passenger seat and Logan held the rear door open for her. "Would you like a proper seat or are you happier clinging onto the tailgate?" A smirk lit his eyes and Hana glared at him. She opened her mouth with a rebuke on her tongue and caught sight of a flash of metal in her peripheral vision.

"Logan!" she screamed and he turned, pushing his elbow through the youngest Dressler boy's nose. The crow bar clanged to the floor and the young man followed it face first. When his brother started to run forward, Nev emerged from the passenger door and leapt over the bonnet.

"Come on then!" he shouted, teeth gritted as he took a fighting stance. The man slowed to a hesitant walk and then backed off, beckoning to his brother. Hana's heart pounded with the adrenaline release as Flick's boy clambered upright, his hand held under his nose. He staggered back towards his assembled mates, none of whom attempted to help him.

"Any more?" Logan asked, opening his arms and cocking his head.

"Na, bro'," someone answered. "We heard about you, dude. We're good."

"Let's make sure it stays that way then!" Logan snapped. Bending, he retrieved the crow bar and hurled it towards them, smiling in satisfaction at the sound of metal scarring metal as it dented the first vehicle's paintwork. He jerked his head towards Nev and waited until he and Hana closed their doors against the dark car park and shadowy danger. Then he made a rude gesture and climbed into the ute, gunning the engine and sending a spray of grit flying up behind them.

Hana breathed out through pursed lips and swallowed the sense of regret at seeing Caleb in all his treacherous glory. She remained silent even after they entered the school site and watched the automatic gates clang shut behind them. Creeping indoors she went upstairs to bed without speaking to anyone, seeing Logan and Nev laughing about Flick's boys through the slats of the bannister rails.

"You're an idiot, Hana Du Rose," she breathed to herself in the darkness as she undressed and exchanged her torn nightdress for a pair of pyjamas.

53

An Ill-advised Alliance

Hana sat on the porch steps and listened to her son pad around behind her on his hands and knees. Short breaths panted from his lips as he exerted himself, crawling away from her and then back again. He crept behind her, his breathing giving him away as he tapped her back with his forehead. She turned with her eyes wide and her hands raised, shouting, "Boo!" even though he couldn't hear. He jerked backwards at her face expression and a delightful belly laugh erupted from his slender body, his lips dribbling saliva and his eyes squeezed tight shut. Hana tickled him and then turned her back, waiting until he crawled away and sat on his puffy nappy. She faced him again, making the movement sudden and he jumped and squealed, the laugh rocking his whole body until the hiccoughs began. Hana turned away and heard him set off towards her again, stifling her giggles until he got close. She waited, but he didn't touch her and she swivelled around in alarm.

Lincoln Haines stood on the front door mat, clutching her son in a grip which displayed his lack of experience with babies.

Mac didn't appreciate being held at arm's length and appealed to Hana with his eyes and a series of pitiful wails. She stood and moved towards the towering male, seeing only the need to retrieve her baby. "Give him to me!" Her green eyes wide and wild with desperation, they flicked to Mac and then back to Lincoln. "You hurt him and I'll kill you!"

"I'm not gonna hurt him!" Lincoln looked horrified, his face paling to a sickly white. "What do you think I am?"

"You tell me." Hana edged closer. "You walk into my home, watch me being attacked and then use that fact to threaten me. Now you're holding my baby, who clearly isn't enjoying the experience." She gritted her teeth and held her arms out, watching as Mac pitched forward in an attempt to meet her embrace. "Give him to me right now. If you hurt him, it will be the last thing you do." Lincoln drew his arms closer to his body but Mac still dangled in mid-air, his agitation growing. "I mean it." Hana cast around for a ready weapon and saw an abandoned tree support lying inside the balustrade. She reached down and seized the stake, eyeing the spiked edge where it was meant to be hammered into the ground. "Say goodbye to your nuts!" she snapped and Lincoln took a step back against the front door.

"Don't be stupid, woman! You'll hurt the kid."

"I'll take the risk." Hana stepped towards him, jousting the hefty stake at groin level. Better an injured baby who fell on a springy deck than never seeing him again.

"I'll drop him!" Lincoln gasped as the spike touched the front of his jeans along his zipper. "Don't be an idiot!"

"Don't you threaten me!" Hana raged. "You make me sick. He can't hear you; he doesn't understand what's happening, you dumb cowboy! He's deaf!" She swallowed at hearing the words spoken aloud and saw the confusion on Lincoln's face. She pressed the stake harder into his groin, hoping she caught Mac if he dropped him and Lincoln saw the determination in her face.

"Okay, okay, I'm sorry. Take the kid." He held the squirming baby out to Hana and she clasped him to her, the embrace too hard for the child's liking. The stake dropped to the ground and Lincoln kicked it away. "Geez, you're a psychopath!" he exclaimed, inspecting the dirty mark on the front of his jeans.

Hana snorted. "Says you! Blackmailer, adulterer, murderer, general asshole! Do you want me to go on?"

Lincoln swallowed and held his arms outstretched, palms facing Hana. "I wanna call a truce. I need to talk to you."

"Whatever!" Hana snapped. "Get out of my way and off this property before my husband gets here." She eyed the livid bruise encircling Lincoln's right eye and smiled in satisfaction. "I see he already taught you a lesson the other night. He'd love the opportunity to finish it."

"Don't call Logan!" Lincoln shook his head. "I never expected you to tell him. I trusted you."

"Trusted me!" Hana raged. "Trusted me to do what you wanted under threat? Grow up, man. Nothing is more important than my marriage and children so think again, loser."

Lincoln stepped away from the front door mat and Hana felt relief thudding through her chest. She made a dash towards it but didn't get the heavy door closed before Lincoln pushed his cowboy boot into the gap and shoved his way through. "You're gonna listen to me!" he huffed, "You have to." He slid on the inside doormat and cannoned into the staircase, groaning in pain as his shoulder took the force. Holding his hands up in supplication, his body language showed defeat. "I get it, Hana; I get it. Just give me a chance to talk to you, please?"

"Why should I?" Hana demanded. "You men think because you're bigger than me that you can be overbearing, threatening and make me run on fear." She shifted Mac to her other hip and started in surprise as he used his little hand to make the sign for hungry. "Hungry?" Hana asked, pride blossoming in her chest. She positioned her empty right hand as though holding a cup and moved it from her throat to her sternum. "You hungry?"

Mac grumbled and repeated the action, his hand movements jerky and inaccurate. Everything in Hana softened at his efforts to communicate with her and nothing else mattered in that moment. Ignoring Lincoln as he hovered near the bottom of the stairs, Hana turned her attention to her son and walked towards the kitchen, rewarding his attempt to communicate by letting him choose a biscuit from the tin in the pantry. His tiny fingers flickered over the assortment of wonderful biscuits and his green eyes narrowed in concentration. He frowned at Hana before drawing out a chocolate digestive and poking his tongue over the treat.

"You've made me want one now." Hana took one and popped it into her mouth in three bites, abandoning the tin on the counter. "Let's get you in your chair and I'll grab some warm milk." Her voice sounded muffled as she spat biscuit and she winced at her bad manners. Hana made her right hand into a fist by squeezing the fingers closed and then opening them like she milked a cow. "Milk?" she asked and Mac wiggled his legs and dropped his head forward and back. "Gorgeous boy." Hana pressed her lips to the side of his soft face and he grinned at her through chocolate coated lips.

"Don't suppose I could have something to eat?" Lincoln slipped into the room and Hana cringed. "Logan turfed me out so everything I own is in my car."

"Do you expect me to feel sorry for you?" Hana poured formula powder into a feeder cup and added hot water from the kettle. She topped it off with sterile water from the fridge to cool the temperature. "Here you go, baby. Milk." She made the motion with her fingers again and he licked the biscuit and a coy expression settled over his features. "Yeah, you know more than you make out, little man. You're like your father."

Lincoln edged towards the counter and selected a plain biscuit. Hana heard his stomach growl from across the room. She raised an eyebrow. "So, you couldn't stop at a burger place? Logan took your wallet too, did he?"

"Na." Lincoln hung his head. "I wasn't hungry until just then. Lost my appetite."

"You only have yourself to blame." Hana clapped as Mac lifted the beaker two handed and supped the warm milk. He beamed in response. "I might have helped you if you'd asked me." She raised an eyebrow at Lincoln. "But I'm tired of being bullied by men. It's not happening anymore."

Lincoln nibbled the biscuit and watched her from under his lashes. "I heard you were a maverick; you did what you wanted even if it went against your hoa tāne's wishes."

Hana shrugged. "I used to, but it was foolish. Logan told me to leave situations alone and he was always right. I've learned the hard way." She sighed and watched her son munch on his treat. "I wish my life was as simple as choosing a biscuit."

"Mine too." Lincoln pushed the last mouthful between his lips. "Please can we start again? I'd love for you to help me find the fifth man and discover who killed Pania."

"What will you do if you find the answer though, Lincoln? Will you show the cops your evidence and let them put that person in prison? What then?"

"I don't know." Lincoln raised his hands and let them fall to his sides with a slap. "I haven't thought that far ahead."

Hana pulled up a chair so she could sit opposite Mac and pursed her lips. "I don't know how to help you, Lincoln. I already asked Logan and Leslie what they remembered and came up with nothing. For what it's worth, Logan still believes you're innocent."

"That will make me feel a heap better when I'm bedding down in a homeless shelter tonight."

Hana shrugged. "Feel free to take a few extra biscuits."

Lincoln sat at the table and watched her play with her baby son. "I wanted children," he said and his voice lowered almost to a whisper. Hana turned to meet his gaze and compassion filled her eyes until they shone a soft green.

"I'm sorry," she replied. "Some women need to feel ready; it's a huge commitment."

"It's not an excuse, but it's the reason I started sleeping with Pania. Fiona and I couldn't communicate. We didn't want the same things and I should've left then, but I loved her. I've thought about it heaps since and realised maybe I wanted her to find out." He gave a low, sardonic laugh. "Just not like that."

Hana nodded in understanding but kept her mouth shut, unable to share his pain. Lincoln ran a hand through his hair and left it sticking up on end. "Do you hate me?" he asked, biting his lower lip as though making it bleed might drain away some of the misery. "I know you hate cheats."

"I don't have the energy to hate you," Hana sighed. "Nothing excuses adultery. You could've left and found someone who wanted your children. Destroying your wife achieved nothing."

Lincoln nodded. "You're right. Fiona wrote me off when she found out I'd cheated. She sent the divorce papers while I was on remand. I signed them the day they found me guilty. She deserved better."

"People in the town think you gave up." Hana smiled at her son and watched him prod crumbs around his tray.

"I did." Lincoln sighed. "But not because I wanted to. He visited me in prison, a man I'd spent my whole life being a friend to and told me to plead guilty."

"Who did?" Despite herself, curiosity budded in Hana's breast. "Who visited you? What did they say?"

Lincoln looked exhausted as he faced her across the table and he ignored her probing. "Am I wasting my time, Hana? Should I just get on with my life? I could go somewhere new and start again." He rubbed his eyes with the backs of his fists. "Only I can't, can I? Nobody wants a convicted murderer on the payroll. Logan was my last hope." He looked at Hana with raw expectation in his face.

"No," she replied. "I won't undermine Logan's authority. I've learned my lesson."

Lincoln nodded. "Then I have no choice but to prove my innocence by finding the real killer." He stood and pushed the chair under the table and stopped at the kitchen door to give Hana a tired smile. "Thanks for your time."

"Hey," Hana rose and turned her body to face him. "You didn't say who came to see you or what they said."

Lincoln shrugged. "Kane Du Rose paid me a visit. He brought divorce papers from Fiona and the guards let me have them after he left. He said everyone knew I did it and those who donated to my defense fund were stopping. My wife didn't want me and the town didn't either. He said they'd hurt the ones I loved and less than twenty-four hours later, my mother died."

"An overdose of antidepressants? I heard. It doesn't mean Kane killed her; it might've been an unfortunate accident."

"But I'll never know, will I? After Liza told me, I refused to take the stand and defend myself. The judge directed the jury to find me guilty of manslaughter and I accepted my punishment. I still loved Fiona; why put her at risk too?"

"But you were friends with Kane. Why use him as the messenger?"

Lincoln shrugged. "The fifth man in the group sent him with a warning; inside or outside the prison, I was a dead man."

Hana shook her head. "Logan wasn't the fifth man, Linc. You're grasping at straws. If Kane delivered the message, then you already knew that. He wouldn't do jack for my husband, let alone be his messenger. You need to look elsewhere and I can't help you."

54

Confessions of Guilt

Hana opened the door with a slice of toast in her hand, Mac clinging around her neck and making fumbled grabs at the buttery bread. Sleeping late after a disturbed night, she'd awoken to find the older children and Leslie gone again. Another day of pondering Lincoln's dilemma left her no nearer to solving the mystery. The others ate dinner and then went to get Macdonald's sundaes as a treat for pudding and Hana stayed home, force feeding herself toast. She gaped at the sight of the visitor. "Hi. Come in." She stepped back and reached to close the front door, relinquishing the toast to her grasping son's tiny fingers. Mac gave a grunt of satisfaction and pushed a corner into his mouth, sprinkling Hana's shoulder with crumbs.

"Are you hungry?" she asked her guest, waiting while the woman glanced around the hallway. Hana indicated the open kitchen door with her hand and nodded encouragement. "The kitchen's through there. Go ahead and I'll make us a drink."

Anahera Du Rose set off in front of her, steps tentative and lacking confidence. Shaking fingers pushed the door open and she pressed through, standing in the centre of the room as though lost. Her clothes looked at least three sizes too big for her and the trainers on her feet flopped without laces to tighten them. Her vacant expression sent waves of panic through Hana's chest.

Putting Mac in the high chair to eat his spoils, she set the kettle to boil and eyed her sister-in-law through lowered lashes. "What brings you here, Anahera?" She kept her voice light and reached behind her for her phone, sending Logan a quick message. *'Anahera's here!'*

"Tea or coffee?" Hana asked the question and Anahera jumped, not seeming to know the answer.

"Wine." She gave a small, tight-lipped reply and Hana swallowed.

"I have none, love. How about some tea?"

Anahera nodded without caring. "Tea."

Hana pushed tea bags into a teapot with a chip in the spout and waited for the kettle to boil. Mac coughed on a toast crumb and she patted him on the back. He turned to her with a grin of victory and waved the soggy bread at her. "Clever boy," she cooed.

Anahera slumped into a kitchen chair and the wooden legs scraped against the floor, jerking Hana back to her present dilemma. "Everyone's been looking for you, sweetheart. Where did you go?"

"Go?" Anahera's brown eyes filled with tears and she nodded. "Yes, I need to go." She stood. "Can we go now?"

"Go where?" Hana put her body between Anahera and Mac. The unhinged look in the other woman's eyes made her want to snatch up the baby and run.

"Away from him." Anahera shook her head. "I can't pretend anymore. It's too hard; I can't do this."

"Away from who?" Hana's voice sounded hoarse and she wished for her husband's reassuring presence, willing him to burst through the house like a human tornado and scoop her up. "Who do you need to get away from?"

"Him!" Anahera's eyes looked wild and she cast around her, the too-big shirt flapping around her thighs. "Help me?" She hugged herself, her frail body shivering in paroxysms of some emotion hidden from view. Assuming it was fear, Hana stepped across the distance and wrapped her arms around Anahera, feeling something akin to volts of electricity course through her.

"You know I'll help you if I can," Hana breathed into her hair. "Wiri's desperate to see you."

Anahera sank forwards with her hands covering her face. "My son, my son." She rocked herself to and fro, lank hair touching the surface of the table. "I miss him. I miss him so much."

"He'll be here any minute. They nipped to the Macdonald's drive through to get ice creams; they won't be long." Hana knelt in front of her, peering up into the gaunt face and eyes filled with disturbance. "What can I do for you, Anahera?"

"Keep my son safe." Sanity tracked back into the dilated pupils and urgency replaced madness. "Look after Wiremu; whatever happens, don't let his father take him. Promise me?" Anahera fixed her fingers on Hana's shoulders, pressing through her sweatshirt and digging into flesh. Hana winced and nodded.

"I promise, Anahera. I promise."

Satisfied, Anahera let go and her gaze followed Macky's frantic movements in the high chair. He sat the floppy slice of toast on his head and then set about searching for it, his arms not quite long enough to reach his crown. Confused, he looked across at Hana and catching her attention, lifted his tiny hands up with the palms facing the ceiling in a sign of, *'Don't know where it went.'* Returning Hana's smile he reached for a stray crumb on the tray of his high chair and the action sent the toast plopping in front of him. He jumped in fear and his face crumpled, morphing into a happy grin as he recognised the object.

"He's funny," Anahera breathed, releasing a lungful of tragedy which enabled her haunted expression to fade. "He looks like you."

"Thanks. I'll get you a cup of tea?" Hana stood and walked towards the counter, tapping her fingers on Macky's tray as she went past. His gaze followed her fingers up her wrist to her arm and then her eyes and he squeezed his lashes together and beamed. Hana dipped her face, kissing the bridge of his nose and smiling at the muffled 'pah, pah' sounds he made.

Anahera seemed to settle, accepting the mug of tea and sipping it with her brow creased.

"How did you find us?" Hana asked, leaning against the counter and stroking Mac's red fringe back from his forehead. "You didn't go all the way to the hotel, did you?"

Anahera shook her head. "No. Linc visited. He said you'd come back to Hamilton and brought Wiri." She shuddered and her gaze strayed to Hana. "Keep him for me? Please? I know it's a lot to ask but keep him for me?"

Hana nodded and looked for conversation, finding nothing in the ensuing silence broken only by the sound of Anahera's exaggerated breathing. Curiosity drove her to ask a question which as she heard it emerge from her lips, knew she shouldn't have. "I noticed Wiri has Lincoln as his middle name. Is that after Lincoln Haines?"

Anahera's eyes shuttered and she choked on her mouthful of tea. Hana fought the urge to bang her on the back but guilt blossomed in her chest. "You don't have to answer that. It's none of my business."

"He's not Linc's son." Tears filled the chocolate brown eyes and Anahera stood.

"I know!" Hana raised her hands, mortified at the veiled accusation her words contained. "I know. He can't be; it's not possible. Wiri's six and Lincoln's been in prison for the last five years and on remand for two years before that. I didn't mean to suggest something improper, Anahera. It was just a question."

"I had to." Anahera's fingers writhed beneath the long cuffs of the shirt. "He's my friend. We grew up together and he's been kind to me." Her fingers went to her mouth and she floundered.

"I can't do this; I can't live with this anymore. I need to tell them. I need to tell the counsellors. They say I can't get better until I tell them." She put her hands up either side of her ears and closed her eyes. "It's there all the time; it won't go away."

Mac's face crumpled as he abandoned his toast and picked up the tangible waves of distress in the room. It fed on the two women like hungry calves at the teat, robbing the air of oxygen and forcing the molecules to spark like static electricity. Mac's whines of sadness cut through the atmosphere and Hana reached for him, hoisting him out of the chair and offering comfort even as he spread butter over her shoulder. His fingers sought her lips, looking for speech vibrations and answers to the peculiar change in his happy home. "Tell them, then." Hana's anxious face searched Anahera's as the poor woman fought internal agonies below the surface. "If they think it'll help then do what they say."

"I can't!" Anahera's scream echoed around the kitchen, her eyes wide with horror. "He won't let me!" She opened her mouth to speak again but the door behind her burst open and Wiri hurtled through, wrapping his arms around his mother's thighs in a bear hug.

"Ma!" he cried, ice cream sundae and chocolate wiping off his lips and onto her shirt. "Ma! Is you stayin' wiv us? I started a new school. I got pictures to show you." His eyes sparkled with excitement and fear that she might deny him. As she squatted in front of him, Hana saw the glistening of tears in the brown eyes and sensed she would break the child's heart again.

"Anahera," Hana said, her tone already begging. "Spend time with him. Let him show you his drawings. He's desperate to see you."

Logan entered the room with a tired Phoenix over his shoulder. Anahera's eyes widened in horror and Logan gave a polite nod in her direction. "Hey," he said and smiled. She stared at him with something akin to fear before her body relaxed with belated recognition. His glance at Hana told her he'd alerted the crash team from mental health services and her heart sank. She hoped they left it long enough for Wiri to enjoy a few stolen moments with his mother.

"I might put our two into bed." Hana jiggled Mac on her hip and he rubbed his buttery nose on her shirt.

"No! Don't leave me." Fear bubbled out through Anahera's lips and she took nervous side glances at Logan. His lips parted in hurt surprise and he took enough strides to put a good distance between them.

Wiri squeezed Anahera's leg and kissed the front of her jeans, his rosebud lips puckered in pleasure. "Don't be scared, Ma," he whispered. "This is lovely; we're all together again." His eyes crinkled at the edges and he stepped back, pulling open the kitchen door. Putting his face through the gap he hollered, "Papa! Ma's here. Come and see."

Something in Anahera's eyes snapped and insanity flooded back over the brown irises, darkening them with the strokes of an unseen brush which coloured them black and fathomless. "No!" she hissed, shooting a look at Logan and then the door. She launched at Hana with such suddenness, the other woman almost dropped the baby in surprise, clutching him one handed at the last minute. The slap left her head spinning and Anahera dragged her forward with gargantuan might, using a handful of Hana's auburn locks as a rope. Hana felt the follicles give way above her ear and cried out, her lower back hitting the counter as she pinged upright before being yanked downwards again. Anahera's insane screams filled the kitchen as Logan deposited his daughter on the floor and dragged the flailing arms behind his sister-in-law's back, pinning her against his chest while she thrashed and bucked. Twice she kicked backwards into his shins and he swore and held her still.

Wiri ran in terror, cannoning into Neville's legs as he entered the room. The child bounced off like a rubber ball and tried to escape again, finding himself battling the fabric of Leslie's copious skirt as she followed Nev into the kitchen. Wiri kicked against her as she hoisted him skywards, abandoning his bid for freedom as Leslie buried him in her breasts. Mac wailed in misery at the attack on his mother, his cries insatiable as strands of auburn hair floated from Anahera's struggling fingers down to the floor.

"Are you okay, Hana?" Logan held the struggling woman away from his body, avoiding Anahera's kicking feet and writhing arms. "Hana!" He snapped at her as short breaths locked up her lungs and sent scant oxygen coasting up to her brain. Logan's eyes darted to a stunned Nev as he lurked in the doorway, his face pale and his grey eyes translucent. "Nev! Take her." Turning Anahera towards her husband, Logan let go and gave her a hefty push. The final scream died in Anahera's throat as she plummeted into Nev's chest and slid down his legs to the floor.

"Sorry!" she wailed, kneeling in front of him with her hands pressed to her face. Chunks of Hana's long hair trailed from her fingers. "Sorry! I'm sorry!"

Hana watched the scene as though through another's eyes, her breath coming in heaves as her lungs struggled and shock fed its chemicals through her system. Mac screamed in her left ear and clung around her neck in terror, unable to hear or understand the awful scenario playing out before his eyes. Hana's right cheek stung as if the flesh hung loose and her scalp buzzed with the effect of the traumatic hair loss.

"Breathe, Hana, breathe." Logan's cheek against her forehead and his soothing arm around her shoulders gave her enough protection to relax. She heard Anahera begging for forgiveness from her husband and Wiri's tortured sobs, but closed her eyes against the child's compounded misery. She put her right hand up to her head and Logan pulled it away. His strong arms encircled her and the hysterical baby and Mac pressed his face into the broad chest and hiccoughed with distress.

"Phoenix." Hana spotted her daughter's blue shoes from underneath Logan's arm and gave his bicep a shove, not wanting a circle of love which didn't include Phoe. Her lungs stopped fighting her and took in oxygen, helping her mind to clear. Her daughter's gaze fixed on something behind Logan, her face set in a mask of disgust. Grey eyes flashed the colour of pebbles as Phoenix set off marching towards the ruckus, skirting the dining table and scattered chairs. Logan let go of Hana and turned, watching as the tiny girl stood in front of Anahera, unmoved by the tears and snot decorating the woman's face. A slender arm raised and an index finger pointed to the open kitchen door.

"Stop. It. Go. Away!" The child formed each of the words, giving them independent weight and momentum. Her slender body tipped forward and a plastic toy from a Happy Meal peered out from beneath her fingers, its childishness incongruent with the adult way Phoenix regarded her aunt. Anahera lifted her face to look at the child, appearing stunned at what she saw there. She shrank back, pulling her body into a tight ball, her eyes never leaving Phoenix's face.

"I'm sorry," she muttered again. "Help me kuia, help me."

Phoenix wagged her finger in Anahera's face. "You don't hit my ma!" she said with authority.

"Phoe." Logan's use of her name reigned her in and she pursed her lips and marched back towards her parents, righteous indignation in her grey eyes and the little blue shoes slapping against the kitchen floor. Hana gave herself a shake, cuddling her son and giving Phoenix a watery smile.

The sound of hammering on the front door sent Leslie scuttling from the room, cradling a distraught Wiri like a baby.

"I'm okay, Phoe," Hana told her, hearing the wobble in her voice. "Accident."

"Not. Accident." Phoenix ground her teeth and her dark eyes flashed like coals, her father's inherited temper near the surface. She felt rigid next to Hana, placing herself on voluntary sentry duty, her eyes straying to Logan's face for guidance and back again. As she wiped a tiny fist across her mouth, Hana glimpsed the small girl's namesake in the determined stance; Kuia Phoenix Du Rose lived on and would one day become a force to be reckoned with.

The crash team weren't what Hana expected. They didn't wear white coats and wrap Anahera into a strait jacket. A male and three female nurses turned up in an unmarked ambulance and collected the stricken woman from the kitchen floor without fanfare. Nev seemed paralysed by the whole event and hung on the fringes of the small group, his complexion white and sick. He made no attempt to comfort his small son and eyed his long time wife as one might a rabid dog.

"Did she have any medication on her?" the male nurse asked and Hana shook her head.

"I don't know, sorry. She wasn't here for long." She paused, listening to the hitching of Wiri's breaths as Leslie tried to comfort him in the lounge next door. Her voice murmured low endearments and his replies sounded hysterical. "Her son's desperate to see her but when he ran in, she freaked out."

The man nodded, his brown eyes soft and kind. He pointed towards Hana's right cheek. "Did she attack you, miss? I can make a report."

Hana shook her head and switched Mac to the other side to distract the man from his intense focus on the red mark blossoming from temple to jaw. "She didn't mean it. Anahera begged me to help her and I promised I would. I thought she meant me to keep Wiri for her but when he came home, she went crazy. It's my fault; I've misunderstood the kind of help she wanted from me." Hana's eyes roved to the open door and the sounds of a van door closing. "Will she be okay?"

The male nurse took a step towards Hana with his hands raised and Logan's face clouded as he body blocked him. "I want to look at her eye." The man sounded surprised as Hana's family closed ranks around her.

"Fine." Logan hefted Mac onto his hip and made room, taking Phoenix by the hand to pull her away.

Tilting Hana's head to one side and peering into her right eye, the nurse tutted. "The eyeball is scratched, possibly from her fingernail." He shook his head. "Bathe it every couple of hours with salt water. Use cooled boiled water from the jug, not the tap." He let go of Hana's chin and released a heavy breath. "Get some ice on that eye and do the same for the scratches on your face. If anything starts to blow up over the next few days get medical assistance. Okay?" He raised his dark eyebrows and Hana nodded, not quite comprehending what he meant by her eye blowing up. Her fingers strayed to the side of her face and the agony of burning in her hair. The skin felt wet and came away coated with clear, sticky liquid tinged with blood. "It's gonna hurt like a bitch," he commented and turned to leave. "Are either of you two gentlemen Anahera's husband?" He spun on the spot, taking in Logan and Neville. Logan's protective stance invoked instant dismissal and he turned his attention to Nev. "Can we have a word outside please, sir?"

Nev galvanised himself and let go of the counter he clung to like a drowning man. He followed the nurse into the hall without words. As the kitchen emptied, Hana felt a wave of sickness and blew out a slow breath. "Why me?" she hissed at Logan. "Why is it always me?"

"Shh," he soothed, kissing the good side of her face and crushing Mac between them. He held Phoenix's little hand and it prevented him wrapping his arms around her. "What the hell was that about?"

Hana shook her head and her heart quailed. "I think Nev killed Anahera's sister."

55

Twists and turns

"That can't be right." Logan's eyes narrowed and confusion crossed his handsome features. "Why would Nev kill his sister-in-law? It makes no sense."

Hana shrugged. "Logan, didn't you see her face when you walked in? For a second she thought you were Nev and when he appeared, she really flipped out. Before you got here, she said the counsellors wanted her to talk about something that bothered her. She said she couldn't get better until she told them. When I suggested she do it, she shouted at me that someone wouldn't let her."

"What did she say exactly?" Logan rocked his son and bent down to scoop Phoenix into his embrace. The little girl looked lost and Hana held her arms out to her, gratified when the child pitched forward into them.

"I love you, baby," Hana whispered in her ear and arms like spindles wound around her neck and coiled the hair at her nape in busy fingers. Hana fought for concentration as the sound of the front door closing echoed around the hallway. "She said, 'He won't let me.' Yeah, that's what she said." Hana sighed and kissed the side of Phoenix's downy head. She lowered her voice and mouthed the sentence to Logan, not wanting her daughter disturbed more than she must already be. "I bet she gave him an alibi for the night her sister got you-know-what and that's why she's in agony. That's why Linc went to see her; he suspected she lied for someone. I wonder if it's at the root of her depression; guilt."

Logan shook his head. "This isn't lining up, Hana. Nev wouldn't let Linc spend ten years in prison for something he did; it's not who he is."

"We don't know who he is though, do we?" Hana pouted and narrowed her eyes. "I thought he was a decent man, not someone who showed no affection for his little boy and stood by with indifference while another family raised him. What's that about?" She cocked her head. "And that's another thing; I asked why Wiri's middle name was the same as Lincoln's and Anahera got defensive like I'd accused her of fathering another man's child. When I clarified what I meant, she gave the impression she didn't have a choice." As Logan raised an eyebrow, Hana searched her memory for Anahera's exact words. "She said, 'I had to.' Those were her words." Hana listened for sounds from next door and hearing nothing, patted Phoenix on the back. "Do you think Nev went with them?"

"I dunno." Logan rolled his eyes. "Let's attempt to put these kids to bed, not that I think they'll stay there after tonight. I need a chance to think."

"You also need to talk to your brother." Hana watched as Mac's head lolled against Logan's shoulder before he jumped awake and gave a strangled cry. She gave Logan a wilted smile. "I bet there's five of us in our bed tonight."

Logan quirked his lips up on one side, revealing a hidden dimple beneath the stubble. "Yeah, well it'll stay at five too. If Leslie crawls in, I'll get out." He set off towards the kitchen door and Hana let out a shaky sigh. Something told her she wouldn't do much sleeping either.

56

A Big Mess

"That's a big mess." Leslie watched over Logan's shoulder as he squatted in front of Hana and daubed her eye with cotton wool soaked in saline. He glared up at her.

"Thanks for that. Really helpful."

"Well, it is. Big, big mess." Leslie shook her head and continued to crowd Logan until he snapped at her.

"Why are you here?" he demanded. "Why are you living in my house, eating my food and sticking your nose into my business?"

"I help Hana." Leslie looked scandalised. "And I left your father. He's a big pig." She tapped Logan on the top of his head. "I take my mokopuna to school and pick them up. I'm doing helping."

"Doing helping? That's not even English." Logan shook his head and Hana watched the patience drain from his eyes. She tensed, waiting for the inevitable fight to begin. Her gaze drifted across Leslie's face until she registered the peculiar lumps dotted along her forehead and the side of her face.

"Are you having an allergic reaction to something?" Hana squinted through her good eye as Logan sealed an ice pack over the painful right one. "You've got strange lumps sticking out of your face."

Logan stood and looked down on his step-mother, trying to peer at her olive complexion. "Yeah, come to think of it you look different. What's going on?"

Leslie jutted out her chin and set her jaw in a determined line. "I don't like to be old and wrinkled." She glared at Logan in challenge.

"It's a bit bloody late to turn that ship around," he snorted. "It sailed years ago."

"Shut up, nasty boy!" She slapped his chest and touched a lump with tentative fingers. "I got buttocks in my face."

"Ha!" Logan spat in victory. "I could've told you that. Face like a cow's ass."

"Logan, stop it." Hana stood, keeping the ice pack over her eye and squinting at Leslie. "Do you mean Botox?"

Leslie waved her hands and took another swipe at Logan. "That's what I said. Buttocks."

"Is that where you keep disappearing to with our ute?" Hana let her fingers drift up to the sore patch near her right ear where Anahera ripped out the biggest chunk of hair.

"No, not all the time." Leslie swung her hips. "I take the wee boy to those gardens at the bottom of town. We feed the ducks. He likes it when they flap their wings and do handstands in the lake."

"Handstands!" Logan threw his hands up in the air. "Botox. Bloody hell, woman. What's wrong with you? Just take your hundred-year-old face back to Alfred and sort your life out." He jabbed an index finger at her. "Everything was fine until you turned up with that drop-kick in tow. Just go back to the mountain and stay away from me."

"Can't." Leslie pouted and stuck her chin in the air. "I've got one more appointment with the doctor." She plumped up her breasts by shoving her forearms beneath her wobbling mounds and jiggling them. "Then I'm gonna bag me a fit dude who can take me dancin'."

"But what about Alfred?"

"What about him?" Leslie looked at Hana in surprise as though her husband possessed no authority over her life decisions. "He told me to leave and I did. He's on his own from now on and I'll be getting jiggy with a younger model."

Hana laughed, but the smile died on her lips at the sight of Logan shaking his head. "Don't encourage her!" he said, his tone edgy. He turned back to Leslie and slapped her hands away from her breasts as she peered down her own cleavage and admired the view. "While you're here, you can tell us what you know of a prostitution ring involving men from the township."

"Why would I know something like that?" Leslie puckered her lips and Hana sighed.

"Because you know everything, Leslie. Did you know Anahera's sister performed sex acts for cash?"

"I can hear te pēpe crying." Leslie sounded convincing as she turned and ran for the kitchen door and Hana listened, hearing nothing. The monitor on the kitchen counter showed no change in sound level which meant Mac still slept. Logan got there first and body blocked Leslie, his grey eyes flashing like a stormy sea.

"No, you can't!" he snapped. "Answer the question."

"Yes, I knew," Leslie admitted. "She started while you were away and managed to keep it quiet. Lincoln Haines was only one of her regulars; I know there were others."

"Who?" Logan's biceps tensed as he anticipated Leslie's onslaught, but she stayed a good metre away from him, fearful of what he might do if she touched him again. "Who were the others, Leslie? Was Nev part of it?"

Leslie's jaw dropped. "I don't know. Why are you asking me that? He's your brother and Pania was his sister-in-law. That's disgusting!"

Thoughts of Caroline and Kane went through Hana's mind. "It's not the worst I've heard about this family," she muttered and Logan raised an eyebrow and gave her a warning scowl.

"Tell me the names, Leslie." Logan tipped forward to allow his threat to hit home. "You tell me right now or I tip you out of here and I don't care where you go."

Leslie swallowed and Hana saw her spine tense through her flowery blouse. "Fine then! But two of thems is dead."

"Reuben?" Logan named his father and his expression looked sick.

Hana pressed the dripping ice pack to her face in an attempt to hide her surprise at not having even thought of Reuben. Her mind strayed to her single meeting with him before he died, tall, still handsome and in possession of the X factor he'd handed down to his son. She shook her head. "Don't be ridiculous, Logan. Reuben wouldn't get involved with a sordid arrangement like that. He didn't need to."

"Sure didn't." Leslie's eyes grew dreamy and Logan recoiled in disgust.

"Euwgh!"

"What? Your father was a fine figure of a man but he had Miriam so no, he wasn't involved."

"Who then?" Logan ground his teeth and Hana saw the bone work through the skin of his jaw.

"Jack." Leslie put her hands on her hips. "And don't you be castin' no judgement on the dead." She crossed herself and drew the action out for maximum effect. "Lincoln. Then there was your cousin who runs the restaurant near Rangiriri."

"Alex!" Horror flitted across Logan's face. "But he's been married for years!"

"Yep, him." Leslie looked unrepentant. "The other one was a boy from the town who worked in the mechanic shop. You remember him, don't you, Logan?"

Logan ran a hand through his hair. "The Irish guy? Did he die? You said two of them died."

"Yeah, youse remember! He got in a car accident and died from his injuries."

"I didn't know. That sucks." Logan's shock looked genuine and Hana felt his sadness vibes from across the room. "So, who's the fifth?"

Leslie shook her head. "Na, only those dudes." She shrugged. "Pania looked hot and she offered it. Do you think she put buttocks in her face?" Leslie's glance at Hana looked hopeful and she pretended not to see. The idea of Leslie's voluptuous body being ridden for cash heated her cheeks and made the ice pack melt faster.

"This is so messed up." Logan forgot his sentry duty and stalked across the kitchen, hurling himself into a chair next to Hana. "How did I miss this?"

"You weren't here." Leslie continued to face the door despite Logan's defection, looking like a naughty child from behind. A very round, naughty child. "You lived in England tāne and then when you came back, you lived on the north shore." She turned then, her eyes wide as she regarded Hana.

"Don't mention that woman's name!" Hana pressed the ice pack to her head with more force than necessary, focussing on the external pain to distract her from mention of Logan's former fiancé. "I'm having a dreadful week and I don't need reminding of her, thanks."

Logan chewed his lip and skirted over Hana's outburst. "We must find out who that fifth guy was."

"Where's Nev? Let's ask him." Hana took the ice pack away and turned towards Logan. "Does this look better?"

He wrinkled his nose. "A little. Nev went outside with the crash team; I didn't hear him come back in. Did you?"

"I'll find him." Leslie's pudgy fingers clasped the door handle before she finished her sentence and she rushed out, banging herself on every piece of architrave in her haste. Hana let out a snort, but extinguished it when Logan didn't see the funny side.

"Nev?" He turned to Hana, an agony of emotion in his voice. "Not Nev. He's dead straight, Hana. He wouldn't cheat on Anahera, especially not with her sister and I can't imagine him killing someone. Na, it's not right."

"Then he'll say so and we can look elsewhere."

Hana looked up as Leslie wobbled back into the kitchen. "His car's gone. Maybe he went to the hospital."

"Well, I hope he comes back," Hana said, her tone grave. "Wiri needs him right now, especially after tonight. I can't imagine how he feels; seeing his mother go loco like that."

Leslie shrugged. "Well, Nev's gone now." She pointed at the ice pack in Hana's hand. "Are you done with that? I has got a big pain in my face."

"Is it killing you?" Logan's lips quirked upwards and Hana willed him not to add the punch-line. Too bad. "Coz it's bloody killing me. You should be knitting wahine, not sticking bacteria in your face!"

"Bacteria?" Poor Leslie looked sick. "It's not bacteria."

"Yeah, it is. It's made from the bacteria that causes botulism. It doesn't get rid of the wrinkles; it paralyses the muscles that move and create the wrinkles." He squinted across the room at his step-mother. "You look like a stegosaurus. Are you sure you used a registered doctor?"

"Yes! Shut up nasty boy!" Leslie flounced from the kitchen without the ice pack which Hana held out to her.

"That's mean," Hana chided Logan and he shrugged.

"You have no idea what a bitch that woman was to me as a kid. If she didn't quit, I would have fired her; marrying Alfred is an unwelcome complication." He turned to Hana. "When's she leaving? She's doing my head in."

"Let's deal with things one at a time." Hana chewed a corner of her lip and reached out a tentative hand, stroking Logan's tense thigh with gentle fingers. "You need to talk to Nev."

Logan looked at her, his eyes wide with surprise. "Really? I know, I'll call him up and ask him if he shagged his sister-in-law and then killed her. What should I do when he says yes, Hana? Call the cops?"

"I don't know." Hana put her head in her hands and then remembered her sore eye. "I don't know." She stood up and left the room, pulling the door closed behind her. Leslie wasn't in the lounge or any of the other downstairs rooms they used. Hana put one foot on the bottom step and felt the vibration of her phone buzzing in her jeans pocket.

"Hello?" Not recognising the number, she spoke with caution.

"Mum." Bodie's voice emerged from across the airwaves and Hana's heart clenched, knowing this conversation could go either way.

"Hey." She kept her tone light. "How are you?"

"Good. Thanks. Look, I wanted to apologise for the other night. You're right; I take you for granted. I hate being at odds with you."

"Me too." Hana sat on the bottom step and massaged her left temple. "What's going on, Bo?"

He sighed. "I borrowed money from Logan a while ago and haven't paid him back. I feel embarrassed when I see him."

"He's never said it was a problem from his side. Obviously you need to repay him."

Silence filled the airwaves before Bodie spoke again. "I know. I'm trying to save it up, but stuff keeps happening and eating into it. So now, I feel I need an excuse to see you so it's not awkward but then it makes it worse. I know you dread seeing me."

Hana swallowed. "I don't dread seeing you, Bo. I struggle when you walk in, say hello and then dump the children on me. I'm getting older and I have two small children of my own. I adore Jas and Hope, but it might be nice to see you at the same time so we can interact as a family."

"Okay, fair enough."

"I know you resent Wiri." Hana tested the sentence in her head first, not sure how long lasting Bodie's repentance would prove to be.

"Na, not really," Bodie protested and she cut him off.

"Bodie, I know you do. Jas is unkind to him and pushes him around whenever they're together. He gets that anger from you."

"I didn't know." Bodie sounded contrite.

"It's because you're not here. I spend hours keeping the boys apart and stopping them from fighting. Last time I tried to talk to you about it, you didn't want to know. Jas picks up the resentment from you. When I visited last month and only brought Phoenix and Mac, he commented how much nicer it was without the other fake son. That's straight out of your mouth, Bodie. You're not a little boy anymore and it's ridiculous to be jealous of a six-year-old child who just watched his mother carried out of our kitchen by the mental health crash team."

"I guess."

"We're supposed to be friends, you and I by now, Bo. I shouldn't need to parent you anymore, not at your age."

"That's what Allen said." Bodie sighed and Hana bit back her surprise.

"You saw Pastor Allen? How is he?"

"He's counselling me, actually." Bodie sounded embarrassed. "Amy threatened to leave and take the children if I didn't get help for my anger issues. Allen thinks it stems from guilt in that last year before Dad died. I knew he was cheating on you and should've said something. It eats me up that I didn't."

"Oh, Bodie." Hana sighed. "I'm sorry."

"It's okay. I've gone back to church and I see Allen twice a week at the moment. You should come while you're in town; I know you go to that church which meets in Rangiriri school hall, but just while you're in town, it would be good."

"I will; it'll be great to see everyone again." Hana blinked her right eye and the scratchy feeling made it water. "I wish you'd told me all this the other day. Neither of us needed a bust up."

"I meant to." Bodie clicked his tongue. "But then I saw Logan and I felt embarrassed about the debt. It popped into my head on the way over that we needed someone to mind the kids the next day and before I knew it, the argument began." The smile in his voice sounded genuine. "You're stronger than you used to be, Mum. I don't want to admit it, but I think Logan's good for you. Being a Du Rose suits you."

"Thanks, Bo. I feel it does." Hana thought of the confidence her husband gave her. She closed her eyes and let her fingers trace the tendons and sinews of his forearms in her memory, bulging veins feeding the work hardened muscles. Love bubbled up from her centre and she stood and turned, wanting to go back to the kitchen and sit on his knee.

Her forehead crashed into a hard chest and the strangeness of his scent told her it wasn't Logan's, even before she looked up. The phone slipped from her fingers, skittering into the panel at the bottom of the stairs and popping the back open. Hana opened her mouth to scream but a meaty hand covered her mouth. She felt a draught from the open front door behind her and a piece of cloth passed before her eyes. Feeling momentarily stunned robbed her of immediacy and she failed to use any of the defense strategies her son taught her. Too late she kicked back, contacting a hard shin and achieving a grunt from its owner. But the white cloth descended over her nose and the hand over her mouth blocked oxygen from any other route. A heady chemical odor filled her sinuses and made its way into her lungs.

The last thing she saw was Wiri's frightened face peeking down from between the bannister rails at the top of the stairs. Tears streaked his cheeks and glinted in the lamp light and trauma filled his eyes. She wanted to reach out to him and tell him not to cry, but her feet went out from under her and she left the old gatehouse backwards.

57

Friends and Enemies

Hana opened her left eye after lying awake for a while. The right one felt swollen shut. The drowning sensation faded enough for her to stop feeling nauseous and she peered around at white walls and a dirty ceiling. Her moan of discomfort at the pain in the side of her head evoked movement within the room.

"Hana, are you okay?" Caleb's voice sounded fearful and he used one crutch to scoot across to her, sitting on the bed beside her feet.

"Where am I?" she asked, her throat scratchy and sore. "What happened?"

"They came back for you." Caleb patted her sock and Hana cast around further, trying to sight her shoes.

"Who took my shoes off? Where are they? I need to go." She pushed herself upright and leaned against a wooden headboard, rubbing at the crick in her neck.

"You didn't have shoes; just your slippers. They're over there." Caleb pointed and Hana groaned at the sight of the useless woolly boots. "It's okay, you're safe here. He only wants the best for you."

"Who? Who's he?" Hana rubbed her eyes and hissed in pain as she pressed the right one. "Where's Logan? What about the children?"

The memory of Wiri's shadowlike face at the top of the stairs pushed guilt into her chest. He looked terrified, but he might at least get help. Unless he saw the incident with Anahera as her fault. Hana sighed, unable to predict the future and grateful for it.

"The kids are fine; he's looking into a way of grabbing them too."

"What? No! Leave my kids alone." Hana drew her legs back away from Caleb and he looked hurt.

"He just wants the best for you," he repeated.

"Who does?" Hana felt the panic building and reached out a hand to touch the ridge of her pacemaker. She wondered if it went wild during her unnatural, drug induced sleep. The room seemed dim, the heavy curtains at the window ripped enough in a few places to admit a watery, pathetic light. She closed and opened her eyes again, trying to make the right one work. "It can't be evening already."

"You slept ages. Who did that to your face?" Caleb asked. "You bled on the sheets."

"Sorry." The automatic apology seemed ridiculous in the circumstances. "I want to go home."

Caleb shook his head. "We're all gonna be together, like a family." He smiled, a look of genuine pleasure.

"I've got a family!" Hana remembered the ground breaking call from Bodie and tears pricked her eyes. "He thinks I hung up!" Her voice came out as a wail. "He told me how he felt about everything and I ended the call!"

Caleb shrugged. "It's okay, Hana. You've got us now."

With a groan, Hana swung her legs off the bed and her socks contacted a worn 1970s carpet, the psychedelic pattern making her head hurt as it repeated over and over. "I want my slippers." It seemed important to get them. With something on her feet she could run away.

Caleb reached down next to the double bed and pulled at the grey woolly boots Hana wore around the house. Rubber soled so she could hang out the washing or walk to the outside dustbin, they were still slippers for eighty percent of their construction. She groaned and put her head in her hands.

"He said you'd feel like this for a while. But it'll be okay when the kids get here."

"You touch my kids and I'll hurt you." Hana gritted her teeth and her green eyes flashed danger, despite one being only half open.

"He'll only bring your two." Caleb ran a hand over his sparse, teenage beard growth. "He doesn't want the other one."

Hana stood, the room pitching around her. She used a rickety cupboard to lean against while she pushed her feet into the slippers. The house felt cold and damp and she shivered, unable to control her body temperature. "What did you do to me?"

"Not me." Caleb jerked his head towards his crutch. "It wasn't me." His vague responses induced anger in Hana's psyche and she lurched for him, grabbing the collar of his sweatshirt and hauling him forwards. For a second he looked fearful and then relaxed. "You won't hurt me. It's not the way you're wired."

"Really?" Hana pitched forward so their noses almost touched. "I once put a shard of crystal through a man's forehead. Do you want to go there with me? Do you?"

"Spirited as ever. I see you've met my son." The gentle male tenor stopped Hana in her vengeance and she dropped Caleb's shirt.

Turning, she met Robert Dressler's steady gaze, blue eyes and dirty blonde hair. He smiled, his handsome face curving upwards and Hana felt relief flood through her. "Help me, Bobby," she pleaded, padding towards him and hurling herself against his chest. "They're going after my children. Help me get away."

Bobby's arms felt strong around her shoulders and he kissed the top of her head. "I came back for you, Hana," he said, his voice hushed. "I couldn't stay away."

58

Unrequited Love

"What?" Hana tried to disconnect but he drew her closer, his arms locking around her back. "This is you? You did this?" She struggled with more spirit and he seized her beneath the armpits as she dropped to the ground in a perfect imitation of one of Wiri's tantrums. Hana let her legs turn to jelly and crumpled, dragging Bobby with her.

"I think they gave her too much, Dad," Caleb said, scuffing his crutch around the carpet with the toe of his good foot. "She's woozy."

"You can't do this!" Hana screamed, thrashing and kicking as Bobby dodged her legs. "I want to go home! Let me go home!"

"Hana! Hana, stop! You know I won't hurt you," he breathed, everything about his voice and his smell promising safety while his actions dealt a different hand. "You know I love you, sweetheart. I'll get Phoenix and the baby and we'll go away together."

"I love Logan!" Hana screamed, her chest tightening in a heady mix of terror and fury. "And if you touch my kids, I'll kill you!"

Bobby stood, his expression a mask of raw hurt. "You don't love him, Hana. You think you do but you don't."

"Don't you tell me what to think!" She clambered upright and moved towards him, noticing with satisfaction how he edged backwards. On the offensive, she shoved at his rock hard chest and managed to tilt him backwards. "You don't know what I think!" she shouted into his face. "I thought you were my friend!" Her shoulders slumped. "I saw you at the hospital. Why did you come back?"

Bobby shook his head. "I want to be more than friends, Hana. I always have. I've followed you for the last few days." He lifted his hand to stroke her cheek and she ducked out of his way. His fingers clamping around her chin meant business and she stilled as he looked at her swollen eye, his scrutiny moving to the grazed skin at her hairline. "Who hurt you, Hana?"

"Not Logan!" She replied through gritted teeth and twisted out of Bobby's grasp. Moving to the far corner of the room, she pressed herself against an ancient wardrobe which creaked against the pressure. "I'm going home and you can't stop me."

"Want me to use more stuff, boss?" The deep male voice came from a small gap between the door and the frame, a bulbous face pushing through to get Bobby's attention. Hana recognised the man from her hallway and the moment seemed like days ago. "I can quieten her down if you want."

"You might have to." Caleb looked resigned and his betrayal sent acid into Hana's throat.

"Judas!" she hissed, but he avoided eye contact.

"Na, just leave her for now; she'll calm down." Bobby gave her a smile, the same one he used to offer as they rode through the bush or laughed about some silly thing one of the stockmen said. Hana closed her eyes against the emotions it evoked, knowing she'd pay a terrible price for letting him get too close.

"How can you do this to me?" She heard the pathos in her voice and detested herself. "You saved me and my son; you promised to help me and now this?" Her outstretched arm encompassed the dingy bedroom and ancient furnishings.

"We're not staying here, Hana. I just need to get the kids and then we'll go."

"Go where?" Hana wrapped her arms around her and hugged herself, feeling cold right through to the bone. "Leave my children alone; I won't come with you."

"You don't have a choice." Bobby turned to leave and jerked his head towards Caleb. "Come on, you don't need to be in here anymore, kid."

"Flick, I can drug her." The big man pushed through the doorway, a bottle in one hand and a face cloth in the other. "It worked last time."

"She's got a heart condition; you can't keep doing that." Bobby shook his head with regret and observed Hana. Her gaze darted across the room as Caleb hauled himself upright. The name reverberated through her brain; Flick, Flick, Flick.

Flick, short for flick knife. He always carried a blade even in the bush. Hana's mind worked to remember his habits and where he kept it. In her mind's eye she saw a ripped saddle cloth trailing around a frightened horse's legs and Bobby soothing it while he reached for the knife. Right handed. She watched a kinder, more gentle man poke a sun browned hand into his right pocket and take the knife, pressing the switch to release the blade even before it fully left the safety of the fabric. He slit the cloth with ease and threw the ragged pieces behind him, stroking the mare's long nose with steadying fingers.

"God help me," Hana breathed, forcing away the panic which affected her thought processes. She cursed herself for not mentioning the sighting at the hospital to Logan. The man disappeared into the crowds so fast she couldn't be sure, but everything about his stance screamed recognition. In avoiding conflict with her husband, she'd invited catastrophe.

Hana watched Caleb hop from the room on the single crutch. He'd found a knife in the bush hut. Did that mean Flick no longer followed the habit of a lifetime? She forced herself to look at the sagging right pocket of his jeans, desperate to see the thin outline of a blade. She couldn't tell, the dirty worn material hanging as though filled with all manner of lumpy objects.

"We're going out to get food; the bros are hungry." A taller man elbowed Caleb through the doorway and walked through the gap, his confidence way beyond cocky. "Everyone's restless, Dad. We need to move on."

Hana recoiled at the sight of an old enemy, pressing herself back against the wardrobe. She shook her head in disgust at Caleb and Bobby, not masking her disappointment and misery at their life choices. "You all make me sick!" she spat.

"Just drug her and come with us." Paul Dressler jerked his head in Hana's direction. "Or finish her; you could use the practice." He tapped Bobby's right pocket and Hana's heart soared in victory.

"Don't tell me what to do, son. This is my show, remember?" Bobby's fists balled at his sides.

"Well, it's a stupid one." His son shrugged his shoulders and turned towards the burly man who chloroformed Hana in her hallway. "Come on, Duke. Let's get dinner. There's a Macdonald's not far from here."

Bobby's jaw worked in uncertainty as he faced Hana's glare. In the end, he relented. "You lot go and I'll stay."

His son snorted and Caleb raised his eyebrows. "You're not gonna hurt her, are ya? She's been nice to me."

"I'm not gonna hurt her. Go."

Hana stayed in her corner listening to the sounds of the house empty around her. The echoes betrayed it as a two storey structure and she tried to map out the wooden creaks and groans in her head. Noises from the window told her the front door was to her left and at ground level. If only she could get to it.

Bobby leaned his backside against the wall and stuffed his hands in his pockets. "I didn't want it to be like this, Hana. But Logan made sure I couldn't come back for you."

She kept silent, working out how to snag the knife from his pocket without getting herself killed. Reason gave way to self-preservation and she decided she no longer cared. Her willingness to die trumped a life of imprisonment. Bobby continued to speak. "Logan put me on a plane with false documents and an address to go to in Brixton." His lips peeled back in a snarl. "He knew I'd never get away from them without a fight. Your husband couldn't risk me coming back for you."

"I'm not staying with you and you're not taking my kids." Hana's voice wavered but her resolve held. "I don't love you; I love my husband." Her words hurt Bobby and he winced.

"You can grow to love me."

"Really? You think so. As a hostage? How romantic." She closed her eyes and leaned her head back against the wardrobe. Logan's frequent warnings about the feral stockman reeled in her head and she wished she'd listened. She wished she'd listened about a lot of things and her crimes lined up before her like a list of misdemeanors. "I should've left Caleb at the hospital."

"He's a good kid." Bobby looked pleased. "My eldest told me about him and I made plans to come back. I remember his mother; nice girl."

"Someone else's life you've messed up." Hana glared at him, green eyes flashing like emeralds in her porcelain face.

Bobby shook his head. "Na. He's turned out fine. Thanks for taking him in." His face softened. "It's good to be all together."

"We're not altogether!" Hana snapped. "This is your family; not mine." Her fingers writhed against her stomach. She whimpered and clutched her collarbone. "My heart, it hurts." Dropping to her knees, she kneaded her chest. "I don't feel well."

"Sorry, sorry. What can I get you?" Bobby knelt down next to her and Hana held her breath.

"I need my medication."

He swore. "How the hell do I get that?"

Hana didn't answer, breathing through pursed lips and massaging the space between her breasts, emitting convincing groans of pain. Bobby leaned closer. "What can I do, Hana? How can I help?"

"Get my pills." She kept her speech ragged and implored him with her eyes. "I need them."

"Which ones? How do I know what to get?"

Hana groaned and tipped her forehead onto her arms.

"She's faking." The tone sounded acerbic and Flick's younger son stood in the doorway watching the floor show. His father shot him a look of disdain.

"I thought you went for food. She isn't faking. Find out what pills she needs and rob a pharmacy or something."

"House," Hana moaned, running her fingers up to touch the pacemaker. "Ensuite."

"See." Flick's son sounded victorious. "She thinks you're gonna take her back to Hamilton so you can front out her husband. She's faking."

Hana shook her head, the effort of holding her breath making her vision foggy. "No. Hotel."

Bobby's head nodded on his shoulders. "Yeah, that's right. There'll be some at her other house." He knelt up, engaging his son in excited conversation. "I'll go back to the mountain and get them." He shifted backwards and Hana settled her fingers over the lip of his right pocket.

"Need them now." She accompanied her plea with a heartfelt groan, the strain in her chest beginning to feel genuine.

"I'll take her with me." Bobby sealed his hand over hers, his face showing pleasure at Hana's voluntary contact. "I'll take your car."

"No." His son sounded resolute and Hana's heart sank. She made a pretense of retching onto the awful carpet, making the younger man recoil in distaste and Bobby lean forward in concern. Hana gripped his pocket and writhed on the ground, pulling him down on top of her as she spat onto the carpet. Loose change and a battered driving licence tumbled to the floor and Bobby put a hand out to prevent its escape. Hana groaned with genuine relief, her cries muffled by the filthy fibres beneath her face. She grasped the heavy flick knife which slid into her palm and moved it beneath the cuff of her sweatshirt, gathering the ribbed material into shaking fingers. Lifting her arm, she wiped the sleeve across her mouth, feeling the comforting weight drop into the space between her forearm and the soft, fleecy material.

"It hurts," she whimpered and felt Bobby's hand pat her back.

"How long will it take me?" he asked and his son shrugged. Hana watched through her lashes as he shook his head at his father.

"You're not taking her, Dad. Go if you want but I'll stay here with her. The contractors will arrive soon and you need to get moving. I've paid them half up front and if you don't show, they'll go without you." He looked at his watch and his thin lips quirked upwards in a way that sent terror rushing into Hana's heart. "There's too much riding on this."

"What do they know?" Bobby took car keys from his son's outstretched hand.

"Nothing. As far as they're concerned it's just a removals job."

Hana's breathlessness ceased to be feigned and became real. "Don't leave me with him," she begged Bobby as he turned to leave. She grabbed his ankle and held on. Strong fingers detached her grip.

"Help me get her back onto the bed," Bobby ordered, resuming authority. "She needs to drink something; she's had nothing since last night."

"This is a fool's errand, Dad. Give her more of that stuff in the face cloth; she'll be fine until it's over."

"No. Help me, Dominic. She's got a pacemaker. It's serious. She almost died a couple of years ago."

"Whatever!" With a disgruntled sigh, Bobby's son helped to lift Hana back onto the bed. She rolled onto her side and trapped the arm with the knife beneath her.

"Water," she begged and Bobby stroked her hair back from her forehead.

"Okay, sweetheart. And I'll be back in a couple of hours with the tablets."

"I won't last," she whispered. "Need them."

"I'll go now!" Bobby ran to the door and Hana gave a sigh of relief as his feet pounded down the stairs. Logan wired their vacant house at the top of the mountain with security cameras in their absence. Anyone entering the property would activate a silent alarm in the hotel reception and draw the attention of the staff. The burly men Logan employed to protect the property and its guests were seasoned veterans looking for a more peaceful existence with their families, loyal men who would apprehend Bobby and contact Logan. He'd know.

"Where am I?" Hana tried to sound muddled and confused. "Where is this?"

"Still Hamilton." Bobby's son squatted next to her and handed over a glass of water. "Horsham Downs to be exact. Do you want the postcode? It won't help you."

Hana sipped the water and coughed. "Logan came here the other night looking for Asher."

"Yep." Dominic's eyes widened in amusement. "Stupid kid promised us weed and information. But when it came to it, he couldn't give us either."

"Logan would've known you." Hana coughed again.

"Yeah, that's why we hid. We're not stupid."

"Why are you doing this to me?"

Dominic Dressler shrugged and shook his head. "I don't care about you." He pointed to a long cut on the bridge of his nose. "See this? Your husband did it the other night. I don't care about you but I do wanna see him squirm."

"None of this makes sense." Hana took a bigger gulp of tepid water and coughed again. Droplets went down her windpipe and she felt the pain in her chest for real, clutching at it in fear. Dominic leaned forward and collected the glass as it tipped in her fingers.

"My dad's an idiot. But if you're part of the deal, then so be it." He shrugged. "It's no biggie. We'll get far enough from Hamilton to be safe and then set up again. I've got a house in Auckland we'll go to."

"You won't want to drag me around with you." Hana rubbed her chest and her mind thought up solutions and then disregarded them. "My children will need to go to school; someone will find us."

Dominic nodded. "Whoa lady, you're thinking way too far ahead. You were just the bait to bring my father back home where he belongs. You'll find yourself involved in a little accident soon and he'll be inconsolable." His smile looked evil, lips curled back from his teeth in a sneer. "You made it real easy for me to get rid of him by demanding those pills. The contractors aren't taking you and him to a new place, miss. They've got strict instructions on how to get rid of you."

Hana shook her head. "My husband knows some bad people." She fixed a steady gaze on his youthful face. A smattering of beard hair sprouted from his chin like dirty blonde fluff. "He'll send the Triads after you. They won't ask questions; they'll just float your battered body in Auckland harbour in a suitcase. That's what they do. I'm begging you, leave my children out of this or you'll be sorry."

Dominic laughed. "You talk some smack, missus. Triads!" He scoffed and Hana allowed a look of amusement to part her lips. It was enough to make him think again. "Your husband don't know no Triads." He sounded less convinced.

"Mr Che owes Logan his life. He always responds to requests for help."

Dominic sneered. "Whatever!" His brow knitted. "Why does he owe him his life?"

Hana uncrossed her legs and moved her arm so the knife fell into her cuff. She used the other hand to pull the sleeve loose and the knife slipped into her palm. "Mr Che suffered a heart attack and Logan resuscitated him and kept him alive until the ambulance arrived. Mrs Che runs security now and Logan only has to call her. They'll flush you out in very little time and make you wish you'd never been born."

Dominic's lips curled back in a snarl. "You're bluffing lady. I think you need a gag to stop you fantasising about big scary friends who don't exist." He stood up and backed towards the door. "Get ready for another sleep, Hana," he said. The door clicked shut behind him and Hana heard a bolt shoot closed. She knew he'd gone to fetch more of the chloroform they'd used on her before.

With shaking fingers, she pulled the blade from her sleeve and examined it for a switch to extend it. Turning the metal shaft over in her hands she heard Dominic moving around downstairs. "Where is it?" she hissed, pressing every part of the knife's surface in panic. "Maybe it's push, not press," Hana corrected herself as she moved a metallic decoration in the shape of a running horse. She eased it towards the top of the shaft and the blade shot out, moving through a ninety-degree angle at speed. The razor sharp edge nicked the palm of her other hand. "Fantastic!" she groaned as blood pooled in the thin wound.

Heavy footsteps pounded up the stairs, robbing Hana of the chance to run behind the door. Her gentle nature fought with survival instinct and by the time the bolt slid back and the handle started to turn, she felt paralysed by indecision.

Dominic closed the door behind him and held the filthy rag outstretched in his hand. He paused a moment to cup it in his palm, ready to close over Hana's mouth and nose. Seeing the terror on her face, he looked apologetic. "It doesn't hurt. Just think of it as a good sleep until the contractors arrive. It might even do you some good."

Hana's head wobbled on her neck as fear claimed her muscles and reduced her to inactivity. "No," she begged. "Please don't." She shook her head and tried to back up further on the bed, holding her hand out in front of her. "I don't want to do this. Please don't make me."

"It's okay." He leaned over her, reducing her options to just one. Keeping the knife clenched with the blade protruding downwards from the bottom of her coiled fist, Hana jabbed in a hammer action like a child gripping a pencil. The knife slipped into Dominic's upper thigh with so little effort, Hana only realised she'd stabbed him when blood soaked her hand and dripped onto her jeans. Dominic looked surprised and then angry, clasping the wound one handed and grappling for Hana with the other.

"Get off me!" she screamed into his face and slashed at the hand trying to restrain her. Dominic inhaled and removed it, staring in horror at the blood streaming from two of his fingers.

"You bitch!" He backhanded her, spreading his blood over her face and the collar of her sweater. He snatched at her hair and Hana struck out with the knife again, catching him on the forearm. Dominic bellowed in pain and fell backwards onto the bed. The blade skittered from Hana's blood soaked fingers and loath to retrieve it, she seized the damp cloth which Dominic dropped on the floor. Leaning over him she shoved it into his face, holding it over his nose and mouth, even though he thrashed and writhed. When his body stilled, she slid to the dirty carpet next to the bed and sobbed with guilt and regret.

Hana checked for a pulse in his wrist but felt nothing through her shaking fingertips. Dominic Dressler looked dead, sprawled on the bed and bleeding. Hana spotted the rectangular shape in his jeans pocket and pushed her fingers between the gap. "I'm sorry," she sobbed. "I'm sorry." Grasping the phone in her blood stained hands, she peered at the screen which jumped to life and saw it asking for a password. "I don't know it," she wailed.

Dominic's right foot twitched, sending Hana scuttling across the floor in horror. She gathered her wits about her and ran for the door, fumbling with the bolt on the outside whilst realising how foolish the action seemed as she imprisoned a dead man. Once in the hallway, the layout confused her. With no recollection of entering the house, it looked impossible to find her way out. "Think, think!" she urged, forcing her feet to walk forwards. "It's two-storey; there must be stairs."

Hana found four more bedrooms before the hallway opened out to a stair well. She crept down, checking around the corner of a dog-leg for more of her captors. Knowing time marched against her, Hana found the front door at the bottom of the stairs and tried the handle. She panicked when it didn't budge and ran her hands over her face. "Open, damn you!" she begged. Locked from the outside with a key, it remained firm, awaiting the return of Bobby or his men. Hana searched out a rear door. She found a ranch slider in a downstairs lounge and sobbed with relief as the lock clicked up and the glass slid open at her touch.

She closed it behind her, trying to give herself time to get away. A pretty garden opened out behind the cedar wood house and post and rail fencing gave way to wide paddocks bathed in moonlight. The house next door looked unlit and deserted and Hana swallowed, unable to trust anyone. "I need Logan," she hissed, running her thumb across the phone screen again and getting only the password request.

The sound of a nearby car snapped her to attention and she cleared the garden in seconds. The post and rail fence proved easy to clamber over and Hana fled, alarming a small group of steers who jumped and ran away from her. Her legs felt like jelly as the adrenaline coursed through her veins and her heart rate doubled. Every few steps she looked over her shoulder, dreading the moment when the men appeared and came after her. She didn't stand a chance.

59

Desperation

Hana fell numerous times in the damp grass, bruising those parts of her body not already wrecked. The wool of her slippers became heavy with evening frost and she slipped and slid despite the rubber soles. The cows ran away and then returned, trotting after her and bucking and kicking as though playing a game. Knowing they'd attract attention and make her more visible to her pursuers, Hana climbed a nearby fence and entered the garden of a single level house with a swimming pool. She hid between the silky fronds of a silver fern, pushing herself backwards into the clustered native plants and praying she couldn't be seen. Clutching the phone again, she saw the screen come to life and noticed another message at the bottom. She obeyed the instruction and pressed the three numbers guaranteed to bring help without requiring a password. 'Press 111 for emergency.' When the operator answered, Hana's voice cracked with emotion.

"Please, help me. Help me. I need cops and an ambulance."

"What's your location, madam?"

"I don't know, I don't know." Hana peeped through the bushes, seeing a bulldog peering in her direction from behind the glass of a ranch slider. Light shone from behind it and it barked and put its front paws against the slippery surface, falling off sideways and trying again. "There's a dog. It's going to get me." Hana let out a sob. "Please, they're coming. You have to help me."

"The dog's coming madam?"

"No! The men who kidnapped me. I stabbed one of them. Please come and get me."

"You stabbed someone? Are they still alive?"

"No! He's dead. The others went for dinner so I stabbed him when he tried to smother me with the sleeping drug."

"What's your name and the number of the phone you're calling from?"

"I'm Hana. Hana Du Rose. Please send help."

"What's your phone number, Hana?"

"I don't know. I took it from the man I stabbed." The operator asked more questions and Hana sat in the bushes and panicked, unable to process her words or reply with anything more than short, panicked breaths. "Horsham Downs," she said as a memory returned. "He said they brought me to Horsham Downs, but I'm hiding in someone's garden and there's a dog."

"Can you knock on the door of the house?" the operator asked. "Is anyone home?"

"No, no!" Hana looked down at her sweater and cringed. "I'm covered in blood."

"Is it your blood, Hana?"

"No, it's his."

"The man you stabbed?"

"Yes, it's his. Please, is anyone coming? Help me." Hana dropped the phone onto the ground and put her face in her hands. She smelled the metallic scent of blood and the last of her resolve left her. Cradling her head in the crook of her elbow and drawing her knees up tight to her chest; Hana admitted defeat and waited for the inevitable moment when the householder released the dog and it made a beeline for her. "Logan," she whispered into the soft fronds of the silver fern. "Logan, I need you."

The muffled sounds of the dog sent shivers down her spine and she contemplated moving. The bare paddocks offered no protection if the men set off across the grass after her and Hana clamped her teeth over the back of her fist to muffle the cry of misery building in her chest. If they followed her, the barking dog would give her away. Hana reached for the phone again and held it to her ear, hearing static from an open call. "Are you still there?" she asked, her voice small. "They'll arrive back in a minute and search for me."

"I'm still here." The woman's voice sounded reassuring. "Hana, we know you're missing. Everyone's looking for you; you aren't in trouble. The police and ambulance services are on their way to the Horsham Downs area, but I need some indication of where you are so I can help them find you. What can you see?"

Hana peeked between the fronds and cast her eyes around the back garden, trying not to focus on the silhouette of the enraged dog hurling its body against the window. "There's a dog," she said again, unable to tear her gaze from its open maw and the mess it made of the glass with slobber and hair.

"What else?" The operator sounded calm and Hana peered around her. "A swimming pool."

"What shape, Hana?"

Hana swallowed, realising how dry her throat felt. "I'm thirsty." Her voice cracked.

"What shape is the pool, Hana? Describe it."

She shook her head. It sounded such a stupid, irrelevant question and other things vied for attention. The question came again with more insistence and Hana concentrated on the shape of the swimming pool. "It's dark but I can see that it's round. No, like a kidney bean." She poked her face through the bushes and the dog stilled for a moment before renewing its territorial fury. "There's an in-ground spa on the edge nearest the house and it's got a turquoise lid on it." Hana pulled her face back and dropped the phone. She retrieved it and raised it to her ear, streaking orange clay over her cheek.

"Hana?" The operator's voice sounded urgent. "Look at the house. What colour is the roof?"

"I don't know." Reluctant to draw the dog's attention again, Hana leaned back against a woody trunk and watched an ant crawl up her sleeve.

"It's important, Hana. I'm looking at satellite photos. What colour is the roof?"

Hana lifted her right hand and parted the fronds above her head. The cornflower blue aluminum roof matched the metal frames of the windows, contrasting against the untreated cedar. "Blue," she replied. "Blue roof, blue windows and the house is cedar wood. Can I talk to Logan? I want my husband." Hana's voice broke and she gave a disgusting sniff. "I want to go home."

"I know, Hana. Stay with us, love. Help's on its way."

Hana's body jerked with a series of involuntary movements, exhaustion and dehydration catching up with her. She heard movement behind her and yelped as strong arms clamped around her shoulders, pinning her arms to her side. He lifted her up and she bent her knees, trying to ram her feet backwards into his legs. One of her slippers fell off and her attacker tripped over it, toppling her sideways. She dropped the phone and it skittered beneath a lazy jasmine which rambled over the fence and beyond. "I've got her." The man spoke to someone else and Hana jerked her head back, trying to break his nose. She hit his collar bone and he hissed but didn't let go. "I need help," he said. "Bring the car round and get ready to take her; I need to sedate her. Yeah, I walked across the paddock and heard her talking. I dunno. Maybe herself. I can't see a phone."

Hana let out a scream and sausage fingers clamped over her mouth. She bit the fatty flesh and received a smack in the nose for her trouble. The cloth covered her mouth again and she groaned as sense and reason exited with her next inhale.

60

Sons of Regret

Hana woke to the sound of yelling and felt the vehicle slew to the left. "Control it!" a male voice insisted, met by aggression from the driver.

"I'm trying! This road is crap and I'm avoiding the sirens."

"How did they find us?"

"Helicopter?" A third voice interjected from next to Hana on the back seat. "Or Google Earth. She must have called the cops somehow and given them landmarks."

"How? You found her hiding in a bush. She couldn't have."

"I don't know!" The man sounded huffy. "I told you I heard her talking. Look, we've stayed hidden and switched vehicles. Now we need to leave. Just drive. We've got a job to do."

Hana sat up and tried to look out of the window, groggy and uncoordinated. Her own reflection met her, the dark outside making vision poor. The man next to her put an arm across her chest to help her stay upright. "She's awake!" he shouted as though it mattered.

"Give her another dose of that stuff then; we don't need her causing problems."

The driver swore and pointed to a haze of blue and red lights leaving a glow on the low cloud a few kilometres ahead. "They've cut us off. I need to get away from the main road."

"We could dump the car and go on foot. We need to finish this job."

The man next to Hana rolled his eyes, the whites looking ghoulish in the dim light. "Best not drug her then or she won't be able to walk. I can't carry her. How far's the river from here? I know he wanted her dumping at Port Waikato eventually so she doesn't wash up anywhere along the riverbank, but they wouldn't know if we got rid of her earlier."

A popping sound broke the silence of dusk and the car lurched sideways off the road and travelled longwise into a ditch. Hana's head hit the window and her brain thrummed for a moment. When her senses returned, she heard running water below her and panicked.

"What did you do that for?" her seat passenger railed and the driver ignored him, struggling to force his door upwards so he could get out.

"It's too heavy." He turned the key in the ignition and nothing happened. "I can't get out! The windows are electric." He scrabbled around pushing at the handle and managed to open the door a crack. "Help me!" he shouted and the front passenger leaned across him and used his weight against the door. Between them it shifted with an ominous creak and the driver clambered out onto the muddy bank and held it open for the passenger. He groaned and cursed at the weight of gravity which worked hard to force the door closed.

"What about us?" The man next to Hana unclipped his seatbelt and plummeted sideways into her. Hana groaned with the impact and her head banged the window again.

"Just wait. We gotta prop this thing open."

"Don't have time." The driver peered into the vehicle and licked his lips. "Hand her out first and then it will distribute the weight enough for you to crawl forward."

Hana's seat companion snatched at her with rough, sausage hands and shoved her through the narrow gap between the front seats. Her slender body passed through, but the weird angle of the car made movement difficult. She clambered up the front seat and as the men held the door at an upwards tilt, she pushed herself out and face planted in the dirt.

"Now me." The rear seat passenger pushed himself into the gap between the seats but his wide girth proved impossible to shove through the small space. He grunted and complained but remained stuck, his pale face pointing upwards with a look of desperation.

The haze of blue and red became fixed in a single spot up ahead and the driver panicked. "We don't have time for this. Sorry, dude."

Hana watched as the men let the door down until it clicked shut and their companion's cries became muffled. "He'll drown," she stated and the other men glanced at one another and ignored her.

"Why did you drive into the ditch?" the passenger demanded as both men cast around them, trying to get their bearings.

"I didn't!" The driver sounded indignant. "The tyre popped. I dunno why. I couldn't hold the steering straight after that." He pointed towards the driver's side tyre which still spun in midair as the vehicle sank further into the ditch on its side. "Look. It's flat."

Hana slipped and slid on the bank, her lone slipper burying itself deep into the soggy mud. The bubbling stream looked too near for comfort and she pulled her foot out with a sucking sound, battling to free the other with its unsalvageable sock.

"Grab her. We'll go off-road and hide until our back-up gets here."

"Gets where? Where the hell are we?" The passenger lurched for Hana and she stepped away and fell onto her backside.

"There's a place near here. We pick up another vehicle if we get into trouble."

"Where's here? Why pay us to move her under a hundred kilometres? It doesn't feel right. We need to get nearer to the main state highway."

"We're north of Hamilton. We need to hide for a few days and then finish her off like he said. He can't give us the rest of the cash until he gets paid."

The passenger lurched again for Hana and she wiggled away backwards, leaving him stuck in the mud. "Help me with her. We need to get moving."

"Hey!" The muffled cries of the rear seat passenger grew louder as the vehicle gave a lurch and became more immersed in the ditch. Water ran over its front left headlamp, making the waves and bubbles shimmer in the dim light.

"What the hell's that?"

Hana peered over the side of the ditch, seeing the rural road stretch out before her like a flat piece of grey string weaving away into the darkness ahead. The red and blue police lights flashed into the night sky. Her eyes struggled to focus as the passenger lurched for her hard, his feet slipping and causing him to slam her face first into the bank again. He landed on top of her and blood pooled on her top lip from a bleeding nose.

A black figure appeared in the centre of the road, its lower half obscured by tufts of grass and the uneven bank in front of Hana's face. The lights from the police blockade back-lit its progress. She wriggled out from beneath the flailing man, roots and rough stones grazing her skin through her clothing. Closer, closer the dark shape moved towards her in her peripheral vision and she held her breath.

"There's someone there!" The driver's voice hiked as the newcomer walked forward at a confident pace. Fearless he came, his outline picked up in the headlights like a ghoul. He held a shotgun in front of him, his eye already against the sight and a black balaclava pulled over his features.

"What should I do?" The driver spun on the spot and slipped sideways, almost taking the recovering passenger back down with him. "Who is it?" No answer.

"It's a cop. He won't shoot us," the passenger snarled.

"That's not a cop." The driver's eyes widened and his irises glinted, reflecting the light from the single unbroken headlamp.

"Back up boys." The gun barrel moved from one to the other and the men cringed. "Don't think I won't do it." The voice sounded low and emitted as a snarl. "I'd love to spray your ugly faces all over this car."

"Help!" The man inside the vehicle sounded frantic, his body looking like a failed planking session in the half-submerged car.

The newcomer snorted and his eyes narrowed behind the balaclava. "Turn around and put your hands against the car."

"It's slipping!"

"Hold on tight then."

"You shot out the tyre!" The driver slipped onto his backside and his right leg became stuck beneath the car. He gave a blood curdling wail of pain.

"You doubled crossed us; we want the rest of our money," the passenger griped. "You can't just take the woman."

"Shut up." The stranger kept the gun trained on the men one handed. His easy confidence with the weapon showed that firing wouldn't be a problem. He bent at the knees and offered Hana his other hand. When she shrank back from him, he wiggled his gloved fingers in the universal motion of 'come here.'

Hana heard him sigh with annoyance. "Take my hand."

She yelped and lurched at the offered lifeline, letting him haul her up the dirty bank. The only part of his body showing through the balaclava was the space where his eyes glared through. Hana steadied her breathing and tried to ignore the pain of her soaked and threadbare sock on the rough road surface. The gun levelled at the face of the passenger who looked up at him and the newcomer's eyes narrowed to slits. "Wait here and don't look back," he snarled. "I'm not alone and my colleagues will blow you away without a second thought."

Another man appeared from the shadows and aimed a bigger gun at the two men plastered against the sinking vehicle. With a nod, Hana's new captor grabbed at her sleeve and tugged her towards him. "Walk," he snapped, authority in his voice. Staring back at the half submerged vehicle, she watched as her assailants turned as one and lurched towards the slight man left on guard. They failed even before they clambered two steps up the slippery bank. He felled them both, the first with a swift kick to the head and the second, by grabbing his hair and smashing his face into the black clad knee. Hana gasped and gave a tiny yelp. "Don't look back." The man's gloved hand reached out and clasped her freezing fingers, closing them into his palm and yanking her away.

She stumbled behind him as he picked up speed, alarmed when he veered off the road and plunged into a wooded area. "Wait!" she cried and he halted for a second and then ploughed on. "I don't have shoes!"

He tutted and returned for her, wielding the shotgun in his left hand as he dipped his body and tipped her over his shoulder in a fireman's lift. Moonlight filtered through the trees and Hana watched the rugged ground pass beneath her. They moved with stealth and the bushman's heartbeat aligned with hers, carrying her as though she weighed little more than a bag of flour. The red and blue emergency lights faded into the distance and Hana sighed with relief. At a clearing open to the night sky, the man bent and allowed her feet to touch the ground strewn with fern fronds. Hana's legs gave out and she crumpled into a ball in a circle of five black clad figures.

"Hey." Logan pulled his ski mask off and squatted on his haunches next to her. "How're you doing?"

Hana nodded and wiped her nose on her cuff. "I killed a man."

Logan smiled. "Na, ya didn't. I'm real proud of you, wahine."

A silent tear rolled from the eye furthest away from Logan and Hana's chest hitched. "I want to go home," she whispered and Logan nodded.

"I know, babe. But right now, you need to leave with these guys."

"No!" Hana shrieked. "Don't leave me!"

Logan reached in and kissed her bloodied lips. "Don't worry, sweetheart. I won't go far." He hefted the shotgun across his knees and jerked his head towards it. "But if they find me here and realise I shot out the tyre with my grandfather's unlicensed gun; you know they'll arrest me."

"The men said there's a helicopter." Hana spoke as the circle of figures pressed closer.

"Na, just road cops." Logan lowered his voice. "But I can hear the sirens, Hana. I need to get out of here."

"They'll know who you are," she hissed and he shook his head.

"Na, they won't." Logan hefted the gun in gloved hands. "This is Poppa Henri's old shooter. I'll take it home and hide it. But I need to go now or you know what will happen to me."

Hana nodded and accepted another kiss. "What do I tell the cops?" she asked with a disgusting sniff.

Logan inhaled. "Tell them everything but not Dressler's name. I don't want the cops looking for his sons either or they'll hear how I gave Flick safe house, knowing a warrant existed with his name on it."

"Then they'll get away with it." Hana's eyes widened in futility. "He'll come back for me and I won't escape a second time."

Logan's lips drew back in an ugly expression. "No, he won't." His eyes resembled lumps of dark coal in the moonlight. "Trust me, Hana." Jaw flexing and teeth grinding, he bent one last time and pressed his lips against her forehead. Hana clung onto Logan's dark jacket until it slipped through her fingers. He melted into the darkness and Hana swallowed as the nearest figure reached for her. She shrank back but his grip felt insistent and exhaustion forced her into submission.

"We get you to children." The voice sounded muffled through the mask and Hana nodded.

"Children," she repeated.

"Come, Meese Du Rosa," the Asian voice said and Hana stood and accepted his outstretched arm.

61

An Old Adversary

The paddocks between Horsham Downs and Lake Road took an age to traverse. Hana trudged without awareness, allowing herself to be led by the small man in front and flanked by the other four. She fell and they picked her up. She stumbled and they righted her. Bruised and bleeding, with one foot sodden and the other numb, Hana made the journey without complaint.

Clouds scudded across the sky, shielding the moon's face from revealing the small company of travellers. Vehicles moved up and down the road parallel to their path, headlights sweeping the route like snow ploughs. The final paddock ended at a hawthorn hedge and the lead man halted the group with a simple hand signal. "Wait!" he hissed when Hana missed the cue and she found herself hauled backwards and a hand slipped over her mouth.

The first man breached the hedge at the junction between two bushes, clearing the post and rail fence without touching it. Hana strained her ears and heard an engine start and the first man's face appeared in the gap, a pair of eyes peeking out through his balaclava. "Come!" he ordered Hana, beckoning with a black-gloved hand. Doubtful, she turned to look at the other faces, taking in the slanted Oriental eyes and the single-minded fearlessness in their expression.

"I don't know," she started and as one, they pushed her towards the fence. A smaller man tapped her on the shoulder and inclined his head.

"You will be safe, Du Rose daughter. Trust."

Hana closed her eyes. There it was again, that word she couldn't process. Trust. She inhaled, exhaled and nodded with determination, seeing the collective pairs of eyes around her turn upwards in smiles. "Okay," she whispered, her voice croaky and sore. "Thank you."

As one, they bowed low and then helped her over the fence. Her body proved clunky and awkward, refusing to obey even the simplest of instructions. She fell in the gravel on the other side and picked herself up again. The first man followed her over and helped her to her feet, waving his arm towards the vehicle parked in the layby. "You go now," he said and bowed again.

The rear door of the limousine slid open with a gentle whir, untouched by human hands. Hana shielded her eyes from the glare of the bright interior and took a sharp intake of breath at the woman reclining in the rear seat. "Mrs Che," she breathed.

"Meesa Du Rosa," the Triad queen replied, beckoning with a long, slender hand adorned with enough gold to snap the delicate bones. "We should get you home, no?"

Hana swallowed and took a step towards the plush vehicle, embarrassed about the state of her dress. Mrs Che raised a perfect black eyebrow and inclined her head. "Do not worry, Meesa Du Rosa. You are welcome here."

Hana clambered into the seat opposite and the door closed behind her with the same electrical whirr. She held onto the edge of the seat as the Limo pulled out onto Lake Road and picked up speed. "Where are we going?" she rasped, watching the Waikato landscape whip past.

"To your home at the school," the formidable woman replied. She glanced at Hana's feet. "You escape and walk there. Tell policemen that story. Your husband is waiting for you." The old lady extended a manicured hand towards the seat opposite and inclined her head. "Change your attire. Your clothing contains DNA and that is now my concern."

Hana swallowed. Their last encounter weighed on her heart, tainted by suspicion and fear. "How did you find me?" she asked and Mrs Che chuckled, a low sinister sound.

"It is our role to know everything," she murmured. "We listen to the chatter and wait to help our favourite son. Logan Du Rosa is my husband's honourary érzi. I know you do not like it, but we will always respond to his call to action."

Hana nodded, reaching for the bag of clothes. She glanced at the passing landscape and Mrs Che smiled. "Nobody will see through windows," she said, her narrowed eyes holding a glint of pleasure.

Hana stripped off her soiled outer clothing but left her underwear on, pulling the clean hoodie over her head. She swayed with the movement of the vehicle as she eyed her filthy socks against the laundered tracksuit pants. "I think my feet are bleeding," she said, looking up at the oriental princess opposite.

"Leave on your socks," Mrs Che ordered. "The police will get only mud from them."

Hana accepted her direction and pushed her feet into the legs of the pants, hauling them up over her thighs and bottom. She forced reluctant toes into the dirty slipper and then sat, feeling awkward under the woman's scrutiny.

Her eyes drooped as she clung to the seat as the driver made the turn onto River Road and started back towards Hamilton.

The limo ran over a pot hole and the jerk startled Hana back to wakefulness. "I'm grateful to you," she said, as Mrs Che observed her through dark, gimlet eyes. Hana shrank back against the plush leather seat. "What will happen now?"

"We drop you on road outside school where there are no cameras. You go home."

"That simple?" Hana wiped her nose on her sleeve. "It can't be that easy."

"Life is easy." Mrs Che folded her arms. "We make it hard for selves. Is easy if we stay focussed. Concentrate only on what matter. All else, disregard."

Hana accepted the advice given in Mrs Che's stilted English and swayed in her seat. Soft classical music played through a small speaker near her head and lulled her into a sense of security so profound, it felt impossible to leave. When the vehicle slowed on Maui Street and the door next to Hana opened, she slid her foot out onto the rail and stood. "Thank you," she said, inclining her head to the regal woman who ran security for her husband's illegal business in Auckland's underbelly. "Please give my regards to Mr Che. I'm not sure we'll meet again, but I'm very grateful for your help."

Mrs Che blinked slitted dark eyes and her thin lips quirked up into a smile. "We will meet again," she replied and bowed her head. Hana stepped back in surprise as the door closed in her face and the sleek car slid away even before it clicked shut. Tinted windows muted all light apart from the glowing red reflectors on the tail lights.

Hana stood on the pavement next to the iron railings surrounding the school grounds and peered down at her feet. The cleanliness of the fresh pants seemed incongruous against a sock which looked indistinguishable from the ruined slipper. She turned towards the main gate a hundred metres along the road and began her slow trudge back to her temporary home.

62

Treachery

"Mum!" Bodie stood in the hallway speaking on the phone and jumped as Hana walked through the unlocked front door. He looked exhausted and his police shirt hung from his waistband like a curtain. "She's home. Gotta go." He ended the call and ran to Hana, scooping her into his arms. "Mum, I'm so sorry. Let's start again, can we?"

Hana nodded, the movement restricted by his arms around her head.

"She's back!" Bodie yelled, so loud above Hana's ears the sound pained her. "It's Mum!"

Leslie caused a bottleneck in the kitchen doorway, her round backside preventing anyone else leaving the room. She screeched in Māori and waved her arms around until Logan gave her a shove out of the way.

"Hana." He stopped in front, waiting for Bodie to release her. The younger man let go and Logan's arms replaced his. "Everything's gonna be okay," he whispered in her ear. "It's over."

Hana nodded and glanced down at his faded blue jeans and the white tee shirt he favoured. Her brow knitted in confusion and he gave a slow shake of his head to silence her. "We've been so worried," he said and his voice faltered. His acting skills looked honed to perfection, but the sentiments beneath the words held truth.

"What the hell happened?" Bodie urged, ever the policeman.

"Just give her a minute, will ya?" Logan's eyes flashed danger and Bodie stepped back.

Hana's heart sank as a familiar shape appeared in the doorway and Detective Chief Inspector Odering leaned against the frame, arms crossed at his chest. "Mrs Du Rose," he said with a frown. "Where do we begin this time?" He wielded a police radio in one hand and chattered into it to announce her arrival.

"With a shower, I hope," she said, her throat rasping from lack of fluid. "And a drink. I need a drink."

The inspector raised an eyebrow at Bodie and Hana's son cringed. "Sorry, Mum. We need your clothing for evidence."

Hana sighed and nodded. "Yeah. I know the drill." She looked around Logan and her eyes raked the hallway for someone else. "Where're the children? They said they were coming for the children."

"Amy's got them up at Culver's Cottage, Mum. They're safe. Nobody can get them there; you know that."

Hana nodded and her face flooded with relief. "I'm so tired," she said and used her forefingers to pull at the sides of her eyes until they resembled slits. "What do you want from me?"

"Your clothes and then a statement." Odering's smile looked false. He glanced at Logan. "And this time, I won't leave until I get both."

Logan shrugged. "I'm not stopping you. Can she take a shower?"

Odering narrowed his eyes. "No. We'll go to the police station and my officer will wait outside the bathroom. Mrs Du Rose can pass her clothing out to him."

Bodie bridled. "Sorry, Sir, you need to find someone else."

"What?" Odering's face changed colour, moving through shades of pink to an angry red. "What do you mean, Senior Sergeant Johal?"

"I'm off duty." Bodie put his hands on his hips and glared at his superior. "And this is my mother."

The lanky inspector glared at his protégé with malice and Hana's brows knitted. She wanted to urge Bodie not to worry, to protect him from Odering's ire, but something about his protest honoured her role in his life and she kept silent. "Fine!" Odering snapped. "I'll stand outside the bloody bathroom."

Logan rolled his eyes out of sight of Odering and Hana saw his desperation to get her by herself.

"Actually, let's do a statement first." Odering's lips curled back in a snarl. "I'd hate for you to suffer amnesia whilst in the shower."

"Sod off!" The look Logan gave him threatened violence and Odering took a step back.

With a shake of his head and an exaggerated sigh, Bodie closed Hana off from view, aligning his body with Logan's to shield her. "I'll do it. Don't put her through it with strangers. I'll bring the clothes."

"If she's got injuries, they'll need to be photographed," Odering cautioned and raised his eyebrows. "I'll ask the doctor to make her way to the station. We'll leave in a moment."

Hana nodded with understanding and sat on the bottom step to at least remove her filthy footwear. "I have to take these off," she pleaded. "My feet sting." She held out the ruined woolly slipper and destroyed sock and Bodie took them, dropping them into a clear bag. The skin of her toes looked crinkled from the wet mud, their surface littered with scratches and shallow cuts. But when she pulled the remnants of the other sock from her foot, even Odering gasped in sympathy.

"That looks painful," he commented, leaning in closer to look. Hana's hands shook as she pulled broken fern fronds from between her toes and tried to ignore the rawness of the skin on her heel and the ball of her foot.

She attempted to make a joke. "Phoenix would've managed just fine. We can't get her to keep shoes on, can we Logan?" She glanced up at her husband and his wooden nod affirmed her statement. Hana groaned as the air kissed the raw skin, the outer layers of the blisters peeling away with her sock. She put it in Bodie's bag and tried to stand, holding onto the bannister rail and hopping on the better foot.

A soft knock on the door heralded the arrival of another officer and she nodded at Odering as he pulled it open. "Car's not far off, Sir," she said in an official tone. Hana noticed Odering's gaze follow the tall, blonde woman's lithe figure as she turned and stepped out onto the driveway.

"Let's go," he said, his face all business and short on compassion.

Logan carried Hana onto the porch to save her walking on her painful feet. She wrapped her arms around his neck and let his courage embolden her. They travelled in the back of the police car with Odering riding shotgun and Logan held Hana's hand the whole way there. Bodie followed with Leslie in his vehicle after a short delay, during which the thoughtful old lady packed a bag of clothes for Hana.

"I've done this too many times for one lifetime," Hana sighed as the female police surgeon photographed her superficial injuries. "I've had enough."

"Yeah, I know, I know." Logan squeezed her hand, the mud from her fingers sticking to his.

"I can't do this anymore," Hana sobbed from the shower as she washed dirt and blood from her body.

"Believe me, I get it, Hana," Logan replied.

Through the glass she saw him close his eyes and heard him mutter, "Nor can I."

Hana's hair tangled without a wide toothed comb and she gave up, piling it onto her head in the clip the kind police surgeon gave her. She hid her cuts and bruises beneath the familiar clothes Leslie sent from the front waiting room and hobbled around in the small washroom until she felt ready to emerge. "Let's get it over with," she sighed and Logan placed his hand on her arm. He glanced across at the doctor as she put her copious bag of plasters and pain killers back in order and gave a slow shake of his head. Hana nodded in understanding, the tight smile making her sore lips crack and bleed.

Hana's statement wove a version of the truth until the moment the car plunged into the ditch, although she managed not to mention names throughout. Odering sat forward and increased the intensity of his stare. "Officers apprehended three men at the scene of the accident." He drew in a loud breath of exasperation. "They claim that ninjas took you."

Hana's bark of laughter embarrassed her and she reached for the glass of juice the doctor brought into the interview room. "Ninjas?" She laughed again and frustration built in Odering's blue eyes. He straightened his tie and gave her a quizzical look.

Contemplating her six feet and four-inch husband as a black clad ninja touched something ticklish in Hana's stomach and she sniffed and snorted while the men sat and watched her, their collective eyebrows furrowed. The woman police officer looked sympathetic and hid her own smirk. Every time Hana thought she'd calmed enough to continue, Logan's ninja image ruined her resolve and she dissolved again.

"Hana, stop!" Logan's eyes widened and he nudged her with his elbow. "It's not funny, babe."

Her head bobbed on her shoulders and she rubbed her eyes with a tissue. "It is, it is. Ninjas." She inhaled and achieved some semblance of control, Logan's alarm communicating itself to her. "It was aliens, actually," Hana said, clearing her throat and avoiding Logan's gaze.

Then the lying began in earnest, wrapping her in a web of deceit accompanied by prayers requesting forgiveness. "The tyre blew out and we ended up in the ditch. I didn't wear a seatbelt because they put me into the car drugged." She touched the side of her face with tentative fingers. "The driver and passenger escaped first and managed to pull me between the seats and through the driver's door. It took both of them to lift it and the car slipped a few times." Hana blew out a pursed breath as she relived the moment, watching her every word for flaws which might betray her husband.

"Take your time," Odering said, his tone gentle. "There's no need to rush."

"I'm tired." A wave of exhaustion rolled across Hana's shoulders and she appealed to Logan for help. "They drugged me heaps of times." She touched the sore spot on her temple, the result of her many clashes with the side window. "Ninjas," she breathed, as though to herself.

"How did you get away from your kidnappers?" Odering's voice stayed level but Hana heard the excitement beneath.

She sighed. "The third man got stuck trying to get out. He was too fat to go between the seats." She closed her eyes and envisioned him there, flailing and drowning. Her eyes popped open. "Did he die?"

Odering shook his head. "No. He just got a little wet. What happened then?"

"I ran away while they tried to get him out. It needed both of them to hold the door up and the man still couldn't wriggle through."

"So nobody appeared with a shotgun and held them up while you escaped?" Odering's eyes narrowed and Hana felt tired of the never ending game. Bone weary tired.

"No." She exhaled. "The tyre blew out and we crashed. He drove like an idiot and I hit my head against the window a couple of times." She rubbed her eyes and hissed at the pain in her right one. She saw pure irritation flit across Odering's expression as he realised once again, he wouldn't get what he wanted. Logan twitched in his seat and the policeman smelled defeat. "I ran up onto the main road. The gravel cut my feet, so I stuck to the verge. The men wanted to get to the main highway and I didn't want to go with them. I headed for my wee church because I woke up as we passed it and when I stepped into the road a car almost hit me. I looked a mess and she offered me a ride."

"Who?" Odering's brow narrowed.

"The old lady." Hana blinked. "She gave me a ride home."

Odering leaned forward. "Police dogs tracked you for miles across country onto Lake Road. You're saying you didn't go that way?"

"No." Hana faked surprise. "I told you, the old lady drove me."

"Describe her." Odering sat back and folded his arms.

Hana sighed. "Asian, maybe Chinese or Korean? Yes, Korean I think. She had dark hair slicked back from her forehead and tied into a bun." Hana closed her eyes in concentration. "I don't think she understood me very well, but she took me back to school." She reached for the orange juice glass and fumbled it, knocking the liquid over and producing a sticky pool. "Sorry." Hana put her hands over her eyes and wished she could project herself home; her proper home on top of the mountain.

"What did she say?" Odering's voice rose a few octaves and Hana heard hysteria brewing.

"Say? She asked if I was okay and I said not really. She planned to head for the Cambridge night market and I asked her to drop me off at the far end of Maui Street."

"Why didn't you call the cops or get her to?"

"She didn't have a phone. I told you, she was an old lady and didn't speak very good English."

Odering stood and walked to the furthest corner of the room. Logan tensed as the policeman kicked the wall with his polished shoe and Hana jumped. "I want to go home now."

"No!" Odering sounded vitriolic and his co-worker shifted in her seat, chewing her lower lip with anxiety. "You're lying!"

"My wife is the victim here!" Logan stood and the pattern was set.

"I'm sick of this!" Odering yelled. The blonde officer scrabbled to turn off the recorder. "You always bloody do this!"

"Do what?" Logan tilted his jaw and the decades old game begun in a schoolboy fight, reared its ugly head. "I'm sick of this. We fought in school and you've dragged it on for years. How long will you hold it against me? I didn't know Michael got your sister pregnant. He didn't show up to fight you and I didn't want my family name dragging through the mud as cowards, so I stepped up."

Odering's fists balled next to his thighs. "I hate your family, Du Rose. I detest every one of your miserable asses. Wanna go again? I'll finish it this time."

Logan shook his head in disbelief. "This is messed up, man. We're grown-ups!"

"Yeah!" Odering lurched towards the table and rested his knuckles on its laminated surface. "I can break your nose again."

"Break my nose?" Logan scoffed. "Lucky punch, dude. But that's what happens when you fight a kid who's younger and smaller than you. I would've kept going if Angus hadn't hauled me off and you know it."

Odering closed his eyes and let out a sigh. His shoulders slumped. "Yeah, you would." He ran a hand through his hair. His body language oozed desperation. "Sorry. Please can we just do this interview? I know in my gut that it all goes back to that very first case three years ago. Robert Dressler formed a big part of that. I don't understand how it hangs together but this reeks of him."

Logan swallowed and Hana tugged at his sleeve. He glanced down at her fingers in irritation and his expression changed to one of concern. Slumping into the seat next to her, he turned her hand over and examined her palm. "You're bleeding."

Hana's brow knitted and she prodded the saturated plaster over the knife wound. "I want this over, Logan. I want it over as much as he does."

"Okay." Logan reached into his jeans pocket and retrieved a white handkerchief ironed into a triangle. He pressed it over the plaster and soaked up the excess blood. "How do you feel?" He lowered his head to hear her reply.

"Tired and fed up."

Logan caught Odering's gaze. His grey eyes shone with a stormy hue. "Five more minutes; then we walk out."

"Fine, fine." Odering held his palms out in front of his face. "Let's go back to when you disappeared. What happened?"

Hana groaned in frustration. "I already told you!"

"I want to cover it again." Odering's face clouded in anger and Hana sighed and went over the same ground for him.

"My phone rang and I talked to Bodie. Half way through the conversation I felt a draught and realised the front door was open. Before I got a chance to turn around, I felt a cloth against my mouth and nose and woke up in a house somewhere."

"There's no sign of forced entry, Hana. Did you let them in?"

"No!" she snapped and then heaved out a sigh. "Living on the mountain got me out of the habit of locking doors. I went out to the rubbish bin earlier and it's possible I left the front door unlocked."

"Did Robert Dressler kidnap you, Hana?"

She shook her head and told the truth. "No. Other men I've never seen before. They said they'd take my kids." Hana stood. "I need to see my children, please?"

"In a minute." Odering made notes and then looked up, studying Hana through narrowed eyes. "We lost track of Robert Dressler after he attacked you a couple of years ago." He underlined a date with his pen, almost putting the point through his paper and onto the next page. "Nothing. No sightings, none of his usual antics and then he's spotted at Auckland airport a week ago. Now you're targeted again. Hell of a coincidence, don't you think?"

Hana winced and looked to Logan for support. He gritted his teeth and she saw the bone protrude through his cheeks.

"You're doing great, babe," he said, his acquiescence to the cop surprising her. She floundered, wondering how truthful Logan wished her to be. His eyes flicked to Odering. "If you saw him at the airport, why didn't you arrest him then?"

Odering shook his head. "An off duty officer saw him and called it in as soon as he got into arrivals. He should've just told customs and let them grab Dressler, but he didn't."

"Maybe Dressler went overseas," Hana offered. "He went there for a while and then came back." She shuddered. "I hope I never see that man ever again."

"Why did these men take you, Hana?"

"I don't know." Hana rubbed her eyes again, remembering at the last minute not to touch the right one. Her head shot up with the sudden thought. "Didn't you catch him at the hotel?" She looked at Logan and then Odering, the fear in her eyes genuine. "He went to the mountain to get my heart pills."

Odering glanced at Logan. "Who," he demanded.

Logan shook his head and his brow knitted in confusion. "It's alarmed to the hilt. The security guys would've called me."

"Make the bloody call, Du Rose!" Odering snarled and Hana cringed, realising she'd slipped up.

Logan's chair grated back and he reached into his pocket for his mobile phone, turning it in his fingers and dialling the number for the hotel. He slipped through the outer door into the corridor and Hana saw him pacing up and down with one finger in his ear.

"I stole someone's phone," Hana said, staring at the table as her mind worked overtime. "I talked to an emergency operator, but it fell in the bushes when the man found me."

Odering nodded and pushed a sealed plastic bag towards her. "This one?"

She nodded with enthusiasm. "It looks like it."

"It's a burner phone. We can't get anything from it."

The sense of defeat rode over Hana and she sighed. "I thought I'd escaped, but he came from nowhere and pulled me out. They kept drugging me. I feel so tired and disoriented now. When will it wear off?"

"I'm not sure." Odering chewed his lower lip and glanced at the female officer. "Why would Dressler come back for you? I know this is his work. Where has he been, Hana?"

"I don't know." Hana sighed and felt her chest tighten. The lie stuck in her throat but if she sent him after Caleb, the teenager would crumble with cowardice and tell Odering how Logan employed Flick to work for him, knowing he was a wanted felon. She shrugged. Leaning forward, she lowered her voice. "What about the man I stabbed? Did he die?"

Odering's brows knitted. "What stabbed man? We found nobody at the house you described. The family live in the UK and say nobody lives there. A family member left it in their will and it's awaiting renovation before being rented."

"I stabbed him," Hana insisted, showing the detective her palm. "It's how I did this."

"So you say." Odering folded his arms. "What was the man's name?"

The lie tripped off her tongue. "I don't know. They didn't say names." It galled her to protect Dominic Dressler, but she'd already slipped up once. Hana glanced backwards through the glass into the corridor. Logan looked deep in conversation on his phone. She forced herself to relax, reasoning if the cops didn't find Dominic at the house, then he didn't die and she should pay him no more attention.

"We'll get his DNA off your clothes, I guess." Odering sighed. "I feel like you're keeping things from me, Hana."

"You always think that." She pouted and made herself sound grumpy. "What did the three men in the car say? They must know more."

Odering's lips pulled back in a snarl. "Contractors!" he spat. "Known to us and nothing more than hired muscle. They allegedly didn't see who sent them after you, but received a hefty fee up front and another to follow on delivery. Apparently the ninja double crossed them when he took you away."

Hana shook her head. "Ninja!" she scoffed. "It must be embarrassing to admit a girl defeated you twice."

"So, you'd never seen those particular three men before?"

"The ones in the car? No." Hana chewed the side of her thumb. "But there were lots of men in the house. I only saw two or three."

"We'll have a go at them again. They must know more than they're saying." Odering shook his head. "Was it about money, Hana?"

"Money?"

Odering snorted out a laugh. "Yeah, Hana. Your husband is a rich man. Did it never occur to you that you might become a very lucrative hostage?"

She shook her head as the thought sank in and mixed with the confusion in her heart. Her green eyes shuttered with the realisation she'd been a pawn yet again in the sick game of ruthless men. Dominic Dressler's words returned to her with sudden clarity and she repeated them for the detective. "He said, 'There's too much riding on this.' You think it was over money?" Her face paled. "They were taking me to Port Waikato and then planned to kill me and dump my body in the estuary."

A vein pulsed in Odering's forehead as he observed Hana's expression of abject shock. "Of course it was about money, Hana. What else is there?"

Logan walked back into the room and shook his head at Odering. "Nothing. The house is secure."

Hana put her head down, covering her eyes with her hands. "He says they wanted money. I have a dollar value." The sobs began as fake hiccoughs but dissolved into genuine misery.

63

The Way of Lies

"I'm so sorry, sir." The blonde cop ran her hand through her hair and shifted on her feet in agitation. She watched Odering's retreating back and raised her eyebrows as he punched the wall of the corridor in anger. "I don't know what's got into him."

"I do," Logan stated. "And next time it will be my fist."

"I'll organise a ride home." She chewed her lower lip in anxiety. "I'm so sorry. You're welcome to make a complaint."

Logan snorted. "I can't be arsed. And we don't need a ride."

Bodie rose from the seating area outside the main reception and poked Leslie in the ribs. She sat up like Medusa and her wobbly buttocks let loose an unpleasant fart. Bodie shuddered and helped Hana stay upright. She shuffled like an old woman and Logan's impatience got the better of him. He swept her off her feet and carried her through the front doors. She sniffed into his shirt and wondered when the fake tears became so real. As though he heard the mental question, Logan kissed her temple. "You're just tired," he breathed into her hair. "You did good, babe."

Hana remembered nothing of the journey back to the school in Bodie's flash car. Logan undressed her and put her to bed, kissing her forehead. "I need to go downstairs and smooth things over with your son."

"No, don't leave me!" Hana snatched at his shirt and dragged him closer. "I need to know what happened. If you walk away, I'll follow you downstairs."

"Hana." Logan sank onto the bed next to her and stroked her hair back from her forehead. "It's over, babe."

"But Flick went to our house." She lowered her voice. "I thought the cameras might pick him up and the boys would go after him."

Logan shook his head. "He didn't get to our house, Hana." He sneered. "You think I'd let him set foot on the mountain?"

"How did you find me, Logan?" Her green eyes stared at her husband's face, seeing the irritation in his expression. "Did you know this would happen?"

"Not exactly." Logan shook his head. "A few days ago, Che phoned me and asked for a meeting. He monitors immigration for his own reasons and knew Dressler arrived back. He had him watched and as soon as he started moving south, alerted me. I sent Caleb away straight after the meeting. I didn't want him around us, but should've guessed he'd align with his rotten father once I did that. It's possible his older brothers sent him to watch us as part of their bigger plan to kidnap you. You rescuing him and moving him into the house proved a bonus."

"Why didn't you say something?" Hana pushed herself back against the pillows and knitted her brow. "A warning might have helped. I'd have locked the front door for a start."

Logan scoffed. "Really? You'd never believe me. All you see is the good in people and one day it'll get you killed. You'd invite Flick round for dinner like an old friend just to prove me wrong. Get real, Hana."

She tightened her jaw and kept silent, betrayal and sadness cloaking her heart like a shroud. Logan shook his head. "Despite a new identity and a job, Flick still couldn't make it work, Hana. He screwed up so bad in England there was no place left for him to hide. You were his next meal ticket."

"He didn't say that." Hana dragged her fingers through her fringe and seized a handful of hair, closing her eyes against the animosity emanating from her husband. "He never mentioned money."

Logan stood and put distance between them. At the door he turned and his grey eyes sparkled in the lamp light. "You never learn, do you Hana?" he said, the words cutting deep into her soul.

Hana swallowed and pushed the covers back. "I want to see my children," she said, her tone hostile.

"Tomorrow," Logan said, his voice cold. "Amy's put them to bed at Culver's Cottage."

"You can't keep me away from my kids." Determination fostered belligerence and Hana fought back, her painful feet smarting against the rug at her bedside.

Logan lifted his index finger and pointed it in her direction, his jaw working through his cheek. "For once, Hana!" he snapped. "Just do as you're bloody told and accept someone else knows better than you."

She opened her mouth to speak but he left the room, closing the door behind him. Hana climbed back under the cool sheets and turned her face into the pillow, physical and emotional pain attacking her in equal measure.

64

The Curse of the Rescuer

"You said we'd get the children." Hana hobbled behind Logan as he walked to the edge of the ridge and looked down over the cool, green sea. "I need to see my babies, not take a walk on Raglan beach." She frowned at the black sand metres below, the surf licking the rich iron ore with a white tongue.

"I want to talk." Logan's tone sounded rigid, his hunched shoulders silhouetted by the watery sun.

Hana snorted. "You never want to talk; you issue orders and expect everyone to follow. That's not talking."

"Whatever!" He strode away and sat on a ledge, dangling his legs over a terrifying precipice. The area of grass formed a circle of land like a table, jutting out over the sea on three sides. After a short delay, Hana stumbled after him and sat with a distance between them. The plaster over her heel rubbed into a painful watershed and she removed her flip-flop and yanked it free. Air hit the raw skin like a blast of pain and she regretted the decision, struggling to flatten it out and reattach it.

"You let him get too close to you." Logan chewed on the blade of dry grass and observed her through cool, grey eyes. "How did you think it would end?" He gritted his teeth and his jaw worked through his stubbly skin.

Hana stared at him, her mouth open and disbelief on her face. "You're kidding me!" It emerged as a shout and Logan started in surprise.

"Well, you did. You're a rescuer. Everyone's salvageable in your eyes and some people just aren't."

Hana swallowed the accusation and stood, latent anger tightening her throat. "I did not let him get too close to me, Logan. You did. This is down to your pig-headedness and let's make no mistake about that."

"How is it my fault?" Logan sneered and Hana balled her fists, struggling not to wipe the ugly expression from his face with a well-aimed slap. She backed away from him, feeling the emotional chasm grow wider than the physical distance.

"You started this; all of it." The realisation helped her mind clear and she saw the path to ruin spread out behind her, leaving its muddy footprints throughout the delicate carpet of her marriage. "Not only did your ex-fiancé breathe down my neck for the first year of our relationship, you took the man who attacked me back to the home you then expected me to occupy. You turned a blind eye when he showed me attention. Not satisfied with all that, you moved Sylvia into the hotel; into our bedroom!"

Logan gaped. "It wasn't like that."

"Like hell it wasn't!" Hana shook her head and backed away further. "You're not truly sorry for any of it. And now you sit here and accuse me of bringing it all down on my own head."

Logan scrambled to his feet. "I have no control over who works with me! Caroline got a job at the same school as us; what did you want me to do?"

"Exactly what I did," Hana spat. "Get her fired."

Logan shook his head. "No, she got caught with that sports teacher, what was his name? I fired him the next year, remember?"

"No! I told Angus about her affair and he made sure the trustees knew. I got her fired, Logan. Me. You just acted like a rabbit in the headlights and expected me to believe your promise that she wasn't carrying your child. You did nothing, the same as you did nothing when Sylvia turned up with her fake hair and lies, pretending Ryan was your son. You pushed me out like I meant nothing to you."

"I never touched either of them." Logan's expression looked haughty, his sense of injustice filling him with false confidence. "I did nothing wrong."

"I. Didn't. Know. That." Hana spoke through gritted teeth and it hurt her jaw. Fury blossomed in her chest like a spreading sickness, clouding her judgement as she backed away from Logan and towards the edge of the cliff. "How dare you say I let him get too close to me!" The words ached in her throat. "You let him get too close to me. He was there when you weren't!" Hana let out a sob mid-sentence and the sound increased her sense of humiliation in the face of Logan's blindness. "You don't see it and you're not even sorry!"

She took another step backwards and heard small stones tumble behind her. Alarm crossed Logan's face and he held his arms out, palms facing her. "It sounds bad when you list it like that." He swallowed and took a step towards her. "You're right. I should have got Caroline fired or quit myself. I should've done that for you. I should've put you above Flick and thought about how you felt having him around and I didn't notice when he started falling for you. I headed it off too late by sending him overseas. And the Sylvia thing." Logan let his hands fall to his sides. "There's nothing in my life I regret more than letting her walk in and disrupt our marriage on a lie."

"You shouldn't have let her do that even if Ryan did turn out to be your son. Anyone else would've done DNA tests and kept her at arm's length, but you don't see your own faults, do you? You let another woman take control of our lives! I meant nothing to you against the promise of a shiny new son." Hana rested a hand over her empty stomach. "I spent Mac's pregnancy miserable and alone while you played happy families with another woman. I sent Sylvia away, Logan. Me!" She jabbed her own chest with rage in her eyes.

"Hana, come away from the edge."

She bridled at the authority in his voice which didn't sit right against the fear in his eyes. Anger flashed but the warm salt water on her cheeks surprised her and she swatted the tears away with her fists. "You ask me to trust you," she said, her chest hitching. "Trust me, trust me, Hana. You say it all the time." Her voice cracked. "But you're the hardest man in the world to trust. I can't trust you. How do I end up in the wrong over this? A crazy guy flew all the way from England to kidnap me, saying he could give me a better life than the one I had. What does that tell you about how my life looks from the outside, Logan? Like an endless list of excuses and apologies and me walking through the consequences of your actions." Hana gave an ugly sniff and sighed. "No wonder he thought he could do better." She wagged her finger at Logan. "But apparently it was all about money. I'm a meal ticket for unscrupulous men. Now, you're blaming me. I'll never forgive you for saying that."

"Hana!"

Rocks skittered from beneath her as she took one step too many backwards. The earth tilted on its axis, the ground crumbled and Hana flailed with nothing to grab hold of. Time stilled and she regretted having no final chance to say goodbye to her family or plead her miserable case with God.

The earth caved and Hana pitched forward, smashing her face into the ledge as gravity claimed her body. The taste of blood and a terrifying weightlessness occupied her brain, along with a sense of dismay at the ironic closing of her life's journey. So many had tried to kill her and yet she'd done it herself by accident. Her hands stopped scrabbling for purchase on the crumbling ledge and she stilled, giving in to a peace which traversed mortal understanding.

A vice around her left wrist sent searing pain as far as her shoulder and the fragment of glass in her vein moved under the pressure. But her downward momentum ceased and she hung in midair like a rag doll as mud and dust passed her, taking grass and moss with it.

"I've got you," Logan gasped. "Trust me, Hana. Trust me."

Hana tilted her head back and saw the corded muscle and tendons sticking out from his neck. Sweat beaded on his forehead and she heard the toes of his cowboy boots scrabbling against the surface as he dug in to bear her weight. The view she'd admired with such abandon spread out beneath her like an open grave and she felt paralysed; by life, by loss, by experience and by love.

With grunts of effort and straining biceps, Logan hauled her upwards. Her left cheek grazed the jutting rocks as he pulled her over them, never letting go of her wrist. When her knees hit the craggy edge, Logan wrapped his arms around her waist and hauled her backwards until they lay on the grass nose to nose. Still Logan pulled, adjusting his body until she slumped on top of him. His breath heaved and he panted with exertion and the aftermath of terror. His grey eyes looked opaque, adrenaline spreading his pupils in an inky circle to occupy most of the area between his dark lashes.

Logan swore and then he cried, regret washing from him like a river. "I'm sorry," he said over and over. "I'm so sorry."

65

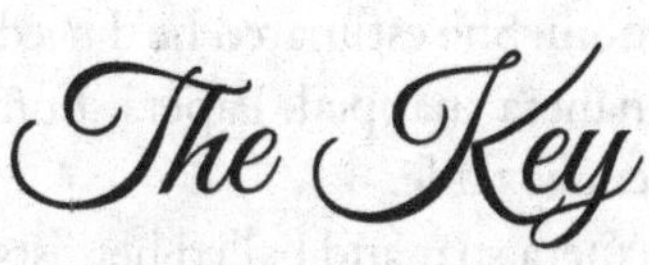

"Anahera." Hana's quiet words made the woman jump and she turned in position, her blank face dropping into an expression of guilt. The fingers of her left hand plucked at a loose thread in her sweater.

"I'm so sorry," she gushed, swallowing and glancing towards the door. Her brown eyes raked Hana's face and she raised a finger to point at the cuts and bruises. "Did I do that?"

"No." Hana glanced around the pretty day room in the secure unit and selected a seat. She kept herself far enough away to escape, but not so far as to appear rude. "I've had an eventful few days."

A male nurse winked at Hana as he settled in a chair across the room. The files on his knee served as a legitimate reason for his presence, but his acknowledgement betrayed otherwise. She shifted in her chair, ready to run if necessary. "I need to speak with you about Wiri."

"My son." Anahera's voice cracked with emotion and she gave Hana her full attention. "Will you keep him for me?"

"But what about Nev?" Hana asked. "He's Wiri's father and when we find him, he needs to step up."

Anahera looked confused. "Nev's missing?"

"Yes." Hana nodded. "He drove off the night you visited and nobody's seen him since."

Anahera closed her eyes and filled her lungs with air. She puffed herself up and Hana tensed, feeling the nurse watching from across the room. She estimated he'd need five good strides to reach her if Anahera snapped. Papers shuffled as he laid the files on a nearby coffee table.

"Coward!" Anahera spat and balled her fists. She opened her eyes and fixed a steadfast gaze on Hana. "Keep my son. Please. If you can't do it for me, then do it for Wiremu."

Hana exhaled. "Logan and I talked. We need to concentrate on our own family from now on." The hard conversation resounded in her ears and she hated the closing of the Du Rose portcullis, knowing the agony of those left outside. "It's for the best."

"Not for him! Not for Wiri!" Anahera stood, agitated and upset. Hana winced and the male nurse appeared by her side as if by magic.

"Hey," he soothed. "Let's get you back to your room."

"No, no." Anahera calmed, seeing her window of opportunity closing. "I'm calm, I'm calm." She thudded into her chair and wrung her hands, accepting the presence of the man in her peripheral vision. "I'll explain."

Hana glanced at the nurse and swallowed, her expression imploring him to stand next to her as a buffer. When he nodded, she pushed her bum back in the seat and forced herself to relax. "Okay," she said. "Explain."

Anahera's tale slipped from her lips like silk and left Hana reeling. With each spoken word, the Māori woman's tense demeanour changed and peace crept in, replacing the anxiety and guilt. The male nurse cringed as her story gave him a different problem and he whispered in low tones to another attendant, who checked on him a few moments into the confession.

"I didn't know he cheated on me with my sister."

Hana's eyes widened in shock and she glanced at the nurse. He shook his head and gave a reassuring smile.

"Nev grew distant and I suspected something but never seemed able to catch him out. I tried so hard to be a good wife but I don't believe he ever loved me. He blamed me for not giving him another son and I felt relieved when I fell pregnant so long after Asher." She swallowed. "It wasn't a good pregnancy and I spent most of it sick. A kuia from our community visited one day, concerned about my sister, Pania and her behaviour. She lived opposite and saw local men visiting; her suggestion caused me shame and I did nothing. The old lady died a few weeks later and I helped her daughter to clean house after the tangihanga." Anahera's voice wobbled. "That's when I saw my husband enter my sister's house without knocking. The way he checked the street and seemed so uneasy made me understand what the old lady tried to say. She wanted me to know my husband was cheating with my own sister. Pania couldn't help with the cleaning because of work. When I saw Nev, I just knew. He was her work."

Anahera released a shuddering breath and balled her fists in her hands. "I watched him leave, a smug look on his face and I hated him with all my heart. I left the kuia's daughter and went home, wanting to challenge him and appeal for my children."

Hana held her breath and felt her chest lock up. Anahera touched her olive forehead and sighed with the memory. "He laughed at me." A stray tear rolled down her cheek and off her chin, the misery so old it stank of death. "He said he loved her and wouldn't stop. He walked out and I felt sure he'd gone to her. I left Asher with Rueben and drove back to my sister's house to confront them both together. I parked on the driveway of the old kuia's empty house and saw Lincoln Haines get into his car. I waited for him to leave. I found Pania tidying her bedroom. The room reeked of them both and she was changing the sheets. When I confronted her, she shrugged. 'It's good money,' she said. 'It's easy.' She'd destroyed my world and she didn't care. 'I don't want him,' she replied. 'Just his cash.' I followed her into the lounge still shouting and she turned and slapped me so hard I lost my balance."

Anahera's jaw tightened. "I felt something snap inside my stomach and I knew." The eyes which turned to Hana channelled heartbreak. "The doctor's said my daughter was already gone by then." Anahera touched her abdomen and winced. "I'd felt different for a few days, better somehow." Her voice shook. "She died and my body felt better. It betrayed me." Her eyes searched for answers. "How can that be right?"

Despite her fear, Hana reached out and touched Anahera's hand. The other woman noticed and took the solidarity, gripping her fingers like a lifeline. "I felt a click in my brain and remember attacking Pania. I pushed her shoulders with such force she fell backwards and smashed her head on the hearth. She made no sound. I stood and watched as her blood made patterns in the carpet and my heart felt numb. Neville preferred her and now he wouldn't be able to have her." Anahera stuck her nose in the air, her face hardening. "I saw Linc's wallet on the coffee table and knew he'd miss it and return. I left through the back of the house and collected my car. He arrived as I reached the other end of the street; he didn't see me. I didn't go back to the mountain, but drove myself to the hospital and my poor kōtiro came later that night. She looked so peaceful. Reuben picked me up from the hospital. He took care of the tangi and dealt with the arrangements. I've often wondered if he knew what I did, but he never said. The police came for the men one by one and then they arrested Linc. I felt nothing, not until I held Wiri in my arms and then I felt everything." Anahera clutched her chest. "I feel it all the time now; it's here."

Hana swallowed as Anahera's grief travelled through their joined fingers like a seeping darkness. Still, she didn't let go. "I've wanted to tell someone for so long." Anahera let go of Hana's hand and looked at the male nurse, touching her fingers to her delicate chest. "It feels good to speak the truth."

"Does Nev know?" Hana asked, her voice a low whisper.

Anahera shrugged. "Yes. He put pressure on Linc to take the blame and serve the sentence meant for me. He sent a man to the prison but I don't remember details." She sighed.

"He sent Kane," Hana whispered and Anahera nodded.

"Maybe. It will be the reason Nev's left. He grew anxious I might confess when he visited me a few weeks ago. He returned and threatened me after Linc visited and said he'd never let me see my boys again if I told the truth. I went shopping with an orderly and hid from her in a clothes shop. I needed to see you."

Anahera looked at Hana, sanity in her eyes. "Linc lost everything. Fiona divorced him and his mother killed herself. I gave Wiri his name. Do you think he'll understand how I tried to make up for it? I wanted to tell you so many times. The men say you're the kuikui of the family and I knew you'd put it right."

"I'm no matriarch," Hana sighed. "I can't even fix my own life, let alone someone else's."

"Take Wiri for me?" Anahera's eyes begged for help and Hana's brow knitted, denial already in her face. "You don't understand," Anahera persisted. "Please, listen to me and then take him."

Hana leaned back in her chair and sighed, knowing she already regretted the visit and the weight the confession placed on her shoulders. "Okay."

"I never let my husband near me again," Anahera breathed, her voice little above a whisper. "I repaid him in kind. Wiri is not his son."

Hana's jaw dropped open and she shook her head. Everything about the child screamed Du Rose and the possibilities sickened her. "Not Reuben?" she pleaded and Anahera answered with a determined shake of her head.

"No, but he knew." She swallowed. "He knew and he never told."

"You paid Nev in kind?" Hana closed her eyes against Anahera's slow smile. "Who then?" Hana demanded, hysteria leaking into her voice. "Whose child is in my home?"

She knew even before Anahera uttered the name and sickness roiled in her guts. Standing, she bolted from the room, leaving the nurse to calm Anahera and work his way through the machinations of the justice system.

Hana's passage to the outside felt fraught with obstacles as the secure exits took an age to navigate. By the time she reached the car and Logan's open arms, her world had already collapsed.

66
A New Start

"Come in, come in!" Hana's brother opened the door and waved them through, stooping to kiss Hana on the cheek. Logan accepted the outstretched hand and gave an upward jerk of his head in acknowledgement. "This is a nice surprise." Mark ushered them through to a simple but expensively dressed lounge.

"Neat house." Logan looked around him in approval, his eyes drifting over the evidence of bachelorhood; a car magazine on the coffee table and black cushions on the sumptuous sofa. The place oozed maleness.

"Yeah, it's amazing," Hana said, giving her husband a smile of thanks for his effort.

"I just bought it," Mark announced and Hana's lips parted in surprise.

"You decided to stay? I thought you were renting it."

"No, I'm staying here. I've made my decision. The owner was happy to sell without brokers' fees."

"I'm so pleased." Hana stood to embrace him and Mark patted her on the back, feeling the wince as her body tightened in pain. He lifted her face with a finger beneath her chin and examined her red eye and the surrounding bruising. His gaze strayed to the scratches on the side of her face and he lifted a lock of hair and knitted his brow at the patch of scalp showing through underneath.

"What the hell happened?" He ran his fingers down her arms as though checking a horse and pulled her hands up to his face. The wound from the flick knife blade showed as a thin red line on her palm and Mark's attention travelled up to her wrist. Moving her sleeve back, he examined the scar tissue concealing the shard of glass he tried, but failed to remove. As always, his nose wrinkled in displeasure. The hard look he gave Logan spoke volumes and his harsh tone communicated his own guilt. "I hoped you'd take better care of my sister!"

Logan gritted his teeth and emitted a rough exhale of annoyance and Hana tensed. "It's not his fault." She swallowed, not wanting to discuss her ordeal. "I'm fine." She pushed Mark's hands away with deliberate gentleness, working hard not to offend. "Tell me what you've been up to. How's your new relationship?"

Mark's face broke into a grin which almost split it from ear to ear. "I don't remember ever being this happy."

Hana met his smile and backed up towards her husband, her soul craving his nearness. "That's amazing, Mark. I'm happy for you. When do I get to meet her?"

Mark's smile never wavered. "Soon. Shift ended about half an hour ago, so not long."

"Great timing then." Hana backed far enough for her spine to contact Logan's chest and stomach and she heaved a sigh of relief. Remembering her injuries, she touched her face. "Maybe it's not great timing. We should come back."

The sound of the front door closing sent Hana's spine rigid and she snatched at Logan's hand in fear. His arms fixed around her chest from behind, bringing comfort and security. Mark wagged a finger at her. "You need to tell me the story about all these injuries, Hana. I'll get it out of you."

Her nod appeared half-hearted as her attention fixed on the open lounge doorway. Hana readied her expression in expectation of meeting Mark's new love interest, hoping the woman saw past the cuts and bruises. Logan's hands slipped to her stomach and he caressed her waist with gentle strokes of solidarity.

67

The Strange and the Wonderful

"Whoa! Bet ya didn't see that coming," Logan hissed in her ear as Hana gaped, her jaw dropping in a most unladylike manner. He jabbed her in the ribs and she tensed and galvanised herself to meet the newcomer.

"Hi, I'm Hana, Mark's sister. Well, cousin actually, but I only discovered that recently." The colour rushed to Hana's cheeks in her awkwardness and she heard Logan snort at her verbal diarrhoea. Everything about Mark's new partner threw her and she didn't know how to react.

"We've talked about it all; don't worry." Mark looked pleased with himself and electricity sparked in the air around him as he gave a goofy, love struck grin.

"We've met, I believe." Mac's specialist shook Hana's hand and gave her a wink, making her blush to the roots of her hair.

"Yes, we have." Hana turned, imploring Logan for help. "This is my husband, Mac's father. Logan, this is the doctor we saw at the hospital."

Logan gave an upward jerk of his head and accepted the outstretched hand of greeting. Hana held her breath, sneaking a look at Mark. Her brother chewed his lower lip with nervousness and his eyes darted from Hana to his boyfriend and back again. She saw a world of agony in the seconds during which the mask slipped and he revealed his vulnerability. Catching her looking, he fixed a smile of bravado on his face and faked joviality. "I'll make us some drinks," he chorused. "What does everyone want?"

"Water please," Logan said and while Hana floundered, "she'd like tea."

"Okay, okay!" Mark clapped his hands together and gestured towards his companion. "Could you help me a moment, Dean?"

"Yeah, sure." The handsome doctor turned and followed Mark into the hallway and she heard their footsteps going into the next room.

"Bloody hell!" Logan hissed. "He's gay!"

"I kinda worked that out," Hana said. "I'm so confused. He said he met someone at the hotel and they worked at Auckland hospital but were transferring to the Waikato. I swear he said it was a woman!" She cast her mind back but came up empty. "Actually I think I assumed it was a woman. When I met him at the hospital, I knew I'd seen him before. Remember that night we went to Alex's restaurant and we saw a group of men from the conference, that's where I saw him." She cringed at the memory of her bathroom crazy moment. "Great, now he's seen me crying my eyes out twice. How do I handle this?" The colour drained from her face. "Oh my goodness! My father will go crazy!"

Logan shook his head and put a reassuring hand on her shoulder. "I think you'd be surprised how accepting older people can be." His lips quirked upwards in a smirk. "I'm glad it's your family and not mine; damned if I'd know what to say."

"Thanks for that. Not helpful." Hana chewed on her lip. "When I think about Mark's history and all his problems, it kinda makes sense. What if that's why he's spent his life searching and making mistakes? Because he wore a persona which didn't fit him?"

Logan shrugged and sat on the leather sofa. "I don't know, Hana. I grew up in a whānau which didn't tolerate difference. I have no blueprint for this; sorry."

Hana rolled her eyes and sat next to him. "I need time to think and accept this. It feels awkward drinking tea and chatting about the weather."

"You can't leave. He'll assume you're judging him. You've got a great relationship after twenty-six years of nothing, so don't sacrifice that."

Hana nodded. "You're right. He might not be my brother but I do love him."

"Then what else matters?" Logan ran his fingers across her thigh and leaned his head back against the seat. His eyes closed and Hana watched as his mind switched to another location, dealing with farm issues and costing solutions in his head.

"I can't believe you just said that."

"What?" Logan opened one eye and squinted at her. "That only love matters? Yeah, I can't believe I said it either."

Mark walked into the room as Hana slapped Logan's stomach and her husband grunted in mock pain. "Beating my brother-in-law up again, are you?" Mark said with a smile in his voice. "It never ends does it, Logan?"

Logan sat up and accepted the ice water from Mark's tray. "Nope." He winked at Hana. "But it's better than being on my own. Sometimes," he added, drawing a hiss of indignation from Hana and a laugh from Mark.

Dean put his head around the door frame and gave a wave to the room in general. "I'll leave you to chat. I need a shower anyway." His head disappeared and Hana felt relief at his tact.

"I love what you two have," Mark said, his expression sobering as he looked from Hana to Logan. "I never dreamed I'd be capable of loving someone to that extent, but I'm beginning to believe I am."

Logan squirmed in discomfort, receding inside himself and concentrating on his water. His scarred index finger traced a line around the rim of the glass. Hana's giggle brought him out of it with a jolt. "You're talking to a Du Rose," she said to Mark. "Du Roses don't talk feelings or emotions. They just hit things and it somehow makes them feel better."

Mark's brow narrowed. "Yes, like that poor young man up at the farm."

Confusion reigned in Hana's expression. "What poor young man? What farm?"

"Your place." Mark shifted in his seat. "I think he said his name was Archer, but he cried so hard it made him difficult to understand. After he shared so much of himself it seemed impolite to ask his name again."

"Asher?" Hana peered at her brother over her mug and felt Logan sit up straighter next to her. "What about him?"

"Sorry, I shouldn't interfere." Mark shook his head and busied himself with pouring tea and stirring in far too much sugar for a practicing doctor. "You've taken my news so well that I thought...it doesn't matter; forget I spoke."

"I can't." Logan's tone sounded acerbic and Hana watched the dangerous tick begin in the vein in his neck. "Finish it, now you've started."

Mark writhed in discomfort. "He's a homosexual. The poor boy's lost, Hana." He appealed to her gentler nature and avoided the rolling storm in Logan's grey eyes. "He's convinced his family will disown him and he's angry; so angry." Mark ran his fingers over his chin. "Just like I used to be."

Hana watched the stiffness of Logan's body as he processed the news. His face darkened and closed and she sighed as the portcullis crashed down over his feelings, freezing her out. She hoped it would be temporary and not rob her of their recent closeness. As Logan remained silent and the awkwardness grew, Hana floundered.

"Will you speak to him?" Mark asked and Hana cringed.

"I don't know, Mark."

He looked disappointed. "If you do, give him my best regards and let him know I had his best interests at heart. No malice intended."

"It's fine." Hana shook her head and brushed it off. "Asher attacked me at the house a few days ago; he's not welcome at the moment." She chewed her lip, the reason for his anger and hatred of the family laid bare. Reaching inside herself, Hana found a thread of compassion for him and tried to nurture it. "If I see him, I'll tell him."

They parted at the door on good terms and Mark stroked Hana's cheek, his eyebrow raised in question. "You'll tell me the story of this another time?" he asked and peered at her sore eye.

"For sure. How about coffee? Text me?" She understood his question reached further than the bruises and scratches on her body; seeking acceptance like a drowning man. Her willingness to meet with him pushed confidence into his expression and his hands shook with relief.

"I will, I promise." Mark let her go. "Am I still Aasshole in your contacts' list?"

Hana grinned and followed Logan's retreating back. "Not telling." She watched her husband open the passenger door for her and climbed onto the rail, waving to Mark over Logan's shoulder. Her husband slammed the door and gunned the engine, backing out onto Hammond Street and not waiting for the automatic gates to slide closed before driving away. Hana glanced at him sideways and bit her lip. Marriage to a Du Rose taught her not to press for confidences while Logan still felt raw. Instead she watched through the window as Hamilton drifted by, the industrial metropolis giving way to green paddocks and dairy herds.

She leaned her head back against the head rest and closed her eyes, auditing her various injuries and declaring herself sound. Despite that fact she craved the peace of the mountain, the solitude of the museum she built from the remnants of Du Rose history and the raw reliance on the earth which came with farming the craggy landscape. "How long till we go home?" she asked, turning her head to meet Logan's tortured eyes.

He relaxed, thoughts turning to his legacy and dispelling disappointment and fear. "Nine weeks, four days, twelve hours, ten minutes and about fifty seconds." he replied with a sad smile. "And it can't come soon enough."

68

Another One Down

"Why do you both have tissues in your ears?" Hana stared at Wiri and Phoenix in disbelief. Logan walked into the kitchen behind her and pulled a face.

"Where's Nonie?" he asked, using Leslie's self-styled title of 'Grandma' with reluctance. The children ignored him, tucking into cheese and crackers without hearing. Every time Phoenix moved her head, the tissues fluttered like ear extensions and Mac pealed with laughter in his high chair.

"What?" Wiri pulled the fluffy end of the tissue and the balled up piece popped out of his ear hole.

"Pardon," Hana corrected. "What's with the ear defenders?"

"The what?"

Hana felt herself growing irritated. "Why do you have tissues in your ears?" she repeated.

"Oh." Wiri squeezed the waxy-looking end of the tissue and wedged it back into his ear. "Nonie's doing horrible singing. We're protecting the instruments in our ears."

"What instruments?" Baffled, Hana turned to see Logan grinning.

"Ear drums." He squeezed her shoulder and leaned over Wiri for the tissue box. "If she's singing opera, this is a grand idea." He balled up the ends of two tissues and shoved them into his ears, leaving the long white tufts sticking out past his hair and joining the white mouse lookalikes at the dining table.

Leslie bustled back into the room, her cracked soprano well past its sell by date as she sang to Hana. "I just nipped to the toilettttttttt! Would you like a cup of teaaaaaaa?"

Hana winced at the sound and managed a nod. "Yes please. Why are you so happy?"

"Ah." Leslie's expression drooped. "Sorry, Hana but I'm going home. My Alfie called while you were out. He misses me. We've been talking on the phone a lot this last week."

"Oh. That's great." Hana glanced across at her husband, not doubting his skill at lip reading when he balled his left hand into a fist and pumped the air.

"Yesssss!" he hissed and Hana glared at him in warning.

"I'll miss you of course, but you should be with your husband."

"How will you manage?" Leslie seemed to be talking herself out of the idea. "Will you get a housekeeper and a nanny to replace me?"

Hana shook her head. "No. I'm sure I'll manage."

"I can stay if you want."

Logan narrowed his eyes and gave Hana a silent warning which made her smile and feel tempted to defy him just for the sake of it. But the thought of running her own family, taking her own children to school and kindy and imposing her own moral standards over their behaviour felt too good to be true. "No thanks," she replied. "It's been amazing having you to stay, but I'll be fine."

"That's good. This life with youse is far too exciting for my poor old heart." Leslie handed Macky another cracker, a lump of cheese glued to it with butter. She added a burst of rusty soprano to the action. He laughed at her open mouth and Hana winced.

Glancing across at Logan, she watched as he licked the tip of his index finger and drew a line in midair. "Another one down," he mouthed.

69

Whānau or Family

Leslie left the next morning and Hana and the children waved her off. Then they walked to school, enjoying the fresh spring air. Wiri and Phoenix held hands and tried to skip; Phoenix fell more than she skipped and arrived at kindy with holes in her woolly tights. While Mac slept, Hana gutted the house, collecting the abandoned belongings of their interlopers and leaving them in a pile by the front door. Logan arrived home after a staff meeting to find the children in their pyjamas and a hearty casserole in the oven. Hana's face glowed with the renewed freedom of being queen of her own castle. "I forgot how nice it is to have law and order," she beamed as Logan kissed her forehead and gave her a sultry wink.

The little family ate their dinner in silence, each consumed by their own thoughts. Phoenix wielded her fork like a shovel, dropping a lump of potato on her leg and Hana watched as Wiri leaned across and scooped it onto his finger. She cringed when he popped it into his mouth.

Logan's phone rang and he fished it from his pocket, glancing at the caller and then sending them to voicemail. He smiled at Hana and turned it off. "Who was that?" she asked and he winced.

"Alex. I don't want to be in business with him anymore; he's not the man I thought he was. He would've got my solicitor's letter this morning."

"But what about the French restaurant?" Hana's brows knitted in confusion at Logan's sudden decision.

"What about it?"

Hana blanched at the challenge in her husband's eyes. His action sent her a coded message; he wouldn't cheat and nor would he align with others who chose to.

"Uncle Logan?" The Du Rose grey eyes with flickering dark lashes stared at Logan with serious intensity and Hana braced herself.

"Yup?" Logan pushed vegetables into his mouth and waited.

"Do I get your blood in me?"

"Ooh! Dat's yukky." Phoenix opened her mouth in horror and Hana shook her head until the tiny jaw snapped closed, hiding the mouthful of half-chewed food. The child swallowed. "I got bloods. Look." Phoe clambered onto her chair and lifted her knee for all to see, displaying the graze and the Mr Bump plaster covering most of it. "I got bleeds today. I did crying like this." She took a deep inhale and Hana cut her off.

"Sit down at the table, Phoe. Daddy can guess how it went."

Phoenix shrugged and abandoned her fork to use her fingers on a carrot stick, chasing it around the bowl like a paper boat in the gravy.

"Yeah, we share blood." Logan's gaze fixed on Wiri and the child considered the answer for a moment.

"How?"

"Poppa Reuben was my dad. You're my nephew."

Wiri sighed. "I miss Poppa Reuben. He taught me fings like fishing and riding and climbing."

Hana saw the flash of hurt cross Logan's eyes at the things he missed out on through the awful Du Rose secrecy.

"Climbing? Wow! Climbing! I wanna do climbing, Mama."
Phoenix munched on the carrot.

"That's nice." Hana smiled at her daughter. "Use your spoon,
sweetie."

"What's climbing?" Phoenix looked at Wiri and he snorted.

"Monkeys do climbing."

"You're a monkey?" Phoenix looked confused and her brow
knitted beneath her curly fringe.

"We talked about whānau in school today." Wiri smiled at
Logan. "I said I finked we shared blood but Mr Rōpata said it
doesn't matter. You can be family without blood. You just have
to open your eyes and your arms and whānau will find you."

Hana's eyes widened in shock and she thought of Bobby,
Tama, Ryan, Caleb and the small boy in front of her. She
opened her arms and got hurt. Maybe the secret was to keep her
eyes open too. She sighed.

"Youse my iwi then, ain't ya?" Wiri continued and Logan
nodded.

"Yep, we're the same tribe." He smiled at Wiri and the boy
drew himself up with pride.

"Good. I'm pleased about that." He jabbed his knife in
Logan's direction. "Youse got the tō rangatiratanga then. Youse
the leader. I'm gonna call you Rangi."

Logan laughed and Hana relaxed. Her gaze strayed to his
gorgeous face as he smiled at Wiri and ate the dinner she'd
prepared, dark locks flopping into his eyes and his strong jaw
working through his cheek. She opened her mouth to speak and
then closed it again, saving her insight for another time. He'd
built a new house on the mountain, not a physical structure
as he'd always believed but a new, thriving house of Du Rose.
Because the house of Du Rose happened wherever Logan
resided and Hana thought about the family members included
in it. Michael's sons, Tama and Ryan, both grandchildren of
Alfred Du Rose, both sons in her home. Logan and Wiremu
represented the other of Kuia Phoenix's sons, Reuben Du Rose.

It wasn't money which united the mountain but compassion, acceptance and love. Love made a family, not blood.

The old diaries of a tortured woman spoke of the prophesied threat hanging over the future of the house; a threat and not the curse Hana once believed. '*The sons will be the ruin of this family.*'

Hana smiled at her baby son and received his eager response as he fed himself with a plastic spoon. Squashed potato glistened on his cheeks and a pea had found its way into his ginger hair. He squeezed his eyes tight shut in an expression of happiness and Hana sighed with pleasure. It was done. The sons might once have ruined the family but united, they wouldn't now.

"What are you grinning at, Mrs Du Rose?" Logan asked and Hana started, meeting his steady gaze with confidence.

"Tell you later," she answered with a smile, not yet sure if she would. She rose and excused herself, taking the rubbish around to the spotless wheelie bin at the side of the house. Dumping the bag in, she turned to meet the sunset with a sense of overwhelming peace.

"It's done, Kuia Phoenix," she whispered into the air, the breeze carrying her words north to the urupa where the old lady's body lay waiting for the resurrection of the saints. "Alfred and Reuben are united, just like you wanted. It's messy and not at all conventional, but he did it."

The promise of spring kissed Hana's lips one last time as the sun plunged behind the boarding house in the distance. She watched as an unseen hand brushed the sky with reds and oranges; it offered her a floor show which nothing but the naked eye could capture in its fullest beauty. She heard her husband and children laughing through the open window and felt grateful for the compassion Logan showed when hers failed.

Kane Du Rose's little son ate at their table in glorious oblivion and Logan allowed him, banishing the curse and completing the whānau, just as Kuia Phoenix Du Rose always believed he would.

Proverbs 15:17

He pai ake te tina puwha ko te aroha hei kinaki, i te kau whangai
e kinakitia ana ki te mauahara.

Better is a dinner of herbs where love is, than a stalled ox and
hatred therewith.

Du Rose Vendetta

CHAPTER 1

"She what?" Logan Du Rose squinted at his wife, an expression of surprise lighting his grey eyes from within. "Say that again."

Hana sighed, wishing she hadn't started the conversation. Her friend had shared a secret and already Hana felt nausea rising into her throat at betraying her so soon. Four hours, twenty minutes and about five seconds. "Forget it," she said, pushing her feet beneath the sheets and snuggling into the comfortable bed.

"No way!" Logan snapped his book closed in a motion which made Hana wince. She closed her eyes and feigned sleep. A click sounded as Logan whipped off his reading glasses and placed them on the nightstand. He slithered beneath the sheets and propped himself up on one elbow facing her. The corded muscle beneath his shoulder flexed and Hana reached out a finger to trace the tattoo snaking around it. "Start at the beginning," Logan said, his tone soothing.

"No!" Hana squirmed with discomfort. "She told me in confidence and I shouldn't have said anything. I promised not to." She sighed. "But we tell each other everything and I didn't want to spoil things by keeping a secret, especially one that wasn't mine." Her eyelashes fluttered against the pillow and she pouted. "You'd know, anyway. Then we'd get into a vicious cycle of you trying to find out and me struggling to stop you. Before we knew it, we'd argue and then who knows where we'd be."

Logan smiled, his lips curving upwards in a gentle arc. He reached out his hand and placed it on Hana's soft cheek. His thumb caressed her lower lip. "And then we'd get divorced and then you'd bury me under the patio and then and then and then. I'm always amazed at how far your surmising goes." His dark eyelashes fluttered and amusement created crow's feet at the corners of his eyes. "What comes after that?"

Hana wrinkled her nose. "We don't have a patio. And you're too tall to go under the deck."

Logan gasped. "Geez wahine! You've thought about it." He jerked backwards and the voile canopy lining the ostentatious four poster bed rustled.

The laugh bubbled up from Hana's chest and banished the guilt for a moment. The genuine horror in her husband's expression made her snigger. She only stopped when he shifted onto his back and stared at the twinkling lights overhead. The tiny bulbs emitted an ethereal glow which bathed his olive face and smoothed out the contours. "Sorry." She forced his arm up and snuggled beneath it, wrapping her legs around his like a koala. "I've no plans to bump you off, I promise."

Logan grunted and closed his eyes and Hana felt chastened. He shook his head and his hair swished against the pillow. "It's okay," he breathed. "I can build a patio."

Hana snorted and jabbed a finger into his ribs, feeling him curl inward and snatch at her hand. She sighed. "Husbands don't count, do they?" Her voice held an edge of pleading. "I know you won't tell anyone."

"No," Logan concluded. "I won't."

Hana sighed. "Libby told me something today and I still feel shocked." She paused and considered her words. "She's a mistress."

Logan's hair swished against the pillow as he turned his head. "I thought that's what you said, but assumed I heard wrong. A mistress of what?"

"Of a man. Her boyfriend is married." Hana shifted onto her stomach so she could gauge his reaction, suspecting it would mirror hers earlier. But Logan's face remained impassive and he displayed his impressive ability to mask his emotions. "She says their arrangement suits her. They enjoy each other's company and he goes home to his wife. He doesn't expect her to take care of his dirty washing or look after him when he's old and infirm. I looked her in the eye and believe she's genuinely satisfied."

Logan twisted his lips and his brow furrowed. "So, it's just sex. There's no emotional attachment?"

"She says she loves him very much. They've been together five years. They have rules around their relationship. He texts and if it suits Libby, he visits her place. She only texts him in emergencies. They go out for dinner and to the movies like a normal couple. They just make sure they go to Auckland and not Hamilton."

Logan snorted. "Except they're not a normal couple. He has a wife."

"I know." Hana reached out and fingered the St Christopher around her husband's neck. The chain slid through her fingers and the fine hairs of his chest tickled her palm. "I was that wife once."

"You told her that?"

Hana nodded. "Yep. That's why she came clean. She said she values our friendship and didn't want to base our relationship on a lie."

"How did you leave things?" Logan stilled the soft fingers as the chain slithered across his skin. He clasped her hand. "Are you still friends?"

"Yes. Much as I dislike her revelation, I still like her. I feel as though we'd clicked on a deeper level. It's lonely up here sometimes and she filled a gap. I'd started to rely on her."

"It's lonely because you're married to me?"

"Yeah." A wistful smile parted Hana's lips and she placed a gentle kiss against Logan's muscular shoulder. "You're a Du Rose and if the local women don't already work for you, they spend their time lusting after you. It puts a distance between me and most of the women my age. I craved someone with shared life experiences who I could relate to and Libby seemed to fit. I still like her but I'm not sure how to move forward."

Logan snorted. "So, she doesn't work for me and doesn't lust after me." He scratched his chin and shot Hana a sideways look filled with mischief. "What's wrong with her?"

Hana released a sigh of exasperation. Logan's grey irises sparkled with understanding and his expression became serious. He pulled her close. She pressed her face against his downy chest and relaxed, a barrage of thoughts and emotions shifting around in her brain. "Do you want some advice?" His voice held a tenderness only Hana and his children ever heard. Gentle fingers stroked her hair as she nodded. "Base your opinion on her role as a friend. She's an adult making adult decisions about her life. That need not involve you. If her relationship status bothers you then have that conversation. You can explain you want no part of it but wish to stay friends. If she's the person you believe she is, she'll settle for that."

The tick of a clock filled the silence as Hana pondered Logan's words. She sighed. "It's difficult. We've been friends for six months without issue and I knew she had a boyfriend, just not the circumstances. It didn't bother me that she hadn't introduced us. I value her friendship and the children adore her, but what she's doing is wrong. There's another woman somewhere whose heart will break when she finds out." Hana's arms snaked around Logan's trim waist and she placed a kiss against his chest. "But you talk sense sometimes, Mr Du Rose."

"Do I?" He pulled away so he could gaze at her, his lips quirking upward into a knowing smile. "So, the toy-boy knows a thing or two then?"

Hana snorted. "Don't throw my age in my face, young man." She jabbed a crooked finger into his ribs and heard the satisfying sound of him groan as his muscles tightened. He was usually much quicker than her to react. "No night-time privileges for you now."

"Says who?" Logan threw the sheet over their heads and burrowed them both deeper into the bed. Hana squeaked as strong fingers slid beneath the waistband of her pyjama shorts and coasted across the delicate skin of her hip. His lips found hers in the darkness, tentative and searching. Hana blossomed beneath his attentions and allowed the burden of someone else's adultery to fade from her list of immediate concerns.

Dear Reader,

I would love it if you could leave a review at your usual retailer.

I find the opinions of readers helpful and constructive. Reviews are the Holy Grail to an author as they cause our work to sink or swim. It is the bench mark for other readers and can determine whether our work will be successful and reach many or none. It doesn't have to be an essay or a literary criticism. A few words about what you liked would be most appreciated. The shortest review I ever received for my work was, 'Great,' accompanied by five stars and the longest was a whole video from a gorgeous woman in the USA. My favourite to date has to be the lady who said, '*I read until my eyes fell out.*' I keep looking at that one because it makes me laugh.

You can review on my website, ktbowes.com.

Go to the book's buy page where you can follow through to your own retailer and leave a review for me.

And hey, let me know when you've done it. I'd love to hear from you.

About the Author

K T Bowes is a bestselling teen and women's author.

Her novel, *A Trail of Lies*, was the winner of the genre award for Author's Cave in 2014.

Phoenix Du Rose was considered for the prestigious Ngaio Marsh awards for 2021 and *Her Quiet Legacy* in 2022.

K T Bowes is an Englishwoman in exile in New Zealand, swapping rugged cosmopolitan for mountain ranges and terrifying rivers. She loves Māori culture and has learned to weave flax using traditional methods. Her other passion is Rongoa Māori, which involves creating medicines from native plants. She is a student of Te Reo Māori.

Say Hello

You can find the author hanging out on social media in the following places.

Check in and say hello. Maybe suggest she gets back to writing and stops watching cat videos.
FACEBOOK
https://www.facebook.com/NZauthorKTBowes/
INSTAGRAM
https://www.instagram.com/k_t_bowes

Also by this Author

The Hana Du Rose Mysteries Series:
Logan Du Rose
About Hana
Hana Du Rose
Du Rose Legacy
The New Du Rose Matriarch
One Heartbeat
The Du Rose Prophecy
Du Rose Sons
Du Rose Family Ties
Du Rose Vendetta
Phoenix Du Rose
Wiremu Du Rose

The Calculated Risk Series:
The Actuary
The Actuary's Wife
The Actuary in Trouble
The Heart of The Actuary

Troubled series for teens:
Free from the Tracks
Sophia's Dilemma
A Trail of Lies
Gone Phishing

Escaping the Back Country NZ Series:
Pirongia's Secret
Deleilah

Standalone novels:
Artifact
Demons on Her Shoulder
All Saints
Her Quiet Legacy

Humorous Cozy Mystery Series from New Zealand
Dead Straight
Bad Hair Day
Side Parting